the Potluck Club

A NOVEL

Linda Evans Shepherd
and Eva Marie Everson

Revell
Grand Rapids, Michigan

D0109040

© 2005 by Linda Evans Shepherd and Eva Marie Everson

Published by Fleming H. Revell
a division of Baker Publishing Group
P.O. Box 6287, Grand Rapids, MI 49516-6287

Third printing, December 2005

Printed in the United States of America

Library of Congress Cataloging-in-Publication Data
Shepherd, Linda E., 1957–
    The potluck club : a novel / by Linda Evans Shepherd and Eva Marie Everson.
        p.   cm.
    ISBN 0-8007-5984-2 (pbk.)
    1. Women—Societies and clubs—Fiction. 2. Female friendship—Fiction.
  3. Prayer groups—Fiction. 4. Women cooks—Fiction. 5. Colorado—Fiction.
  6. Cookery—Fiction. I. Everson, Eva Marie. II. Title.
  PS3619.H456P68 2005
  813'.6—dc22   2005006687

The lyrics on page 224 are from "Sweet Hour of Prayer," words by William Walford (1845) and music by William B. Bradbury (1861).

The lyrics on page 323 are from "This Is My Father's World," words by Maltbie Davenport Babcock (1901) and music by Franklin Lawrence Sheppard (1915).

To the woman I called "Grandmother," a fine lady who knew her way around a Southern kitchen and who taught me much about loving Jesus. I love and miss you!

—Eva Marie Everson

To my wonderful mother, who cooks even better than Lisa Leann Lambert. Also, to the sisterhood of AWSA (Advanced Writers and Speakers Association). I love you, girlfriends. And a special thanks to my dear friend Eva Marie. You and your characters rock!

—Linda Evans Shepherd

Contents

1

Oh, the ladies
of the Potluck Club . . .

Clay Whitefield sat in his usual spot at the Higher Grounds Café and shook his head as he jotted notes on a clean sheet of his reporter's notebook. The Potluck Club. This was a group so exclusive, he'd seen country clubs easier to get in to—a group led by a sassy old maid named Evangeline Benson.

Evangeline Benson, Clay Whitefield thought. *Now there's a piece of work . . .*

Evangeline

Ingredients   Brown Rice

1 can beef bouillon soup
1 can onion soup
1 c rice
1 sm. can mushrooms or fresh cut-up
mushrooms
2-3 pats of butter or margarine

Pour together in a greased casserole dish.
Put pats of butter on top. Bake 350 for
1 hr. covered.

2

Simmering the Past

Maybe I should begin by telling you what the Potluck Club is, exactly. More than twenty years ago my dearest and oldest friend in the world, Ruth Ann McDonald, and I started praying together on a regular basis. We'd meet once a month at my house. I'd make coffee, and Ruth Ann would make one of her near-famous coffee cakes. While the aroma of good-to-the-last-drop Maxwell House wafted through the kitchen and into my dining room, Ruth Ann and I sat waiting at my grandmother Miller's old cherry dining room table, our Bibles spread out before us. I'd read a passage or two—perhaps something the Lord had given me since last we met—and then we would share the issues that needed our prayerful attention.

"I think," Ruth Ann said at our very first meeting, "that we should begin by praying for Annice Brightman's daughter, Julie." She reached for the pad and pen she kept tucked in her Bible's cover.

I watched her push her large-frame glasses up the bridge of her petite nose before she jotted "Julie B." on the pad.

"Why? What's going on with Julie?"

Ruth Ann shook her head sadly, without so much as a "only her hairdresser knows for sure" blond hair moving on her head, then looked back down to the paper and began to retrace the name of the girl who needed our prayer.

"That boy she's been dating?" I asked.

"That boy she's been dating."

This, of course, was the Lord's confirmation.

10

I pressed a hand to the dark brown hair I wore pulled back in a French twist. Ruth Ann said that with my thin frame I looked like Audrey Hepburn when I wore it that way, but the truth is, it was easy, and around Colorado's high country, women are into "easy." Today I keep it cut short with just a hint of curl. Now people say I look more like Shirley MacLaine when she played in that movie about being the late president's wife who got kidnapped. I think that's supposed to be a compliment, but I could be wrong.

"How should we pray, then?" I asked Ruth Ann.

Ruth Ann looked up and raised her brows. "We'll pray she sees the light."

And we did. We prayed just as hard as we knew how, but Julie Brightman and Todd Fairfield ended up getting married anyway, bringing into the world a precious child—if there ever was one—Abby, about six months later. Not that I'm gossiping. I mean, after all, that child is nineteen years old now, going to school at the same university where I received my degree in business education on an academic scholarship. (The child, not me.)

Months later Ruth Ann declared we should pray for Janet Martin. "Poor thing," Ruth Ann said. "She's got cancer."

"How do you know so much, Ruth Ann?" I asked her. "Do you stand with your ear to a glass pressed against the world or something?"

Ruth Ann sipped at her coffee before replacing the cup in the saucer. "Very funny, Evangeline. But I'm telling you, I heard it from a reliable source. She was seen in a doctor's office."

Well, that much was true. She was seen in a doctor's office, only it wasn't because of cancer. It was an extreme case of vanity. In other words, Janet was getting a nose job.

So that's how the Potluck Club began: two women, a pot of coffee, some coffee cake, and enough misinformation to bring down a church. And it would have too, had it not been for Yvonne Westbrook, the godliest thing you'd ever meet, and I'm not kidding.

Yvonne had been a classmate of Ruth Ann's and mine, but Ruth Ann and I hadn't been especially close with her growing up. Then Ruth Ann went off to the Great Lakes with her new husband, and

Vonnie and I ended up going to the same college and becoming sorority sisters. While I was studying business management, Vonnie worked toward getting her RN. In our senior year, Vonnie decided to go to Berkeley (I can't imagine why, but she did), but she didn't stay long. Before I knew it, I heard she'd gone back to Cherry Creek College to finish school.

After graduation I came back to our sweet little town of Summit View, Colorado (God's country), and started a home-based tax service, and Vonnie eventually went to work for Doc Billings. Of course, that was before everything around here changed . . . before the "Rushies" moved to town, bringing us out of simple life and into a more modern existence.

I imagine you'd like to know a little more about Summit View, wouldn't you? Well, know right up front that if anyone in this town has the authority to inform you, it's me. After all, my daddy was, at one time, the mayor.

Summit View, Colorado—population 25,000—is pretty as a picture when it comes to scenic mountain towns. It was established during the Colorado Gold Rush in 1856, about ten years after the California Gold Rush.

I remember sitting on my grandmother's front porch, rocking in a rocker, listening to Grandpa telling us the stories he remembered being told himself back when he was a child.

"Back then," he said, "we had gold mines, all right, but we had some of the best gambling joints and houses of . . ." and then he'd look at me sideways and say, "ill repute."

"Daddy, why on earth do you say things like that?" my mama implored. "Why encourage her natural curiosity?"

"She's twelve years old, Minnie. Don't you think she knows what a house of ill repute is?"

I nodded. "I know what a house of ill repute is, Mama," I said, though I had no idea. I had to go ask Ruth Ann, who went to her older brother, who told us, giggling, then called us innocents too. I suppose we were, and I suppose that's not a bad thing. It's a shame to know your beloved little town used to harbor things like that.

But we also have lost gold mines and stage coach robberies. The stories about those have delighted our children. Not a generation has come and gone but what some pack of kids hasn't wandered around the hills, looking for lost bags of gold or mother lode never found.

With or without the gold, we have some of the most beautiful mountains, true testaments to the creative hand of God. Summit View is just two hours west of Denver, near Breckenridge. The town sits on Lake Golden, which is actually over an old mining site. And you can see the ski runs in Breckenridge if you stand on a high spot overlooking the lake.

When I was younger, if you lived in Summit View, you knew everybody and everybody knew you. Of course, that was before the Rushies came to town.

"We're calling them Rushies," I told Vonnie one evening while I stood at the kitchen table folding some laundry that was still warm and soft from a recent fluff-'n-puff in the dryer. "You know, all these new couples moving here from California with all their West Coast ways."

Vonnie chuckled in that soft, little girl laugh of hers. "That's a good name for them, Evie. I understand you have a couple of them moving into the house across the street from you."

I gave my best *humph*.

"Have you gone over to meet them yet?"

I grabbed at a towel in the clothes basket atop the kitchen table. "Now, why in the world would I want to do that? I don't like all this . . . you know, people coming in here. What's wrong with just settling in Breckenridge or Vail? That's where most of them work, isn't it?"

"What's wrong with getting to know them, Evie? I lived in California. Remember? And I'm not a bad person."

"Maybe you weren't there long enough to be affected."

"And maybe inviting them to church or to one of our suppers on Wednesday night in the social hall might be in order."

I laid the folded towel on top of the others at the far end of the table without responding.

"Do they have children?"

13

"How in the world should I know?" I paused. "One."

Vonnie giggled again.

The extended cord of the phone kept bopping me on the elbow, so I grabbed at it and tucked it under my arm. "I saw a baby crib going into the house, okay?"

Vonnie laughed hard then. "Oh, Evangeline. You are so funny. Now, don't you think that if they have a baby, they might like to know we have a lovely church right here in town?"

We do have a lovely church—that much is true—though at one time Grace Church, a charming but small white clapboard structure, was the only church in town. We have a few more now, mainly because of the Rushies coming in and starting up their own fellowships. But none of them have the history of Grace Church. None of them were established by Father Dryer, the famous circuit preacher who visited his churches by cross-country skiing through the mountains. We have the stained glass windows to prove it too. Each one depicts a scene from the skiing preacher's ministry.

Okay, so yes, I did invite the neighbors, and they did graciously attend our services for a while, but like I said, that was before so many moved into Summit View and changed everything, including the cost of living.

We prayed about this during one of our Potluck Club meetings. By this time our twosome had grown to a foursome. After all, Jesus said (and I quote), "Again I say unto you, That if two of you shall agree on earth as touching any thing that they shall ask, it shall be done for them of my Father which is in heaven."

That's Matthew 18:19 in King James Version, if you need to mark it, and Ruth Ann and I figured that if our two prayers were reaching the heavenly Father, then surely four would reach him all the faster. So that's when Vonnie and Lizzie joined us. Like Ruth Ann and Vonnie and me, Lizzie Prattle had grown up here and had attended school with us. She hadn't been the most popular girl in school, and she wasn't the smartest or the prettiest, but she always loved the Lord, and that was good enough for us.

And she makes a wonderful apple pie. Plus, her husband is the president of the local bank and on the finance committee at Grace, so she's good to have around. Okay, okay. All that, and she's so often the voice of reason. Like Vonnie.

Around this time, I was throwing in a dish from one of my mama's recipes, usually some sort of vegetable, Ruth Ann was bringing some of her nice homemade melt-in-your-mouth buttery biscuits, Vonnie was bringing along Mexican tamales (which she said she learned to cook when she was at Berkeley), and Lizzie was bringing the pie or a cake.

While we prayed about the increase in taxes, we also prayed for Ruth Ann, who hadn't been feeling well. We prayed the Lord would give her more energy, and then when she went to the doctor, we prayed that the doctor would find the cause. Then we prayed when he found that she had cancer. They wanted to operate, so we prayed about that, and we prayed while she was in surgery. And then we prayed a few days later as we wept at her funeral in the pews of Grace Church, wondering why God answers some prayers just like we want and doesn't answer others the right way at all.

At least not the right way as far as we can see. But God's ways are not our ways. No, they are not. And one of these days when Ruth Ann and I are sipping on coffee and nibbling on coffee cake in the Great Beyond, I'm going to understand why my best friend in the whole wide world had to leave me all alone at such an early age.

By the way, I'm not married and I never have been. Not that I didn't want to find that special someone. I did—I just never found him.

"It must be wonderful," I said to my sister Peggy on the evening before her wedding. "To have found Matthew and to be so in love."

Peggy, older by three years, and I were burrowed under the thick comforter on her bed. This would be our last night to sleep in the same bed together as sisters. We had the covers pulled up to our chins, lying face-to-face, whispering in her moonlit bedroom.

She smiled and sighed deeply. "It is wonderful, Evie. But don't you worry. You'll meet Prince Charming soon enough and fall in love and get married just like me."

15

Either Prince Charming never came to Summit View or I was too busy to notice him, but either way, here I am, alone in a rambling old house, Mama and Daddy's before they were killed in an auto accident. I have good friends, and I'm active socially and civically, and I'm the president of the Potluck Club, which by the way is having its meeting tomorrow.

Now, about the PLC. Nothing—and I do mean nothing—about the Potluck Club is as it used to be. What began as two and then boomed to four has all but exploded to five.

Make that six.

We have another transplant in town—Lisa Leann Lambert, if you can buy that name—and she's invited herself to the group. How she managed to sidestep her way in is another story. Goodness, even our pastor's precious wife, Jan Moore (who, like Lisa Leann is also from Texas, but we all love and adore her), can't get an invitation into our group. I've come to the conclusion that Texas women are either "sweet as pie" or "pushy as cowpokes."

Donna Vesey is neither. Another of our members, Donna . . . well . . . humph. Deputy Sheriff Donna Vesey, daughter of Sheriff Vernon Vesey, that girl, in a sense, cost me a husband.

But I won't go into all that now.

Then there's Goldie Brook Dippel. She was also a transplant, but from Georgia. She married Jack, who was from Denver, back in the early seventies. They moved to Summit View when Jack got a position with the Summit County Board of Education as head coach at the high school. Goldie has been an asset to our community (in spite of her no-good husband) and a good friend ever since. So, even though she wasn't born here, she's really a local.

The funny thing—and no one has dared breathe a word about it—is that I, Evangeline Benson, the president and founder of the Potluck Club, hate (and I do mean hate) to cook.

Simply hate it. But God in his infinite wisdom has made me queen bee of the PLC.

The Gold Rush Grocery Store is in the center of downtown Summit View, right next to the old Gilded Age Movie Theater. I drove my old but faithful Camry through the streets and blessed God for the parking space right up front. I put the car in park, shut off the engine, and scurried out, making my way into the heated grocery as quickly as I could. Fortunately, Vernon Vesey saw me coming and opened the door for me.

"Good afternoon, Vernon," I greeted him. Vernon, a 1963 graduate of Summit View High, gave me my first kiss during a game of spin-the-bottle back when we were twelve. We played this at Ruth Ann's birthday party, after most of the guests had gone home and the adults thought we were just talking and drinking RC Colas in the backyard. When it was Vernon's turn, the bottle landed on me. We held hands and, as was required, walked around Ruth Ann's daddy's toolshed. There was an old plant pot in the middle. When we got to it, we were supposed to kiss, which we did, not that we had a clue as to what we were doing. What I remember most is thinking that Vernon Vesey kissed like a chicken, not that I'd ever kissed one of those either. At any rate, Vernon was my first sweetheart, a passionate affair that lasted all of two days until Doreen Roberts told him she'd kiss him for five full minutes if he'd break up with me and go with her, which he did. And I've never entirely forgiven him for it.

"Good afternoon, Evangeline. Can you believe it's snowing already?"

I shook a light dusting of snow off my coat. "One never knows what one will get in Summit View," I replied.

Vernon, dressed in his uniform and a leather jacket, reached for one of the baskets kept stacked up near the door and just before the shopping carts. "Basket or buggy?" he asked with a smile. I have to tell you that Vernon Vesey—even after all these years—has managed to keep the most endearing smile I've ever seen. No matter how hard I try, I can't resist him when he smiles at me like that.

"Basket," I said. "I'm just here to pick up a few things." He handed me the top basket, and as a way of being pleasant, I asked, "So, how's your daughter, Vern?"

"Good. Good."

The door opened about that time, blowing in more of the crisp cold along with two Rushie women and their little ones. You know a Rushie woman when you see one; she's the one with frosted blond hair cut in some style fresh out of a magazine, wearing some sporty outfit and enough makeup to get that new woman Lisa Leann Lambert so excited she can practically see herself sitting in a pink Mary Kay Cadillac.

"Good afternoon, ladies," Vernon greeted them.

"Good afternoon, Sheriff," they said, reaching for carts instead of the baskets.

I crossed my arms. "So, how's Summit County, Vernon? Any new crime waves going on while the good citizens are sleeping?"

Vernon shook his head. I noticed his hair seemed to be sprinkled with a little more salt since last I'd seen him, which was about two weeks ago. Funny how I always notice things like that.

"Not as long as I'm the law in this town."

I patted him on the arm and then started to walk away. "You're a good officer, Vern. Just like your daddy and his daddy before him."

Vernon began walking beside me. I cut him a sideward glance. "I see you have neither buggy nor basket there, Vernon."

"Oh, I thought I'd just walk along with you for a minute, Evie-girl," he said, using the endearment by which he'd called me since we were sweethearts. "Anything wrong with that?"

I frowned. "No, nothing I can think of. Unless you think I'm going to shoplift or something."

Vernon laughed. "Evie, tell me something. What was I thinking all those years ago when I let Doreen talk me out of going steady with you and into going steady with her instead?"

I stopped dead in my tracks, which, fortunately for me, was right in front of the soups. "I don't know, Vernon. What were you thinking? As a matter of fact, what were you thinking years later when you met her at the altar?"

His eyes twinkled. "Oh, I don't know. Probably the same thing I was thinking when she ran off with the church's choir director. What kind of fool am I?" He sang the last line. It was off-key, but appropriate. Of course, he was right there. The whole incident gave the entire town something to talk—or pray—about.

18

I reached for a can of soup. "A big one, I'd say. All because she'd kiss you for five full minutes."

He nudged me with his shoulder. "And full on the lips too."

I opened my mouth in indignation. "I kissed you full on the lips," I all but hissed, then blushed and pushed his shoulder with the flat of my palm. "Vernon Vesey, how do you manage to rile me up so?"

"You know you'll always be my first love, Evie."

I walked away, heading for the canned goods aisle. "Shut up, Vernon."

"Wanna go to the movies later tonight?"

"I do not."

"Tell you what, I'll pick you up at 7:00, we'll have dinner over at the diner, and then I'll take you to the Gilded Age."

I reached the canned goods, but the peas, carrots, and mushroom cans all seemed to blur together. This wasn't the first time Vernon had made a pass at me since Doreen left him, and it wouldn't be the last. Shame on me, but I did get a kick out of it, and what was the harm, after all? "Vernon—"

"We'll sit in the back row, and you can prove to me that you can kiss a good five minutes like you said you'd do when we were twelve. You owe me one, Evie-girl."

I blushed appropriately. "Vernon, if you don't hush . . ."

"Come on," he whispered, leaning dangerously close to my ear.

I giggled. "No."

"Why not?"

"Because I need to get ready for tomorrow's Potluck meeting."

Vernon straightened. "Oh yeah. The Potluck Gossip Club."

I spun around, my vision suddenly crystal clear. "You take that back, Vernon Vesey. We are five women who pray fervently for God's children."

"I hear from Donna that tomorrow you'll be six, what with Mrs. Lambert joining you."

I huffed. "That woman. The nerve."

"It won't hurt to add one more pray-er, I don't suppose. Who's on the slaughter block this week?"

19

"Oh, ha-ha. And if you must know, we pray for anyone and everyone who calls and lets us know they need prayer. Sometimes we pray for folks who don't ask, but we know they need it. We even pray for you." I added the last part for good measure.

Again he chuckled. "I could use it, Evie. The good Lord knows I need all the prayer I can get."

With that he walked off, leaving me to wonder what was going on to make him say such a thing.

"What do you think made him say such a thing?" I asked Vonnie on the phone later. I was making the brown rice, starting off by measuring a full cup of dry white rice into Mama's old measuring cup and pouring it into a buttered Corningware casserole dish.

"Well, I wouldn't know. I haven't seen Vernon in over a month and haven't had a decent conversation with him in I don't know how long."

"He looked healthy."

"I'm sure he's fine, Evie. I'm also sure you were shamelessly flirting."

I reached for the utensil drawer and pulled out my can opener so I could open the cans of onion soup. "So? He's not married anymore, and I'm not married period. Where's the problem?"

"You know the answer to that as good as I do. It's not fitting for a woman of our age . . ."

Not fitting. I poured the two cans of soup over the rice and thought how easy it is for a married woman to say how a single woman should act. What does she know about the loneliness or the emptiness? What does she know about eating cold sandwiches in a dark living room by the light of the television or holding a pillow close to her breast and pretending a warm body is next to her? "Maybe he's got financial problems."

"Evie . . ."

"Or maybe he's bored with his job."

"That I can imagine."

I pulled the telephone cord as I walked across the kitchen toward the pantry, where I pulled two cans of beef bouillon soup off the shelf and returned to the counter where the rest of the necessary items waited.

"Poor Vernon. In all these years not one serious felony."

"Thank the good Lord."

I picked up the can opener and began to open the third and forth cans of soup. "Vern's probably thanking the good Lord for tourists. If he didn't have them and all the problems that come with them, his sole job would be dusting the courthouse all day."

"At least he has his work with the volunteer fire department. That keeps him out of trouble."

"Yes, what would we do without our snow bunnies who manage to get lost in the mountains at least once before they go back to wherever they come from." I added the soups to the mixture, then popped the top on the mushrooms and threw them in as well. Cooking the way I like it. Simple, simple, simple. "I'm done with the rice. Other than cooking it, I mean, and I don't really have to do that part. What are you bringing tomorrow?"

"I have a new pork chop and potato dish."

I sighed.

"What's wrong with that?" she asked.

"Well, I'm making rice."

"And?"

"Rice and potatoes?"

Vonnie laughed. "Remember, sweet one, that our purpose is to pray, not eat."

I laughed along with her. "What do you think that Lisa woman is going to bring? Some Texas dish, I'll bet."

"Evie. Lisa Leann is a nice woman. A good woman."

"I called Jan Moore about it."

I heard a slight gasp from the other end of the line. "You didn't."

"I did. She told me she thinks she might have been somewhat responsible for Lisa Leann inviting herself."

"In what way?"

"I don't know. That's just what she said. Had that 'I'm sorry' tone in her voice. Well, I'm not happy about it, but who in their right mind could ever be angry with Jan Moore? She's the sweetest thing . . ."

"That she is. The more I know her, the more I love her. I don't even want to think about the Moores leaving us for another church. Not ever."

"They won't leave. Though if Jan lets one more person into my group, I may drop-kick her through the goalpost of life." I laughed at my own humor, Vonnie with me. "Still, I say we ought to be able to find some way to get Mrs. Lambert out of the club. After all, this is her first meeting, and she wasn't even invited."

"Evie, we are a Christian prayer group."

"All right. Let me get this in the oven, and I'll see you tomorrow."

"Sounds good."

I covered the casserole dish with its glass top. "And Vonnie?"

"Yes?"

"Don't mention to anyone about Vern, okay?"

"Of course not."

I hung up the phone, then walked the Corningware over to the oven. As soon as I slid it on the center shelf and shut the door, my telephone rang.

"Hello?"

"Aunt Evie?"

"Leigh?" It was Peggy's daughter, my twenty-five-year-old niece.

"Hi, Aunt Evie."

I could hear a cacophony in the background. "Where are you?"

"I'm in O'Hare."

I swung around and rested my bony hip against the counter. "Say that again?"

"O'Hare."

"What in the world are you doing there?"

"I've left home."

I decided we must have a bad connection. "You've done what? You've left home?"

"I'm coming to Colorado, Aunt Evie. I'm coming to see you . . . to stay with you for a while, you know what I'm saying?"

So much for lonely, I thought, closing my eyes. Still . . . "Leigh, you can't be serious."

"I am serious, Aunt Evie."

My eyes widened as if to take in what Leigh was saying. So this was why Peggy had been so quiet lately when I asked her about Leigh. She was always open and honest about her boys, but lately she'd been very secretive about Leigh. "Are you having problems with your mama?"

"Aunt Evie—"

"Answer me, Leigh. You can't just come out here without telling me something."

"I'll tell you when I see you. I arrive in Denver in a few hours. I'll take a shuttle to Summit View; you don't have to pick me up at the airport. I don't want you out this late." She paused for a moment. "Aunt Evie, they're calling my flight number. I have to go now. I'll see you tonight, okay? I love you."

"I love you—" The line went dead before I had a chance to finish. "Oh, Lord, what in the world?" I hung up my phone and picked it up again, dialing Peggy's number.

"Hello?"

"Margaret Benson Banks, would you mind telling me what's going on out there?"

"Good afternoon to you too, Evie."

I walked over to the kitchen table and sat in one of the chairs. "I just received a call from Leigh."

There was an audible sigh from the other end. "I should've known she'd go there."

"And?"

"And what?"

"What's going on?"

"I think you'll have to talk to Leigh. All I can say right now is that she has broken our hearts, Evie. She has nearly destroyed her father and me."

"What does that mean?"

"Evie," Peggy's voice dropped an octave, "you know how Leigh has always been. Wild . . ."

"Spirited."

"Spoiled."

"Unconventional."

Peggy sighed again. "You've always seen Leigh as you want to see her. I'm her mother . . ."

"And you've always wanted her to be just like you. Why not let her be who she is?"

"Because." Peggy's voice was up again. "You know what, Evangeline? You just keep your condemnations to yourself. I don't see how you can possibly judge me when you've raised not one single child of your own, especially one who came along late in life. I don't see how . . ." she trailed off. "Why don't you just call me tomorrow after you've talked to Leigh and then we'll see how you feel about all this?"

I was almost too stunned to respond, but I did, in the most cutting way I knew how. "I think I will. I'll just do that. I have to go now, Peggy. I have to get your old room ready for your daughter. Looks like I'll have a child to take care of after all."

"Yeah, well. I hope you do a better job of that than the job you've done caring for Papa and Mama's graves."

I slammed the phone down. *How dare she? So I don't like cemeteries. She didn't have to get mean about it, now did she?*

Leigh wasn't really a child, but to me she'd always be a precocious little girl in blond ringlet pigtails. She's got large blue eyes you could just drown in and the softest, prettiest skin ever to grace a young lady. There were framed photographs of her all over my house, so it didn't surprise me, either, that she would come here. She'd always known how I felt about her.

I busied myself for the next few hours getting her room ready, then waited in the living room, reading our Beth Moore study book. I just love Beth Moore. She's—how does Vonnie say it?—deep. The sky had long ago grown dark, so I got up and turned the front porch light on, then walked over to the front window and peered out just in time to see a passenger van pull into my driveway. I turned away, rushing to the front door so I could open it for Leigh as soon as she got up to it. The weather was bitterly cold, and I didn't want her out there even a second longer than she had to be.

As soon as I heard her nearing the porch, I swung the door open wide. "Hurry. Hurry," I said as she stepped into the foyer. I closed the door and turned to take a look at her. She carried a small suitcase in her right hand and had a purse slung over her shoulder. Her hair, dyed dark red and cut short and spiked all over her head, carried flakes of snow. When she shook her head, snowflakes fell to the shoulders of her wool coat.

"Let me get you out of that coat," I said, reaching for it. "Then we'll go into the living room, where I have a nice warm fire going."

"Thanks, Aunt Evie," she said, setting the suitcase on the floor, then turning around as she unbuttoned her coat.

I pulled it from her shoulders and turned toward the foyer coatrack so I could hang it there to dry. I heard Leigh heading toward the living room, and I called after her. "Are you hungry?"

"No. I grabbed something at the airport."

I frowned, walking into the living room, where she stood facing the fireplace. "Why did you do that?"

She turned to look over her shoulder and smiled at me. "I was hungry."

And then she turned all the way around.

What can I say?

There she was, my beautiful Leigh, with a belly as round as a basketball.

3

Does she know
she's infamous . . .

That Evangeline and the Potluck Club. As ace reporter of the *Gold Rush News*, knowing what he knew . . .

Clay Whitefield shook his head and tapped his pen on his lip. Well, a man could weep at the sorrow of it all . . . or crack up laughing.

Clay was chuckling.

The legend of Evangeline and Sheriff Vesey was nearly as famous around Summit View as the stories of the old gold rush days—not that Clay believed Ms. Benson knew just how infamous she had become over the years. *Because if she did,* Clay thought, *well, she wouldn't set foot anywhere in town, much less in her beloved church.*

The ladies of the Potluck. One day he'd crack their story, no matter how many days he had to sit in this one spot, keeping his eyes peeled and his ears open. Or how much he had to imagine before he got to the truth.

Lisa Leann

Best Oven Barbecued Brisket

Ingredients:

5-6 pounds brisket (or a 3-4 pound
eye of round roast)
1 bottle liquid smoke
Garlic salt
Onion salt
Seasoned salt
1 tsp. flour
1 oven bag
1 bottle barbecued sauce (onion flavored
1/2 cup mild picante sauce)

(over)

4

On a Roll

As I powered down my window to back my Lincoln out of that tricky parking spot in front of Mac's Video Store, I noticed the sky was sputtering something that looked like slush again. *Doesn't the weather around here ever make up its mind?*

Just that morning, as I sat in the cedar rocking chair on my balcony and tried to read from the Psalms, the sky was a blazing September blue. The groves of aspen zigzagged glowing yellow up emerald-green mountains. The whole mess reflected like a postcard into the silver mirror they call Golden Lake. Scenery like that called Henry and me to this state of wonder. But now that we've actually sold our exclusive home in the Woodlands, near Houston, I'm still in a state of wonder, wondering, *Why? What were we thinking?*

I, Lisa Leann Lambert, am only forty-seven years old and still in my prime. I'm not ready to retire to that little ol' rocking chair. But that's just what Summit View, Colorado, has done to me. It's turned me into a rocking-chair granny. Now, I don't cuss like a cowboy, never have. But shall I daresay Summit View has been a rocking chair . . .

"H-e-l-l-o, Donna!"

Henry says I wave too much. But I can't help it if I'm friendly. Besides, most folks wave right back. Even Donna Vesey. Seeing her standing out there doing her job, I had to think she looked great decked out in her sheriff deputy's uniform. Why, see there, she was almost pretty despite that scowl she was wearing. Of course, if I was

28

standing in the icy rain, writing speeding tickets to men in little red sports cars, I'd scowl too. I'd bet that was a rental car, straight from a DIA rental lot with a California driver behind the wheel. That ticket served him right. *You go, Donna girl!*

The chill made me power up the window and turn on the heat. While I was at it, I hit the windshield wipers. I turned on the stereo, and Sandi Patti belted out "Majesty," one of my all-time favorites; and it certainly described the scenery in my new subdivision, Gold Rush Townhomes. None of those puppies around Golden Lake sell for anything less than three quarters of a mill—they're some digs, I can tell you.

Of course, the thing about our frequent afternoon rain showers is that they always manage to streak my Lincoln Continental with dust. I probably should've gotten the tan Lincoln instead of the maroon, but this one has a lot more gadgets, like heated leather seats. And I just know that will come in right handy in a month or two.

This town may not have an automatic car wash, but at least it has a mom-and-pop video store. I guess it would be too much to ask that it carry DVDs too. Thank goodness I kept my old video player.

That night's entertainment was *You've Got Mail.*

I'd seen it a hundred times already, but my copy was still in some unpacked box stuck high in the garage rafters. Not that I was depressed, but that movie had a right sweet way of cheering me up. Who could ever grow tired of seeing Meg Ryan and Tom Hanks falling in love all over again? When I watch it, it's just like I'm falling in love right along with them.

And I would too, that is, if I weren't married to Henry Lloyd Lambert. Henry's my husband of twenty-five years, but at times it seems like a hundred. He's almost ten years older than me and retired from his job as a manager over at the Exxon Oil. He really lucked out, though; he got his retirement all in a lump sum, just before Exxon announced their retirement package cutbacks. So you could say dear ol' Henry and I are set, at least financially.

But not only is Henry retired from work, I hate to say it, but he's retired from our marriage. Of course, we're not divorced—we're

Baptists. But that man only gets excited about rainbow trout and the Dallas Cowboys. I don't seem to fit in anywhere.

I'm not really sure how that all happened. But I guess it happened sometime between the kids' soccer practice and one of my service sorority's fund-raisers. Or maybe it happened when I was down at the First Baptist Church for choir rehearsals. But how could I help being so involved in community life? Those folks absolutely relied on my leadership. I've been president of every organization I've ever been a part of. I show up, and zap—I get the tap to wield the gavel.

The truth is, if I'm not in charge, I'm not happy. As my family's had to figure out: if Mama ain't happy, ain't nobody happy.

But one day, while I was off leading the herd, I looked back and found that Henry had just quit following. The man reminds me of a faded curtain that's blocked the sun for too long. He's still there, but barely.

When he is home, I can find him in one of two places: in front of the television buying fishing rods and hand-tie flies on QVC, or on the computer buying them on eBay. It seems his motto is to never miss a good chance to shut up or to shut me out.

On my way home from the video store, I drove past my new Grace Church, the cutest little white clapboard you'll ever want to see. Too bad it's not Southern Baptist, even if it does have pretty stained-glass windows. There is a Southern Baptist church that meets at the town library, but a church in a library is just not my speed. Neither is the Catholic church or the Church of Christ down on Main Street, not that there's anything wrong with either denomination. Still, I'll probably never step inside those buildings unless I have to attend a funeral.

But back to Henry. He's a fine Christian man. He'd been a good father, though disinterested, perhaps. He doesn't swear, and he's certainly never laid a hand on the kids or me. So I really can't complain, not like those from the women's shelter that my society friends and I used to collect hotel shampoos for. Some of those women actually cried at the sight of hair conditioner. Imagine! Crying over a necessity like hair conditioner. What's the world coming to?

But then I'm always doing charitable things like helping poor women who only want a good shampoo. Besides, that's what Jesus would have me do.

Anyway, Henry left me to my leadership roles, and in return I let him play his golf game every Saturday morning and Sunday afternoon.

Golf I can handle. But unfortunately, Henry's new game is fishing. He spends most of his waking moments up on Gold Rush Creek, up to his waders in rushing water. The only movement you'll see from him is an occasional flick of his line or the sun glinting off the fishhooks covering his cap, the cap that says "Go Cowboys," of course.

It wouldn't be so bad, but he's not into the catch-and-release routine. He actually brings home those slimy fish, all beheaded and gutted. G-R-O-S-S! Our garage freezer's already full of those nasty, frosty trout. I'm a good cook, and I won't stand for those fish smelling up my new kitchen. However, he's determined to fry a couple for himself every night. Imagine, being married to a gourmet cook and settling for pan-fried fish that he has to cook himself.

I passed our little Gold Rush Grocery Store, and while I didn't need anything, I was surprised to see Donna's daddy, Sheriff Vernon Vesey, opening the door for Evangeline Benson. *My, my, but don't they look friendly.* I'd have to tease Evangeline about that when I saw her tomorrow. *Gotta boyfriend, Evie?*

She probably had to run into the store to pick up something for some horrid little potato dish like she had brought to the all-church supper. That dish was so dry it scraped the hide right off the roof of my mouth. Too bad about that. All that dish needed was a little TLC, some butter and maybe a dash more milk. Tomorrow at the Potluck Club meeting, I'd have to find a tactful way to tell her so.

Besides, all wouldn't be lost. I was bringing my barbeque brisket special. I started making it the day before. First I soaked that six-pound round roast all night in a bottle of liquid smoke. Just before I left the house for my movie run, I sprinkled it with garlic, onion,

31

and seasoned salt. Now that brisket was simmering at two hundred degrees in my oven. And there it would stay until the next morning. Then I'd drain off the juice and boil it with an entire bottle of onion-flavored barbecue sauce and a half cup of picante sauce. Finally, I'd bake it another hour.

To tell the truth, I'm glad I was able to worm my way into the Grace Church Potluck Club. God knows they need me and my barbecued brisket. And soon, I can guess, I'll be in charge of the whole shebang. I'll be Queen of the Potluck, all right.

I love the sound of that—and the sound my gold bracelets make every time I reach for the turn signal. I just love noisy baubles or anything that sparkles, like the two-karat rock I wear on my left ring finger. I had to do some fancy talking to get that one out of Henry. But I managed to get my way, as usual.

Speaking of sparkle, that's exactly my plan for the members of the Potluck Club. I'm going to give those pale-faced women a Mary Kay makeover. It's not like I need a pink Cadillac. Shoot, I'd sell that makeup at cost just to improve the scenery around here. I want to rescue those drab women from their dry skin and wrinkles. The Colorado climate is a bit harsh, and some of those women look like well-weathered sailors. But I'll fix that with my soothing layers of creams, pink foundation, and a bit of rosy blush. I can't wait till I can get those gals together with a tube of lipstick. Let's see, I think I'll paint Evangeline's lips a luscious bashful berry. Vern might even want to kiss lips like that.

I always check my rearview mirror when I laugh, and now was no exception. My teal blue eyes look good with laugh lines, not to mention with my copper and gold eye shadow. I still look pretty good, despite the fact I haven't even had my first face-lift. And even though I like to cook—like my mama before me—I don't eat most of what comes out of my oven. I have to work hard to wear those size four petites. I never miss a day of Jane Fonda leading me in a workout, either. That's unlike some of the Colorado "native" women around this town, who are, let's say, a bit pudgy? No, I've never seen them on the hiking and biking trails around here. Maybe that's what makes the trails so lonely.

Yes, it's a good thing I'm here. Why, I'll shape all those little darlin's up and put a bit of sparkle on them to boot.

I have to admit it; the Potluck Club was a hard nut to crack. My lands, it wasn't that difficult to become a member of the Woodlands Country Club. If it hadn't been for Pastor Kevin's wife, Jan, I'd still be out in the cold. These Colorado women are so cliquish! But not Jan Moore or her husband, Kevin. Really, the Moores are darlin'. Like me and Henry, they're retired Texans. All the local folks of any character are, of course, from Texas. And it's only natural for Texans to migrate to these parts. In 1836 Colorado was part of the Republic of Texas. Texans only come here to check up on their former claim and to put some life back into the place.

But thinking back to the Moores, I can't help but admire them. They're in Summit View on kind of a working retirement. They've got the right idea, really. They're only in their fifties and they've got a purpose. I use to have a purpose too—after all, I was the president of my community service sorority, the president of the soccer club association, and the president of the church choir, not to mention the mother of two children. Sure, I miss my clubs, but they're behind me and my kids have outgrown me. My son, Nelson, is a nineteen-year-old sophomore at the University of Texas, a surefire party major, and twenty-three-year-old Mandy has been married only a year and will soon be a mother herself.

I've got to get my purpose back. And I think I've found it at the church. After Henry and I visited Grace Church for the first time, Kevin and Jan drove up to our townhouse for a cup of coffee and some of my famous cinnamon rolls. But I have to give credit where credit's due. Warm cinnamon rolls always help a friendship get off to a good start, and it certainly helped put me on Jan's good side.

Still, I had to work like a dog to find out what the social scene in the church was all about. Finally, Jan let the news of the Potluck Club's existence slip right through her sticky fingers.

"No one at the Potluck Club can cook like this," Jan had said, taking another bite of a warm roll.

33

Aha! I could tell that Jan hadn't meant for that little tidbit to slip. And as I've always said, it's much easier to get the cat out of the bag than to put it back in.

"Potluck Club? I love potlucks!" I said sweetly.

Jan was wearing a white T-shirt with scalloped edges. Her cheeks suddenly glowed pink beneath her big brown eyes. Those liquid eyes of hers are fringed by salt-and-pepper bangs, and that short, wavy haircut makes her look like a million dollars. But Jan looked uncomfortable as she crossed her petite legs under her broomstick skirt. That pink skirt absolutely blended with my velvet-covered Victorian chair.

She cleared her throat. "The Potluck Club? Well, it's a tradition, really, with some of the church's old-timers."

"Do tell."

"Well, they meet once a month for potluck lunch and prayer. But I think it's a closed group."

I just pushed my red curls out of my eyes and stared her down . . . sweetly, of course. "What would it take to get an invitation?" I asked.

"Lisa, I'm the pastor's wife and I'm not even a member."

Right then I reached for a pad of paper. "Honey, just give me their names. I'll handle the rest."

I'd tried not to laugh at the list of corny names. And the funniest of all had to be Evangeline Benson, the Potluck Club president. I could just imagine Evangeline, a plain-faced spinster with her graying hair pulled up in some painful-looking twist. I love a challenge and made a point to meet her the very next Sunday. Of course, I didn't go empty-handed. I came armed with a paper plate full of warm cinnamon rolls. And honey, you just can't ignore rolls like that.

That Sunday, just before I pulled my rolls from my oven, I'd dressed in a long but simple V-necked chenille dress in a delicious cobalt red. It was belted with a gold metal coin belt that showed off my slender waist. Once at the church, I caught up with Evangeline in the parking lot—one of the parishioners, an elderly gent, had helped point her out. Though his help hadn't really been necessary.

I would've recognized Evangeline Benson anywhere. I'd been right about the plain face and the hair (except that her hair was cut short and still plain), but I could never have imagined her clothes. That burnt orange and white polka-dotted polyester pantsuit had to be working on at least three decades. At least it was topped off by a lovely white silk scarf. And with that scarf, one could almost forgive such a flagrant fashion violation. But even so, it was hard to forgive her tacky pinecone brooch that held her scarf in place.

Me in my camel-colored fashion boots skipped across the gravel to where Evangeline stood with a cluster of polyester-clad women. "Evangeline, darlin', I thought I'd bring you these buns."

Evie eyed me with suspicion. "Do I know you?"

Naturally I ignored her question entirely, the point being that she may not know me now but would certainly know me in the future. "They're still warm from my oven. Try one." I shoved the plate closer to Evangeline's nose so she'd get a better whiff of heaven on a platter.

It didn't take long for Evangeline to pull back the foil. She slid a warm pastry into her mouth. When her eyes sparked, I said (just as pretty as you please), "I'm Lisa Leann Lambert, and there's more where that came from, darlin'. I made these special just so you would know what a great addition I'll make to your little Potluck Club."

Evangeline almost choked, but to her credit, she managed to swallow that first bite. But there she stood, tempted between another gooey bite or a quick getaway. It's not hard to say which one won.

An expert at handling awkward moments, I said, "Evie, darlin', isn't that what they call you? Evie? You should taste my brisket. Could I bring one with me, next . . ."

Before Evangeline could help herself, she'd responded, "Saturday."

I smiled in triumph. "At your house? What time?"

Evangeline looked a bit like a trapped animal. Imagine . . . there she was, holding a plate of warm cinnamon rolls, poised to take one more mouth-watering bite. Poor thing. She'd even looked to

35

her friends for support. I saw that their faces registered both shock and admiration for my cleverness. And now, in front of an audience of her peers, holding sticky buns dripping in icing, Evangeline had not been able to refuse my question.

"Noon, and bring your brisket."

So that's how I got into Evangeline's club, which of course will soon be my club. All it'll take is a couple of briskets and maybe a couple of slices of my mom's daffodil cake. Yes, the daffodil cake. Heavy artillery, I know, but I'm going to need it. Donna Vesey's been a bit standoffish so far, but she'll get used to me. And I have to admit my gratitude to Jan. She's just the sweetest thing. I'm sure I'll be able to wiggle her into the club too. Some of the Potluckers weren't so sure about me, but Jan has treated me like a long-lost friend. Yep, that Jan's from Texas, all right. She may have lost her accent, but she still has class.

These women may have history, but I've got the goods.

The ringing of the phone interrupted my reverie. The lake being all misty, I'd decided this night to grab a blanket and sit in my rocker for a spell. What I thought was mist turned out to be a snow squall just over the lake. I moaned, thinking it was too early in the season for snow. Then again, this is wild country up here, so who knows.

Anyway, maybe Henry was calling in from the creek to see what's for supper besides fish. I grinned as I reached for the phone, thinking that pretty soon the lake and creek will be frozen and Henry won't be able to fish at all. That is, unless he's figured out a way to cut a hole in the ice. *Oh, dear Lord, do people do that around here?*

"Hello?" I answered when I'd reached the phone.

"Hi, Lisa, it's Vonnie."

Ah, Evangeline's sidekick. She's one of the polyester gals who shared in those warm cinnamon rolls that Sunday morning in the parking lot.

"Lisa, something's come up. I'm afraid tomorrow's club meeting is off."

"Off? What's up, Vonnie?"

"Evie has unexpected company."

36

"Really? Who?"

"I really can't say."

Can't or won't? "Thanks for calling; you're a darlin'."

"Bye, now."

Unexpected company? I sat down on the pink Victorian. I figured this may work to my advantage. I'd long ago figured out that leaders have to actually serve the group before they could expect to be in charge. And just think, there I sat with my mouth-watering barbecued brisket in hand. Briskets are even better than warm cinnamon rolls in terms of persuasion. This could be my first attempt to win over Evie before taking over the Potluck Club's presidency. She'd never know what hit her.

5

Invader, that's
a good word for her . . .

Clay sat at his scarred desk, pecking away on his laptop.

> From the minute Lisa Leann Lambert invaded the city limits of Summit View . . .

"Invaded, now there's a good word," he said to his two gerbils, Bernstein and Woodward, who dutifully watched their owner from the cage atop the desk. There was sure to be a tug-of-war between Lisa Leann and Evangeline Benson.

"Evangeline doesn't take kindly to anyone treading on her beloved Potluck," he continued the conversation with "the boys," focusing more on Bernstein than Woodward, who was climbing into the cage's wheel for his nightly run.

Bernstein blinked back at him as though interested in the rest of what his owner had to say. "No one has even dared. Even Donna Vesey treads lightly. Between you and me, I wouldn't have even thought that lady knew how . . . to tread lightly, I mean." Clay jutted his neck forward. "Why are you looking at me like that?" He reached for a nearby can of cashews, dug into it with his beefy hands, and then dropped a few nuts into his upturned mouth, saving one and slipping it between the wires of the cage. Bernstein took it greedily while Woodward continued his jog.

Clay—using only his index fingers—continued his typing.

Even as the number of the Potluckers has increased, it's been by invitation only. Women whisper at the diner about it, sure. Everybody who is anybody wants to know what really goes on at those meetings. But not one has ever dared invade it.

Until now.

Goldie

Mother Dippel's Chocolate Cake

1 cup Shortening
1 Stick Butter
3 cups Sugar
3 cups cake flour
4 TB Cocoa
~ ~ ~ ~ ~ ~

½ ts Baking Powder
1 cup Milk
1 TB Vanilla
5 large eggs)

~ ~ ~ ~ ~ ~ ~ ~ ~ ~ ~ ~

Cream shortening, butter and sugar. Sift
flour (today you can get some cake
flour that doesn't have to be sifted, so
watch for that), cocoa and baking powder
together. Add alternately to creamed
mixture with the milk, vanilla and
eggs, lightly beaten together. You'll want to

6

Chilling Report

Life wasn't supposed to turn out this way, Lord.

Not that I'm questioning your ways. I'm not. I'm just telling you what's on my mind. In my heart. And what's on my mind and in my heart is that life wasn't supposed to turn out this way.

I felt a lonely tear slip down my cheek and quickly brushed it away, hoping my husband Jack wouldn't come into the kitchen so early in the morning and find me sitting at the table, Bible spread out before me, crying. He wasn't that big on women who cry. He wasn't all that keen on women who get up early to read the Word of God and pray, either.

But more than that, he wasn't too keen on me, I didn't think.

Maybe that's too harsh of a statement. Lord, is that judging a man's heart? Because I don't mean to judge his heart, you know. I'm just saying how I feel. And if I can't talk to you about this, who can I talk to?

Anyway, I stole a quick glance to the microwave's digital clock to check the time. It was nearly 6:00 in the morning. Jack would be stirring any minute, shuffling his way into the bathroom, where his usual morning grunts and groans would be emitted. Then, as always, he'd step a little livelier down the hallway and into the living room, where he'd sit with an "ahhhhh," reach for the remote to turn on *Fox and Friends*, and then call out, "Goldie, you got breakfast started?"

Not "Good morning."

Not "Well, hello Mary Sunshine."

Or even, "Did you sleep well?"

Just, "Goldie, you got breakfast started?"

And what would I say? The same thing I say every morning. "Almost done, Jack."

I stood from the table, closed the Bible, and walked it over to rest on a nearby countertop next to the recipe book I'd pulled off the shelf the night before. After I got Jack off to work and the house straight, I'd be preparing a dish for the Potluck Club's luncheon and prayer meeting, so I'd gone ahead and laid out the recipe book and ingredients I'd be needing for sweet corn pudding.

With a final, *Well, I guess I asked for it, Lord. Laci told me Jack Dippel would break my heart one day, and he sure did that,* I closed my morning chat with God and got busy in the kitchen.

People around Summit View don't think I know the truth about Jack. Either that or they think I know the truth but choose to ignore it. Doesn't matter how one believes. Either way, I'm pretty pathetic, aren't I? But just to keep the record straight, yes, I know what a womanizer Jack Dippel is. I've known about all the women he's bedded since probably the first affair he had on me . . . in spite of the fact that I'm sure he considers himself discreet.

And "Christian." Why, Jack Dippel wouldn't miss a Sunday sitting that flat fanny of his in a pew at Grace Church. Looking sharp, I might add. Jack Dippel is nothing if not a fine-looking man. Which is, of course, what attracted me to him in the first place.

I met Jack during my high school senior trip to Washington, D.C. I grew up in the little town of Alma, Georgia—born in nearby Douglas, Georgia, in 1955, which makes me nearing fifty now. I would have to say I was sheltered most of my life. Daddy and Mama had some farmland and made a pretty good living off it, raising three boys and two girls, me being the oldest of the girls but the third child born. Daddy and Mama were just plain good people back then, and they still are. With the exception of Hoy Jr., we're all still here and we're all good Christians.

Hoy Jr. died in a work-related accident. There was never a finer man than Hoy Jr., except maybe our daddy. Hoy Jr. and Daddy were two peas in a pod.

Daddy and Mama made sure we were in church every time the doors opened: Sunday school, church on Sunday, prayer meeting on Wednesday nights. When we got old enough, we got to go to Friday night YIF meetings. YIF stands for Youth in Fellowship.

My best friend back then was Laci Hopper. Laci and I did everything together, and most of it was good. The only thing I can think of right off the top of my head that might have been slightly sinful was the time when we were about eleven years old and decided to try smoking. Laci's daddy smoked, and she managed to slip two cigarettes from his pack of Winstons while he was taking a shower and her mama was cooking supper. That Friday I spent the night at her house, and as soon as we thought her parents and little brother were asleep, we slipped out her bedroom window and ran across the yard to where her mama's potting shed was. When we got to the back side of it, we slid down low, lit up, puffed like two magic dragons, and then threw up the rest of the night. We didn't want Mr. and Mrs. Hopper to know what we'd done, of course, so we had to stay outside in the dark and the cold, retching in a hole Laci dug with her mama's little potting shovel.

Cured me of ever wanting to do anything even slightly sinful again.

Until I met Jack Dippel.

Laci and I managed to work the entire summer before our senior year at one of the two restaurants in Alma so we'd have enough money for the annual trip to D.C. When the big day finally came, we loaded up on the bus with the other seniors, anxious to see where the "Law of the Land" was made and to tour the great old government buildings. When we arrived at the hotel, our teacher, Mrs. Sanderson, said to go right up to our rooms, take a shower, and get dressed and ready for dinner. We were to meet back in the lobby by 5:00 sharp.

Laci and I raced upstairs, giggling the whole way. When we got to our room, we opened our luggage and began pulling our clothes out, hanging up the ones that needed to be hung and putting the rest in the dresser drawers. That's when I spotted a really cute lavender sleeveless sweater of Laci's and said to her, "That would go so great with my slacks I'm wearing tonight."

"Want to wear it?" she asked, already handing it to me.

"Do you mind?"

"Don't be silly," she said with a toss of her dark hair. "Let's make a deal right now that we can borrow, okay?"

I took the sweater in one hand and shook her hand with the other. "Deal."

So it was that on that particular evening, when I'd showered and dressed ahead of Laci, that I decided to go ahead and go on down to the lobby to check things out. What happened, though, is that I got checked out instead, which I now suppose is understandable, considering Laci's sweater was a bit too small for me.

As it turned out, Jack Dippel was in the same hotel, though he was traveling with some college friends. Unlike me, he was unchaperoned, which I suppose I found somewhat exciting and dangerous.

After looking around the gift shop and perusing the lobby a bit—and not having seen one single familiar face—I took a seat in the center of the room so I could get a feel for the place. I'd hardly been there two minutes when Jack walked up and sat in the chair next to mine.

I took notice of him immediately. What red-blooded girl wouldn't? He wasn't very tall, but he was muscular in a sort of chiseled kind of way. His hair was silky straight and blond, his eyes were blue, and his skin was tanned. He looked like he'd walked off the pages of a Coppertone ad. When he sat—wearing tight jeans and a pullover shirt—he rested his elbows on his knees, turned his face my way, and said, "You've got the prettiest red hair I believe I've ever seen."

My hair. If there is ever anything in my life that has gotten me noticed, it's my hair. In fact, my real name is Nancy, but my whole life I've been called "Goldie" because my hair is "the color of the setting sun on an autumn afternoon," as Daddy used to say. Knowing it to be my greatest feature, I had taken good care of it and had let it grow until it reached my waist in soft waves.

At Jack's words, I reached behind my neck and pulled the length of it over one shoulder. "Thank you," I said.

45

"What's your name?"

"My friends call me Goldie." I pressed my lips together.

"I can see why." He smiled then, showing off twin dimples. "Where are you from?"

"Georgia. What about you?"

"Colorado. I'm here with a few friends, taking a break before summer semester starts."

"You're in college?"

"Yeah. You?"

"I'm a high school senior. This is our senior trip." I gave the lobby a sweep with my eyes, wondering if any of my classmates might have wandered down. I knew one thing for certain: I didn't want Mrs. Sanderson to catch me talking to this guy. She'd call Mama and Daddy before I even had time to blink, and Mama would meet me back home with a belt in her hand. Mama didn't take to me talking to strangers, especially when they were young men.

It wasn't that I hadn't dated yet. I had. But they were all boys from church, and so far I hadn't been allowed to date by myself. It was always group dates with guys and gals from YIF. Up to that very moment, that had always been fine with me.

"Well, hello Miss Senior from Georgia," Jack said, reaching a hand out to shake mine. "I'm Jack Dippel."

I took his hand, then released it and brought mine back, immediately catching the scent of English Leather. "Hello, Jack Dippel. I'm Goldie Brook."

Jack gave me a sideward smile. "That name deserves to be in a book somewhere. Or on a movie screen. Goldie Brook."

I giggled. "Well, I doubt it."

"So what are you doing tonight?" he asked. "Out to dinner with the class?"

I nodded.

He leaned closer, like he wanted to whisper something to me, so I leaned nearer to him. "What are you doing after that?"

I shrugged my shoulders. "I guess we're coming back here and going to bed."

He held my green eyes captive with his blue ones. "I'd really like to get to know you better, but I'm going out for dinner too." He moistened his lips with his tongue. "Tell you what. Meet me back down at the pool at 11:00."

I shook my head. "I can't."

"Why not?"

I smiled at him. "What if we got caught?"

"Got caught? Got caught doing what? We're just going to sit at the pool and talk." He held up his hand as though he were taking an oath. "I swear."

I bit my bottom lip and looked up just in time to see several of my classmates stepping out of the elevator. "I gotta go," I said, standing.

Jack stood too, taking my hand in his as though we were spies passing notes. "Meet me," he whispered. "Come on."

I gave him a coy look from the corner of my eye. "Maybe," I said with a smile, knowing I would indeed somehow, some way, manage to be at the pool at 11:00 that night.

Jack was right. All we did that night was talk. And the next night, and the night after that. By the fourth night, though, we were all over each other. Not in a bad way. We just started kissing, and we kissed all night long . . . or at least until about 1:00 when I went back to the room, where Laci waited for the nightly report.

When we left D.C., I cried. Jack and I exchanged addresses and phone numbers and promised to stay in touch, but I felt like my insides were coming out and that I might as well go home and die. No boy from Alma, Georgia, would ever compare to Jack Dippel.

As soon as we got on the bus, Laci handed me a little gift: stationery she'd stolen from the desk in our hotel room and a pen. "Go ahead," she said. "Start writing him. You know you want to."

I couldn't mail letters to Jack from the house, so every day when I went into town for my shift at the restaurant, I'd drop a sealed-with-a-kiss envelope in the mailbox outside the post office. I told him he'd better not send letters to my house but instead send the letters to Laci's with no return address, which is what he did. He'd also call me every Friday when I spent the night at her house, and we'd talk, me stretched out on Laci's satiny bedspread with tiny goose bumps up and down my body. Jack Dippel had a way of doing that to me.

I should have known a relationship started on secret meetings and deception would lead to disaster, but I was young and foolish and so in love I couldn't see straight. That included when fall came and I took a clerical job with Dr. Thomason. I told Jack I wasn't planning to go to college right away because I was unsure what I wanted to do, but the truth was my parents couldn't afford to send me and my grades weren't good enough to get me a scholarship. Truth be completely told, what I wanted more than anything was for Jack to somehow arrive in Alma and take me away.

Laci and I talked about it all the time . . . what it would be like to be Mrs. Jack Dippel. We continued to hold on to that dream even when Jack told me he was dating a girl in college but still had feelings for me.

"I just want to be honest with you, baby," he said during one of our Friday night long-distance marathons. "It's not that I don't love you, because I do. You know I do."

Tears welled up inside me. "I know you do," I whispered.

"Are you crying? Oh, man. Don't cry. Baby, please don't cry. I can't stand it when a girl cries."

"I won't," I said, crying all the more. Laci was in the room. Her brow was furrowed as she brought me a box of tissues from her dresser.

"I swear to you, it's just to have someone for parties and things like that. She's not you, Goldie."

"Okay."

"She's not even pretty."

I coughed out a sarcastic laugh. "I have trouble believing that."

He paused then, quiet so long I thought he'd hung up on me. "Tell you what. What if I come to Alma next month for Christmas?"

My heart literally stopped beating. "What?"

"Seriously. I want to meet your family anyway, and it'll give us a chance to be together again. I'll come the week before so I don't mess with my mother's plans for the holidays."

By this time I'd sat straight up on the bed. "What?" I asked again. "Jack, don't you know my parents don't know about you? Haven't you figured that out?"

"Don't you think it's time they did? I mean, after all—"

"After all what?"

He paused again. "Look, baby. We'll talk about that later."

"We'll talk about what later?"

He laughed then, the soft, adorable little laugh I'd come to love so much. "Who loves you?"

"You do," I said so softly I'm surprised he could even hear me.

"That's my girl."

Jack came at Christmas that year and met my family—a tenser Christmas there has never been since the birth of Jesus. Hoy Jr. was living back then and in his own place with his wife and their baby, so I talked him into letting Jack stay with them. By the end of the second day, Jack had sweet-talked Mama into loving him and had nearly won over Daddy too. By the time he went home—me crying like a lovesick fool—he'd won over the entire family, our pastor, and half of Alma.

Jack Dippel is just plain good at winning people over. The only person by this time who didn't love Jack was Laci, and I guess with her knowing everything, she saw right through him. Sometimes I wish I had.

Two years, five "other girlfriends," and a college degree later, Jack and I got married. We honeymooned in D.C. for the sake of sentiment, stayed in the same hotel, and, at Jack's insistence, "met" by the pool at 11:00.

"We'll make out a while then go upstairs," he said, nibbling on my neck as we rode the elevator to the seventh floor.

We stayed in room 714. I'll remember that number till the day I die, I think.

"Where you will really become Mrs. Jack Dippel," he concluded, his eyes all twinkly. My goodness, how that boy could sweet-talk.

"You are the most romantic thing I've ever known," I said back to him. "Marriage to you is going to be so wonderful."

Yeah, well. We've been married nearly thirty years now, and it's been anything but wonderful.

Not that I regret marrying Jack. We have a beautiful daughter, Olivia, and the most precious grandson anyone has ever seen on God's green earth.

Olivia and her husband, Tony—who owns an antique shop over in Breckenridge—named the baby Brook, after my family. Brook is almost three years old, and—as my mama would say—he's a cap pistol. He's also the near spitting image of his grandfather. God help all the girls who will fall into his spell when he grows up. I can only pray to the good Lord that he doesn't sin like "Grandpa Jack."

When we came home from our honeymoon, it was to Summit View, where Jack had taken a position at the local high school as the football coach and eleventh-grade history teacher. With his charismatic ways, he soon had everyone eating out of his hands and thinking he was the best thing since sliced bread. Jack's family lived in Denver, so every Sunday after church we'd pack ourselves into his Ford Pinto and drive the two hours to spend the rest of the day with them.

Jack had two younger brothers who still lived at home, though the older of the two was already attending Regis University. The younger was a sophomore in high school and cuter (if you can imagine) than Jack. All that to say that Sundays at the Dippel home were loud, with Dad Dippel and his sons watching whatever sport was being aired that day and Mother Dippel and me working our fingers to the bone in the kitchen, trying to keep up with them.

I remember well the afternoon Mother Dippel and I finally grabbed a quiet moment to talk. She'd made a pot of coffee to go with the chocolate pound cake she'd baked the afternoon before. When we'd finished serving the men, we retreated to her sewing room, where she kept a little love seat and a black-and-white television set. We curled up, both of us, on either end of the love seat, our hands wrapped around the coffee mugs, and began talking like we were old friends.

Like Laci and I used to do. How I missed Laci.

That's when she told me. "You know," she said quietly. "You know that Mr. Dippel has never been the most faithful of husbands."

My mouth dropped open, I'm just sure it did. "What do you mean?"

She looked me straight on. Like me, she was short in stature, but a bit rounder—what with three kids having lived in her womb. She was by no means unattractive, though. She kept her hair styled, and though she didn't wear any makeup, her face was just as pretty as it could be.

Mother Dippel stretched out her right hand, showing off a brilliant emerald and diamond cluster ring. "Affair number one," she said.

Up until that moment I'd always admired that ring. She didn't wear it a lot—it seemed she had so many rings she could accessorize every outfit she owned with a different one. That wasn't the end of it, either. Rings, bracelets, necklaces, earrings. You name it, she had it.

"Affair number one?"

She withdrew her hand, using it to point to the emerald and diamond earrings dressing her ear lobes. "Affair number . . . what was it . . . five, was it? Yes, five."

"Mother—"

Before I could finish, she jutted her wrist toward me. "Affair number eleven," she said as the diamond bangle bracelet winked at me from where it teetered.

"Why are you telling me this?" I asked, truly confused.

Her lips formed a thin line. "Listen to me, Goldie, and listen good. Jack's father is a good man in every way but one. He works hard, provides well, and has never once laid a hand on me in any way other than sexually."

I blushed, thinking I'd never heard my own mother speak of sex in any form or fashion—not even when she was talking about gender. Now . . . Mother Dippel . . . this . . .

"He's a good man," she repeated. "He just has this . . . need, I guess. He's always been discreet about it, and goodness knows this city is big enough I don't ever have to run in to any of these women, whoever they are."

"Then how do you . . . ?"

"How do I know?"

I nodded.

"I know because there's absolutely no other reason for a man to shower a woman with so many baubles when it's not her birthday, their anniversary, or Christmas. That's how I know."

I bit my bottom lip so hard I nearly drew blood. "But why are you telling me?"

She took a thoughtful sip of her coffee. "So you'll know what to look out for."

"Me?" I squealed, sitting straight up.

Her lips grew thin again. "Jack is a good boy, but he's his father's son. I'm no fool, Goldie. Don't you be one, either."

I thought about Mother Dippel's words all the way home, casting glances over to Jack in the driver's seat, him looking as handsome as ever, I thought. I'd promised Mother that I wouldn't repeat any of our conversation to anyone, and I'm certainly a woman of my word, so when Jack said, "What are you thinking about so quiet over there?" I answered, "Just thinking how lucky I am to be married to you."

Which of course garnered a dimpled smile. He leaned over for a kiss, and I obliged, wrapping my arms around the strong biceps of his right arm. "We're happy, aren't we, Jack?"

"Of course we're happy."

"I mean, we're really happy."

"I'm really happy. Are you really happy?"

I nodded in answer. "These have been the most glorious ten months of my life, Jack Dippel," I said. "I can't imagine being any happier."

He looked at me then, taking his eyes off the road long enough to draw me in closer to him. I squeezed his arm, then kissed him near his ear. "I promise you I'll make you the best wife forever and ever."

"You've already done that," he said sweetly. "You're the best a man could ask for."

The following year—in our fourteenth month of marriage—Jack surprised me with a pair of diamond stud earrings.

For no apparent reason.

Except one.

7

That woman is loyal to a fault . . .

From his usual spot at the café window, Clay Whitefield saw Coach Jack Dippel drive by. *Wonder where he's off to*, he mused with some suspicion.

As far as Clay was concerned, Coach Dippel was a snake, no two ways about it. Back when Clay was in high school, he'd been the idol of nearly every guy on the team, but once those like Clay had grown up and learned the truth behind the legend, they weren't so impressed.

How a man could do a woman like Goldie Dippel the way Coach had was anyone's guess. She'd always been the kind of lady who bakes cakes and pies—good cakes and pies—and takes them down to the boys at the volunteer fire department and to the nursing home.

"The kind of woman you hope to find for yourself one day," Clay had heard himself earlier that day saying to Tate Tucker, an ex-team member and the current nursing home administrator. Clay had just made his weekly visit to get the necessary stories for "News from the Home Front," a keeping-you-informed gossip column about the elderly who lived and died there.

Tate was munching on a homemade cookie fresh and hot from Goldie's kitchen.

"You got that right," he said, nodding then pointing to the basketful of goodies. "Loyal to a fault and sweet as Southern pecan pie."

SPICEY APPLE CIDER

2 CUPS WATER
2 CINNAMON STICKS
1 Tbs. WHOLE CLOVES
1/2 tps. WHOLE ALLSPICE

2 QUARTS APPLE CIDER
1 LEMON-SLICED THIN
1 ORANGE-SLICED THIN

COMBINE WATER AND SPICES IN A LARGE
POT ON STOVE AND BOIL. STRAIN MIXTURE
AND POUR SPICED-WATER INTO CROCK-POT.

ADD APPLE CIDER, LEMON AND ORANGE AND
COOK OVER LOW HEAT TILL WARM.

MAKES 10 CUPS

8

Steaming the Locals

I pulled my white Ford Bronco into the Gold Rush RV Park, just two miles west of town. I usually enjoy this area by moonlight, the tall pine forests standing like giants under the twinkling stars. Trouble was, I couldn't see the stars with the glare of all the artificial lights. The overhead beams look like spotlights on the great white motor homes scattered around the picnic tables and jungle gym and trampoline. Trampoline? Now, there's a lawsuit waiting to happen.

I looked back at the campers. It appeared to me that the great whites, as I called those monstrosities, had thinned out—probably because of the snow shower earlier in the evening.

I picked up the radio and spoke to dispatch. "Arrived at 10-20 RV Park, 10-23 till I talk to manager."

The manager, Bob Burnett, was already striding across the gravel to my window. When I lowered it, he popped his scowling face so close to mine I could smell a whiff of beer on his breath. He's a funny, bald bird with eyebrows that jump so high up his forehead they could be mistaken for a streak of hair. As comical as he looks, I never laugh. A snicker from me would send him on another one of his world-famous tirades about respect. I've heard his speech often enough in the hallways of Grace Church; I didn't have the patience for it tonight. Oh, no doubt, Bob believes in respect, especially when it comes to him. How he feels about women is an entirely different story. However, I've noticed he doesn't hesitate to send for me when he needs someone.

"Deputy Donna, it's those kids again. They ain't on our property but close enough to drive my customers to leave for home. There are several truckloads of them over down by the river. They got their music blaring, and worst of all, I think they've been trying to start a campfire."

Not good. With the fire conditions this extreme, even a spark could kick off a forest fire. The early evening snow shower helped, but not enough to dampen this parched timber. It was too little moisture, too late in the season. The way things stood, this forest was nothing more than an inferno waiting to happen, that is, until we got a real blanket of snow. And a fire this close to town could burn it down.

Polite as always, I said, "Thanks, Bob, I'll drive over and look into it."

"Oh, and Donna, the next time you see Miss Evangeline at your Potluck Club meeting, give her my regards."

I fought the impulse to roll my eyes. "Sure, Bob, I'll tell her."

He gave me what appeared to be a shy grin as I closed my window. *Bob must be lonelier than I thought*, I decided as I circled my Bronco around Bob's office and store. I shuddered. What anyone could see in Evie, well, that would take some imagination.

A quarter mile on the freeway, I pulled onto a dirt road. Just a couple of hundred yards ahead, I spotted them, about a dozen teenage boys blinded by my headlights. Talk about disturbing the peace. Truck stereos blared to the same heavy metal station while a couple of boys fed a small campfire pinecones and twigs.

I parked and stepped out of my truck. "You boys know we have a fire ban here?" No sense in elaborating—everyone knew about the fire ban unless they'd just landed from Mars. The forest fire threat had the whole county on edge. Besides, I could tell these boys were locals, judging by the old beat-up pickups with Colorado tags. They certainly weren't driving the fancy red SUVs or sports cars the tourists pick up at DIA before driving up I-70 to visit us.

The boys stared at me without answering. I've seen that look plenty of times; it says, *"Well, little lady, so what?"*

Little lady. That's what the fat, balding Texan tourists call me whenever I pull them over for speeding. I hate it. Maybe I'm short at five foot two; maybe I look petite even when I wear my gun. My voice doesn't help my authority status either. I'm not as bad as the woman rookie in the movie *Police Academy*, but to these boys, I'd sound more like their irate mother than a law officer. And I know my blond hair doesn't help, though I crop off my curls to keep it air force short. This effect makes me look like Tinker Bell, maybe, but nevertheless, it's a major mistake to think I'm anything but tough. These boys would soon discover that.

Things could get interesting, I hoped.

I took my power stance. Hand on my holster, legs spread apart, my voice loud and commanding. "Boys, put out that fire *now!*"

A tall, lanky teen with a yellow streak dyed into his cropped hair slowly undraped himself from the hood of his truck and stood to his full six feet of height to peer down at me. The other boys did the same. Yellow Hair stepped closer.

"You think you're going to make us?"

"That's right, or I'm taking all of you to jail."

The boys laughed among themselves and crossed their arms as they looked me up and down.

"And just how are you going to arrest us all?"

Keeping my hand on my holster, I stepped back, never taking my eyes off the boys. I reached under the seat of my truck and pulled out my twelve-gage shotgun.

Casually as you please, I cocked it and emphasized my words. "Oh, I won't have to. I'll only have to arrest those of you who are still standing."

That shocked those boys into silence. Of course, I would never make good on that threat, not unless they came at me. But that wouldn't happen, because they were worried now that I might be crazy, an assessment not far from the truth.

They stared. I stared right back. Suddenly, one of the boys turned and kicked dirt onto the fire. Another boy poured his bottled water on the small blaze. As it sizzled out, other boys stomped on the hot twigs, grinding them into the dirt.

Then, slowly, one by one, they spit their tobacco juice onto the ground, then climbed into their pickups and drove past me to the highway. Only Yellow Hair made eye contact as he slyly topped his head with a Rockies baseball cap, adjusting it with a one-fingered salute. He was a daring one, all right.

I sighed with relief as I walked over to investigate what was left of the campfire. I kicked a couple of blackened pinecones into the river, then walked back to my Bronco to grab my fire extinguisher. One final squirt of white foam, and the fire was officially out.

I probably should have called it in, or at least called for backup. Even a small campfire like this would make front-page news, with wildfire being such a threat. But a call to dispatch would have taken too much effort. Besides, I'd have to spend the rest of the evening writing up a report. Then the *Gold Rush News* reporter, Clay Whitefield, would call me first thing in the morning, waking me from my well-deserved rest, just to get a quote. Nope, I'd handled things just right. I don't need anyone's help, except maybe when it comes to cooking something for that Potluck Club. Why I go, I'll never know.

Okay, that's not quite true. I know exactly why I show up—with some lame dish in hand—month after month. And it's not to say hello to Miss Evangeline Benson. That woman hates me, but I'm long past trying to win her approval. Besides, that was all resolved in sixth grade one Sunday at church.

There I was, all of twelve years old, dressed in one of the only dresses I owned, an olive drab A-line that was probably wrinkled and too short. Miss Evangeline Benson, dressed in her new orange pantsuit, walked right over to me, pinched my cheeks, and blurted, "Donna, dear. Someone needs to take you shopping. But, oh, I guess since your mom left your dad, you have to fend for yourself, poor, dear child."

I stared at the woman, totally speechless, and stepped back into plump Vonnie Westbrook, my Sunday school teacher.

Vonnie stiffened, and one glance told me this lady was angry! Her voice shook as she spoke. "Evangeline Benson, that's no way to speak to this fine young lady." She'd put her arm around my shoulders and whispered in my ear. "Never mind Evangeline, dear. She's just a bitter old maid."

"I heard that," Evangeline charged.

"Good." Short Miss Vonnie never seemed taller. "Now you know how it feels when folks don't mind their manners."

With that, Vonnie and I stomped off together, though I somehow peeked over my shoulder to see Evangeline's livid face.

That was probably the first time that old biddy had been told off in a very long time, and that it was Vonnie, one of her perpetual sidekicks, who did it just made it sweeter.

And Vonnie, truly a lady of grace, the very next week drove me down to a Denver Sears store and bought me a new dress for Sunday, a couple pairs of shoes, plus new tops and pants for school. She even managed to talk Dad out of two hundred bucks to perform this miracle.

"Vernon, Donna is a young lady now, and for that reason alone she needs new clothes. Now, don't argue. I know you're good for two hundred, and I promise to bring you the change."

To my astonishment, Dad forked over the money without batting an eye. He said, "I appreciate the help, Vonnie. I'm not much on shopping for girls."

Even today, I consider Vonnie Westbrook my best and possibly my only friend. She's the reason I attend the Potluck Club. It was Vonnie who took my motherless self under wing.

I once had a mother. Deep inside my mind, I can still catch a glimpse of her swirled within watercolored fog. I wish I could remember more. Did she ever tuck me in at night? Did she ever tell me she loved me? I don't know.

But I do remember she was a petite blond with a soft cloud of curls that framed her blue eyes. I know those eyes well because I see them every time I look into the mirror. But it's my mom's voice I remember best; a voice that sang sweet songs around the house, a voice that sang solos in the church choir.

I remember the time, one Sunday morning, when I was all of four years old; my father squeezed my arm, a warning to stop my wiggles as Mom sang from the pulpit of the church. That's my last clear memory of my mom, and even now, it's like a grand dream. Her voice rose in sweet glory while the choir director, Mr. Shelly, flapped his skinny arms as the choir's voices rose to embrace my mother's pure song. Suddenly, the choir director turned and stepped into the pulpit with her, completing the hymn in unbelievable harmony as the choir's voices faded to silence. I stopped wiggling then, not because of the warning hand on my arm but because I was lost in the utter beauty of the song.

In fact, that moment is probably the last memory most people have of my mother and the choir director. Instead of going home after the service, they'd hopped into Mr. Shelly's car and headed for the interstate to start a brand-new life together, a life that didn't include me or my dad.

But what I still want to know is—why? Was it me? Was I just too wiggly for Mom to manage? Or was it because she and Mr. Shelly thought their college-trained talents were wasted on the people of Summit View and Grace Church?

No one really knows, but it was rumored they had headed for Nashville in hopes of becoming big recording stars. Maybe she meant to call; maybe an eighteen-wheeler hit her before she reached her destination. All I know is she left me with a brokenhearted father who, if you ask me, still grieves for her, though he never shows it anymore. But the worst part of it all is the rejection. To be rejected by your own mother, wow, that hurts today as much as it did twenty-eight years ago.

But dear, sweet Vonnie didn't abandon me. She and her husband, Fred, have been like family. I was the child they'd wished for but never had. It's their friendship, especially Vonnie's, that's kept me from giving in to the demons that continue to haunt me today. In fact, they've haunted me ever since the night that . . . Well, it would take too much energy to explain that right now.

Even so, Vonnie doesn't know the thing that happened to change me so much. She doesn't know why I resigned from the Boulder County Sheriff's Department and came back to Summit View. She'll never know if I can help it. I couldn't stand to be abandoned by her as well. Now my pain is bearable. It hurts, but I'm tough. Though there's no point in asking God for help. He's allowed my mother to leave me, and he's never once been there when I needed him. Oh, I'll go to church and pretend we're on speaking terms. But we're not, and we never were. The way I see it, who needs a God who fails?

People like Evangeline Benson serve a God like that.

Evangeline Benson, the old flirt, always saying things like, "Oh, Vernon, you look so powerful in your uniform!" Once, after dinner, Dad asked me what I thought of Evangeline. As the chief cook and dishwasher, I'd been busy scraping cold spaghetti off the bottom of one of my best cooking pots. Even though I was only nine, Dad talked to me like I was a grown-up. There he sat, with his gun tucked safely on top of the refrigerator, reading the paper and sipping the remainder of his iced tea. He looked up. "Donna, do you know Miss Evangeline, that woman from church?"

I'd been surprised when he'd mentioned the church. He hadn't darkened the church door since Mom and Mr. Shelly had publicly humiliated him with their great escape. If it hadn't been for Vonnie picking me up every Sunday, I probably wouldn't have gone back to church either.

When I didn't answer immediately, he'd asked, "Do you know the woman I'm talking about?"

Did I ever. Miss Evangeline had always made me feel lower than a squashed bug.

"Yes," I'd finally answered, "I know who she is."

"She invited us over for pie tonight. But I told her I'd check with you. What do you think?"

"I wouldn't eat her pie if she paid me a million dollars."

Dad looked over his paper with an arched brow. "Wouldn't you, now?" He chuckled. "Fine, then. I'll tell her we have other plans."

That was the day I thwarted Evangeline's intentions to marry my dad. And that was the day the real war between us began. Apparently, Miss Evangeline, being fairly sharp, had traced the rejection back to me. I could tell the very next Sunday.

"Donna, dear, don't you like pie?"

"No ma'am. Not your kind."

To think, after all these years, I'm a member of Evangeline's own Potluck Club.

Okay, I take back what I said earlier. There are actually two reasons I take part in this silly gathering. The first reason has already been stated: I love Vonnie. The second reason is I love to rub Evangeline's failure into her face. And that's just what I represent to her. I'm the family she couldn't have.

Her pointed looks no longer bother me, because I've learned the real secret to life. True power comes from dispassionate hate. Such an emotion has the power to keep the whole world at bay.

I flipped on my radio. "Dispatch, 10-8. All clear."

Now to the real problem at hand. How about a store-bought crust filled with a can of cherries?

No, I brought that last time.

What about a carton of Blue Bunny ice cream?

No, too little effort.

I zipped up my leather jacket against the evening chill. What was I thinking? It was autumn, after all. *It's time to bring a Crock-Pot full of my spicy apple cider.*

Yes, that should go over very well.

I glanced over at my mounted portable computer jutting out of the dashboard of my Bronco. My shift ended at 3:00 a.m. If the evening slowed down, maybe I could slip behind the old Gold Mine Bank and enjoy a good game of solitaire. Besides, who would know? And who would dare to complain to the sheriff?

I'm still his daughter, after all.

It was about 1:00 in the morning when the trouble started. I'd been trying to entertain myself by watching the drunks as they left the Gold Rush Tavern. I knew most of these repeat offenders, and I often dropped by near closing time to scout out for those who needed a ride home, especially on Friday nights. That's when I noticed the red Ford Mustang, Colorado tag Z15–991. It was the same rental car I'd stopped earlier in the evening. That's a stop I'll never forget. I'd just finished writing the ticket when Lisa Leann drove by in her Lincoln Continental. With a jolly wave, she plastered me with icy slush.

There I stood, trying to seem authoritative, when suddenly I looked like a drowned rat. But I didn't get soaked as bad as the man in the Mustang. A Mr. David Harris had taken it right in the kisser.

"Is this a Colorado welcome?" the stranger sputtered as he wiped his eyes then his mouth with his sleeve.

I handed him his speeding ticket. "Nope, I've got your welcome right here. Sign, please."

Mr. Harris looked up. "Can't you give a guy a break?" he asked, pen in hand.

"Sorry. No breaks allowed for Californians. Not around here, anyway."

"I didn't know we were outlawed."

He must have caught my hint of a smile; he cleared his throat. "Say, while I've got you . . . I'm looking for someone."

"A missing person? I haven't gotten a briefing about anyone who's disappeared around here. A friend of yours lost out in the backcountry?"

"It's not like that. And I don't have a lot to go on. I'm looking for a woman . . . Jewel?"

Whoa. This guy could be some sort of stalker. I looked at him hard and mentally rehearsed the statistics I had just read on his driver's license. For starters, he didn't look as goofy as his photo, even with a splash of muddy ice on his cheek. And according to his license, he was born in 1968, was five foot eleven, with black hair and brown eyes. Dispatch had informed me that he had no priors or warrants, at least not from Colorado. So he might be on the level. But one couldn't be too sure.

Before I could ask for more details, an eighteen-wheeler baptized us once more. That did it. I tucked my soggy ticket pad into my back pocket and headed back toward the Bronco. I called over my shoulder, "I don't know any Jewel, but good luck."

That splash-down had happened in the afternoon, and now many hours later, there was Mr. Harris's car parked near the back of the tavern. I should have known a good-looking guy like that would hit the bar. That meant he was single—or married and on the prowl.

If he was looking for trouble, chances were he'd find it, especially this time of night, and especially with Wade Gage's pickup parked in the lot. That meant trouble for just about anyone, especially anyone from California.

Suddenly, I spied Dippel and his girlfriend coming out of the joint. It wasn't bad enough he was dating a local; he was taking her out in public. Practically under Goldie's nose. To make matters worse, these two were having a rather loud lovers' quarrel. Here was a fine example of a Grace Church member if I ever saw one. Another case in point as to why I don't take the business of God very seriously. Jack Dippel was just another instance of God's failure.

Charlene Hopefield was drunk and angry. "Jack, you jerk! It's my birthday and all you could buy me was a lousy beer or two while your wife sparkles like a jewelry store? Don't I mean anything to you?"

"Honey, of course you do. I took you out on the town, didn't I?"

Dippel looked over his shoulder and spied me. I nodded and lowered my window. "Evening, Jack. Charlene. Problem?"

Charlene slurred her words. "The problem is my boyfriend here's a jerk."

I got out of my car and glared at Dippel with my hands on my hips. "Obviously."

Dippel cleared his throat. "Sorry, Donna, it's not what it looks like. This is my brother's girlfriend—people often mistake my brother and me, and Charlene here is a little tipsy. Allen's still inside. You know, my brother from Denver?"

Now that was lame. If his brother was in there, then my instincts were so far off I might as well become a beautician.

I smiled sweetly and looked at Charlene. "Well, now, is that so?"

Dippel answered for her. "It's so, unless she never wants to see my brother again."

Charlene's anger turned into fear of abandonment. She sighed, then meekly followed Jack to his Expedition and slid in the passenger's side of the car. Jack said, "Deputy, I'm just going to run Charlene home, then come back for my brother."

I stared hard. "Sure, Dippel, you do that."

The car slowly pulled out of the parking lot and onto the highway. I sighed. How I'd love to arrest that man, but what could I do? Being a no-good liar wasn't a crime. If it were, this whole town would be behind bars.

It continued to amaze me the way people I'd known my whole life lied right to my face. Practically everyone but Vonnie had done so at one time or another.

The barber would say, "Donna, I wasn't speeding. Your radar must have picked up that car that passed me when you hit your radar gun."

Right.

Larry, the short-order cook from the grill, told me, "Donna, I put my credit card in the gas pump before I pumped the gas. It must have malfunctioned. You've known me since grade school; I'd never drive off without paying, not on purpose."

I rolled my eyes and wrote the ticket.

Somehow my skepticism makes me a bit unpopular. But I don't care. I'm mad at this town for lying to me. How dare they be mad at me for calling them on it? That's my job.

Besides, I only have the people of Summit View to thank for helping me create my life thesis, which states: "Most folks are liars, period." And those who claim to be honest? Well, I just hadn't caught them in the right circumstance yet.

I watched Jack's Ford disappear. When it didn't wobble, I breathed a sigh of relief. I knew Jack wasn't too drunk to drive Charlene home.

Good thing, because if I arrested him, well . . . I could just imagine the scene. I'd pull him over, take him and his honey to jail, then call Goldie to pick them up. I snickered at the idea until I thought of Goldie. Though it would serve Jack Dippel right, it would certainly not serve his wife well.

I turned to walk back to my Bronco and glanced at the Harris car. Something was odd there. I walked over. There was Harris slumped over his steering wheel.

I tapped the window. "Harris?"

No response.

"Harris, are you okay?"

He seemed too young to be a heart attack victim. Maybe he was dead. Or dead drunk.

I tried the handle and found the door to be unlocked. I swung it open, then shook the unconscious man. "Harris, David Harris?"

He wasn't wearing a seat belt, so with a tug, I jerked him part of the way out of his car. Suddenly, he bolted upright and stood, albeit wobbly, in front of me.

"Harris, are you okay?"

"I . . . I must have fallen asleep."

I pulled my flashlight off my belt and shone it in his eyes. "Have you ingested narcotics or alcohol?"

He blinked and looked away. "What? No, no, I wasn't feeling well. I pulled over to rest."

"Are you sick?"

"Maybe, but I think it was just the enchiladas from Rosey's Mexican Food."

I nodded. "That could be. I try to avoid that health violation myself."

Harris looked down at his shoes, then back up. "Say, I hate to bother you again, but you're the deputy here. Are you sure you don't have any knowledge of a woman, probably in her late fifties, named Jewel?"

I squinted my eyes. "Who's this woman to you, Harris?"

I saw him swallow hard before answering. "My mother." He grimaced and touched his stomach.

I clicked off my flashlight and jammed it back on my belt. "Harris, on a scale of one to ten, how sick are you?"

"I'd say a two. Mainly I just need to be near a restroom. I'll be okay in an hour or two."

"I could take you to the ER."

Harris rubbed his eyes and stretched. "No, I'm fine."

"Then why don't I follow you back to your hotel and make sure. Where are you staying?"

"My California bank canceled my credit card when it picked up both a California and then a Colorado charge today. They said they considered the card stolen until they could confirm my whereabouts. Never mind that they had me, in person, on the phone, telling them I was indeed in Colorado and needed to use my card." He laughed bitterly. "They just said they were sorry for any inconvenience but had to follow bank protocol." He sighed. "I didn't know I needed my bank's permission to travel."

"So, you're saying you don't have a place to stay?"

"Not till tomorrow, when I get this mess cleared up."

"Well, then, I see you've got two choices: I can either haul you to jail for loitering or take you to the ER."

A loud voice called out from the tavern doorway. "Deputy Donna, is this man giving you trouble?"

I cringed. I knew that voice all too well. Without turning around, I said, "Wade Gage, how are you?"

"Half drunk, as usual."

I turned to look at him. Wade is a good-looking man. There he stood, six foot tall, his muscular silhouette framed in the doorway, his blond hair backlit in a golden halo. Of course, he was wearing his signature Coors belt buckle, his brown cowboy boots, jeans, and a black muscle tee.

I pretended to be glad to see him. "Wade, you're just the person I've been waiting for. Let me make you an offer. My friend Harris here is sober. That is correct, Harris?"

"Yes, ma'am."

"Now, Harris will run you home, so you won't get arrested for DUI, if you let him stay tonight in that spare bedroom of yours."

Wade walked up to Harris and gave him the once-over.

"I don't know. He ain't a Texan, or worse yet, a Californian, is he?"

I put my hands on my hips. "Wade, I don't see that's any of your business. However, Harris doesn't feel too well, and his credit card down at the hotel is temporarily out of commission. Besides, I don't think he's even got a record. Do you, Harris?"

The man's eyebrows shot straight up. "No. No, ma'am."

I turned back to Wade. "So, how about playing the good guy for once and giving him a bed. Your act of kindness will win you a get-out-of-Donna's-jail-free card, especially if you don't cause any trouble tonight."

Wade stared at me, then said, "That would make you indebted to me, now wouldn't it?" He flashed his white teeth into a grin. "Now, a guy like me could get along with a proposition like that."

"Don't get any ideas," I snarled.

"Of course not, Deputy. Why, I would never dream of laying a hand on the meanest woman around, even if she is as cute as you."

I felt my face color. I swallowed down my displeasure. "Well, good. Then, Harris, you're driving?"

Harris walked over and opened up his passenger door for Wade. "Yes, ma'am."

Wade ducked into the car as Harris said, "Just tell me the way home."

As I watched the two men drive into the night, I felt pretty good. Most people think my job is all about arresting criminals, but actually, I see it as problem solving. It also means I don't have to waste my time writing reports. Problem solving seems to be my so-called "spiritual gift," as Vonnie would say.

I couldn't help but think about Harris. Like mine, his mother had apparently abandoned him. As for the mystery of who she was, I figured he must have been adopted, probably through one of those private arrangements complete with instructions never to reveal the identity of the birth mom. But somehow, through hook or crook, he'd managed to discover her name and maybe a possible location. Somehow, I hoped he'd find her.

By 3:00 in the morning I felt half dead. It would be so good to hit the shower and climb into my bed. My telephone message light was blinking when I got home, but at that point, I couldn't care less. For now, all I wanted was a ham sandwich and to sleep till 11:00 in the morning. Then I would grab my Crock-Pot, stop at the grocery for apple cider, and head for Evangeline's house for the next installment of our little Potluck Club.

9

No one can call her
a cream puff . . .

If Clay had said it once, he's said it a thousand times: *Donna Vesey is no cream puff. She doesn't tread lightly, and she says just what's on her mind.* "Believe me, I know," he said to Larry, Higher Grounds's chief cook and bottle washer. "I've been on the other side of her sharp tongue enough times to testify."

"Who hasn't?" Larry asked with a wry grin. He leaned over the countertop of the bar, resting his elbows against the edge. "Knowing that girl can leave a man with scars he doesn't want to talk about."

Clay nodded in agreement. "But on the flip side," he said, "I know enough about Donna Vesey to write a book . . . and I just may one day. I'd call it *Feisty*, because that's a good word for her."

"That ain't what I'd call it," Larry said. "But I can't repeat what I'd call it." He grabbed at the damp cloth nearby and stepped back. "Gotta get back to work before Sal fires me," he said with a wink.

Clay gave him a "take care" salute, then flipped open the notebook he kept handy at all times.

"Donna Vesey," he scribbled, then rested his chin in the palm of his hand. Nah, he wouldn't ever write that book. He and Donna

71

went way back. Too far for him to say much else, because, like it or not, he considered himself a gentleman.

"*PLC*," he jotted, then shook his head. A smart guy like him couldn't help but wonder what a girl like Donna was doing in the Potluck.

Among other things . . .

Lisa Leann

Apple Cinnamon Bread

Ingredients:
1 cup water
3 Tbsp. Apple juice concentrate (frozen)
1/2 cup Applesauce
1 tsp. Cinnamon
1 1/3 Tbsp. Sugar, brown
1/2 tsp. salt
3 Cup Flour, whole wheat
2 Tbsp. Vital gluten
2 cups Flour, bread
1 tsp. Yeast
2 tsp. of Flour & baking at high alt.
(over)

10

Barbecuing the Competition

When my alarm went off at 6:00 a.m., I bounced out of bed. Fortunately, I didn't have to worry about disturbing Henry; he'd gotten up at 5:00 and had already left for his favorite fishing hole. That meant I had the place all to myself. I flipped on the radio to K-LOVE, a godsend of contemporary Christian music that somehow reached this remote mountain town. I turned up the volume to sing with Michael W. Smith as he belted out one of my favorites, "Place in This World."

The coffee's automatic timer had already started my first pot of coffee brewing, and my trusty bread machine with its automatic programming had just finished baking a loaf of apple cinnamon bread. It looked perfectly risen with a cinnamon tan. I checked the brisket. It had been in the oven simmering for more than ten hours. In a couple more hours the tender slab of barbeque would be ready to serve. My home was a symphony of aromas and music. I felt sorry for Henry. Imagine, he was missing all this wonder just to stand in his waders in a freezing river.

After I sipped my cream-swirled coffee, ate a slice of fresh bread with apple butter, and danced with Video Jane, as I call Ms. Fonda, I returned to my bathroom and warmed up the shower. I slipped out of my gold satin pj's and stepped under the hot jet. Hmmm.

This did beat a hot, muggy morning in Houston. Things would almost be perfect here. Almost, if only it weren't so lonely.

After my shower, I slipped into my designer teal blue sweater with the fringe around the bottom, my size-four blue jeans, and my kicky black leather boots, then I applied my makeup with the skill of an artist. After that, I combed my hair to curl just so around my face. Happily, in this mountain air, it would be dry in no time. Next, I grabbed my Bible and headed for the deck with my favorite comforter.

The morning was crisp, and the sky already a brilliant blue. The lake sparkled with reflections of the mountainsides. Gone were all traces of yesterday evening's snow shower, except for a couple of white patches hiding in the shadows. It was amazing how fast the weather could change around here. Like last evening, one minute we had swirling snow and the next minute we had brilliant stars. It was all spectacular.

I took a deep breath and thanked God for this beauty before I turned to the first chapter of James. Verses 2 through 4 jumped out to me, just as if God meant the words to go right to my heart: "Consider it pure joy, my brothers, whenever you face trials of many kinds, because you know that the testing of your faith develops perseverance. Perseverance must finish its work so that you may be mature and complete, not lacking anything."

Wasn't that precious of God to comfort me when I'm going through this difficult move? It's true, when I read my Bible, God speaks to me. It was too bad that I never had much time for Bible reading in Texas.

I went back into the house and poured myself another cup of coffee and turned on *Fox and Friends* as I readied my presentation of brisket surprise. First, I pulled out the brisket, added the barbeque sauce and onion salt, lowered the heat, and slid it back in. Secondly, I covered a large shallow box lid with foil that would serve as my tray. Next, I papered the bottom of the tray with baby blue contact paper complete with pink and gray roses. Lovely. I opened my cupboard to peruse my disposable aluminum foil serving dishes. I selected two. A small one for Henry, in case he got tired of eating fish, and a large one for Evangeline and her company. Then, I cut the fresh apple cinnamon bread into thick slices with my electric knife and rolled the slices into a tube of foil. Finally, I added a small, unopened jar of apple butter.

I opened the oven door and pulled out the brisket. It looked perfect. I slid the hot pan out of the oven and put it on my cooling rack. Soon I filled both of my disposable pans to the brim with hot brisket, then covered the tops with foil.

I stepped back to admire my handiwork. Of course, I hadn't planned any side dishes, but with luck, Evangeline had already made that little potato thing of hers. Besides, the aroma was magnificent! This was a meal that would open any door. Who would be able to resist?

After clearing the kitchen of dirty pots and pans, I slipped into my black leather coat and headed for the Lincoln. I glanced at my watch: perfect timing. I should arrive at about 11:30 at Evangeline's front door, where I would present her with lunch and win a chance to solve the mystery of her secret visitor.

And it was a mystery. I just knew Evangeline wouldn't postpone her club for just anyone. If she were entertaining friends or family, she would probably just invite her guests to join our luncheon, unless there was a compelling reason for secrecy.

I couldn't help it. I absolutely shivered with excitement. This was my most intriguing Summit View adventure yet! I couldn't wait till I called my mama to tell her about it. She and Daddy still lived in Denton, Texas, even though it had been six years since Dad retired from teaching history at North Texas State University.

It was pathetic, really; my mom and I had always been close, though I hadn't always invested the time to call her on a regular basis. But since I'd moved to Colorado, I practically lived for our daily phone visits. And to speak frankly, Mom's had been the only friendly voice I'd heard since I moved to Summit View. Too bad that voice originated from a cozy Texas kitchen almost two thousand miles away.

A few moments later, I pulled up in front of Evangeline's hundred-year-old clapboard Victorian house. It was complete with a steep roof of red shingles with lacy white woodwork beneath the peaks. I loved the wraparound covered porch with its ornate white columns.

Simply adorable. The whole house was framed by yellow-leafed aspens that had spilled a blanket of liquid gold all the way to the front door. Surely, this was all a sign from God that I was walking in his will. He had even rolled out the carpet for me.

Carefully, I pulled my tray of brisket and bread out of the trunk and walked down the golden path. I climbed the steps and managed to use the brass knocker on the red-painted door. I could hear the hardwood floors squeak as Evangeline came to answer. She opened the door only a crack. Intriguing.

I smiled my best Lisa Leann smile into Evangeline's frown. Evangeline spoke first. She sounded exasperated. "The meeting is off. Didn't you get the message?"

"Yes, I did. But when I heard you had company, and me with all this hot barbecued brisket and homemade apple cinnamon bread, I *had* to drop by. That's okay, isn't it?"

Evangeline stared at my tray. The door opened a bit wider as she smiled what appeared to be a tense smile at my lovely presentation. "How thoughtful. Let me just take it here at the door, so as not to disturb my guest. I would invite you in, but . . ."

In the background, I caught a glimpse of a young woman making her way down a mahogany staircase. "Who's at the door, Aunt Evie?"

Aunt Evie? The girl's steps landed her behind the half-closed door. Before Evangeline could react, the door had swung wide open. And there before me stood Evangeline's very own, very tall, and very pregnant niece. Ta-da! Mystery revealed.

I was delighted. This young woman was tall and practically glowed with white porcelain skin and bright blue eyes, which were lined dramatically with black liner and heavy mascara. Her lids were polished with blue, silver, and ivory shadow that helped create a wide-eyed charm. Her cheeks shimmered with a rosy blush, and I loved her pouty lips. They were heavily outlined in deep maroon with a luscious rose filling. She could teach the other Potluckers a few things about makeup, I can tell you. She was dressed in a long black dress—slimming, but not enough to hide her blossoming belly.

"You must be Evangeline's niece," I chimed. "I heard you were here, so I thought I'd drop by to bring you some of my hot barbecued brisket."

"Wow, and just in time for lunch too," the girl sang. "Aunt Evie, invite her into the kitchen. I'm starving."

Before Evangeline could stop me, I was following my invitation down the hall. As I proudly carried my offering, I couldn't help but notice that Evangeline's home was impressive. It was full of mahogany antiques and quaint maroon velvet sofas with large original paintings of mountain meadows full of Indian paintbrushes and columbines. Lovely.

The kitchen was charming too. Of course, it had been updated, and I simply loved the whitewashed wooden cabinets with their glass fronts. Through the glass, I could see rosy china and Depression glass stacked in neat arrangements. I adored the big iron sink and the oak kitchen table decked with hand-crocheted placemats of Dutch-blue yarn.

"Evie, this is truly charming," I said, turning to see her pale face.

"Thank you for bringing over the meal," she said. "I'd invite you to stay, but you must be busy."

"Oh no, I'd love to join you," I said as I removed my leather jacket and slung it over the kitchen chair I was claiming as my own.

The niece busied herself setting the table, while I began to unwrap my gourmet lunch. Evie seemed at a loss for what to do but soon found herself pouring the tea into glasses of ice and setting butter on the table.

"Leigh, honey, put the sugar on the table too," Evie said.

Leigh. Now I had a name to go with this beautiful young woman. Of course, her hair was a bit too apple red, not to mention a bit too spiky for my taste, but she'd certainly fit in with my Nelson's party friends. And she looked to be Mandy's age, and pregnant too. Seeing this girl made my heart pang in longing for my own daughter and soon-to-come first grandchild. Maybe this was God's offering to me. A gift to fill in for my daughter who was so far away. But I couldn't jump to conclusions; I'd have to wait to see.

I had been wrong about the potatoes. Instead, Evangeline re-heated a tasty rice dish, a perfect complement to the barbeque, though a nice salad would have enhanced the meal.

We sat around the table, and Evie managed the prayer. "Dear Lord, be with us today and protect us from the enemy. Amen."

Of course, I wasn't sure if Evie meant Satan or me. She probably hadn't decided. And who knows, maybe she's right in her fear of me. After all, I planned to take control of the Potluck Club, and if I were really lucky, I might soon proudly own her niece's friendship.

It was time to make my first conversational move as Evie and Leigh tasted my delectable barbeque. I waited until Evangeline's mouth was full.

"Leigh," I started, "how long do you plan to stay?"

"Probably until after the baby comes. Maybe longer."

I couldn't help but notice that this comment seemed to alarm Evie. But I pretended not to notice. "Then your husband will be joining you?"

"No. I'm not married," Leigh answered.

Evie almost choked on her mouthful of barbeque.

"Then you're planning on raising your baby yourself?"

Leigh glanced at Evie. "Of course. All I need is a supportive place to call home."

With that, Evie jumped up to get some more bread off the kitchen counter, almost spilling her glass of tea.

"Oh dear" was all she said.

"No one's ever accused me of being shy, so I'll ask: have you thought about adoption?" I said, like this was the most natural conversation in the world.

"I won't even consider it."

"When's the baby due?"

Before Leigh could answer, the doorbell rang. Evangeline ran to answer it.

Leigh confided in her absence. "A couple of months."

I know that's when I lost my eyebrows under my red curls, but I just couldn't help it. For I could see this young lady didn't have a clue as to what she had gotten herself into. It was like my daddy had always said: "There are two kinds of people—the ones who learn by reading and observation, and the others who have to touch the fire to see if it's really hot."

Leigh was about to get scorched if, for heaven's sake, she didn't have a friend like me.

Suddenly, I heard Donna's voice at the door. "Canceled? I didn't know. I knew I should've checked that phone message before I drove all the way over."

Aha. Another one of my potential projects had arrived. I stood and walked to the kitchen door. "Hi, Donna," I called.

Donna looked perturbed, but surely not at me. She was off duty, dressed in jeans, tennis shoes, and a floppy white T-shirt with the word *dangerous* emblazoned in red. Heavens. If only she'd pat on a little makeup and let that hair grow a bit, she wouldn't look so much like a young boy. I bet she'd have lovely curls. Like mine.

I called again, "Evie, invite Donna in. Let's have our own party."

"What smells so good?" Donna asked as she accepted my invitation and walked toward the kitchen, lugging a Crock-Pot and grocery sack, much to Evangeline's irritation.

"My barbeque brisket," I said as I hurried to grab another plate. Leigh stood and helped with the silverware and napkins. Donna busied herself with her apple cider and Crock-Pot. "For dessert," she announced. She turned to look at Leigh, and her eyes popped.

Evie offered, "Donna, you remember Leigh, don't you?"

Donna quickly adjusted to her surprise as she sat down. She scooped a large helping of my brisket onto her plate, then buttered her apple cinnamon bread. "Little Leigh? You were all of sixteen the last time I saw you. You're from West Virginia, right?"

Leigh smiled at Donna. "That's right. I just flew in yesterday."

I leaned back in my chair and almost let my happy sigh escape my lips. This was perfect. The conversation wouldn't need much direction from me, and I could concentrate on studying each of these women. Though, I couldn't help but feel sorry for Evangeline. Here was a woman who loved control, and that control had just slipped through her fingers. Which, to tell the truth, was all right with me.

Soon, Evangeline's world would be my domain. And as for Donna, she was a woman who ate a meal without so much of a prayer or blessing. There was a lot more to her than her dear Grace Church friends suspected. I detected a lot of pent-up anger. But why? A dark secret, perhaps? Whatever it was, not only was I going to find out, I would somehow manage to give her a much-deserved makeover. I could hardly wait to get started.

11

She's got some nerve . . .

Clay had seen Lizzie Prattle in the Higher Grounds Café earlier that day, so he knew the Potluck Club had been canceled. The news had caused a bit of a stir among those, like him, who were sitting there nursing hot cups of coffee and finishing off plates of the daily breakfast special.

"Everybody knows that Evie doesn't call off the meeting for just any reason." Sal, the owner of Higher Grounds, was poised with coffeepot in hand as she refilled his cup for the fifth time that morning. "That's just odd," she continued. "Wonder what's going on over at Evie's?"

"Maybe she's not feeling well. Cold weather coming in . . . some people are getting sick," someone from behind Clay said, though he wasn't sure who.

Lizzie shook her head. "Evie's fine. Whatever the reason, I'm sure it's a good one."

But when Clay saw Lisa Leann's car heading toward Evie's side of town, he spoke out loud but to no one in particular. "There goes trouble." In spite of himself, he chuckled a bit. *For a little bitty thing,* he thought, *that woman carries a lot of nerve.*

Not too much later, Donna's Bronco passed by the café, heading in the same direction. This time, Clay nearly fell out of his chair.

"What's so funny?" Sal asked from the counter.

He shook his head. "Nothing," he answered. "I just got a mental picture of three hens fighting in a coop."

Sal frowned. "You need help," she said.

"Someone does," he said, reaching for his notebook and pen. "But it's not me."

Lizzie

Oven Fried Eggplant

1/2 cup fine dry crumbs
9/4 tablespoons grated Parmesan Cheese
1/4 teaspoon salt
1/4 teaspoon pepper
1/4 cup mayo
eggplant

Combine first your ingredients in shallow dish. Peel eggplant and cut into 1/4 inch slices. Spread both sides with mayo. Dredge in breadcrumbs. Bake

12

Mincing Words

It didn't take long after our canceled Potluck Club meeting for us to know why the postponement. Evie's niece coming to town seven months pregnant jolted us to no end; I won't lie about it. After all, this was Leigh whose swollen belly we were suddenly staring at a whole day later in the middle of the church parking lot. Leigh, who'd come to visit every summer and who'd played with my own daughter, Michelle.

Michelle and Leigh are the same age. When Leigh came to visit Evie alone for the first time, the girls were about eight years old. Evie explained to Leigh that there was a little girl she could play with, but that the little girl—my daughter—was deaf. Couldn't hear sounds and couldn't speak well enough to always be understood, though she does have a voice. I think it's a beautiful voice.

Leigh wasn't the least bit intimidated by this. We brought the girls together, my old chum and I, and allowed their hearts to blend in a very special way. In no time, Leigh was attempting to learn sign language, and by the end of the summer she'd pretty well mastered it. For Michelle, it was more than merely gaining a new friend, or even a hearing friend. Michelle attended Denver Institute for the Deaf in those days, so she had plenty of deaf friends. They seemed to have so much in common.

The girls loved Barbie. And Cabbage Patch dolls. And biking on warm afternoons. They spoke of their friends; Michelle's from the Institute and Leigh's from West Virginia. During the school year they wrote letters to each other and, eventually, when personal computers became as common as television, they emailed. The passing years only added to their camaraderie. They shared favorite movies and music, stories of boyfriends and future plans.

To my knowledge, however, they'd never talked about being unwed mothers.

I asked Michelle about it as soon as we returned home from church that autumn morning.

"Did you know?" I signed to her.

She shook her head no, then started up the staircase toward her bedroom. I knew she wanted to avoid the conversation, but I worried about how this might affect her.

I reached for her hand and turned her toward me.

"Don't walk away from me, Michelle," I said, signing "don't" and "Michelle" with my free hand as firmness registered on my face.

Michelle spoke out loud in a voice that, although nasal and strained, is angelic and pure. "I don't know anything, Mom. I was as shocked as you."

Michelle uses her voice when she's emphatic about something, so I knew she was telling me the truth. I released her hand. "Okay," I said.

Michelle sat on one of the stairs then, wrapping her arms around her knees, buried her head in the circle of her arms, and began to weep.

"Oh, Michy . . ." I cooed, though I knew she couldn't hear me. I sat beside her, slipped my arm around her shoulders, and drew her close.

"I feel bad for her," Michelle signed when she'd gained her composure.

"Me too."

I waited, not wanting to rush my daughter's feelings or expression of emotion. "I think I should talk with her, but I don't want her to think I'm prying," she signed.

I raised a finger before I signed back. "Why not go over later this afternoon . . . spend some friendship time with her . . . let her know you're here for her if she needs you." I shook my head. "But don't question her. Just listen."

Michelle eyed me funny. "You won't beg for the answers?"

I laughed at her. "No, Funny Face. I won't beg for the answers."

Michelle brushed her cheeks with her fingers, pushing the remaining tears away. "I love you, Mom," she said out loud.

"I love you too," I said as she stood and, turning, bounded up the stairs just as her father walked through the front door and found me sitting there alone.

"Let me guess," he began. "You've fallen and you can't get up?"

I smiled at the handsome devil I'd married thirty-six years ago. Though his hair is silver (well, so is mine) and mostly flushed down the drain or swept up in my Hoover, he still has a way of setting my heart to flutter. After all these years—four children and five marvelous grandchildren—he and I still desire the presence of each other over any other person in the whole wide world. "No. I was just sitting here talking to Michelle."

Samuel's glance went up the staircase and back to me. Joining me on the stair, he said, "I suppose you were talking about Leigh Banks."

I nodded.

"Pastor Kevin and Jan called me into his office after the finance committee and I had finished with the morning offering to ask me how I thought Evie was handling it."

I ran my fingers through one side of my short but full hair as I propped my elbow on one knee. "What'd you say?"

"Well, I said I thought once the shock wore off she'd be okay . . . but we certainly need to pray for her."

"Of course."

"I think Evie has her hands full right now. She's always put Leigh on such a pedestal. She probably never expected to have to deal with anything like this from her."

"I might have expected it from one of Peg's boys but not Leigh, no."

Samuel reached over and kissed my cheek. "We know how Evie feels, don't we, Mother?" He stood and began to ascend the stairs.

"I'm going to lie down for a while. Want to call me when lunch is ready?"

"*Want* to or *will* I?"

"You know what I mean," he said with a chuckle.

I listened to his footsteps as he mounted the thickly carpeted stairs and then finally disappeared down the hallway toward our bedroom.

Yes, we did know about that; we weren't the first and we obviously wouldn't be the last. Although the Brightmans and the Fairfields were the first in our church community to struggle with it, our youngest son, Timothy—now thirty-one and most commonly called Tim—and his lovely wife "had to get married," as they say. They'd been high school sweethearts and went off to college together, and while they swore they lived in their separate apartments, Samantha's mother and father felt as we felt: the kids were managing to live together behind our backs.

Who could have predicted that by their junior year of college they would have a little one to prove it? Of course, by the time the baby was born, they were married and more than a little repentant. Today they live in Baton Rouge and have two children—a boy and a girl—so their little family is complete.

Samuel and I have two other children—Samuel Jr. (whom we call Sam) is thirty-three and Cindy (whom we call Sis) is thirty-one. Tim is also thirty-one—and no, they aren't twins. For the life of me, I don't know how I managed to give birth to two children within the span of a twelve-month period, but I did. More than that, I'm not sure how I managed to raise three children with just under three years' difference in their ages.

Then, five years later, when I thought I'd finally be able to catch my breath, Michelle was born, bringing a whole new set of worries and concerns. But God has been faithful and good. As the psalmist said, "His mercy endureth forever." Though I had a pack of children and a husband with the all-important job of Gold Mine Bank and Loan president, I was equally blessed to be the high school librarian, which meant I got summers and holidays off to be with my babies. I taught them the joy of reading, every year encouraging them to win a star-studded certificate from the Summit View Public Library as the top readers in Summit County, which they did, Michelle more than the others. I suppose with her hearing loss, the world of books opened up exciting possibilities to her.

Like me, Michelle is fond of both the Little House books and the Green Gables series. Last year, for Christmas, she gave me a collection of short stories by Rose Wilder Lane, daughter of Laura Ingalls Wilder and great author in her own right, which thrilled my heart.

We also enjoy the works of Daphne du Maurier and the Bronte sisters.

Michelle and I are simply old souls living in contemporary bodies.

Michelle did go see Leigh. As I promised, I didn't pry my daughter for information. I did, however, drive over to Evie's Monday afternoon as soon as I got off from work. In her hospitable way, she offered me a cup of coffee and some homemade tea cookies.

"Leigh made them," she said.

"I figured," I said as I took a seat at the kitchen table. Evie gave me one of her looks. "What?" I asked. "Like I don't know you?"

She nodded her weary head then, casting her eyes to the countertop, where she had set large Dollar Bonanza mugs, asked, "Lizzie, what in the world am I going to do?"

I stood, walking over to her, and placed my hand on her back. "About Leigh?"

She cut her eyes over to me. "No, Lizzie. About the price of tea in China. Of course about Leigh."

I gave a quick look over my shoulder. "Where is she now?"

"Out taking a drive. Said she just needed some air."

"Oh," I said. "Well, it's a nice day for it." The coffeemaker coughed and sputtered as it dripped its last drop of aromatic brew. I jerked the pot out and began pouring while Evie walked over to the fridge for some milk. "Has she said anything about the father?" I replaced the coffeepot and then walked the mugs over to the table, where Evie was already sitting, folding two napkins from the napkin holder that set in the center.

"Only that—and I quote—'it's over.'"

"How can that be? She's pregnant with his child, isn't she?"

Evie began preparing her coffee to her liking, and I did the same. "That's what I said. Apparently he's a businessman. Successful, she says. And wants to take part in the baby's life. Support the child financially. Have visitation rights." Evie's shoulders sagged. "What kind of world are we living in, Lizzie Prattle?"

"You tell me," I answered, taking a quick sip of the hot coffee. "I work at that school every day, and I am here to testify that the children of today are only getting worse. I am fifty-eight years old, and if I can hold out four or five more years, I can retire and be done with the whole lot of them."

Evie patted my hand. "How's Samuel?"

"Good, but don't change the subject. Let's talk about what we can do for Leigh." I took another sip. "Other than pray."

Evie swallowed a gulp of coffee. "Did I tell you that busybody Lisa Leann Lambert showed up here on Saturday?"

"No!"

"Yes." Evie shook her head, then began a high-pitched, drawling imitation of our newest member. "'I heard you had company, and me with all this hot barbecued brisket and homemade apple cinnamon bread, I *had* to drop by. That's okay, isn't it?'"

"She's up to something, that one is."

"Like I don't know it. And then, to make matters worse, here comes Vernon's daughter. Didn't listen to her answering machine, my great-aunt Martha."

I had to giggle. "Evangeline, when are you going to get over your resentment of that poor child?"

"I do not resent her."

"Oh. I see." I reached for the cookie plate, brought a cookie to my lips. "I've just known you since the day I was born, but don't let that get in the way of you telling *me* the truth."

"I don't resent her, Lizzie. I just . . . she could have just . . . You know, every time I see her, I see her mother. What that woman did to poor Vernon . . ."

"You mean besides kiss him full on the lips and then marry him?"

Evie frowned at my humor. "We need to talk about the club. Do you think the girls would be up to coming next month rather than this month?"

"I think you should go ahead and plan for this month, Evie. Don't hide in a closet like you've done something wrong. For heaven's sake, we've all been through bad times together. We all know about Jack Dippel. Prayed Goldie through a dozen affairs and loved her all the more. And don't forget when Tim had to get married. No one was judgmental—"

"That you know of."

"Evie!" I dropped the remainder of my cookie onto my napkin.

"Don't give me that look, Lizzie. You know how people talk."

I retrieved the cookie. "So what if they do? It's not like Leigh is the first unmarried woman to find herself pregnant. The important thing is for us to pray she'll do the right thing. Yes, ma'am. That's the important thing."

"So what do you suggest?" Evie took another swallow of coffee, draining the mug.

"I say give yourself two weeks and then let's have another meeting. Two weeks after that, we'll have another one. Our regular one. Pretty soon, Leigh will have God's answer for her life, and we'll feel as though we've done something pretty important, wouldn't you agree? Maybe we'll even throw her a baby shower."

Evie rolled her eyes.

"Did she say when she's going back home?"

Evie stood and walked her mug over to the sink, where she began to rinse it out. "At first she said she wasn't certain."

"And now?"

Evie turned and looked at me dead-on. "And now she says never."

Another Potluck Club was scheduled two weeks after the canceled meeting. On the Thursday before, I decided I would take my oven-fried eggplant, which I hadn't made in a while. Samuel gave his usual endorsement for my choice by suggesting I prepare it for the family—Michelle, himself, and me—a couple of days before to make sure I hadn't lost my touch.

Funny man. Though I did concur with his idea.

But I would be taking more than my eggplant. I also gathered up my read and reread Christian women's magazines to carry with me. The other gals don't subscribe to every magazine that comes along like I do, but they dearly love to read my discarded copies.

They're equally hip to my other magazines, but I don't share those. Magazines like *Quilter's World*, *Threads*, and *Crazy for Cross-Stitch* stay with me for years on end. My mother taught me the art of needle and thread, and I've passed that on to my daughters as well. What is taught within the pages of patterns and such won't go out of style.

On the Thursday before our now-rescheduled meeting, I made a second decision when I thought to start a new work of cross-stitch, something for a baby. I hoped it would inspire the rest of the gals to think along the lines of a baby shower or perhaps just lighten up a little where Evie was concerned. In my heart I knew there would be some gossip—already had been. Most of it came from the Lambert woman, whom I have managed to keep my librarian's eye on. If it's one thing years in the school system has taught me, it's how to keep a lookout for trouble when it's brewing.

Lisa Leann is one nosy woman. I suppose she's a sister in the Lord, but she's truly upset Evie, and she's even had the nerve to call me up and try to get me to talk about who tithes at Grace Church and who doesn't.

"Lisa Leann," I said matter-of-factly, "just because my husband is the head of the finance committee doesn't mean I know anything about such as that. Besides, that's between our parishioners and the Lord. Not between them, you, me, and the Lord."

Lisa Leann just giggled in that way she has and said, "Oh, but darlin', don't you ever just wonder? I think it's a matter of spiritual maturity, and that's really what I want to know, who at the church is *truly* spiritually mature."

"How are you doing in your new home there?" I asked her, changing the subject rather abruptly. "It's certainly a pretty new subdivision you've found yourself transplanted to."

"It is that. I just love getting up in the mornings, sitting out on my deck, and reading the Bible. I suppose with you growing up here, you might have missed the beauty around you."

"I haven't missed it."

"Take it for granted, I should say."

"I haven't done that either."

"Oh. Well, then."

We ended the conversation somewhere around her asking me about Michelle's deafness. It seems she has a third cousin who is hearing impaired—although not totally deaf—and she'd attempted to learn sign language but hadn't completely gotten the knack of it. I told her it wasn't so easy to learn when one didn't use it all the time. Lightheartedly I reminded her that what you don't use, you lose.

"So what is it Michelle does? I mean, for a living and all?"

Michelle works in management at one of the resorts in Breckenridge, and I told her so.

"That sounds like a wonderful job," Lisa Leann said. "Now, does she live up there or does she come home every night?"

"She comes home. Lisa Leann, I hate to end this conversation, but I've been working all day and I still have dinner to prepare."

Lisa Leann laughed. "I'm so sorry. You know, when one doesn't work outside of the home, one forgets."

I let out a tiny pent-up sigh. "Let's plan to have coffee together soon or something like that. Maybe one Saturday. I'd love to hear more about your children and husband as well." What can I say? Maybe the woman is lonely and just needs a friend. Maybe it's to be my calling for the time being. For such a time as this . . . and all that . . .

No, that's not it. I just wanted this stranger out of my family business. Maybe playing twenty questions is the way they get to know one another in Texas, but up here in Colorado, we tend to stick to our own business. Unless, of course, we just happen to have grown up here and we already know everything there is to know, anyway.

You can't keep a lot of secrets here in Summit View.

Immediately after work I headed for a little craft shop downtown where I buy my cross-stitch materials. Driving there, I couldn't help but ponder why I love Summit View so much. The air is crisp and the skies are an absolute turquoise, a brilliance broken only by the hedge of emerald pines and gold aspens, the rise of the majestic mountains. This time of year I'm often reminded of the days when we were all growing up here in Summit View. The world was ours. We knew it wasn't perfect by any stretch of the word, but it was perfect enough for us. Ruth Ann, Evangeline, Vonnie, and I romped and frolicked as much as we ever read about Laura and Mary Ingalls doing. Sometimes, at my insistence, we put on "Little House" plays for our mothers, who in those days were all stay-at-home moms. Not like today. We're nearly all working . . . and working hard.

As soon as I walked into the craft shop, a restored multileveled Victorian painted golden yellow and trimmed in white, I was met by the scents of cinnamon and candle wax. Dora Watkins, the owner, had come to understand a long time ago that if she were going to survive financially, she would need to sell more than thread. She wisely brought in antique chifforobes and etageres purchased at Goldie's son-in-law's shop, which she stuffed with already-made crafts, crystal and porcelain figurines, silk floral arrangements, hand-stitched quilts, handcrafting how-to books, and scented candles. Dark, antique tables spilled over with linens, crocheted items, and stone coasters. The walls of the store, painted in muted, warm colors, were literally covered in framed and matted prints, cross-stitch patterns, wrought-iron coatracks, and cinnamon-scented brooms.

Dora greeted me from the centrally located customer service area, which was really two oversized tables converted to cutting tables, one with a cash register sitting at the end. She sat on a bar-style swivel chair, surrounded by Christmas merchandise that needed to be set out (and we hadn't even hit Halloween yet), and appeared to be absorbed in the latest in the stack of best-selling Christian literature she kept near the register and that she sold upstairs in the Secondhand Book Nook.

"How ya doing there, Dora?" I asked. Dora's mother had, at one time, owned the Sew and Stitch, and when she died, Dora—who is now in her midforties—took over.

"Doing well, Lizzie. You?"

"Doing fine." I walked past her, taking the two or three steps to the second level of the first floor, past a cutesy display of bunnies and over to the racks of cross-stitch patterns flush against a side wall, next to a door marked "Employees Only."

Dora joined me. "Looking for something special?" Her wide eyes twinkled behind large glasses.

I love Dora dearly—she is also a sister in the Lord—but sometimes I wish she'd let me shop alone. It's almost as if she's too anxious for a sale. And does she have to know every single thing I sew? "Something for a baby," I told her.

"For Evie's niece?" she asked.

I crossed my arms, allowing my eyes to scan the books of patterns. "That's right."

"Such a shame about all that," Dora said, reaching for a book with a somewhat gnarled hand; a hand that had obviously sewed many a stitch and cut a million and one patterns from countless bolts of material. "How about classic Pooh?"

I took the book from her. "Pooh is good."

"Boy or girl. Won't matter. All children love Pooh."

I began flipping through the book until I found the pattern I thought best to start with. "This would make a nice baby pillow," I said.

"You could do the whole thing," Dora said, taking the book from me and flipping a few more pages. "See, you've got the frameable artwork here. A throw. Crib bumper pads. Everything you can imagine for a baby's room. Did you hear Leigh is planning to stay here with Evie for an indefinite amount of time?"

I took the book back from Dora, returning to the original page. "I'll need to get floss," I said. I turned on my heel and headed toward the nearby racks of floss in every color imaginable.

Cross-stitch thread is called floss, and rather than being organized by color, it comes in DMC numbers. I began pulling the appropriate numbered skeins from the little display hooks. About that time the door chimes signaled that another customer had entered. Sight unseen I was grateful. I didn't want to get into a gossip session with Dora Watkins. Being the only craft and sewing store in town makes the Sew and Stitch as bad as a beauty salon when it comes to idle chitchat. I was even more pleased to see that the newly arrived customer was Jan Moore.

"Hello, ladies," Jan called out, immediately making her way over to us, though I knew with Jan's love of cross-stitch she could have just as easily been coming over to check out the latest in floss. Jan has a penchant for angels and has stitched some of the most inspiring works of heavenly hosts you've ever seen. In fact, the ladies room at Grace Church has a set of two quite large angel patterns, hand stitched by our loving pastor's wife, then framed and matted at Christi's Frame Shop.

I have a special place in my heart for Jan; my sister is also a pastor's wife, and I know the lifestyle can be demanding and oftentimes lonely, though I've never once heard Jan complain. She's always bright and upbeat. A positive in a world full of negatives. Jan is also a pretty thing. I'll have to give it to Texas, some of the best-looking women seem to come out of there, and that includes Lisa Leann. But I noticed right away that Jan looked a bit pale this afternoon. Drawn. I wondered if things weren't so good over at Grace Church. Or within her family. I didn't want to pry, because I'm not the prying kind, but like I said, these old librarian's eyes catch everything. "You okay, Jan?" I asked.

Jan reached Dora and me with a smile that belied the rest of her face. "Oh, you know. A little tired. I haven't slept well the last few nights, and I've been a bit nauseous. I think it's just the change in weather." She gave us a wink. "Or maybe just the change of life. Hot flashes and all that."

"It'll get you when you're not used to it," Dora said, not being specific about whether she was speaking of the change of weather or the change of life.

I patted Jan's slender arm, then showed her the Pooh pattern I was going to make for Leigh's baby. "What do you think?"

Jan smiled at me again. "I think it's a wonderful thought," she said. Jan Moore should know a wonderful thought. I doubt she's ever had anything but wonderful thoughts. She is undoubtedly the sweetest woman in the whole world, and we're blessed to have her as our pastor's wife. In fact, we're pleased to have both the Moores. The entire family is special, and there's not a single person in Summit View—no matter where they worship the Lord Jesus—who doesn't love Pastor Kevin and Jan.

"I'm just thinking that maybe if we give Leigh a lot of love and wrap that with prayer, it'll help her to make the right choices where the baby is concerned." I felt more than saw Dora moving closer to Jan and me. "Maybe she and the father can even work out their differences . . . make a home for the baby."

"What do you know about the father?" Dora asked, crossing her arms.

I shook my head, then cut a glance over at Jan. "Nothing really. It's not really our business, so even if I did know something, I wouldn't say."

Jan placed her hand on my shoulder. "Good for you, Lizzie." She then turned to Dora. "Now, then, Miss Dora. What I'm looking for is a long-term project. Something I can give to my own daughter for Mother's Day next year, what with it being her first year as the mother of little Jenny-Lin."

Jenny-Lin is the daughter that the Moores' one and only daughter and her husband adopted from China. This now made them a family of seven—with two of the children being adopted.

But isn't that just like the Moores? This is one wonderful family. All the way around. Whatever goodness they've received from the Lord they deserve and more.

That's what I'm saying.

13

Everyone knows
she's rock solid . . .

*If you take all the ladies of the Potluck and put them in a bowl,
the one that will settle to the bottom first is Lizzie Prattle. She's
rock solid . . .*

Clay typed on his laptop. Behind it, the squeak-squeak of Woodward's wheel kept tempo with the *peck-peck-peck* of Clay's fingers on
the keyboard. Together they made some kind of orchestra, though
not one anyone would pay to hear.

*I used to like to go to the library during school hours just to talk
with her. She was a great reference for studious kids like me. She
always treated me with respect . . . well, heck, like one of her
own.*

Clay knew her kids, of course. Over the years, he'd hung out at their
house after school, football games, and during youth programs the
senior Prattles were always hosting. In his whole life, he'd never seen
two parents more devoted to their children, especially Michelle.

Dora Watkins had come into the café the afternoon after Lizzie and
Jan had gone by. Told everyone within earshot all about the visit.

*Sometimes I think Dora likes to talk about who comes and goes
at the Sew and Stitch so others will drop by for a visit. You might*

97

say it's like a beauty shop. Women go there to catch up on the latest news, and getting their hair done is a bonus feature.

No matter. Clay knew Dora well enough to know she was worried about Jan Moore. "She just doesn't look well, if you know what I mean," Dora said to Sal. "I'm not saying she's sick. I'm just saying she looks completely worn out. After all, one thing I know is 'sick.' When the doctors told me I had cancer I looked like death warmed over, but look at me now. I fought that disease like a cat and came out on top."

Thinking about her words, Clay took a deep breath and sighed. Personally, he was more concerned about Evangeline and her niece than Jan Moore . . . not that he didn't care about whatever it was that ailed Mrs. Moore.

"There's an awful lot going on within the PLC, men," he said to the gerbils. "Not to mention the news around the café about Coach Dippel's latest escapades."

Woodward stopped his running, stepped out of the wheel, and wobbled over to the front of the cage. Rising up slightly on his hind legs, he gave Clay an ominous look as if to say, *Now, there's a story* . . .

Goldie

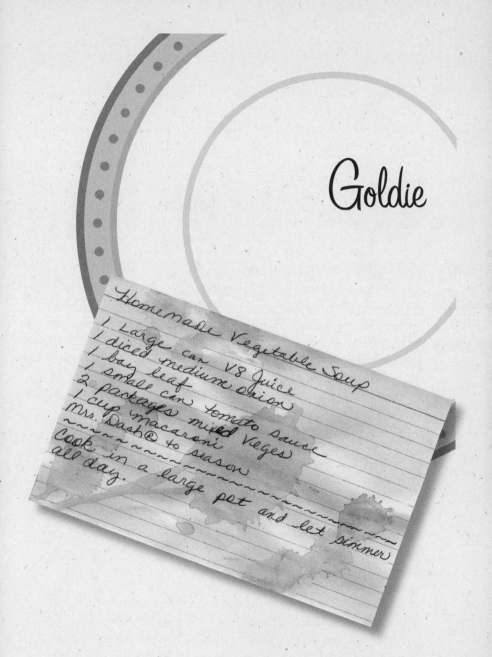

Homemade Vegetable Soup

1 Large can V8 Juice
1 diced medium onion
1 bay leaf
1 small can tomato sauce
2 packages mixed veges
1 cup macaroni
Mrs. Dash® to season
~~~~~~~~~~~~~~~~~~~~~~~~~~~
Cook in a large pot and let simmer
all day.

14

Crushed Hopes

I was glad the PLC had canceled two weeks ago, though if we had met, the focus would have been on Evangeline and not me. I felt pretty sure everyone knew about the scene at the Gold Rush Tavern between Jack and Donna Vesey and that woman Jack tried to pass off as Allen's date.

Charlene Hopefield. I couldn't believe it when I heard about it . . . and I heard about it! Jack has, in the past, kept his affairs to women out of town, but Charlene Hopefield? The high school Spanish teacher? Well, *Dios mio*!

What will Jack do next? Bring her home for Sunday dinner with Olivia, Tony, and Brook sitting around Grandmother Brook's dining room table like some modern-day family? I don't think so.

If you're wondering how I found out, it didn't take Lucy Welch, our down-the-street neighbor, long to call me the day after the incident. Lucy's daughter Jane is some roustabout, hanging out at places like the Gold Rush Tavern, but she sure brings home a load full of talk. Which Lucy just can't wait to share, of course, especially if it involves someone from Grace Church.

Lucy is a heathen.

So, Lucy called me the next day while I was in the middle of making my bed. Jack had just left for work—which she probably knew because she watches for every little thing out her front window—and I was busy getting the house in order, what little bit there was to do. "Goldie?" Lucy began, sounding as if someone in my family had just died. Well, I knew that tone. Knew it well.

"Hello, Lucy."

"Goldie, mind if I come down for a minute?"

"What's going on?" I asked her. Might as well hear it over the phone than in person.

She sighed the death sigh again. "My Jane went to the Gold Rush Tavern recently for a drink or two with her workmates, like they often do. . ."

Mmmhmm.

"And said she saw quite the skirmish between Jack and Charlene Hopefield."

I felt my spine go ramrod straight. "The Spanish teacher?"

"*Sí.*" She attempted humor, but I didn't think this was any time to cut jokes. If she knew what it felt like to stand in my shoes . . . God willing, she never would.

"What kind of skirmish?" Shame on me for asking, but I couldn't help it. I needed to know. At least when people looked at me I'd know what they were thinking.

"Apparently, the two of them—and this is just what Jane told me, but she's a pretty good source seeing as she'd only had one beer to drink—got into quite the fight. Both drunk, of course. Charlene threatening to never see him again if he didn't divorce you . . ."

I gasped at the word. In all these years, Jack had never said one word about divorce, and neither had I. After all, there's Olivia to think about. And sweet Brook all of three years old. What kind of life would it be for him in a small town like this? Everyone would know. Everyone would talk.

"Oh, I'm sorry, Goldie," Lucy now apologized.

No, she wasn't sorry. She didn't care.

"Then what happened?" I asked her, setting my jaw.

"Apparently—and again, this is what Jane said—they went out-side, where Donna Vesey had to deal with them."

Donna Vesey? From my own Potluck Club? God, why are you letting this happen to me? "What do you mean by 'deal'?"

"Well, Jane said that Donna said—"

101

"Wait a minute. If Donna and Jack and Charlene were outside and Jane was inside, how—"

"Jane said it was about time for her to go home anyway, so she picked that moment to leave . . . you know, when Jack and Charlene were walking out with Charlene shouting something about it being her birthday and he didn't buy her anything special but he buys you diamonds all the time, and you know, Goldie, you sure do have a lot of nice pieces, I'll say that much."

I couldn't help but smile, though it was a bitter one. So, Charlene didn't get anything from Jack for her birthday. Other than drunk and a run to the motel, I'm sure. That was probably the night he didn't bother to come home until the wee hours of the morning. Not that it matters to me when he comes home. I stopped sharing a room with the man years ago. So as long as he doesn't wake me, I'm fine with it.

Yeah, sure I am.

"Lucy, I can't thank you enough for calling me," I said, wanting to end the call. I needed a good cry.

"I just felt you should know what was being said. I mean, about the 'D' word and all."

"Thank you again."

"In case you need a good attorney."

"I don't think that will be necessary." I cast a glance out my window. The sky was turning a bit gray. It would snow again later this afternoon. Well, didn't that pretty much set the stage for my day?

"Because if you need a good one, my nephew over in Denver—"

"I'll be sure to keep that in mind. Good-bye, Lucy." I hung up the phone before she could get another slithering word out. As soon as I knew the connection was broken, I picked up the hand piece again, then beat it against the bedside table until it literally shattered, all the while screaming like some wild animal caught in a hunter's trap. When I saw what I'd done, I jerked the whole phone, wire and all, from the wall and threw it across the bedroom.

My bed, half made, was a perfect target of my continued rage. I raked my fingernails across the comforter, dragging it toward me, balling it up as best I could and throwing it to the floor. The pillows were next, beginning with the European shams that were now awry, followed by the equally askew back pillows and matching throw pillows. I was ready to rip into the sheets, the guttural sounds still emitting from deep within my throat, when I heard the phone ringing from the other side of the house.

I turned, almost unsure what to do. Walking toward the bedroom door, I paused when I heard the answering machine inside Jack's office come on. My husband's recorded voice announced, loud and strong, "You've reached the Dippel family. We're not here right now, but you can leave a message at the sound of the tone. Go, Gold Diggers!"

The machine beeped, followed by Olivia's voice. "Mom? Hey, it's me. Where are you so early in the morning?" I began moving through the house, toward the office. "Well, I'm wanting to make your homemade vegetable soup tonight . . . you know, the one with the bay leaf . . . and I wasn't sure—"

"Hello?" I answered the phone on Jack's desk.

"Hey, Mom!"

"Hey, sweetheart."

My daughter paused. "What's wrong?"

"Nothing," I said, though my voice quivered.

Another long pause. "I'm coming over," she said.

"No, Olivia, that's not—"

"I'm coming over." She hung up on me.

I huffed, wrapping my arms around my abdomen, then twisted myself around to lean against Jack's desk. Remembering I had the phone in my hand, I replaced the hand piece, then allowed my eyes to scan over the contents lying willy-nilly on the surface of the desk. Papers. Score pads. Doodles of plays on legal pads. A small trophy next to a larger one. A picture of Brook that needed dusting (this is not a room I typically enter, except to vacuum the carpet). A book, *101 Plays to Think about on the Toilet*, the cover displaying a football coach sitting on the john.

Disgusting.

A brass mail organizer held several opened bills and invoices. I turned and pulled them from their nest, shuffling through them.

The bank statement—we were doing all right—the bill from Ford Motor Credit, the power bill . . .

A photo of my husband and Charlene Hopefield.

Jack, Charlene, and several other teachers surrounded by a number of high school students. But Jack and Charlene, nonetheless.

I drew the photo closer to my nose, focusing my eyes on the blue-eyed Jezebel. Her head was too big. Her bleached blond hair fell to her shoulders like straw. Her smile was fake. Her breasts were fake.

My eyes skimmed down her torso. What was that on her hip? Oh yes . . . my husband's hand. Right there for the world and the photo lab technician to see, resting a little too low, a little too flat. It was as comfortable there as it was attached to its owner's arm.

Before I could stop myself I began shredding the picture, the bills and invoices dropping to my feet. I turned again, grabbed for the phone, and dialed a number I had to search my memory for.

"Vesey," Donna answered. She sounded sleepy but not as though she'd already fallen asleep.

"Donna, this is Goldie Dippel."

Pause. "Hey, Goldie. The club is on for Saturday, isn't it?"

"Yes, yes. I'm calling . . . I need to ask you . . . I'm sorry to wake you or bother you if you were about to go to bed . . ."

"Goldie. You're calling about Jack and Charlene?"

"Yes."

"Who told you?"

"Lucy Welch."

Donna swore lightly under her breath. "I should have known when I saw Jane Welch coming out of that tavern. Aw, Goldie, I'm so sorry. Really. If anyone doesn't deserve this, it's you."

"All I want to know is if it's true."

"I'm afraid so."

"Did the two of them leave together or—"

"Yeah. Yeah, they did. If I could have done anything about it . . ."

"I know." I tucked the phone between my ear and shoulder and—for the life of me I don't know why—began to shuffle the papers on Jack's desk into neat little piles. "I just wanted to know if it was true." I stopped my shuffling, pulling an ad for a beautiful turquoise and diamond necklace. I'd never seen anything so exquisite—or so expensive. *Well, I suppose this will soon be mine,* I thought. Small price for Summit View's Man of the Year to pay, though it would hang like a noose around my neck.

"Again, I'm sorry, Goldie. You're a nice lady . . ."

"Thank you."

There was a long pause before Donna continued. "Hey, let me ask you something. The night all that happened, there was a man—a stranger from California—who came into town looking for a woman. Name of Jewel."

"Jewel? No, I don't know any Jewel. Who was he?"

"I don't know. I heard he hung around for a day or two, then said he'd be back soon." Donna paused again. "Well, if you remember a Jewel from maybe back when you first moved to town . . ."

"I'll let you know." I turned suddenly, hearing the sound of Olivia coming through the front door. "Donna, I have to go. Olivia's here. Thank you, dear. Thank you for being honest. You're a sweet girl."

"Yeah. See you Saturday."

Olivia's voice rang from the foyer. "Mom?"

"Don't say anything about this phone call to the girls," I whispered. "Good-bye."

15

She knows it . . .

Clay was considered a regular in places around Summit View. It was one of the unique elements of being *the* bachelor about town.

There was, of course, the library, where he liked to do some of his research. Something about the smell of musty books intoxicated him, making him even more creative with words than he was by simple talent. And there was Higher Grounds, which practically reserved a table and chair for him. And then there was Sprinkles, the local bakery, where he bought both his bread and a special dessert once a week.

Typically, a birthday cake where the baker had misspelled someone's name or, as he was buying on this particular day, a half-price cake with special icing scrawled on top, reading: "Congratulations, Jody, on your confirmation."

"What should it have said?" he asked.

"Congrats, Mark, on your bar mitzvah," the baker answered with a wince.

Clay chuckled. "I'll take it," he said just as the bells on the front door jingled. He turned his head to see Goldie Dippel entering. Clay cocked a brow. The woman looked just awful.

"Mrs. Dippel," he greeted her.

She raised cocker spaniel eyes. "Oh," she said. "Hello, Clay."

He turned a bit more, resting an elbow on the glass display case beside him. "You okay?" he asked.

She stared at an arrangement of Toll House cookies, then looked back at him. "Hmmm?"

Clay winced inwardly. *Dollars to donuts*, he thought, *she knows about Coach and Miss Hopefield.*

Vonnie

Mexican Tamales

5 lbs. lean pork or beef, cooked and shredded
6 to 7 lbs. fresh masa (corn flour)
1½ lbs. lard
1 Tbls. salt
1½ pts. red chile sauce (store bought)
1 bundle ojas (corn shucks)

Completely cover the meat with water, add salt
to taste, then slow boil in a large covered pot,
until completely done. Next, cool the meat and
save the broth. When meat has cooled, shred
it and mix it into the chile sauce. While

— back —

16

Searing Revelation

Why does the Lord always use Scripture to make me feel guilty? I sat in my recliner and read from my Bible, which rested on the overstuffed arm of the chair, while Chucky, my King Kong–sized bichon, nestled on top my cushy thighs. He snored as I sipped my first cup of morning coffee.

I let my eyes scan over the words. "Praise be to the God and Father of our Lord Jesus Christ, the Father of compassion and the God of all comfort, who comforts us in all our troubles, so that we can comfort those in any trouble with the comfort we ourselves have received from God."

Comfort. My snort caused Chucky to look up at me, then sniff toward my blue coffee mug. The mug was my favorite because it pictured an adorable baby cradled by a cloud.

"You wish!" I said to my groggy dog. I turned back to stare at the familiar words in front of me and sighed. With all the goings-on of late, God couldn't expect me to be much of a comfort to others when I felt so comfortless myself. Sure, I'd try to be of help to Evangeline and Leigh; I'd even pray for them, but what words of comfort did I really have to offer? Zip, that's what.

I'm not saying I don't have a lot of blessings in my life, and for those blessings, well, I'm grateful. After all, I love God. I have an employed husband who's in good health; I have a nice home and friends. But that's where it all ends. Here I am, a fifty-seven-year-old woman without a son or daughter or grandkids to call my own.

We'd talked about adopting but never did. And as both Fred and I were "only children," we don't even have a niece or nephew to hug. Where's the comfort in that?

While it's true that over the years I'd given myself to the little ones in my fifth-grade Sunday school class and even bonded with a few of them, it's not the same as having your own to raise.

I turned to the end table next to Chucky and me, reaching for the yellowed photo in a metal frame. There I was, at least twenty years younger, not quite as plump as now. I looked so "eighties," dressed in a self-belted ivory and red jacquard-print dress topped with a red vest. My still-yellow hair was styled in short waves. There I stood, surrounded by the smiling faces of my fifth-grade Sunday school class. Goodness, they were almost as tall as I was, except for petite Donna Vesey. She stood in front of me while I rested my hand on her shoulder. Her pink, long-sleeved cotton dress was wrinkled, and her tangled hair was in need of a wash.

That was the year I became Donna's surrogate mother. The poor child needed one, as her own mother had skipped town with that no-good choir director. My relationship with Donna has helped ease some of the pain of childlessness. But comfort? My heart still ached for the baby I never held.

With a sleepy sigh and an arm around Chucky, I carefully set my half-empty mug on the brick hearth in front of the fireplace and closed my eyes, thinking I should probably pray. Actually, I should have prayed last night when I'd been busy tossing and turning through my worries.

I leaned my head back and whispered deep in my heart. *Comfort? Lord, just what are you trying to say to me?*

My prayer faded into peaceful slumber until the phone startled me awake. With my heart pounding, I sat upright, lowered the recliner's seat, and then bolted for the kitchen receiver.

I hate to be caught with sleep in my voice, and I hoped my jog across the room would jar me to my senses.

"Hello?" I said a little too brightly.

"Why, hello, Vonnie. It's Lisa Leann. Say, did I wake you?"

"No, no, no."

111

"Well, okay. It is after 9:00 a.m., after all. Hey, I just called to talk to you about the Potluck luncheon tomorrow. I'm so excited to finally get a chance to show off my barbeque brisket."

I rubbed the sleep from my eyes. "Brisket?"

"Brisket's all right, isn't it? I mean, you're not making a brisket too, are you?"

I shook my head as though she could see it. "Oh no."

"Well, what are you bringing?"

"Potato salad?"

"That would be perfect! Say, Vonnie, as this is my first time and all, and as I want to be PC . . ."

"PC?"

"You know, politically correct. Well, I was wondering about Evangeline's niece. Do you think it would be okay for me to bring up that I'm planning a baby shower for her?"

"I thought I would . . . I mean, it's so soon."

"Well, honey, that little girl is going to have a baby, and *soon* is the word. How much longer can I wait? Besides, it's not a secret. Everybody in town knows. You should hear what they've all been saying down at the market. Oops. Hang on, another call is beeping in. I'll call you back, okay?" *Click.*

How is it that whenever I talk with that woman I always feel like I've just had a conversation with a steamroller? But even before I could shake my head, I heard lapping sounds coming from the living room. "Chucky?"

I peeked around the corner just in time to see Chucky lick the last of my coffee from the mug. Now, that's just what I needed, a wired dog leaping about my priceless collections.

"Chucky, no!" I scooped up the mug and took it to the kitchen sink; Chucky followed behind, licking his chops and looking very smug. As I rinsed the mug before placing it in the dishwasher, my eyes swept over the windowpanes, where a half dozen or so stained glass babies tumbled about. I looked past their antics into the bright mountain morning. The glare of the sun hurt my eyes. The intense light was such a contrast to my cozy, albeit dark, home. But I'm convinced my babies love the dim light, which swirled with prisms of rainbows from dangling crystals and dancing stained glass splashes of color.

I turned back to look at what so many describe as "Vonnie's museum." Patches of yellow, blue, red, green, and purple light skimmed across wide-eyed and sleeping faces. Babies. Babies everywhere. Every square inch of my house is covered with them. Antique, new, porcelain, china, rag, and plastic—all babies, in large, medium, and miniature. The babies, of every race and nationality, line my mantle, shelves, bookcases, display cabinets, and piano, not to mention my walls. Many sit on specially built shelves, hovering above my comfy blue sofa, which of course is covered with even more babies. I walked over to the bookshelf and picked up Baby Amanda from her vintage wicker carriage. Amanda, one of my greatest treasures, looked adorable in her ivory lace gown. I stopped to admire her long lashes closed in sleep and her sweet rosebud lips painted on her porcelain face. I sat Amanda back in her carriage and looked about like any proud mother. At last count, I had over 528 babies in my collection, each dressed, pressed, named, and loved. Even so, somehow it seemed that no matter how many babies I took home, I ached for more.

Now that I'm finally retired from Doc Billings's office, not a week goes by that I don't sweep through the local antique stores and yard sales, hoping for a find. And recently, much to my delight, Donna showed me how to search eBay on Fred's computer. From what I've seen there, my hobby's about to get much more expensive, at least as soon as I set up my PayPal account. Good thing Fred's still employed—I'm going to need that paycheck to keep up with our ever-expanding family.

It wasn't hard to remember when my collection started. True, I'd always had baby dolls as a girl. But it wasn't until Evie and I left Summit View for Cherry Creek College in Denver that I'd added my first baby to my collection, a baby I soon lost.

While Evie had majored in business management, I chose nursing. Nursing had been a fascinating study. It became even more so when I took my senior year clinicals at the local Cherry Creek Hospital. There, I quickly discovered that nursing had a lot to offer;

that is, besides emptying bedpans, making beds, and spoon-feeding some of the more feeble patients. Nursing at Cherry Creek Hospital had one bonus that stood head and shoulders above the rest, and his name was Joe. Joe was six feet tall and worked as an orderly. With his good looks, dark wavy hair, and dreamy brown eyes, he had quite the following when it came to student nurses and candy stripers. So I'd been surprised when he sat next to me at lunch one Saturday at the cafeteria.

"Hey, Von. What are you studying?" he asked, pointing to the book spread wide next to my plate of half-eaten spaghetti.

I closed my book. "I'm cramming for a test tomorrow."

He looked over at the cover. "Psych, huh?"

"You've taken it?"

"Last year." He cleared his throat before continuing. "Tonight, after work, how about grabbing a pizza with me on the hill?"

I hesitated before answering. "With clinicals and my studies, I don't have much time for dating," I lamented. "Maybe we'd better not."

"But you do eat, don't you? And judging from all the remains of cafeteria spaghetti left on your plate, I'd like to take you to get some real food."

"And pizza's real food?"

Joe laughed at that. Then he looked at me and smiled in a way that warmed me right down to my toes. When I think back, I'm certain it was his smile that caused me to lose my heart that very moment.

Our pizza date became the first of many enchanted occasions, all of which found us hand in hand, walking the hill across from Cherry Creek College, an area busy with students, hippies (protesting the war, the establishment, or the wearing of a bra), restaurants, and a park on a hilltop that overlooked the city and the mountains beyond. Our evening walks became the highlight of my life. Joe was a source of ceaseless stories about his family life in East L.A. Somehow, Joe made growing up poor sound like a privilege. His father was a busy doctor at a clinic, and though he, his mother, and his three older sisters lived in a modest home, money was always tight. "But we always had enough," Joe would say. "And we had more than enough, we had each other."

One evening, just after we watched the sun set, a bearded young man stopped us. He was barefoot and wearing white striped bell-bottom pants with a dirty tie-dyed T-shirt. His long, straggly hair was held in place with a wide band of braided beads. Experience told me this glassy-eyed man was about to ask us for a quarter, but instead he grabbed Joe's hand like he was going to shake it. "Man, is that your old lady?"

Joe slid his arm around me, but not before he gave me a reassuring wink. "Yeah, man. Why?"

"Well, if I had an old lady, a blond bombshell like that, I'd never go to Nam. I'd make love, not war, man. Do ya hear? Stay in school, man, don't risk it. You've got too much to lose."

My cheeks burned at the idea of lovemaking, but Joe just nodded his agreement and gave me a light squeeze. "Sir, you do have a remarkable point."

But the truth was, Joe was not a student. He had once been pre-med at Cherry Creek College but had taken a year off to find himself after his father died in a car accident. He hadn't gone back home to L.A.; he'd stayed here, in the beauty of Denver, Colorado, beauty he'd hoped would help heal his grief.

His self-prescribed therapy had worked.

One night we sat on a bench in the park watching another sunset over the mountains. Joe cradled his arm around me. "Vonnie, my father had always been my inspiration. He was such a caring man, which is one of the things that made him such a good doctor. But when he was killed by that drunk driver, it was as if everything I had ever found to be true and good died. Even my faith in God."

I pulled back from the crook of his arm. "But, Joe, how could you not believe in God?"

"I believed. But I was angry. But now that I've found you, I just can't stop thanking God for bringing you into my life. You've helped me find my purpose. Vonnie, because of you, I'm going back to school. I'm going to be a doctor and follow in Papa's footsteps."

I could have cheered, but instead I raised my lips to meet his. It was then I experienced one of the most tender, passionate kisses of my life. And yes, I had been kissed before, mainly by my old school chum Fred Westbrook. But Joe's sweet kiss had an intensity that I'd never felt with Fred.

A few days later, Joe received his enrollment package from Cherry Creek College. He jumped into the process of reapplying for the following semester, but the very next afternoon the mailman delivered a letter of "greetings" from ol' LBJ himself. Joe had just been drafted.

I took the news hard. "Joe, Vietnam? Isn't there something we can do to stop this?"

It was too late. Joe would soon be off at boot camp, then war. When the reality of our impending separation hit us, our discreet romance ended in a quick marriage before a justice of the peace and an all-too-short honeymoon in the elegant Boulderado Hotel in Boulder.

It had been easy to arrange. The Friday afternoon we were married, Evie thought I had driven back home to see my folks, and of course my parents thought I was at the school cramming for a test. Instead, Joe and I were saying our vows at the Boulder County Courthouse. From there, it was only a short walk to the Boulderado. Once Joe carried me up the cherry staircase and into our bedroom suite, we were not seen until checkout Sunday morning. Only room service knew where we were for sure. For me, our honeymoon was a time of both joy and despair. We laughed, we cried, we made love. We celebrated each other and our lives as one.

Sunday afternoon was our final day together. In silence, I drove Joe to the Denver train station in my gray Volkswagen bug. Once there, Joe pulled himself out of my arms. "I'll write every day. I love you, Vonnie. Don't worry. I'll be back, you'll see," he called to me as he climbed onboard the late afternoon train that was to whisk him away. He turned to wave, but I could no longer see him through the haze of my tears.

The day Joe left for war, he left a part of himself behind. For all too soon I discovered Joseph Ray Jewel was going to be a father.

I had kept the entire romance and marriage a secret, even from Evie. Mainly because I knew Evie couldn't keep a secret and also because I knew just how my overbearing parents would react. That's why I worked so hard to keep up with my schoolwork. With my good grades and baggy sweaters and uniforms, no one suspected a thing. That is, no one suspected until I arrived home for Christmas break. Try as I might, I just couldn't hide the fact I was with child.

After dinner one night, Daddy asked, "Vonnie, your mother and I are concerned. You're gaining weight and you never feel well in the mornings. Is there something you want to tell us?"

I cleared my throat. "My baby, I mean, our baby is due in May."

Daddy jumped from the table, almost knocking over his chair. Mom dropped her water glass. "What?" she cried.

"It's okay. I'm married, Mama. Daddy, I'm married. I'm Mrs. Joseph Ray Jewel."

"Then where is this husband of yours?" Mother asked. "I don't see him. What kind of man would leave you this way?"

"A nice man, a kind man, the son of a doctor. He was drafted, Mama. He's serving our country in Vietnam."

"This son of a doctor got you pregnant, then left town?" Mom challenged.

"No, Mama," I said, desperate to make them understand so they could share my joy. I sprinted to my room and pulled out a large envelope and came back downstairs. "Look, here's our marriage license."

I pulled out the gold chain that held my wedding band close to my heart. "See, here's his ring."

But Mom could not be consoled, especially when she saw our wedding photo. There I was, dressed in a white miniskirt topped with a soft white peasant blouse with puffed sleeves and a scooped neck etched in colorful embroidery. My long, straight blond hair cascaded over my shoulders and down to my waist. I stood smiling, clutching a bouquet of tiger lilies and Joseph's arm. Joe was dressed in a blue polyester suit with a white shirt and maroon tie.

Instead of smiling at the camera, the camera caught Joe smiling at me. Seeing the love in his eyes brought tears to my own.

"Mama, see how handsome he is?"

"His color isn't right, Vonnie. What kind of man is he?"

"What do you mean, Mama?"

"He's too dark to be American."

"Of course he's American. His father was English, and his mother's from Mexico."

That's when the bomb exploded. My pure-blooded Swedish mother cried, "You are carrying the child of a Mexican? Vonnie! How could you disgrace yourself, your family in this way?"

"Mama, I love him. He's my husband. Don't you understand?"

But my parents couldn't understand. The next day, the Monday before Christmas, I'd boarded a bus and headed for the Los Angeles home of Maria Jewel, Joseph's Mexican mother.

Maria was wonderful. She was shorter than me, and I stand all of five foot two. She welcomed me into her home and treated me like one of her own daughters. She taught me how to make warm corn tortillas and mouth-watering tamales, still one of my most sought-after specialties.

But as my belly grew, I longed for my mother. Even though I wrote her a steady stream of letters, they came back to me marked "Return to Sender."

I had quite the lifestyle change that spring. I had given up my nursing career to live on the poor east side of L.A. But I didn't mind a bit. I was in love and waiting for my baby's father—my husband—to return from war, all the while living the incredible stories of warmth and laughter, the stories Joe had told me on our walks on the hill.

I, with a tummy swollen to full-term, was no longer able to work at the nearby dry cleaner's shop. That's why I happened to be home the day the United States army chaplain stopped by. When his black Ford LTD pulled into our driveway, I raced to Maria. Together we'd opened the door at the chaplain's knock. "Mrs. Jewel?" he'd asked, another man standing by his side.

We both stared. "Yes?" we answered in unison.

Maria and I leaned on each other for support.

The officer continued. "I'm Chaplain Rodger Walters from the U.S. army," he said, showing us his credentials. First he looked at me as he handed me a telegram. "I'm sorry to inform you that your husband," then he turned to the elder Mrs. Jewel, "and your son, Joseph Ray Jewel, has been killed . . ."

I never heard the rest of his announcement. A blood-curdling scream filled the air. The scream and the others that followed seemed to belong to someone other than me. I fell to the ground, twisting in agony. The last thing I remember was Maria bending over me, calling my name, pressing a cold cloth to my forehead. Then I felt the wetness. My water had broken. My time had come.

The difficult labor lasted forty-six hours. During those hours, I slipped in and out of consciousness. There were times I couldn't tell if my screams were from the pain of giving birth or the pain of my broken heart. Finally, it was all too much. My mind gave way to blackness, and I remember nothing more.

It was another two full days before I awoke. Maria was gone. In her place was my own mother, who gently patted my hand. "Vonnie. Vonnie, dear?"

I opened my eyes.

Mom's face leaned over me. "Dear, you're better off," she whispered.

My head pounded. My voice croaked through parched lips. "Mama? What do you mean?"

"The baby." Mother stroked my hair. "The baby's gone. But don't worry, dear, it's all for the best. Now you can come home."

When Chucky suddenly jumped into my lap, I realized I was back in my recliner, holding—okay, gripping—baby Amanda Jewel to my chest. Well, a couple of teardrops probably won't ruin her gown. Even so, I had no business rehashing the past. It's between me and God, and no one else needs to know. Even my dear Fred's never dreamed I've been married before, much less had a baby, albeit stillborn.

I wish I could have seen my child, or at least had the opportunity to say good-bye. But I was still sleeping when they laid him to rest. Mother said he'd been a boy with dark curls, like his dad. How precious. At least I know that Joe and his son are together, and that brings me a bit of peace.

But baby Joe's birth had deeper consequences. Some time after I married Fred, my gynecologist in Denver said the birth had caused too much trauma to my uterus. "Yvonne," he said as he stared at the latest diagnostic report, "I hate to say this, but I don't think you'll ever conceive again. That is unless you believe in miracles."

I did believe. I just knew God would heal my womb. For he was a God of love, and he alone knew just how much I wanted to be a mom. But my miracle never came. My baby would never be.

Eventually I had a hysterectomy, and that was that. It's all quite sad, I suppose. But life does go on.

When I left California, Mom talked me into breaking ties with Maria Jewel and her family and heading back to Cherry Creek College to finish my RN. I'm sorry to say, I walked away from the Jewels and never looked back. My mother even invented a cover story to explain my time in California. She told all our friends I had temporarily transferred to Berkeley until I got homesick. After graduation from Cherry Creek, I worked in Denver for a while, then headed right back to Summit View, just like a homing pigeon. Evie and Ruth Ann were already enjoying life as best friends, and I didn't want to be a third wheel. I was the odd man out. At least in those days.

I lived at home and worked for Doctor Billings, our town's only M.D. In fact, that's how I reconnected with Fred. Being an auto mechanic, he came in to see the doc after he broke his finger when it got caught in a tire jack. It was sort of a fortunate accident—the injury healed beautifully, plus it got the two of us back together. If there were ever two people who needed each other, it was Fred and me.

Fred loves me; I know that. He's loved me since grade school. He stole his first kiss from me in second grade. And though I've never felt passionately in love with him, I appreciate him more each day. It's hard to believe we've been together for thirty-five years. But I must confess, though Fred has been a good husband, faithful, and a good provider, he'll never hold a candle to my Joe.

Mom always liked Fred. He's a medium-built Swede with bright blue eyes and a fine crop of platinum hair; that is, when he had hair. And after all these years, he's still not a bad-looking man, though he's a bit on the paunchy side. But that's only because he so loves my tamales. It breaks my heart to think I never made him a dad. He'd have been a good one. He'd have taught our children about God, the secret life of car engines, and how to fish. In fact, fishing is one of Fred's favorite pastimes. Lately he's been going out with Lisa Leann's husband, Henry.

All in all, Fred's and my time together has been pleasant and sweet. However, I've always wondered: if Fred knew of my past, how would he react? Would he feel angry or hurt or even prejudiced against Joe—like my mother? To even think of it causes me to feel a bit lightheaded. I've betrayed him all these years with my secret love for another man. And as a consequence, my previous marriage stole our ability to have children. If Fred found out the reason or that I never confided in him about my past . . . I can't even imagine.

I looked down at my watch. *Goodness, look at the time.* It was almost noon, and all I had to show for it was a few tearstains on my favorite doll. *Let's see, I promised Lisa Leann I'd make some dish for the Potluck. My famous fruit salad? Probably. I've already picked up the ingredients for that.*

I walked to the kitchen with Chucky at my heels. That dog follows me everywhere, just like a little white shadow. I pulled out the bread for a sandwich and trimmed the crust. As was our routine, Chucky sat at attention while I tossed him bread bits. That dog's amazing. He could catch those bits in midair, unless they bounced off his nose. Then he goes sliding across the slick linoleum to chase them down. I always get a chuckle out of that.

The phone rang, and my caller ID announced Evangeline Benson. Evie was probably calling to make sure I was cooking something for the Potluck. Now, don't get me wrong; I love Evie, I really do. She relies on me for everything. But I suspect she thinks I'm not capable of brushing my teeth unless she directs the event. Evie hasn't always been so bossy, however. Why, back in college, she was so consumed with her failed "romance" to Vernon, not to mention her studies, she never noticed how love had turned my usually grounded self into a woman whose feet never touched the ground.

Once, after I floated in late from one of my secret dates, she gave me a strange look. I merely explained that I had been studying at the library, though I never said what or whom I was studying. And Evie, being all about honesty and practicality, believed me.

We really weren't close back then. I wasn't her best friend. That title still belonged to Ruth Ann, who had headed for the Great Lakes naval base with her new husband, Arnold. However, Evie found that I was a comfortable second choice, not to mention a first-rate sorority sister. Even so, Evie and I didn't become best friends until decades later, some time after Ruth Ann's passing. And in truth, Evie's never quite gotten over Ruthie's death. How could she? Without Ruth Ann, she had no one. Well, except for me. I think the thing that makes us so close now is that we share a bond so secret even Evie doesn't know—we share the bond of loss.

We may be best friends today, but sometimes Evie drives me batty. It seems to me that her number-one goal has been to organize my life. She thinks she's pretty accomplished at it too. But that's okay. I keep my secrets, and I stand up to Evie whenever necessary. A feat I've accomplished on several occasions, especially when it comes to her treatment of Donna Vesey.

Amazingly, whenever I make my stand on the subject of Donna, Evie straightens up. She's never been mean-spirited, only bitterly alone. Despite her hard side, in many ways, she's still that lost little girl wondering how Doreen Roberts stole her boyfriend with just a kiss.

I picked up the phone. "Hi, Evie. How's it going with Leigh?"

"Honestly, I don't know what I'm going to do with that girl. She's planning to come to the Potluck Club."

"And?"

"I don't think I can bear any more questions about her condition."

I chuckled. "Evie, just like Lisa Leann says, this is no secret."

I could hear an exasperated huff on Evie's end of the line. "What else did Lisa Leann say?"

"She said she's bringing her brisket and something about throwing 'you all' a baby shower."

"Oh, she wouldn't dare."

"She would, and she'd have the entire populace of Summit View there with gifts in hand."

"Well, she's got to be stopped!"

"Don't worry, Evie, you'll find a way."

"Yes, of course. If push comes to shove, we just won't go, that's what."

I laughed. "Be tactful, now, Evie. Tactful."

Evie huffed again, then added, "Oh, I almost forgot why I called. What are you bringing to the Potluck?"

"My famous fruit salad?"

"No, that won't do. I'm bringing a peach cobbler. That's too much fruit."

"My baked beans?"

"No, beans make me bloat."

"Corn bread?"

"Perfect. Yes, do your cheesy corn bread. Glad that's settled. I'll talk to you tomorrow."

We hung up. Settled for her, maybe, but now I had to figure out what in heaven's name I'd done with Mom's recipe. Before I could start thumbing through my stack of cards, the phone rang again. This time it was Donna.

"Hey, Vonnie, the Potluck still on for tomorrow?"

"You bet. You'll be able to come, won't you?"

"Yeah, I have to work tonight, though. Got a hunch as to what I should bring?"

"Well, so far, we've got cobbler, brisket, and corn bread."

"Salad. I'll pick up the makings at the grocery."

"Okay. I'll see you at noon."

I hung up and looked at Chucky, who wagged his tail.

"We're going to see our girl," I told him.

I'd swear that dog understands every word I say, and with that bit of news, Chucky seemed to smile with his whole body. But he's always had a liking for Donna. Why wouldn't he? It was Donna who united the two of us in the first place.

Donna had been on duty when I called her to see if she could investigate the mystery of my disappearing picnic lunch. I'd been in the process of laying out a beautiful spread of sandwiches, iced tea, and apple pie for Fred and me. But every time I went back to my kitchen, the food I'd placed on the picnic table would disappear.

Fred was in the house reading the paper when I said, "Something here isn't right."

He looked at me with his eyes a-twinkle and said, "Sounds like a case for Donna. It'll give her an excuse to join us for lunch."

So I called her cell phone.

Moments later, Donna showed up in her sheriff's Bronco, siren off, but lights a-blazing. She came in all official, and even before I could finish describing the crime, she pulled out this frizzy-haired stray from beneath my back porch.

"Mystery solved," she said. "Are you inviting me to lunch?"

"Only if you turn off the light show in front of the house," I said. "What will the neighbors think?"

She grinned. "Sure thing. Gotta rope so I can tie this mutt while we eat? I hate for him to stink up my truck."

But when we tied that pooch to the porch railing, the dog began to whimper and squeal, just like a brokenhearted woman. I just couldn't stand it. He looked at me with those big, brown eyes of his as if to say, "Save me!"

"You know," I said to Fred, "that dog looks like Chucky, the baby doll Evie bought me on her trip to Durango."

Fred stopped chewing and stared at me. "Vonnie, you want that dog?"

I turned to Donna. "Do you suppose it would be okay?"

"Well, he doesn't have any tags. But tell you what, why don't you keep him and if anyone shows up looking for him, I'll let you know. He probably ran off from the campground, and I'm guessing his folks are long gone. It happens a lot."

"You mean I can keep him?"

"Sure. But why don't you take him over to Doc Ivy's to be checked out."

So that's how Chucky became mine. And after a good bath and a brushing and a checkup at the vet's, that terribly matted dog turned into my fluffy, beautiful Chucky.

Aha! I picked up a tattered note card. *Here's the recipe I'm looking for. Now, let me check for the ingredients.*

The phone rang. This time, the ID announced Kevin Moore, the pastor from Grace.

I picked up. "Hello?"

"Vonnie, it's Jan."

"Jan, it's nice of you to call."

"Vonnie, isn't your Potluck Club meeting tomorrow?"

"That's right."

"Well, I've got a prayer request for you."

I grabbed a pad and pencil to take notes. "Anything for you, Jan. What is it?"

Her voice sounded brave. "I haven't been feeling well, have been losing weight. So I finally got over to see Doc Billings. Vonnie, he gave me a bad report this morning." She sighed from deep within before going on. "I've got cancer. Doc Billings says it's inoperable."

I sat down hard on the kitchen chair.

"Jan, no. Are you sure?"

"Yes. That's why I'm calling. I don't want this to go beyond the Potluck Club until Kevin can announce it on Sunday. But please ask the girls to pray. Ask them not to tell anyone else just yet. I still have friends and family I need to tell in person."

"Oh, don't worry. I'll let the girls know. But, Jan, what exactly does Doc say? You know I used to be his nurse, so you can tell me . . ."

"Doc Billings says it'll take a miracle."

My heart stopped at the words.

Miracles never happen. At least not to me.

17

That's her, a mother
without children . . .

Clay sat hunched over a cup of coffee at the café and flipped through
his ever-growing notebook of PLC facts.

Vonnie Westbrook. Who is she apart from her doll collection? He
mused. *The city of Summit View should make that house some sort
of museum.*

Impressive . . . but a bit unusual.

Well, anyway, he had a soft spot where Vonnie Westbrook was
concerned. In a way, she'd been like a second mother to him, always bringing him leftovers. He glanced down at his belly. *Not
like I need them.*

Still, he'd always wondered why a loving woman such as Mrs.
Westbrook hadn't had her own children. Not that it was any of his
business, he'd just wondered.

Evangeline

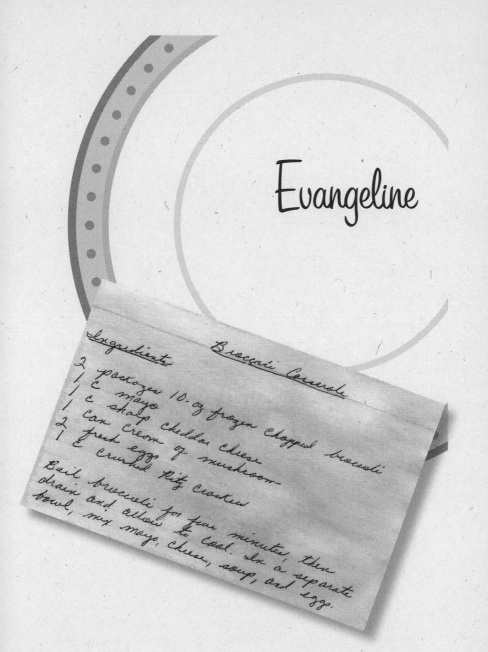

Broccoli Casserole

Ingredients

2 packages 10-oz frozen chopped broccoli
1 c mayo
1 c sharp cheddar cheese
2 can cream of mushroom
1 fresh eggs
1 C crushed Ritz cracker

Boil broccoli for five minutes, then
drain and allow to cool. In a separate
bowl, mix mayo, cheese, soup, and egg.

18

Dirty Dishes

I hung up the phone in the kitchen not two seconds after I'd said hello.

"Who was that, Aunt Evie?" Leigh asked from the kitchen table, where she was folding the linen napkins I bring out only for the PLC meetings.

My palms pressed the front of the new slacks Leigh insisted I buy when we'd gone shopping for nursery items a few days earlier. "That was Vonnie. She's going to be a tad late."

Leigh nodded, continuing in her work. "Something wrong?"

I shook my head no. "I don't think so. Though to tell you the truth, she didn't sound just right."

I stepped from the kitchen into the dining room, where the table was all set and ready for the girls to arrive. We typically keep the food on the kitchen table and eat buffet style. I know I could just leave all the dishes in the kitchen for everyone to pick up and then serve themselves, but I like the looks of a formally set table, and so that's what I do. I set the table. I took a moment to walk around it, making certain all the little flowers on my mother's china pattern were facing forward, and they were. Of course they were; I'd set the table myself.

Leigh walked in with the napkins arranged on a silver tray, nicely folded into a little pattern she told me she'd learned to do when she was waiting tables at some restaurant back home. "See?" she said, holding up the tray. "We'll set these in the center along with a little teapot filled with the flowers I bought yesterday, and we're all set."

"Pretty," I commented, flexing my hands.

Leigh set the tray in its proposed place, never once taking her eyes off me. "What's wrong, Aunt Evie? You keep working your hands."

I looked down at hands that looked more like my mother's with every passing day. "Oh, nothing. A little arthritis, I guess."

Leigh straightened as much as she could with her belly sticking out and it weighing nearly what she does. "I think it's a little nerves, you know what I'm saying?"

I placed my hands on my hips. "What in the world do I have to be nervous about? It's not like I haven't been having this meeting every month since I was not too much older than you."

But she smiled at me knowingly. "You're nervous about people being here, in your home, with your pregnant niece." She ruffled the back of her crop of hair with her fingertips, grinning all the more. "And not a wedding band in sight."

I pointed a finger at her. "Now, you listen to me, Leigh Banks. You may think this is funny, but come two months from now you won't when you're lying up in that hospital without a husband to support you. And what about after that, when *you* have to support the child?"

"I've told you more than once that Gary will support the baby. And believe me, he can afford to support the baby."

I frowned. "There's more to supporting a baby than sending a check."

"I know, Aunt Evie. And he will. He'll see the baby whenever he wants. We're going to get it all set up legal. It's gonna work out. You'll see."

Before I could voice more of my disapproval, the doorbell rang, causing me to flex my hands again. Leigh noticed too. "See," she said with a wink. "Nerves."

That child. When did she grow up and get so smart, that's what I want to know. I turned away from the table and headed for the front door, which was opening on its own. The good Lord help me, the first arrival was none other than Lisa Leann Lambert, who obviously was raised in a Texas barn and didn't know you're supposed to wait for someone to answer the door before you just go barging right in. Unless, of course, you're from Summit View and everyone knows you, and then you can knock and enter. But Lisa Leann is still, in my opinion, an outsider and shouldn't be opening doors on her own accord.

"Helloooooooo," she called out, sticking her head in before anything else.

With all the times I've seen this woman at church and in town, I'm still not used to all the makeup and the hairdo and the flashy clothes, so it took me a second to respond. "You're the first one here," I said, working hard to remember the good manners my mother had instilled in me. "Do you need some help there?" Lisa Leann was nearly weighed down with what smelled like her brisket and a large basket loaded down with six pink-foil gift bags all tied up with gold ribbon with lots of pink and gold swirly paper sticking out. *What in the world is that woman bringing to our prayer club?*

"No, no honey. I've got it. Oh, is that a new outfit?"

Leigh walked in about that time and said yes it was and then commented on the aroma from the brisket as I shut the door (but not before sticking my head out for a quick look-see, hoping against hope that one of the other girls was not far behind. Of course, there was not a PLC soul in sight).

"Wow, that smells scrumptious," Leigh said.

"Darlin', it is scrumptious. I don't cook unless it's scrumptious." Lisa Leann let out a little-girl laugh.

For a moment I thought of Ruth Ann. It was a fleeting thing, and I knew it was caused by Lisa Leann's giggle. *Just like Ruth Ann's,* I thought. Almost an innocence about it . . . *Oh, Ruth Ann, why'd you have to go up and die on me? Why couldn't God let you live long enough to see me through?*

I watched Leigh and Lisa Leann disappear into the kitchen. My shoulders sagged ever so slightly, then came back up again when I heard Lisa Leann remark, "You didn't by any chance get up to Breckenridge for Oktoberfest, did you?"

"No, ma'am, I didn't."

"I wish I would've known about it beforehand. One thing I can do is polka with the best of 'em." Lisa Leann laughed a hearty laugh.

I shook my head at the very thought. *Oh, dear Lord, why don't you and I just start our prayers out right now?* I took a step toward the kitchen, thinking I may as well join them as stand there like a ninny in my own foyer, when I heard a car door slam. I all but twisted myself like a screw, I turned so fast to open the door. A nice push of cold air hit me square in the face as soon as I did, and I thought, *Well, Evie-girl. You deserve that slap.*

Lisa Leann bypassed the foyer altogether. She shot out of the kitchen and into my living room, parting the curtains for a quick look-see. "Who's that?" she asked. "Is that Goldie?"

I didn't answer. "Hurry, Goldie," I called out. "It's dropping colder by the minute."

Goldie ran in, ducking her head a bit while balancing a glass dish covered in aluminum foil. Quite frankly, she looked like she had been run over by a truck, though I would never dare to say so. Lisa Leann, however, was another matter.

"Look at her," I heard the Texan say to Leigh in a low voice. "Looks like she hasn't slept in days."

Goldie stomped her feet on my welcome mat before entering, carrying a white bag of Toll House chocolate chip cookies she'd obviously bought from our downtown bakery, Sprinkles. She extended the bag to me. "Sorry," she said. "I didn't have time to cook anything."

I looked from the cookies to the Lambert woman, worried at what she might say. My sweet Leigh saved the moment with, "I *love* Toll House cookies." She rubbed her swollen belly. "You can't go wrong with the original recipe and a great big glass of milk."

Goldie smiled weakly. "You're a dear and you always were."

"Hello and welcome to the Potluck Club," Lisa Leann chimed in. My eyebrows shot up a good six inches, I'm sure, blending right in with my hairline. Who was she to welcome folks to *my* club meeting?

Goldie must have thought the same thing. "Thank you," she said, then cut a glance over to me. "Am I the second to arrive?"

I placed my hand on her elbow and steered her toward the kitchen. "You are. Let's just put those cookies on a tray so they'll look like you spent hours over a hot stove."

We rounded into the kitchen when Goldie said, "My, what smells so wonderful?"

I pinched her arm but good. "What's wrong with you?" I whispered.

"What?" she asked, then looked me up and down. "New outfit?"

The doorbell chimed, and Leigh called out, "I've got it, Aunt Evie."

I looked from Goldie to the direction of the front of the house. "Thank you," I said, though my niece probably couldn't hear me. I turned back to Goldie. "You okay?"

She got all teary. Before she could answer, we heard Donna Vesey greeting Leigh with a "Hey, girl."

Hey, girl? What kind of talk is that?

I never got a direct answer from Goldie, but I did notice that she and Donna looked at one another like some sort of long-lost mother and child. I narrowed my eyes at the both of them, but my instincts gave up nothing. Still, looks like that can go right to the heart of a matter, no matter what the matter is.

We'd all arrived except Vonnie, and I told the girls she'd be a tad late and I thought it best we wait on her.

Everyone agreed. "Why don't we go sit in the living room?" I suggested. Everyone agreed with that too. Lisa Leann rushed into the kitchen to get her basket of goodies before joining us.

My living room is simple but tasteful. Most of the furnishings— the camelback sofa, various armchairs, and occasional tables—were Mama's. A large picture window at the front of the room allows in plenty of sunshine and gives an overall view of the rest of the old neighborhood. I'd set a fire to going in the fireplace earlier; it wasn't blazing full blast, but it hadn't died out altogether either.

Goldie and Lizzie (who brought the beginnings of a cross-stitch pattern for the baby, which everyone *oohed* and *ahhed* over) and Lisa Leann took a seat on the sofa while Donna sat in the armchair near the window and Leigh and I sat on the opposite side of the windows in two chairs separated by an occasional table. For the first few seconds we said stupid things like "Here we go" and "That's a lovely charm bracelet, Lisa Leann." Then we just sat looking around like we didn't even know one another. I personally think the cause of this was Lisa Leann, being new and all, but who knows. Finally Lisa Leann said, "Girls, I have something for each of you. Why don't I just go right ahead and pass these out?"

The next thing I knew, Lisa Leann was darting about the room, handing out bags like an elf at Christmas. As soon as she said, "Now don't be shy. Just dig right in," the girls immediately began to pull ribbon and paper away from the bags.

The *oohs* and *ahhs* started again, which encouraged the Lambert woman all the more. "What I've brought, ladies, is samples of lipstick and blush. You'll notice that each of you has personalized bags. That's because I chose only colors I know are perfect for your skin type and coloring. Not like those giveaways at department stores. One color does not suit all when it comes to cosmetics."

I narrowed my eyes as I opened my bag, more out of have-to than want-to. Turning the lipstick on its head, I read the name "Bashful Berry" and thought, *Well, how can a berry be bashful?*

"What do you mean, Evie?" Lizzie asked from the sofa.

I jumped a bit. "What?"

"What do you mean when you ask how a berry can be bashful? It's just a name, you know. Like Passion Fruit—which, by the way, is my color. Fruit can't be passionate, but there's something zany about certain fruits. Thank you, Lisa Leann. This is marvelous."

Had I spoken out loud? What else had I said, that I thought I'd only thought? Good heavens!

Lizzie continued. "Speaking of berries, did any of you notice the cute outfit the Berry girl was wearing at services on Sunday?"

Well, of course we did . . . what little bit there was to it.

133

"No bashful there, huh? But a bit too tight if you ask me," Lizzie commented. "What the kids are wearing these days. If I told you girls some of the things I see every single day of the world at the school . . ."

"Like a walking advertisement for early sexual activity," Goldie muttered. She shot a glance over to Leigh. "I'm sorry, Leigh."

Leigh's eyes brightened, and she chuckled. "Think nothing of it. I was pretty much a virgin till I met Gary, you know what I'm saying?"

"Leigh!" My voice was a firm warning.

"Well, I was." So much for the warning. "Besides, these days waiting till I was twenty-four makes me like a freak or something."

Lisa Leann giggled. "Honey, I like your forthright candor." She crossed her legs, and her charm bracelet jingled like a gypsy's tambourine.

Donna leaned over and placed her elbows on her knees, nodding. "I'd have to agree with Leigh. Our generation feels differently about sex than yours does." Her eyes scanned the room, and I noticed they skipped Goldie's altogether.

Lizzie brushed an imaginary piece of lint off her wool slacks. "What's to feel differently about? The Bible says that marriage is between a man and his wife. Period. Anything that deviates from that is outside the will of God." She looked over at Leigh. "I'm not saying you're going to hell or anything, honey . . ."

"Well, let's hope not," I interjected.

"But what I want to know," Lisa Leann piped in, "is if you've asked God to forgive you."

Donna sat straight up. "Forgive her for what, Lambert?"

Lisa Leann met her eyeball-to-eyeball. "For having sex."

"Outside of marriage," Goldie added, though—once again—we could hardly hear her.

"Actually, I have," Leigh answered.

I looked at her sharply. "Is this really necessary?"

Leigh winked at me, which she does frequently. It's her way of saying "Take a chill pill," as she puts it. "Not necessarily necessary, Aunt Evie. But I have nothing to hide." She rubbed her tummy. "Obviously."

She turned her attentions back to Lisa Leann. "I'm not saying I think of this baby as a mistake. Babies are gifts from God; I don't care how they come into this world. But I've asked God to forgive me. I told him I'd be the best mother in the world . . . with his help."

"Then," Lizzie said, "why not marry the father?"

Well, now, wasn't *that* just the $64,000 question?

Leigh became tight-lipped. Looked down at the evidence of her sexual encounter, then back up. "He hasn't asked."

Well, I can tell you right now, my mouth just fell open. Just fell right open. This was the first I'd heard tell of the young man's lack of intentions. "What do you mean 'he hasn't asked'?"

Leigh shrugged her shoulders. "Just that. He asked me to move in, of course."

"Ugh," Donna said, sitting back in the chair. "Show me a good man, and I'll show you a woman in drag."

While the rest of us sat shock faced, Leigh and Donna laughed like Donna was some sort of Phyllis Diller. "Girls," Lizzie said, coaxing the conversation back to a more decent level.

The "girls" sobered.

"It's the truth," Leigh said, more to Donna than anyone else. "Gary—that's the name of my ex-boyfriend—wanted me to move in, you know what I'm saying? Said he loved me, and what in the world was I suddenly becoming so conventional about? But I told him I wanted to do this right. To be right with God again like I used to be when I was a kid. I told him no more—*ahem*—playing around and running around like tomorrow doesn't matter."

"You go, girl," Donna said with a nod.

"Men have to be put in their places," Lisa Leann said. "Have to see the importance of God in the big picture. We women get that. Like I was saying to my daughter just the other day, 'Mandy, think about it, darlin'. Who was the proactive one in the Garden of Eden? The woman was, that's who. She was out there trying to at least *find* knowledge while all Adam was doing was sitting around naming animals.'"

"What does that mean, exactly?" I asked. Call me a stupid old virgin, but I just didn't get a bit of this.

135

"It means women are a lot smarter than men. I, for one, think we have a deeper pull toward God's heart."

"I wouldn't say that—"

"She has a point, Evie," Lizzie said. "Women are more in tune to the emotional side of God. His heart. Women understand the romance of God."

"What does that have to do with naming animals?" Goldie asked.

"More importantly," Donna said, "what does it have to do with Gary and Leigh?" She turned to look at my niece. "So what do you think? He'll come crawling?"

Leigh shook her head. "I'm not saying that's what I want."

"What do you want?"

Leigh shrugged her shoulders again. "I really don't know. Right now I'm just taking it one day at a time."

"I think we should pray for Gary," Lizzie said. She looked at Leigh. "We'll pray for you too, of course, Leigh. We'll pray that God will give you direction. But we need to pray for Gary's heart."

"Is Gary a Christian?" Lisa Leann asked.

"A Christian?" I jumped in. "What kind of Christian could he be?"

"What's new about Christian hypocrites? I've carted more than a few to the Summit County jail," Donna said. I noticed she deliberately avoided Goldie when her eyes swept across the room.

"You *can* be a Christian and not be perfect," Lizzie said. She leaned forward a bit and toyed with her blunt-cut fingernails. "My own Tim is a Christian. They made a natural mistake, is all."

The only face in the room that didn't at least go pink was Lisa Leann's, and that's only because she wasn't around when Tim and Samantha had to get married. I wanted to kick myself all the way to the bedroom, where I could hide under the covers the rest of the day. Goldie patted Lizzie's knee and said, "Tim is a fine man." She took a deep breath and exhaled. "We've all got our fair share of crosses to bear," she said, then looked past Lizzie to Lisa Leann. "Lisa Leann, if you plan to spend any amount of time with this group of women, you'll find out that we not only have enough to pray about within the community but within our own circle as well."

Lisa Leann started to say something—God only knows what—but was interrupted by Donna, who once again leaned forward. "Hey, ladies, let me ask you a question." We turned to give her our attention. "Any of you who've been in town a while know of a woman by the name of Jewel?"

I looked from Donna to the sofa where Lizzie and Goldie exchanged blank glances. "No, why?" I answered.

"A few weeks ago I stopped a man from California. Name of David Harris. Nice looking guy too," she added with a raised brow toward Leigh, who said, "Do tell."

"Mid-thirties. Close to six foot. Black hair. Brown eyes. Looks Hispanic. Maybe Mexican. Mexican-American. Hard to say, really." She ran a palm across the top of her short blond hair.

"A Latino?" Lisa Leann asked. "This Texan can tell you right now I think those men are hot. That Julio Iglesias can park his slippers in my closet any time he likes."

I decided not to comment on that. "Keep on with what you were saying, Donna," I told her.

"Apparently he has a mother here. I'm thinking he was adopted and is trying to find her. This isn't official or anything, but I kinda feel bad for the man."

"I've never heard that name before," Lizzie said. "But I can ask Samuel. See if he remembers."

Goldie shook her head. "This could've been before I moved here." She looked at Lisa Leann. "I married a local."

"Where're you from, darlin'?"

"Georgia."

Lisa Leann smiled. "I thought I detected an accent."

Donna cleared her throat. "Evie? You look like you're thinking about something."

My eyes widened. "No. I'm not thinking anything."

That was a lie. I was thinking about something. Something about the name Jewel . . . but God help me, I couldn't quite put my finger on it. You know, like when something's on the tip of your tongue but it just won't come out? That's how it was, something on the tip of my brain, but it just wouldn't . . . well, whatever. Somebody I knew named Jewel, but not from here. From where, then? And what woman around here could have farmed out a baby thirty-five years ago without me knowing about it?

My inner struggle was interrupted by the sound of Vonnie's car pulling up to the front of the house. "There's Von," I said, standing.

The rest of the girls stood too, following me to the front door. When I opened it, it was apparent the weather had dropped a few more degrees. Vonnie was moving her stocky form uncharacteristically slowly up the walkway. Her face was downcast, keeping a watch on her tiny feet.

I knew it! I thought. *Something is wrong.*

It didn't take long for us to find out what it was, either. As soon as Vonnie had dropped her cheesy corn bread onto my kitchen table—each one of us gathering around her—with the rest of the food that had grown to room temperature, she let out a pent-up sigh.

"What is it, Von?" I asked.

Her eyes filled with tears as she took in the lot of us, all gathered round the table, silent and waiting. "It's Jan Moore," she began.

"What about Jan Moore?" Lizzie asked. "You know, I saw her in the Sew and Stitch not too long ago and thought she looked a little thin. Said she wasn't sleeping well and thought it might be the change."

"The change in what?" Donna asked, which brought a chuckle from us more mature Potluckers.

"The change of life, darlin'," Lisa Leann said.

I watched Vonnie swallow hard. "It's not the change." She took in another breath.

"Well, for crying out loud, Vonnie. Spit it out," I told her.

"Jan Moore has inoperable cancer."

It seems to me that a good lifetime went by before anyone spoke—and that someone was our logical Lizzie Prattle. "Has she seen Doc Billings?"

138

"She has. I put in a call to him myself. I feel sure he'll talk to me about this."

"And?" Goldie asked.

"And he hasn't called me back yet. His wife said he went to Jackson Hole for a family wedding."

"Dorothy didn't go with him?" Lisa Leann asked, leaving me to think, *Well, who cares if Dorothy went with him or not?*

"Dorothy's never much cared for his family," Lizzie answered.

There was another pause, still none of us moving, before Vonnie said, "Well, girls. Here's what I do know: specifically, she has breast cancer."

"Breast cancer?" Goldie repeated. "But there's so much hope for women with breast cancer."

Vonnie shook her head no. "Not in this case. The cancer began in the back of the breasts. She wouldn't have felt anything during a regular self-exam. What happened is that it metastasized. Spread."

"Where?" Donna asked.

"First to her lungs. Then to her liver and spleen."

"How much time are we talking about exactly?" Lisa Leann asked, taking a step closer to Vonnie.

"Six months. Maybe less."

I took in what she said, nodding, thinking about my best friend, Ruth Ann, and how hard we'd prayed that she would beat cancer. But instead it had beat her, and beat her to death too. The pain of burying her, even after all these years, hadn't so much as lessened by a smidgen.

Leigh put a hand on my shoulder. "What are you thinking about, Aunt Evie?"

I looked at my old friends as I answered. "Ruth Ann."

Lizzie and Goldie nodded at their own memories.

Dear Lord, I prayed. *Please tell me you're kidding, 'cause I don't think I can go through this again . . .*

Needless to say, the rest of our meeting was spent with us girls in a stunned position. The food got cold, and the Glade scented candle I'd lit earlier in the day burned down to the bottom of the wick, leaving nothing but a blackened ring at the bottom of the tiny glass bowl. Vonnie kept saying we needed to pray, but no one said anything, just nodded in agreement. Lisa Leann said she'd pray when she got home, and for the first time I actually found myself not being agitated at what was coming out of her mouth. I remembered that Jan felt responsible for Lisa Leann being there in the first place, and I thought, *Well then, she certainly should pray.* Strange as it sounds, it wasn't a bitter thought but a comforting one.

Donna left almost immediately. I guess because she's so young and these kinds of things have to just settle on you gradual-like when you're young. The good Lord knows it had to settle on me when Ruth Ann died. In fact, it's still settling.

Lizzie talked about getting some books for us to read on this kind of cancer. "And on grief, in case we need it," she said, to which I said, "Well, of course we're going to need it, Lizzie Prattle. From the looks of things we're already grieving."

Leigh piped in, "From the looks of things you've already got Miss Jan buried. Whatever happened to faith?"

And with that, Goldie burst into tears like the sky in a rain forest. She cried for a good half hour, but something told me it wasn't just about Jan. Something told me it had to do with Coach Dippel.

That man . . . At times he makes me glad I'm not married.

When everyone finally left the house, I sat down on the living room sofa and just stared at nothing while Leigh began cleaning the kitchen. The scent of lemon dishwashing liquid crept into the room, becoming stronger with every *whir-whir* of the dishwasher. The smell mixed with that pumpkin-scented Glade candle, and the blending reminded me of Thanksgiving Day from years gone by and Mama and Peg and me standing in the kitchen, washing and drying dishes the old-fashioned way, by hand. We'd talk and talk, the three of us, about one thing and then another, our bellies stuffed full of Mama's turkey and dressing, good vegetables, and lots of pie.

That thought made me think of Mama's recipe for broccoli casserole, which made me think of how much Ruth Ann loved that dish as good as anything my mama ever made. She'd sit at the kitchen table and literally scrape the cheesy crust right off the sides of the Corningware with a spoon until the dish hardly needed washing at all.

"Done, Ruth Ann?" I'd ask, giving her a glare that read, *You're embarrassing me.* We were, after all, still in high school, and it doesn't take much to embarrass you when you're in high school.

But Mama would say, "Leave her alone, Evangeline." And she'd walk over to Ruth Ann, give her back a rub, and say, "Honey, you just make yourself at home. I'm pleased as can be that you like my broccoli as much as you do, and it warms my heart to know you're eating a green vegetable." Mama then turned to me. "She'll grow up healthy, Evangeline, eating broccoli like she does."

Now I'm left to wonder why all that broccoli didn't keep Ruth Ann alive . . . and if Jan Moore has been eating well all these years, well, what does the surgeon general have to say about all this?

"Aunt Evie?" Leigh's quiet voice came from around the kitchen doorway. "I'm going to lie down for a while. Is that okay with you?"

I nodded, looking over my shoulder to where she now stood. "I imagine you're getting a little tired."

Leigh rubbed her swollen belly. "That I am. Maybe later you and I can go out to dinner. Want to?"

I smiled weakly. "We'll see."

Leigh nodded, then turned and headed up the stairs toward her room.

I sat silent for a moment, returning to my reflections of the past. *Ruth Ann, Ruth Ann . . .* I thought heavily, then wondered for the millionth time since her death what she'd think if she knew Arnold had gotten married not even eight months after her death. *"Don't blame him, Evie,"* she'd say. *"He just can't live without a woman taking care of him. I understand that."* To which I'd say, *"Why do you always make excuses for that man?"*

I remembered the evening Arnold had called me, talking first about how much he missed Ruth Ann and then, like a knife slipping through soft butter, asking me out for a date. I wondered what

Ruth Ann would say to that, if I ever had the nerve to drive over to the cemetery and tell her.

Of course I'd declined the offer, not only because Ruth Ann had been my dearest friend for life but also because I wouldn't really know how to behave on a date, anyway. Sitting in my living room, in a house where I all but lived alone now, I frowned. *What had it been about me that kept the boys from asking me out?* I wondered. *I'm not a half-bad-looking woman—as good looking as any woman around these parts, I'd say. Was it something in my character? Some wall I'd built around my heart that dared anyone to get close enough to even touch the stone-cold bricks?* The questions disturbed me now as much as they'd ever done; not that I'd ever told a soul—not even Ruth Ann—how I felt about being alone.

I answered my own question with a *maybe so*, then prepared myself to do what I always do when I'm upset: I clean something. Not that my house needed special attention, but somewhere between where I was this morning and where I was right now, I decided my life needed some restructuring, and that began with my closets.

I started with the one in the guest room (Leigh was sleeping in her mother's old room), which at one time had been my parents' room and is now where I keep my off-season clothes. The closet is not an overly large one and the door is just a door, not one of those louvers like I've seen in some of the newer homes around here. I opened it and pushed it all the way to the wall, then began jerking hangers off the cedar bar that hung from end to end. I threw everything on the bed, separating the clothes into two piles, one to take to the church's clothing pantry and the other to keep.

My keeper pile was considerably shorter than my pantry pile. With my hands on my hips, I stood over the bed, wondering what in the world had happened to me in the years I'd been on this earth. As a child I had been a fun-loving girl. I dressed like all the other girls dressed. I did exciting things . . . sometimes. When had I become such a fuddy-duddy?

I turned from the all-too-depressing sight and began pulling shoe boxes from the top shelf, peering into each one, then setting them near the pantry pile. At this rate, by next spring I'd be barefoot and naked.

I returned the few keeper items to the closet and then shut the door, all the while deciding to repeat my efforts in my bedroom closet, where my autumn and winter clothes were hanging. The results were the same—keeper pile slim, pantry pile high.

By the time I finished, Leigh was standing just inside my room, looking fairly quizzical. "What in the world?" she asked, sounding remarkably like her mother.

"I've decided I'm an old fuddy, and I need a new look, like you've been saying."

Leigh took tentative steps toward my bed piled high with clothes dating back two decades and more. "My goodness. What made you suddenly decide . . ."

I began slipping fabric from hangers. "Do you know when I stopped living, Leigh?"

"Stopped living?" Leigh began helping me in my ministrations.

"Yes. Stopped living. I'll tell you when. When Ruth Ann died, that's when. There's no reason, no reason on God's green earth as to why I am like I am, except for one. When Ruth Ann died, I wished more than anything that I'd been buried with her. So I just quit living."

Leigh reached for the next garment on the pile. "What brought this on, Aunt Evie?"

"I was just thinking, is all. I was just thinking that here we go again, now what with Jan Moore's illness. And I was thinking how you got me to buy these new clothes the other day and how some of the girls commented on my new look, and I'm not a half-bad-looking woman, now am I?"

Leigh burst out laughing.

"Why shouldn't Vernon Vesey want to take me to the movies?"

Leigh's eyes widened. "Sheriff Vesey has asked you out?"

I clamped my mouth shut, then muttered, "Maybe."

She jumped up and down as much as a woman in her third trimester can do. "Oh, Aunt Evie! That's awesome!"

"Yeah, well. Whatever."

"You and Vernon Vesey. Who'd have ever thought?"

I took on a stern look. "Plenty of people, I'll have you know, Leigh Banks. For your information, yours is not the first generation to discover the opposite sex. I'll have you know I lived through the sixties."

Leigh stopped in what she was doing, dropping an old orange taffeta dress to the bed. "You had sex with Vernon Vesey?" she asked, her voice in a whisper.

My brow drew together. "I most certainly did not. I've never— I . . ." My words wouldn't come easy. "But he did kiss me full on the lips when we were children."

Leigh's lips turned upward. "Then what happened?"

I went back to busying myself with the work on the bed. "Then Doreen Roberts happened, that's what."

"And that was the totality of your experience with the opposite sex?" she asked, touching my arm with her tiny hand.

I sent her a look that warned her to drop the subject, and she did, but not before adding, "I think the day Vernon Vesey dropped you may have been the day you died, Aunt Evie." When I said nothing, she cleared her throat and added, her voice bold, "This calls for shopping, you know what I'm saying? Why don't we invite Michelle and her mom to join us for a little shopping in Silverthorne next Saturday, followed by dinner?"

I nodded. That sounded like a good idea to me, as good as any idea I'd heard all afternoon.

Later that evening, at Leigh's insistence, I brought out an old box of photographs and my high school and college yearbooks. We sat at the dining room table, laughing at the old black-and-whites of Peg and me, Mama and Daddy. One year, when Peg and I were young teens, we'd gone to the West Coast and vacationed at the beach. Leigh got a particular kick out of seeing her mother and me wearing our quite fashionable (at the time) bathing suits and of Mama wearing an oversized straw sunhat. I explained some of the shenanigans I'd managed to get into during my college years, pointing to photographs of my schoolmates and telling her the stories behind each one.

I pointed to a photo on the left side of the book. "That was Rebekah Noble. She was so pretty. She and I used to go skiing nearly every time we had a spare minute to do so. She loved Breckenridge." I tapped my finger on the photo for emphasis. "She ended up in ministry, as a missionary, to be exact. Over somewhere in Africa or the Middle East. I can't remember exactly. We corresponded for a while and then . . . well, time has a way of separating people you never thought you'd be separated from."

Leigh "mmm'd" an agreement, then jutted her neck a bit, leaning closer to the right side of the book. She pointed to one of the many pictures and said, "Isn't that Vonnie?"

I leaned closer. "Where?"

"There. Sitting on the bench with the hottie."

"The what?"

"There. Right there, Aunt Evie."

I leaned closer still. "Oh yes. That's Vonnie."

"Who's she with?"

"Hmm? Oh, I don't think she's with anybody—" I stopped short, knowing my words didn't match the photo on the glossy page.

Leigh laughed. "You don't think so? They look awfully cozy sitting there, you know what I'm saying? And he's a hottie."

I furrowed my brow. "Why do you keep saying that, Leigh Banks? What does that mean exactly?"

Leigh gave me a quick hug. "It means he's handsome, Aunt Evie."

I looked back at the picture. "He is a nice-looking boy. But, I don't think . . . hmmm."

"Hmmm?" Leigh's eyes twinkled.

I shook my head as though I were trying to rattle something loose. "What *is* it? I remember him . . . something . . ."

Our church's "death patrol" leader is a gal named Sharon Kanaly. She's about fifty-five years old—give or take a year—and is frail and tall and married to Curtis Kanaly, the local coroner/postal worker. Curtis is the guy you call should you have the unfortunate luck to have someone die while in your home, and Sharon is the one who calls everyone on what she calls her prayer chain when you're sick, dying, or already dead. Sharon started her chain years ago after she tried to become a part of the Potluck Club and we wouldn't let her in. It wasn't because none of us like her—though few of us do—but because Sharon has a way of putting a damper on the most positive of times and turning the simplest things into catastrophes.

Take, for instance, the day Clarice Stephens took sick and went home from her job at the drugstore. Clarice had never so much as missed a day of work in her life, that much is true, and when she came down with what we all thought was some twenty-four-hour flu bug and couldn't stand up straight, she went home at 4:30 from her usual 8:30 to 5:00 shift. At 4:30 she was only a half an hour short, mind you. She hadn't gotten in her driveway good but what Sharon was calling everyone on her prayer chain, saying Clarice had that year's deadly virus from some foreign country as yet unknown.

Turned out Clarice had a light case of vertigo. Doc Billings cleaned her ears out good and gave her some medicine, and she was good as new in no time, ringing up Midol for the young girls in town and Preparation H for those of us who'd heard it was good for removing wrinkles from around your eyes, as well as other things.

All this to say it was no real surprise the morning after our Potluck Club meeting that Sharon was ringing her hands and pacing back and forth in front of the church, looking more like death than Jan Moore ever could. I'd hardly slept all night and didn't look much better. Not only was I wrung out from the club being at my house, but also—of course—there was the news about Jan, not to mention that the cleaning out of my closets had left me more than a little drained. It wasn't just clothes I was choosing to get rid of but rather what felt like a lifetime of wrong thinking. Naturally, today I had *nothing* to wear except something dated, but I knew next week would be different. Next week there would be a whole new Evangeline Benson, at least on the outside. I'd still be the same on the inside, somewhat angry with God and willing to bet that after he took Jan Moore from us, I'd be even more so.

Sharon ran to me as soon as I stepped out of the car. The air had more snap to it today than the day before, and I was grateful I'd worn my dress jacket. "Hello, Sharon Kanaly," I said matter-of-factly when she reached me.

Sharon looked first to me, then to Leigh, who pulled her full weight out of the passenger's side of the car, then back to me. "Hello, Mrs. Kanaly," Leigh greeted. "Aunt Evie, I'll go on inside and get settled in our seats."

"Our seats," she'd said, meaning the same seat I'd sat in since I was a child swinging my little legs back and forth—left, right, left, right—and noting the sheen in my shiny Mary Janes against the stark whiteness of my frilly socks. One thing was for certain, when Peggy and I were children, Mama dressed us to the nines on Sunday mornings.

"Did you hear the news?" Sharon asked me, jutting her neck so she looked like one of those birds from down in Florida.

"I assume you're talking about Jan Moore." I began walking toward our tiny church, toward sanctuary I knew would not come easy today. "To be honest with you, I thought it was going to be kept under wraps for a while."

Sharon kept step with me as I looked around, noting the other members as they milled toward the front doors of the church or the side door closest to the nursery, for those who had little ones. "Well, naturally the pastor told Curtis this morning, wants him to find out who they need to contact within the medical community."

I stopped, turning to face her. "This morning? And you know already?"

"Well, Evie. It's not like husbands and wives keep secrets from one another." She blanched. "Oh. Well, maybe you don't know. Well, they don't."

"I see." I started walking again. "Will a formal announcement be made this morning, then?"

"I just saw Jan in the kitchen and told her I thought she should come right out and tell the congregation, no need to keep it a secret. After all, between my prayer chain and your little prayer group, I think we'll have her covered, don't you? I think that's what we're called to do as brothers and sisters in the Lord." The way Sharon said "Lord" was more like "Lower-ed," which made me smile in spite of myself.

"I have to say I agree with you. Did she say what she was going to do?" We'd reached the front doors and were nearly surrounded by other members.

Sharon shook her head no. "But I believe she'll do the *right* thing, don't you, Evie?"

"I'm sure she will," I said, then turned slightly as one of the teenage boys from our congregation opened the door with a "Here you go, Miss Benson." I winced. Like I didn't have the strength to open a door myself. Still, manners need to be observed, no matter how I might be feeling.

I settled myself in my favorite pew next to Leigh, we being the only two in that particular row and on that side of the room. Vonnie and her husband, Fred, sat in front of us, Fred smelling faintly of motor grease and Vonnie smelling like sweet talcum powder. The two scents together made my nose wrinkle, which Leigh caught, and she laughed. As soon as I settled, having taken off my jacket, Vonnie turned to me and whispered, "Did you know that Sharon Kanaly is already aware of Jan's illness?"

I nodded. "She accosted me outside."

Fred turned his heavy-set balding head our way and shushed us. "Girls," he said. "This *is* the house of the Lord."

I frowned at him. "Like I don't know that, Fred Westbrook."

He twisted his neck a bit more. "Good. Then stop gossiping long enough to act like it." He then glared at Vonnie, who said, "Fred's right; I'm sorry." She smiled sweetly at her husband, nuzzled shoulders, and then turned back to the front.

Leigh smiled at me again, waggling her brow just as the choir—all ten members of it, including Goldie Dippel and Lisa Leann Lambert—walked in from a little side door, taking their places in the loft behind the pulpit.

Grace Church begins each service by singing a little "good morning" song. As soon as our pianist, Carrie Lowe, hit the first chord, we began to sing. I found myself choking, however, when we got to the words about rejoicing in the day. How could I possibly rejoice, I wondered, when there in the front row of the church, sitting straight and tall, was one of the best women God had ever put on his green earth and that woman was dying. I stared at the back of her head, watching the tiny movements of it as she sang along with the congregation. I wondered what thoughts might be beating against her heart at this moment and then reflected on how I might be feeling were I her, knowing I was dying.

The song finished. Pastor Kevin—who'd been leading us—called out, "Greet one another in the name of the Lord!" Leigh and I winked at one another and then turned to the pew behind us, where the Fairfields—Todd and Julie—sat with two of their three children. "Good morning, Fairfields," I said. "How's Abby?"

Julie Fairfield took my hand. "She's fine, Miss Benson. Just fine. Loving every minute of school."

"My alma mater, you know," I reminded her needlessly.

"Yes, ma'am." She turned to Leigh, taking her hand. "How are you, Leigh?" she asked.

"Big as a house," Leigh answered.

Julie smiled at her, and I caught a look in her eyes. *I've been where you are*, it said. *Pregnant and unmarried.* I realized Leigh wouldn't know this; it had happened long before she would have caught the gossip, but I thought it might bear telling later on in the morning. "Leigh," Julie said in a low voice, leaning over the back of our pew. "If you ever need to talk . . . I've been where you are. Abby—"

So much for telling her later, I thought, though it took a moment for Leigh to understand. When she did, I watched a light shine in her eyes. "Oh, really? Thanks. I'll do that. I really will."

Julie Fairfield took a deep breath and sighed as though she'd just let the biggest cat out of the bag and it had caught some church mouse. A bit uncomfortable, I turned back to where Vonnie should have been standing but was not. Instead, she was at the front, holding Jan Moore's hand and talking intently to her. Naturally Sharon Kanaly was within earshot, and I couldn't help but frown.

I took a step to join Vonnie (and push Sharon out of the way), but something stopped me. I wasn't ready for this, wasn't ready to take death by the hand again. Instead, I reached for Leigh's, squeezing it with mine, and for the first time thought favorably about the life she carried inside.

19

Her life will never be the same . . .

Clay heard about it first from Donna, who stopped by the café on her way home from the club meeting. She was chalky and visibly shaken and sat on a barstool. But she was close enough that he could ask her, "What's going on?"

At first she just shook her head; then she ordered a cup of coffee to go. Clay stood, walked over to her, and leaned against the counter. "Come on, now," he said, noticing a tear slip down her cheek. That's when she told him that Jan Moore had been diagnosed with cancer.

Clay shook his head. "Dora Watkins was in here the other day. Said she didn't think Jan looked well."

"Dora Watkins," Donna said, eyes wide. "Hey, she beat cancer, didn't she?" Hope registered for the briefest of moments, then settled.

After church services the following day, it seemed everyone in town knew. As Clay ate his Sunday luncheon special of sliced ham, creamy potatoes, and green beans, he listened to the agonized whispers of those who spoke as though they'd buried the lady already.

"Geez O'Malley, there's a lot going on around this sleepy little town" he wrote later. He continued pecking at his typewriter.

> And you don't have to be as observant as I to know that with the birth of Leigh's baby and the possible death of one of the town's most beloved members, life around Summit View will never be the same.
> Especially for Evangeline and the ladies of the Potluck.

151

Lizzie

Lasagna

2 pounds ground beef
1 clove garlic, minced
1 tablespoon parsley flakes
2 tablespoons basil
1 teaspoons salt
1 can tomatoes
1 6-ounce can tomato paste
1 16-ounce package lasagna
1 teaspoon olive oil
3 12-ounce cartons cottage cheese
2 beaten eggs
2 tablespoons parsley flakes

20

Savory Family Dinner

On Monday afternoon I was a woman with a mission. As soon as I'd closed down the computer in the high school's library, tucked chairs neatly around the few tables the county school system had afforded us, and then locked the door leading into the hallway, I walked back through the library and made my way to my office. Without a moment's hesitation, I grabbed my purse from inside a desk drawer, turned out the lights, and slipped out the back door, which led to a corridor used exclusively by faculty and the occasional students who were room assistants. Mrs. Hall, one of the second-grade teachers, was coming down the hallway with a stack of disarrayed papers in her arms. She greeted me kindly with, "Going home, Lizzie?"

"Actually, no. I'm headed for the public library." I turned the doorknob to assure myself that it had locked.

"Oh?" Janet Hall is a pretty young woman—one of our newer educators—with large innocent eyes and a smile bookended with deep dimples. She and her husband of two years are expecting their first child in seven months or so. We all wondered whether or not she'd come back to teach or decide to stay home and be a full-time mommy.

"Research," I said, walking beside her. "I'm going to read everything I can about breast cancer, cancer treatment, cancer centers. Basically anything I can get my hands on in hard copy. I'm going

154

to look up some things on the Internet too. I know I could do that here, but I want the full scope at my fingertips."

"Is this because of Jan Moore?"

Janet is a Methodist and doesn't attend Grace Church, but that certainly doesn't matter. Everyone in Summit View knows Jan, knows her and adores her. "Yes," I answered. "I'm a lover of research, as you may or may not know. I intend to have some information to share with her by this time tomorrow. Hopefully enough to shed some light on the situation. We're not going to take this lying down, you know."

We reached the outside door, and I opened it. "Thank you," she said, to which I replied, "Think nothing of it."

"And what do you think of the situation?" she asked me as we continued toward the employee parking lot.

"I believe . . ." I began, then choked. I took a deep breath and continued. "I believe in miracles," I finished.

Janet raised her eyebrows. "If you believe in miracles, why are you researching?"

Reaching my car, I pulled keys out of my purse, then looked her dead in the eye. "I believe that through modern science we see God's miracles. Now don't get me wrong. I also believe in those miracles man cannot explain. But if you ask me, when a disease destroying a body is brought to a stop by man's intellect—which is God's gift in the first place—then we still have a miracle."

Janet nodded, then moved on. "I can't argue with that. Let me know how it goes," she called behind her, to which I replied, "Will do."

A few minutes later I drove my Acura into the parking lot of the Summit View Public Library, got out, and hurried toward the front door. The temp was dropping again, and I had a fleeting thought about snow, hoping it would hold off at least until I got home.

I walked into the warmth of the large open room dominating the whole of the library. Kristen Borchardt, a librarian and a friend of mine, met me. "Lizzie, I'm so glad you came in," she said.

I stopped. "You are?" I smiled at her.

She motioned for me to follow her to a room behind the U-shaped checkout and returns counters. I walked around to the little half door that swung inward, pushing it with my knee, then followed through. Kristen was already in the room and standing on the other side of the desk when I walked through the doorway. "Come here," she said, pointing to the chair behind the desk. I noted that there were several stacks of magazines and books sitting neatly on top. "I've already gathered together a few books and periodicals for you. Some medical journals too." She tapped one of the stacks with her index finger. "They're all up-to-date. Every single one of them."

I stopped in my tracks. "I take it you were expecting me."

Kristen nodded. "As soon as I got home yesterday from church, I said to Horace, 'Lizzie Prattle will be at the library first thing after school's out.'" She looked down at her watch. "What took you so long?"

I smiled at her. "So you gathered together the information you thought I'd want to read."

"I did." She pointed to a computer desk behind the chair. "The computer is booted up and ready for you to surf the Internet if you want."

"Thank you, Kristen," I said, slipping behind her to take a seat in the desk chair.

Kristen walked toward the door, stopped, and turned. "By the way, the University of California San Francisco is making some wonderful progress when it comes to breast cancer. I've printed out some information and put it on top of the medical journals for you."

I glanced down, nodding. "Thank you. I'll start with that."

Two hours later I was forced to stop in my labors in order to call Samuel to tell him I'd be late returning home. "And dinner would be . . ." he prompted.

"Apparently takeout," I answered with a frown. As much as I love my husband, a few of his absolutes drill on my nerves. The first one is: a woman should first and foremost cook for her family. Nothing else—including work, social, or church obligations—should interfere with this rule. Samuel couldn't so much as boil water if he had to, so I knew he'd be sitting in the family room, reclining in his La-Z-Boy, counting the minutes by the growls of his stomach. "What would you like?"

He paused before answering. "Why don't you just go to the grocery store and pick up some of that already fried chicken? You can put some veggies from a can on the stove when you get home, and we'll call that dinner. Oh, and pick up some of those brown-'n-serves I like so much."

My frown grew deeper. Why didn't *he* set some veggies on the stove? "That sounds good," I said. "I'll be there shortly. I'm just going to gather up my notes and say good night to Kristen."

"I'll be here waiting on you," he said. "I *am* a little anxious to know what you've learned."

That line brightened my spirit. "Good. I'm a little anxious to share it with you."

"Sounds good."

I started to hang up until I heard him say, "Hey!" I brought the phone back to my ear. "Yeah?"

"Michelle's not here. She and Leigh went out for dinner."

"So it will just be the two of us . . ."

"Just like old times," he said with a chuckle, but I knew better. It would never be like "old times" again. When we were newly married we knew nothing of having three children so close together . . . of institutes for the deaf, of learning to speak with our hands . . . (or of dealing with an unwed son who would become a father). Now we had adult children. We had grandchildren halfway across the country we rarely got to see, some right here in town we see all the time, and we worry about them all. I sighed deeply. "Old times" didn't include friends we'd buried too soon and those we were scared we might have to bury soon. *Father God*, I prayed silently. *Please . . .*

It was an hour later before we were sitting across from each other at the kitchen table, plates of fried chicken, Italian green beans, and brown-'n-serves between us. "Do you think Jan and Pastor Kevin know about UCSF?" I asked my husband.

157

"What about it?" he asked, taking a bite of a chicken thigh, his favorite piece.

"They have a cancer center where literally hundreds of clinicians are working toward finding a cure for cancer."

"What about those who have already been diagnosed?"

"They're giving them treatments. I'm sure some are part of the research."

Samuel speared beans with his fork. "I don't know if they know or not. Are you planning on telling Jan?"

I nodded. "I'll call her later." I glanced at the kitchen wall clock. "If it's not too late." Samuel took another bite of beans, and I continued. "Have you ever heard of J. Michael Bishop?"

He shook his head.

"Harold Varmus?"

Again, he shook his head.

"They've discovered cancer-causing genes. According to their research, it's genetic mistakes that cause cancer."

"It's amazing what medical science is coming up with."

I nodded, looking down at my so-far-untouched plate. "There's a lot I don't understand, of course, but there was a paper released recently about some gene that was identified as being key to breast cancer metastasis."

"From?"

I looked around the room for the stack of notes I'd brought home, locating them on the corner of the kitchen counter, lying next to the now-empty chicken box. "Let me get my notes," I said, rising from the table. When I came back, having looked through more than half my scribble, I said, "California Pacific Medical Center Research Institute."

Samuel paused for a minute before saying, "Why don't you let me talk with Pastor Kevin about all this? If all this research is going on close by, he may want to look further into it."

"I think that's a very good idea. When will you?"

"Tomorrow." He looked down at his watch. "For now, *Law and Order* is on. Dinner was passable," he added with a wink, then left me alone at the table.

"Have fun last night?" I asked my daughter early the next morning. We are both forced to rise early in order to get to work on time, Michelle having to leave much earlier than I do. I could easily sleep in a bit longer, but our predawn moments over coffee and cereal have become a favorite part of my day. I love my time with my daughter—and then my time in the Word before I have to head back up the stairs and finish getting myself ready.

Michelle nodded her fisted right hand up and down, signing "yes." She smiled at me, then continued. "Leigh and Evie want us to go to Silverthorne on Saturday for shopping and dinner."

I signed back. "Sounds good. I'll talk to Evie."

"Good," Michelle signed, then went back to her cereal. I watched her for a moment. My goodness, she was so pretty. Long dark hair pulled back in a thick ponytail. Porcelain skin. Large dark eyes that mirrored every emotion she'd ever felt. She was so beautiful . . . so perfect . . . except that she couldn't hear.

Why my daughter? I'd wondered more than a few times over the years. There was no answer for it, of course. Life happens, and life isn't perfect. *"In a perfect world,"* I'd been known to say, knowing it was something I'd never see until I reached the pearly gates.

Michelle looked up at me. "What?" she said aloud. Her mouth was half full of cereal.

I smiled at her. "I was just thinking how pretty you are. Obviously without the cereal hanging out of your mouth."

Her eyes rolled. "Mom . . ."

"I can't help myself," I signed. "I'm your mother."

She swallowed, stuck her tongue out at me, then continued in her conversation. "Speaking of your children," she signed, "your son called me yesterday at work." Michelle's job had installed a TTY telephone system just for her needs, enabling her to send and receive phone calls.

"Sam or Tim?"

"Tim."

I felt my eyebrows lift. "What's up?"

"Not the cost of living. Tim and Samantha have decided to build a new house."

"Why?"

She shrugged her shoulders. "Tim says he wants a bigger house."

I shook my head, bewildered. "But why?" I asked, raising my hands palm up.

"Mom," Michelle spoke aloud. "Ask him. Not me. He's your son." She stood and walked her bowl and spoon over to the sink. "I need to get going," she signed.

I merely nodded at her. *What's going on in Baton Rouge?*

"Have you spoken to Tim lately?" I asked Samuel as soon as he opened his eyes. He was still lying in the bed, flat on his back the way he'd slept as long as I'd been married to him, and I suppose his whole life long before that. How he manages to sleep flat on his back is a mystery to me, but he does.

He yawned. Morning breath hit me square in the face, but I overlooked it. If something was going on with my son, I wanted to know about it firsthand. As far as I was concerned, if Samuel knew that Tim and Samantha were planning to build a new house and had not told me . . . well . . .

I planted my fists firmly on my hips.

"No, why?" Samuel asked, sitting up and swinging his legs over the side of the bed. He stood, stretched, and made his way to the master bath.

"Did you know he and Samantha are planning to build a new house?" I asked, following on his heels.

He stopped and looked back at me. "Really?" he asked, then continued on toward the bath, where he shut the door in my face.

I spoke through the door. "Why in the world would they want to do that?" I asked. "Their house is big enough."

I heard the toilet flush and the sink water run before the door reopened. Samuel stood before me with a tube of toothpaste in one hand and his toothbrush in the other. "What are you stressing about, Lizzie? So the boy wants to build a new house. On his salary he can afford it."

I watched him squeeze a generous amount of Crest onto the toothbrush. "A mother knows when something is up."

Samuel chuckled in a way that bordered on loving condescension, if that makes a bit of sense. "All right, Mother." He turned toward the bathroom sink. "I'm calling Pastor Kevin this morning. What about you? What are your plans with Jan?"

I pulled my nightgown over my head. If I didn't get ready soon, I'd be late for school. "I'm calling her during my lunch break . . . will probably go over after school today. I thought I'd take her some of my lasagna from the freezer."

"Sounds good," he said, his words garbled from brushing his teeth. I heard him spit and rinse as I hung my gown on a hook inside our closet. For a moment I stood in the chill of the house, wearing nothing but my underwear. I just stood and stared at a rackful of clothes and wondered what to wear until Samuel came out of the bathroom and stopped short. "Well, good morning, sunshine!" he exclaimed.

Something told me I'd be late for work after all.

21

The town's most cautious woman—
in a speeding car . . .

Clay took his time getting ready that morning. He even made a cup of coffee, using the hot plate in his room and an instant coffee bag. It wasn't nearly as good as Sal's, but it would do in a pinch.

He sat in his favorite chair—okay, the only chair—a La-Z-Boy recliner he'd purchased at a rummage sale sponsored by Grace Church some five or six or ten years earlier, turned on the television, and watched the morning news for updates from around the globe. He sipped on the less-than-perfect brew and made faces with each swallow, jotting words and quotes in his notebook. He called his editor, suggested they follow the recent news out of Brazil a bit more closely.

His editor agreed, giving him some extra time to check the Internet before heading over to the newsroom. In the old days he would have had to go to the office to check the AP wire. Clay praised the morning for the Internet.

Clay disconnected the line, then got dressed. According to the local weather, it would be a bit chilly, so he grabbed the jacket his mother had given him the year before on his birthday before bidding Woodward and Bernstein good-bye and then slipping out the door.

Moments later, he stood on Main Street, waiting for a slow stream of cars to pass before crossing over to Higher Grounds. When at last there was a break in traffic, he stepped off the curb, ambled about halfway to the center of the road, then jumped to the yellow line in caution as a car nearly plowed him over.

He spun his head around. No one was ever caught speeding in the center of town, and he wondered briefly where the fire was.

Clay's brow furrowed. *Good grief,* he thought. *That was Lizzie Prattle, the town's most cautious woman when it comes to driving safety.* He shook his head as though trying to dislodge a thought, then made the rest of the way over to the café.

"Wonder what that was about?" he said to no one, then pulled open the café's door.

Donna

SAL'S DENVER OMELET

1 Tbs. BUTTER
1/4 CUP CHOPPED ONIONS
1/4 CUP CHOPPED GN BELL PEPPER
1/8 CUP CHOPPED HAM
1/8 CUP CHOPPED BACON
3 EGGS

1 Tbs CREAM
1/8 tsp SALT
1/8 tsp PEPPER
3 DROPS TABASCO
1/4 SHREDDED CHEESE

SAUTÉ ONION, BELL PEPPER, HAM AND BACON
IN HOT SKILLET WITH BUTTER. THEN IN A SM
BOWL, WHIP EGGS LIGHTLY AND ADD CREAM,
SALT, AND PEPPER AND TABASCO. ADD MIXTURE TO
SAUTEED MIX AND LET OMELET BROWN ON ONE
SIDE. FLIP OVER AND BROWN ON OTHER SIDE, (COVER
TOP WITH CHEESE, FOLD IN HALF. SERVE (1 SERVING)

22

Café Chats

My gasp sent the ghost of my breath swirling above the icy river that churned around me. I had somehow managed to pull free of my Bronco as the rapids dragged it into the deeper currents. What had happened? How had I come to be in these frigid waters? Clueless, I could only struggle to survive the freezing torrents.

My next gasp for air was met by an ice-cold wave that pushed my head beneath the raging river. My ears filled with water, and I could only hear the fizzy shush of the roar above me. I pawed at the waves surrounding me, somehow jutting one hand above the icy froth. My hand was met by a strong clasp. I held tight, fighting to break my head free of the pounding surge. My would-be rescuer's face was lost in the glare of headlights beaming through the mist, illuminating my fight to live. The river's icy grip pulled at my body as my fingers, numb with cold, begin to slip from the hand that held mine. I gasped one last lungful of air before my head disappeared beneath the waves as my fingers slipped free. The frozen darkness pulled me downward, engulfing my very soul . . .

My eyes popped open, and I stared at the red digits on my radio alarm clock. It was 9:00 in the morning. In a huff, I turned my back on the time, tangling my legs in the covers. For Pete's sake, I'd only been in bed since 4:00 a.m. It was too early for the dream.

I sat up and rubbed the sleep from my eyes. There was no fighting it now. Once the dream interrupted my rest, it was over. I might as well get up.

My misery was interrupted by a pang of hunger. Of course! I was out of bread last night and went to bed without my ham sandwich. No wonder I was awake. I was starved. Maybe I'd shower, then hit Higher Grounds Café for a good cup of joe and one of their famous Denver omelets. Sal, the woman who ran the place, had once given me her recipe, and I was capable of making one myself, if I had such an inclination. Not!

Besides, it would be good to see some of the regulars that gathered there every morning, though to tell the truth, I kept most of them at arm's length.

The bell above the door of the café jingled to announce my arrival from the autumn morning. Now, a person who had eight hours of sleep under her belt might enjoy how the sun backlit the last of the golden aspen leaves against a sky so blue that only the surrounding mountain peaks could interrupt its horizons. I, however, was not that person.

As I walked in, the *Gold Rush News* reporter, Clay Whitefield, looked up from nursing his cup of coffee and nodded above his copy of *The Denver Post*. Clay was half Cherokee Indian and half Irish, which explained his dark freckled skin and auburn hair. He was outfitted in his gray boiled-wool jacket, still zipped to the top, over a pair of khakis. He was in his mid-thirties, with a slightly receding hairline and a pouch of a belly. He lived alone in a one-room apartment overlooking Main Street.

"Deputy Donna, catch any wild bands of criminals last night?" he quipped, squinting against the ray of sun that followed behind me.

I tipped my Rockies baseball hat. "'Fraid not."

He looked up at me over his reading glasses. "Oh, great. I'll have to scratch my cover story. Got anything else for me?"

I climbed onto the stool at the counter, playing along. "Like what?"

"Jewel thieves would be nice. I'd plaster their mugs on the front page followed by Nobel-Prize-winning copy."

"Sorry, but no. Though . . ." I thought of David Harris and wondered if he had found his missing mother.

"Though what?" Clay asked with hope.

I grabbed a copy of the laminated breakfast menu, though I knew my options by heart. "Though nothing, unless you want to write about how Fred Westbrook lost the big one in Gold Rush Creek again."

Clay snorted a laugh. "Sorry, already wrote and printed that one too many times."

I looked up at Sally Madison, who was already waiting to take my order. Sal had probably landed in Summit View in the sixties, wearing bell-bottoms and a tie-dyed T-shirt that had somehow morphed into a red waitress uniform complete with her name embroidered on her breast pocket. I could almost imagine her forty pounds lighter with flowing blond hair. She could still be that flower child if it weren't for the hairnet, wrinkles, and crisp white apron. Sal lived out behind the café in the Higher Grounds Trailer Park, not far from Wade's charming aluminum home. Of course, the thing that distinguished Sal's trailer from Wade's was the psychedelic vintage peace symbols hanging about her windows. There was, however, another feature that distinguished Wade's trailer from hers, and that was his Coors beer can collection littering the front yard.

"Good morning," Sal said a bit too cheerfully.

I ignored the greeting and grunted. "The usual."

"Denver omelet?"

"And extra strong coffee, if you've got any dregs," I answered.

"Coming right up," she announced before handing the scribbled order to Larry, the short-order cook. He shot me a glare, still steamed over his gas pump ticket. It made me almost hope he didn't poison me. Though my murder might tie up a lot of loose ends and give Clay his cover story.

Sal sloshed a cupful of black coffee in front of me, and I took my first swig. It was nasty. Just the way I liked it.

What was left of my peaceful morning was broken by the rustle of someone sliding into the seat next to me.

"Deputy Vesey?"

I leaned over my mug but cocked my head to the side. "Well, if it isn't David Harris. I wondered if you were still around."

"Yeah, I took all my saved-up vacation to spend some serious time mountain biking and looking for my birth mom. Though, I can't say I found any leads. Time to get back to work. I catch a plane back to L.A. this afternoon."

This time I really got a good look at the man, a rather Julio Iglesias look-alike. Okay, make that Julio's son, Enrique. How had this little detail escaped my attention before?

"What do you do out there? Star in the movies?"

David's eyes sparked. "Nope, though my mom's Harmony Harris, a star in her own right back in the sixties. I'm just a paramedic."

"Your mom's a movie star? I thought you said she was missing?"

"Harmony was my adoptive mom. I just buried her a few months ago. Cancer."

I nodded. "A loss prompting you to look for your 'real' mother," I stated in my matter-of-fact voice.

David's brown eyes met mine as a shy smile spread into a genuine grin, making my heart flutter, a reaction that I found extraordinarily annoying.

"Something like that." He leaned one elbow on the counter and turned to face me. "Deputy, I couldn't help but overhear you say something about Jewel? Were you talking about my birth mother?"

The intensity of his brown-eyed gaze startled me. How could I have missed his smoldering eyes? Maybe it was because he hadn't looked so attractive when he was sick and with slush on his face. At least, not like now. Here he was shaven, his black curls combed back in a most attractive fashion, and wearing a camel leather jacket over a red button-down shirt with blue jeans. I gave him the once-over, for here sat a man who could break a girl's heart. That realization made me determine that he wasn't about to get near mine.

"No, it's been a rather slow crime month. We were just cracking a joke about imaginary jewel thieves stirring up some excitement. Sorry, but I haven't turned up anything about your mother."

169

David pulled out a card and wrote his name and number on the back. "Well, I've got to get back home. But if you should run across any information about my mother, would you please give me a call?"

"Sure. By the way, how was your stay with Wade?"

"I wanted to ask you about that. Is that guy your boyfriend?"

To my chagrin, I could feel a blush creeping across my cheeks. "Now, why is that your business?"

"I don't mean to pry. But . . ."

I swiveled my stool to face him and folded my arms. "But what?"

David shrugged. "It's just that I saw your picture there."

My voice actually squeaked. "My picture?"

"Yeah, of you and Wade. Looked like it was taken back in high school. You were all fancy, in pink chiffon. Wade had his arm around you and looked like a guy in love."

I swiveled back to my coffee and took a sip. "Oh, that."

"You were high school sweethearts then?"

Sal plopped my steaming Denver omelet in front of me. "We were, but that was a long time ago."

"Then you're not together?"

"No, not that it's your business."

"I'm sorry to pry, but that still doesn't explain . . ." He caught my sideward glare and stopped.

I put my fork down and turned back to face him. "What? Explain what?"

David cleared his throat. "The Wall of Deputy Donna."

"What wall?"

"He's got a wall of newspaper clippings about you. You know, from the local paper, like when you first came to town, when you captured the bear that climbed into the mayor's tree, stuff like that. It made for really interesting reading."

I stabbed a bite of omelet with my fork. "No kidding? Well, that's news to me. Wade and I broke up thirteen years ago."

"Oh. Well. When I come back to town, I may look you up. After reading all those stories, I almost feel like I know you." He smiled when he said that, a smile that this time made my heart almost stop.

I wanted to say, "Forget it and good riddance" but instead, I croaked, "Sure."

I watched as David left, catching the smirk on Clay Whitefield's face.

"Donna, I didn't know you had a boyfriend."

"That man is not my boyfriend," I said as I turned back in a huff to face my cooling omelet.

The bell above the door jingled again, and in walked Wade Gage.

Wade folded his tall frame on the stool that David had just vacated.

"Donna! Long time no see. Wasn't that your boyfriend who just left?"

I could hear Clay snicker behind me.

"No," I said casually. "But why do you ask?"

"Well, when I allowed that guy to drive me home the other night, at your insistence, I might add, I had no idea he was going to use my entire stash of toilet paper."

"So he really was sick from Rosey's enchiladas?"

"I'm afraid so," he said with a disgusted sigh.

So help me, that was funny, and, try as I might, I couldn't help but giggle. Wade did a double take. "I'm glad you're amused. Toilet paper don't grow on trees, you know."

I tried to take a sip of my cold coffee, but somehow I managed to breathe it up my nose. I grabbed my napkin as I snorted coffee all over my favorite white tee and jeans.

Wade stared at me. "Donna? Are you okay?"

"I'm fine. I'm sorry, Wade. That just struck me as funny."

Wade gave me one of his most charming grins. "Can't say that it's not a pleasure to see you smile."

I stopped then and looked at him hard. I took another bite of my omelet before asking, "So, Wade. What's this about the Wall of Donna?"

Wade was just taking his first sip of coffee when he choked.

I narrowed my eyes. "Whatever is wrong, Wade? Something I said?"

Wade wiped his mouth with the back of his hand. "That friend of yours told you about that?"

"He wanted to know if you were my boyfriend."

"What'd you say?"

I leaned back and glared. "No! Come on, Wade, we've been over for thirteen years."

Wade stared at me for a moment. "You're right, Donna. I'm nothing but a drunk, and you're nothing but a bitter woman with a permanent case of PMS."

Wade stood and flipped a few bucks on the counter.

I turned to watch his retreat, which came complete with the revving of his truck engine before he peeled out of the parking lot. I caught Clay staring at me. "You know, Donna, if I started a gossip column, your antics alone would pick up my circulation."

I too flipped several dollars on the counter and turned to go. "I'm glad you find my life so amusing. But remember, before you print a word of it, apparently I'm a lady with a permanent case of PMS." I took a step toward the door, then turned back to look at him. "And I carry a loaded gun."

Clay feigned shock. "Why, Deputy, is that a threat?"

I looked out from beneath the brim of my baseball hat. "Just concerned for your safety is all."

With that, I walked back into the brilliant sunshine and climbed into my Bronco. I turned and looked at my onboard official deputy laptop that hung from a pedestal in the middle of the seat and caught today's date. I noted it would be Vonnie's birthday soon. I knew I'd better think of something special for her this year. Besides Dad, she's one of the only people on this green earth I can really count on.

Though I was off duty, I turned on my radio scanner. Dispatch was just calling one in. "Car One, please respond to a disturbance at Summit View High School. We have a report of an altercation in the parking lot, allegedly between two of the teachers."

I shook my head. Charlene and Jack, no doubt. *I'd better head over there, at least for Goldie's sake.* I pulled my Bronco onto Main Street. This was turning out to be a morning I was glad to be awake for.

23

That girl doesn't
embarrass easy . . .

A more interesting morning in Summit View there had not been in a long, long time.

The Wall of Donna. Well, it certainly piqued Clay's interest, letting him know he needed to venture out to ol' Wade's from time to time. And the Harris fellow . . . Well, who was he? Sure, Clay knew he was the adopted son of Harmony Harris, a woman he'd been fairly infatuated with back in his younger days. And this guy David had the fortune of growing up under her roof. Have mercy.

"Now he's looking for his real mother, is he?" Clay noted in his book while sitting at one of the few traffic lights in town. He scratched out the word *real* and wrote in *birth*. What's more, he was looking for her in Summit View. And he'd somehow gotten Donna involved.

"What does she have to do with this? Or him, for that matter?" Clay spoke out loud. And had that been a sign of fluster he'd seen on her face?

The light turned green. Clay dropped the notebook to the seat beside him, slipped his pen over his ear, and pressed on the accelerator. Moving forward toward the Higher Grounds Café, he struggled to think, to reason the whole thing out.

He slammed his palms against the steering wheel. "Man, if I could just reason some of this out, understand these women . . ."

174

He looked out the passenger window and caught sight of the sheriff's office.

If Donna is somehow involved, then someone from the Potluck Club is . . . David Harris's birth mom?

A smile crept over his face. Maybe he was finally getting somewhere after all.

Lizzie

Indian Chai Tea

3   tea bags black tea
4   cups water
1   3-inch cinnamon stick
    1-inch piece ginger root
      cut into four slices
1/2 teaspoon cardamom seeds
1/2 teaspoon black peppercorns
1   teaspoon whole cloves
1   teaspoon whole coriander
      seeds
1   cup milk
    honey

24

Tea Time

"What's the prognosis, Jan?" I decided the best course of action was to just come right out and ask. I'm sure I'm not the only one who noticed that on Sunday, when Pastor Kevin had made the announcement about the diagnosis, he'd avoided the prognosis. He talked about faith in God, faith in the doctors, and having to make choices. "We have some decisions to make," he'd said. "And we'd appreciate your prayers while we make them." *What* decisions were not mentioned, but we could all pretty much imagine.

Jan and I sat in her family room, a room that told more about Pastor Kevin's personality than his wife's. With the exception of framed family photographs and a few of Jan's matted and framed cross-stitched angels, the room was mostly leather and plaid. A large-screen TV dominated one wall. On the right-hand side were two wicker baskets tied off with plaid ribbon. One held video games and the other DVDs. Two identical baskets were on the left-hand side. These were lined in plaid material and filled with magazines and books.

I sat on one of the leather sofas—the love seat—while Jan sat on the nearest end of the large sofa, her feet tucked up under her. Her small hands were wrapped around a mug of hot Indian Chai Tea she nursed rather than drank. Occasionally they trembled a bit, and I saw that the natural blush of her cheeks had all but drained away. I set my mug on the large pine coffee table devoid of anything but a box of tissues, a well-worn Bible, and a short stack of books. I noted that Calvin Miller had authored all of them. Dr. Miller happens to be one of my favorite theological writers, which is probably why I noticed at all.

"Not good," she answered.

I wondered if she'd repeated herself in order to take it all in. Personally, I felt the need to do the same, but refrained. I took a deep breath instead and sighed. "Treatment?"

"I'll get my port later this week . . . then we start chemo."

"Did the doctor mention anything about surgery?"

She shook her head no. "There's really no point."

"My Lord . . ." I looked from her pale face to the large framed print of quail nesting in a field of straw, which was over her head and above the sofa. I took a deep breath, then said what was really on my heart. "Look, Jan. My sister is a pastor's wife, as you well know, and I can't imagine that you are any different from her or any other pastor's wife out there. You think you can't let your hair down, but let's just go ahead and throw that out, okay?"

Jan's intake of breath jerked and hissed. I waited patiently as she looked around the room, avoiding my eyes with hers, which were welling up and spilling over with tears. "I want . . ." she began, her voice whispery and choking back. "I want to . . . to . . ."

I continued to wait, finally saying, "You want to . . ." as I reached for the box of tissues, whipping one from the box and handing it to her.

She took it, thanking me, then blew her nose. "I want to be there for my children . . . my grandchildren."

My heart ached, literally ached. I am a mother and grandmother, so it wasn't so difficult to empathize. She continued, "I'm not doubting God, Lizzie—"

"I know."

"I'm just wondering why? Why? Why me? I'm just wondering . . . I'm just . . ."

I reached for the box of tissues again, this time just handing her the whole box. She grabbed another tissue and again blew her nose, took several deep breaths, then sobered. "I'm sorry," she said. "I didn't mean to break down."

I shifted my weight slightly, turning more toward her than I was before. "Jan, you don't have to be all things to all people." She nodded in response. I pressed my lips together, then asked, "How are the children taking this?" All three of the Moores' children were married with families of their own, living in their native Texas.

"Betsy wanted to drop everything and come up, but I asked her to wait until after I get the port and begin chemo. Randy and Will are flying up together in a couple of weeks."

"That's not really what I'm asking you, Jan."

She nodded. "I know. The boys were very quiet, but I suspect they're just trying to process it. They've called every night since we told them. Betsy has called two or three times a day. She cries a lot . . . and I cry right along with her." She began to weep again. "Pray for my children," she whispered.

"I will."

We sat silent for a few minutes. Jan closed her eyes. Her breathing became so deep, and I thought she'd fallen asleep, but then she opened her eyes, took a sip of her tea, and said, "God is good, Lizzie. With or without the cancer, I may have had only a short time to live." She continued. "I'm trying really hard to be strong for Kevin . . . for the kids . . . but I don't really want to be. Still, in my heart of hearts I hear the Lord remind me that none of us are guaranteed anything. Not a single thing."

"I know, but—"

"If God . . . if God decides that I should go home . . . tomorrow . . . then I will. If he decides that I should live another ten years, I will. Who am I to question God?" Jan brought the mug up to her lips and blew gently. I watched tiny waves form, then subside. "Just promise me you'll pray for my children, my grandchildren. For Kevin."

"I promise. And I'll have the girls at the Potluck Club pray too . . . if that's okay."

"Of course. And you tell them I still believe in miracles." She brought the mug back near her lap, and I thought back to the conversation I'd had with Janet Hall before nodding in agreement. "But," Jan continued, "maybe not the way you all might think of miracles."

"What do you mean?"

"Share this with the girls: I've always believed there are different types of healing. Five different types, actually. First is the body's natural immune system. So many germs floating around out there, so many diseases just waiting to attack. But God has given us an awesome immune system that counterattacks more often than we are even aware of."

"Without it, I'm sure most of us wouldn't survive to our first birthday."

Jan smiled before continuing. "Then, of course, you have the kind of healing most people pray for but few believe in. Even if they see it for themselves, they don't often truly believe."

"Years ago, before you and Pastor Kevin came, there was a man who lived here named Murray Danning. Nicest, godliest man you'd ever want to meet. So kind to everyone, especially the children. He'd go to the schools on Monday and pass out candy to the ones who could tell him they'd gone to church the day before and then quote the Bible verse they'd learned while there."

"How marvelous," Jan interjected, her eyes wide.

"Anyway, Mr. Danning contracted cancer. Brain cancer, they said it was. He had no wife, no children, no real family to speak of. Everyone said, 'Mr. Danning, are you afraid to die all alone in the world?' and he'd say, 'Who said I was all alone? And who said I was going to die? I serve a God who says I'll live forever, and forever started the day I accepted him at his word.'" I watched Jan's eyes mist over with tears as I continued. "Then Mr. Danning would say, 'Besides, I've got way too much to do down here just yet. The doctor may say cancer, but God hasn't, and until God does, I'm not going anywhere.' And do you know, the man lived another ten years, not a cancer cell in sight."

"What happened to him? I mean, I'm assuming he's with the Lord now."

I nodded. "Went to sleep one night and just didn't get up the next day. When the neighbors saw that he hadn't opened his front door like he always did, they went over to check on him. I remember someone saying he had the sweetest smile on his face."

"How merciful is our God, Lizzie."

I mulled the words over for a moment before asking, "You said five types of healing?"

"The immune system, the truly miraculous, and then medical healing. God has been so gracious to give our medical professionals the wisdom and knowledge to do what they do. Medical science is just fascinating. Adult stem cell replacement as a weapon against cancer . . . now who would have ever thought of that? But Kevin and I have read testimony after testimony." She took another sip of tea. "The fourth type of healing is the one that's talked about in 2 Corinthians 12:8–10." Jan reached for her Bible, setting her mug next to mine. She opened the book, easily turning to the near back. "Which says," she continued, "'Three times I pleaded with the Lord to take it away from me. But he said to me, "My grace is sufficient for you, for my power is made perfect in weakness." Therefore I will boast all the more gladly about my weaknesses, so that Christ's power may rest on me. That is why, for Christ's sake, I delight in weaknesses, in insults, in hardships, in persecutions, in difficulties. For when I am weak, then I am strong.' That's a healing of the attitude, which is more important than a physical healing." She closed the Bible, then held it close to her abdomen as if to draw a cure from it.

I began to weep at the strength of faith being shown to me from this tiny woman of God. "And you say you're struggling . . ." I attempted to tease her, and she smiled back at me. "The fifth?" I asked, anxiously waiting to hear the answer. But Jan shook her head as though she were mistaken.

"No, only four. I'm sorry."

I knew she was holding out on me, but this was her game, and we'd play it her way, so I held my breath for a moment before folding my hands together and then leaning over a bit. "Jan, Samuel was to talk to Pastor Kevin about this when they met this morning, but are you familiar with the work that's being done at UCSF?"

Jan smiled. "I am. In fact, we've got an appointment with one of the physicians there."

"Has the doctor spoken to you about your diet?"

"He has."

I felt myself growing excited. "You know, Suzanne Sommers had breast cancer, and she beat it. Completely changed her diet. I heard her talking about it on some talk shows."

Jan gave me a knowing look. "Thank you, Lizzie. Thank you for caring enough to look into all this for me. Kevin and I are so blessed to have friends like you."

I used my cell phone to call Vonnie on the way home. I don't use the phone often—don't like to run up the minutes—but I couldn't bear to wait until I got home to make the call. Vonnie answered on the third ring.

"Vonnie? Lizzie. Got a minute?"

"What's up?"

"Well, I was thinking maybe we should have an emergency meeting."

"What for?"

I turned off Cross Creek Drive, where the Moores live, and on to Aspen Fields Road. "I was thinking maybe we could talk about breast cancer and about what Jan might be up against. And maybe you could talk some about what you know, from a medical perspective."

"Things have changed a lot since I left Doc Billings," Vonnie said.

"I know. And I've got a stack of research to prove it. But maybe you can also call the breast cancer awareness folks and see what information you can get for us. We all—every one of us girls—need to be aware of certain things."

Vonnie paused, and I glided my car to a stop sign. "I think you've got an excellent idea there, Lizzie. I'll make all the arrangements for us to get together at my place one night this week."

I rested at the stop sign for a moment, having looked in the rearview mirror and seeing that no one was behind me. "I'll double check Donna's schedule for you."

"Sounds good. I'll call you later on this evening."

"I'll be home," I said. Which reminded me . . . dinner . . .

25

She's got something
on her mind . . .

Clay drove his jeep to Summit View's small public library. He found an empty parking space, parallel parked, and then scurried toward the door, glancing toward nearby Grace Church and its next-door parsonage. He stopped cold. Lizzie Prattle was sitting in her car, arms wrapped around the steering wheel and her head resting on her forearms. Even from where he stood, Clay could see that she was crying.

She had something heavy weighing on her mind, he could tell. She must have been visiting with Jan, he decided, then breathed a deep sigh through his nostrils. This was one of those things he didn't understand in life . . . about God, and all.

As soon as Lizzie straightened and started her car, he turned, grabbed hold of the front door handle, and slipped inside where he was met by the glare of the eagle-eyed Martha Nell Kincaid, a woman who had served as head librarian since about five minutes after God capped the mountains with snow, and who now sat behind a large oak desk not two feet from the front door.

"Mr. Whitefield." She used his surname as she'd always done, even when Clay had been a boy.

"Mrs. Kincaid," he returned.

"What can we help you with today?" She glanced up at his *Gold Rush News* cap.

185

Clay pulled the cap from his head, felt the cool of the air tickle his scalp. No one could say that Clay's mother had raised him to be rude and manner-less. "Ah . . . I'd like to look at a few of the old yearbooks if it's not too much trouble."

Mrs. Kincaid smiled, showing off a slight overbite. "High school, middle school, or elementary?"

"High school."

She stood. "Year?" she asked, making her way to a small room a few yards away.

"Ah, mid-eighties. Say eighty-six to ninety."

Mrs. Kincaid turned at the doorway, crossing her arms. "Looking for anything in particular?" She seemed to barricade him from entering the room.

Clay felt himself beginning to sweat. "Official business," he said.

"Oh, I see." She turned and entered the room, allowing him to do the same, and a few minutes later, left him alone with a pile of musty books filled with old black and whites, a splattering of color, and enough dreams to fill several lifetimes. With the turn of each page, he was taken back to a time and place when he'd ruled the school's newsroom. A time when he'd determined each item to be placed in the very yearbooks spread out before him.

He pored over every detail of every glossy page, looking for a face he'd always found endearing, noting the times hers was linked with the boy she was nearly always seen with around campus. He flinched. He wished he'd worn more deodorant than he had put on that morning. He wiped sweat from his forehead.

Donna Vesey and Wade Gage had been quite the couple in their day.

Now Clay couldn't help but remember what little he knew about their courtship—and wonder just what had gone so wrong with Summit View's most perfect couple.

Vonnie

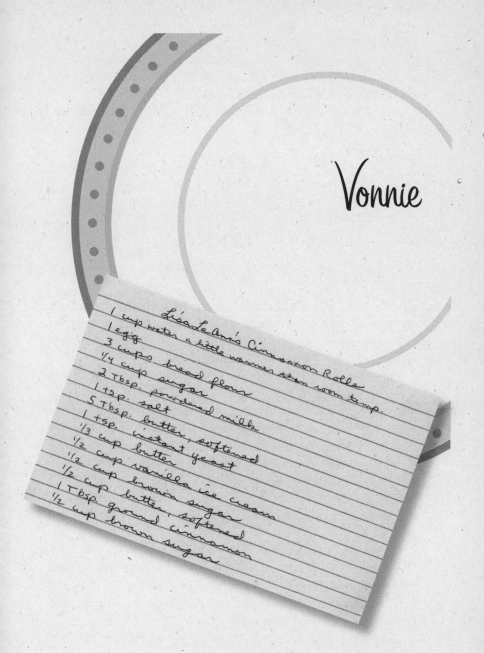

LisaLeAnn's Cinnamon Rolls

1 cup water a little warmer than room temp.
1 egg
3 cups bread flour
1/4 cup sugar
2 Tbsp. powdered milk
1 tsp. salt
5 Tbsp. butter, softened
1 tsp. instant yeast
1/3 cup butter
1/2 cup vanilla ice cream
1/2 cup brown sugar
1/2 cup butter, softened
1 Tbsp. ground cinnamon
1/2 cup brown sugar

26

In a Pickle

I'd really hated to bother the protective coating of dust that covered my home. I secretly felt it wasn't good to disturb the dust bunnies. But with Lizzie conducting an "extracurricular" Potluck Club meeting at my house, it just had to be done.

Other than dust and set up the coffeepot and trimmings, there really wasn't much to do. Lisa Leann had pledged to bring her famous cinnamon rolls, and Lizzie said she'd bring a cake, as this was going to be more of a dessert meeting than a lunch. Lizzie had called this little get-together to tell us Potluckers what she had learned about conducting a monthly breast exam, and I'd been tapped to explain what Jan might be up against.

The doorbell rang, and I peeked out my kitchen window and saw Donna's Bronco. What a dear. She'd arrived early to help me get set up.

I turned to Chucky, who was barking like a dog gone mad. "It's just our girl," I scolded as I hurried to the front door. When I swung it open, there stood my little Donna. Every time I saw her, my heart swelled with pride, and once more I secretly thanked Doreen Vesey for gifting me with a daughter.

"Donna! Come in! Oh my, haven't you been sleeping well, dear?"

I hadn't meant to be critical, but her appearance rather shocked me. The dark circles seemed to punctuate her tired blue eyes, and black definitely was not her best color, though I'd never say so out loud.

"I'm coming off the night shift this week, and it takes me a bit to adjust," she said, looking around at the glints of rainbows that played through my darkened home. "What can I do?"

I opened the nearby closet and handed her a feather duster. "Dust, dear."

I busied myself in the kitchen, and out of the corner of my eye watched as Donna flipped on my lamps and light switches, dusting my babies as she went. I saw her pause when she got to the hearth. She stooped to pick up the picture of the old Sunday school class. I silently enjoyed the smile that played on her lips.

The doorbell rang again, and Chucky repeated his barking routine. I hurried after him. "Hush, Chucky!"

I found Lizzie at the front door; she'd managed to secure a folder of notes under one arm while holding a cake plate topped with a beautiful chocolate cake. Chucky barked at her feet. We tried to ignore him as Lizzie said, "Goldie gave me her mother-in-law's recipe. Where do you want me to put this?"

I took the folder from her and said, "Out back on the picnic table. The day's too beautiful not to go outside."

She nodded and carried the cake to the back door. I held the screen open for her while holding back a growling Chucky with my foot. He couldn't go outside until we all did or else he'd be on top the picnic table in the middle of that cake.

"You really have to do something about that dog," Lizzie scolded me.

I shrugged. "He's a dog. He's just letting you know you've entered his territory."

I turned to see Donna folding her sweater into a neat square, which she carefully placed in a corner.

"It's already seventy degrees out there," she informed me. "This sweater's a bit much with this turtleneck."

Later, after all the arrivals and greetings, the girls gathered around my picnic table, which was covered in a yellow vinyl tablecloth

189

graced with several of my garden pumpkins, paper plates, napkins, Styrofoam cups filled with piping coffee, along with that gorgeous cake and Lisa Leann's rolls. Chucky sighed as he nestled at my feet for a nap. He was totally worn out from announcing every one of my guests with his convulsive fits. I reached down and petted his head. Poor thing. He plopped his head on top of my foot and fell asleep.

I looked around. It was a beautiful autumn day, one of the last before mud season settled upon us. "Mud season" is what we high-country folks call that brief spell between the glory of autumn and the cha-ching of ski season.

But for now, it was still autumn. Fred had raked up our carpet of aspen leaves last Saturday, and the grass still had a bit of green despite its annual summer scorching. My mum beds were in full bloom in ruby and gold along my wooden privacy fence, which was stained the color of redwood. Pine trees stood around us like sentries, swaying their branches with the soft breezes, while the surrounding mountains graced their emerald slopes with dotted traces of fading gold.

Lizzie stood to speak. "First let me say this: breast self-exams are something you can do for you!"

Everyone nodded. Lizzie continued. "The first step is knowing how your breasts feel normally. Secondly, don't do this when it's 'that time of the month,' if you still have 'that time of the month.'" The words brought laughter, and even Lizzie got tickled at herself. "Your breasts change during this time anyway, so you won't have a clear . . . uh . . . feel for things." More laughter. "The best time to examine yourself is seven to ten days after your cycle has ended, but if you've stopped your monthly periods, then set a date like the 1st or the 15th. Think: I pay my car payment on the 15th. Pay my car . . . feel my breasts."

I thought Lisa Leann was going to fall on the floor she was laughing so hard. "What if Henry makes my car payment?"

To which Donna said, "Oh my goodness. This is turning into some kind of freak show."

Lizzie placed her hands on her hips. "Girls, this is serious. Let's keep in mind what's caused us to do this in the first place." Everyone sobered. "Okay, then. You'll want to stand in front of a mirror and examine each breast separately. Note size, shape, color, and contour. Note the direction of your breasts and nipples."

Every woman in the room looked down at her chest. "The direction they are now or the direction they used to be?" I asked.

Lizzie smiled at me. "Now. Forget used to be. I know I am . . ."

The women chuckled again.

"This is fun, you know what I'm saying?" Leigh asked. "Of course, mine are . . . at this stage of my pregnancy . . . well . . ." She looked down.

"Out there," Donna said. "Yeah, yeah, yeah. Rub it in."

Leigh frowned. "I was going to say 'tender.'"

"Who doesn't remember tender?" Lizzie now teased.

"Me," Evie said. "Not once did my breasts get tender when you were pregnant, Lizzie. What about you, Vonnie?" she asked, looking my way.

I'm sure I pinked. "Why in the world would you ask me?"

"Can we get back to this?" Lizzie asked. Again, everyone moved their attention back to her. "Okay, raise your arms over your head . . ." Lizzie demonstrated for us. "Turn slowly—side to side—and look. Now, place your hands on your hips . . ." Again, she demonstrated. "Push your shoulders forward. Look at each breast." She stood erect. "Now you know your breasts."

"Let's throw a party," Donna said, then chuckled at her own humor.

I have to admit, it was funny.

"Ready?" Lizzie asked. "Now it's time for the BSE . . . or breast self-examination. Using the left hand for the right breast, start just below the collarbone. Moisten the pads of your three middle finger-tips with body lotion, apply pressure, and make small circles."

"And be sure to cover the entire breast area," I interjected. The girls nodded. "You'll also want to do this lying down on your back with your hand raised over your head."

"That's right," Lizzie said. "And that's all I have to say."

It was now my turn, so I handed out laminated shower cards with BSE instructions. "Be sure to look for lumps, thickening, red, hot, or orange peel skin—"

"What kind?" Goldie asked.

"Orange peel. Looks dimply like an orange peel."

"Oh," Goldie said.

"Look for an itch, a rash, a sore, unusual pain, dimpling, puckering, bloody discharge from the nipple, a retracted nipple, a change in the direction of the nipple—"

"Gracious," Leigh commented. "That's a lot to remember."

"It feels that way, yes," I said. "But this is important. I don't think it takes a rocket scientist to tell us when something is wrong. Go with your instincts. Remember, most of the time, it's nothing. But sometimes it is something. More than two hundred thousand women in our country alone will be diagnosed with invasive breast cancer in the coming year."

"What does all of this mean for Jan?" Evie asked.

I sighed. "I don't know. Jan's was undetected. I really can't say why . . . it just was. And Jan's has spread." I pressed my lips together. "That's really all I know to say on Jan."

Evie said, "Well done, girls, and with that I'd like to suggest one last thing before we slice into that cake."

"And enjoy my homemade cinnamon rolls," Lisa Leann added.

Evie stared at Lisa Leann for a second and then continued. "Let's take this opportunity to pray for Jan."

We all voiced agreement and, as one, lifted our bodies off the picnic benches and walked toward a grassy space near my pumpkin patch. There, we formed a circle and held hands. Chucky followed and sat at my feet, cocking his head up at me as I closed my eyes.

As I stood next to Evie I felt her hand muscles tense as Lisa Leann led us off. It was as if I could hear her silent scoff, *The nerve of that woman.* I squeezed back my thoughts. *Be nice, Evie.*

"Dear heavenly Father, we come to you on behalf of our precious sister, Jan Moore," Lisa Leann's hushed voice whispered. "Father, we ask that you spare her life and leave her, at least for this season, with us. Father, we know that one day she will spend eternity with you, but, Lord, we just ask that you delay that day as long as . . ."

I heard a loud snap above us. I peeked and saw Chucky spin his body toward the picnic table. His hair stood on end.

I turned my head just in time to see a small black bear lumber down from his perch in the pine tree above the table. Making himself at home, he sat down smack in the middle of my yellow tablecloth.

I'm not a screamer, mind you, but I'm afraid I let a mighty big one loose. My yell was joined by those of my friends as their eyes snapped open to the sight of that bear gobbling chocolate cake. I don't think our initial panic was as much from fear as outrage at our loss. Our voices fell silent as we watched that bear stuff paw after paw of chocolate goo into its mouth.

I noticed Donna's hand reach for her back hip, as if going for her gun. But it was her day off, and her gun belt was probably locked up in the Bronco or at home in that cute alpine cottage of hers.

Chucky bounded across the lawn and landed his front paws on one of the picnic benches as he looked up at our intruder. He barked ferociously.

The bear licked at the chocolate on his paws and stood up, right on top my table, and batted the air with gooey paws. He seemed to say, "You don't scare me, dog!"

Donna commanded us all to go inside, and the Potluckers stampeded toward my back door.

I alone stood in the yard, determined to save my dog. "No, Chucky, no! Come here!"

"Vonnie, you come back this instant!" Evie called from the back porch.

But even before I could respond, the bear pushed off the table in a flying leap, landing a mere three feet from where I stood. The girls screamed, and I froze. Chucky whirled toward us, continuing his high-pitched barks.

The bear and I stared at one another as he sat on his haunches, his brown eyes level with my blue ones. He lifted his head and sniffed in my direction, twitching his black velvet nose. It was as if everything was suddenly in slow motion and I was merely observ-

193

ing. I noted that this was a black bear, though cinnamon in color. I guessed he weighed about 350 pounds. I didn't know if he would really hurt me, because I had once read in one of Fred's hunting magazines that black bears weren't nearly as aggressive as grizzlies. And being nose to nose with this creature, I found that thought to be comforting to no end. As these thoughts played through my mind, I could hear Evie scream, "Run, Vonnie, run!"

I couldn't. I was caught in the bear's hypnotic stare. Mesmerized, I suddenly thought that this creature looked like a fuzzy oversized teddy bear. If it hadn't been for his unbelievably bad breath, though scented of chocolate, I just might have reached out for a hug. Maybe not.

The spell broke as soon as he stood, towering eight feet tall.

There were more screams from the Potluckers as the bear lifted his paws and extended his long, sharp claws. He stepped close, drooling on my tennis shoes as he bared his fangs. I stared up at this apparition, and my heart literally stopped. My teddy bear had turned into a monster.

All it would take was one swat from those extended razors, and my life would be over. As the bear moved toward me, Chucky jumped forward and bit him right on the rump. I'm not sure the bear could really feel that bite through all that fur of his, but nevertheless, it got his attention. To my horror, the bear turned and swatted his razor-sharp claws at my dog. Direct hit. Chucky yelped and flew toward the picnic table. The bear turned and looked at my fallen dog.

I screamed. Was Chucky dead?

No, too much fur padding, I realized as he sprang back to life. With deafening yaps, Chucky circled the bear, dodging in and out of the bear's comfort zone, ready to attack.

The next thing I knew that bear was loping toward my back fence with Chucky nipping at his heels. I watched as it scrambled over the top and out of sight.

The girls streamed back from the house and surrounded me. Goldie spoke for all when she said, "Vonnie, you could have been killed!"

Chucky ran back to me, and I lifted him up into my arms. "Not likely, with Chucky on duty," I laughed, feeling like my legs would buckle.

We all turned and looked at the picnic table. What a mess. Napkins and plates were scattered about the yard, and chocolate was smeared everywhere.

Evie said, "How do you like that, Lisa Leann? That bear didn't care much for your cinnamon rolls."

"Well, he's the only one, then," Lizzie exclaimed. She turned to Chucky, still nestled in my arms. "And I take back what I said about your dog. He's a pleasure to have in our club."

Donna took me aside. "Be prepared for a visit from Clay White-field and his camera later. 'Tiny Dog Scares off Bear' will make the front page, for sure."

Later, after we picked up the mess and Donna had phoned in a report to animal control, I said good-bye to Lizzie at the door. She said, "Thanks for having us, Vonnie; this was one of my all-time favorite get-togethers." She laughed. "This is one meeting that will become part of our Potluck Club lore, I'm sure."

I nodded at her words while I watched Goldie pull Donna aside. I heard Goldie ask, "Donna, any more news from the love and war department?"

Now, that piqued my curiosity. Had Donna confided in Goldie that she had a boyfriend? And if so, why hadn't she told me?

I watched as Donna nodded and pulled Goldie closer. I couldn't hear what she said, but I saw Goldie's reaction. Goldie paled, grabbed her purse, and practically ran out my front door without even a good-bye. Heavens, what was that all about?

Before I could find out, Evie pulled me aside to discuss Lisa Leann's nerve at praying for "our" pastor's wife. Of course, Lisa Leann couldn't overhear us; she had already left, and by the time Evie was through criticizing her, we were alone. Poor Evie. I tried to reason with her, but my pleas of, "Evie, Jan is Lisa Leann's pastor's wife too, you know," fell on deaf ears.

Finally, I was able to wave good-bye as she headed out my front door. I turned to Chucky, exhausted. "Well, boy, care to join me

195

on the La-Z-Boy for a quick nap? The media could show up any minute, you famous mutt you." Chucky followed me to our favorite spot and leaped into my lap. Just as I started to close my eyes, I noticed that Donna had rearranged the photographs on the hearth. What a sweetheart. How lucky I was to have her in my life.

27

Oh, she's got some
stories to tell . . .

Sal had always kept a police scanner in the back of the café, so as soon as Donna called animal control, the news about Chucky and the bear spread faster than butter on Larry's just-made hotcakes.

Minutes later, Donna walked in, taking the heat for allowing a dog to be the hero of the day rather than herself. In her "Donna-esque" fashion, she dismissed them all, then sat across the table from Clay. "Take a look," she said, pushing an old photograph framed in an equally aged brass frame across the table. "Recognize anyone?"

"I certainly do." Wow, did this photo bring back memories.

"I'm going to have it reframed at Christi's," she said, shoulders flung back with a mixture of pride and excitement. "It's Vonnie's birthday. She's going to be so surprised!"

Clay nodded, taking note of all the young faces—now adult men and women—lined up outside the church with their beloved Sunday school teacher. "A lot going on behind this photograph," he said. "A lot of stories to tell." He looked up at Donna. "If we'd only known then what we know now."

CHICKEN MARSALA

4 BONELESS CHICKEN BREASTS
1/2 CUP FLOUR
2 TBS. BUTTER
2 CUPS SLICED MUSHROOMS
3 TBS. CHOPPED GRN ONIONS

2 TBS. OLIVE OIL
1 CUP MARSALA
1/2 CUP CHICKEN BROTH
SALT + PEPPER TO TASTE

MELT BUTTER AND SAUTÉ GRN ONIONS AND MUSHROOMS. REMOVE FROM PAN + SET ASIDE. POUND CHICKEN WITH MALLET - THIN. ROLL CHICKEN IN FLOUR - + SAUTÉ IN OLIVE OIL. ADD WINE, CHICKEN BROTH, MUSHROOMS GRN ONIONS + SALT + PEPPER. HEAT 3 MINUTES. POUR SAUCE ON TOP.
FOUR SERVINGS

28

Fresh Discovery

I patted my black sweater tucked on the floorboard of my Bronco and placed the paper bag labeled "Christi's Frame Shop" on top. I was glad for my stroke of brilliance, totally unplanned, of course. Somehow when I saw that old photo of our Sunday school class in that cheap brass frame, I knew what I had to do for Vonnie's birthday. I would reframe her beloved print.

I'd felt a surge of excitement as I shopped at Christi's. I'd tugged out the photo, then held it next to every frame I saw—gold, mahogany, ornate carved oak, porcelain, and pewter.

Finally Christi herself came over to see what was taking so long. Christi was a natural Colorado beauty who had moved to Summit View from Boulder. She was all of twenty-five years old with long brown hair braided down her back. She wore not a hint of makeup on her peaches-and-cream complexion. Besides her natural beauty, she had it made. She was one of our town's lucky trustfunders. Set for life, she merely played at being a shopkeep by framing scenic mountain prints she photographed herself. Her high prices reflected her good taste.

When I showed her the print, she gushed, "Donna, is that you with Mrs. Westbrook from church from, what, back in the eighties?"

"Afraid so. I want to get this reframed for her birthday next week."

Christi nodded. "Great idea."

"So, what do you think?" I asked, holding up my selections thus far.

Christi looked at my assortment, then suggested, "I'm thinking the wooden frames look best. I could mat it for you too. That would cost a little extra, but it would look really great."

"I don't know," I said. "This wooden carved frame comes with a blue mat, and that looks pretty nice. I think I'll just go with that and do it myself."

"Good choice."

Christi carefully wrapped the frame with tissue paper and put it in the bag for me, along with the receipt.

I felt pleased with myself as I headed my Bronco toward Dad's house. It was our weekly night to get together, and I couldn't wait to show him the old photograph and catch him up on today's Potluck adventures. He loved a good story, though he always seemed a little too interested in any story that pertained to Evangeline Benson, no matter how nerdy I tried to make her sound.

Perched in the back seat was a grocery sack filled with everything I would need to create a chicken marsala dinner. I'd printed out the recipe from an e-recipe book called *Great Chicken Recipes*, which I'd downloaded from RecipeCoach.com. I smiled. This was just the kind of dish Dad would love. We usually ordered pizza, but tonight was to be special because I was celebrating the fact that my rotating schedule had finally returned to the day shift.

I pulled into the driveway. Dad's alpine bungalow was covered in cedar and stained aqua trimmed with gray. I had spent my entire growing-up years here. But since I'd moved out, Dad had turned my old bedroom into his office, filling it with a secondhand desk and chair, along with an old filing cabinet the department had discarded. The walls were bare except for my old Barbie clock, which still kept good time.

I let myself into the house with my key and set my bags down in the kitchen. I then switched on the light and looked around. Over the years, all traces of a woman's touch had somehow evaporated. Dad's kitchen was a case in point. It was neat but painted stark white with no hint of imagination. The living room wasn't much better. Again, Dad had painted the walls white, while his sofa was vinyl brown leather, as was his easy chair. The focal point of the living room was nothing less than Dad's new big-screen TV. His old console was pushed to the side and now housed his twenty-year collection of *On Patrol* magazine.

As I began to prepare dinner, I first pounded the chicken breasts with a meat cleaver I'd found shoved in the back of his utensil drawer. After I sautéed the green onions and mushrooms in butter, I set them aside and browned the chicken. I added the chicken broth and marsala and stirred in the mushrooms and green onions. I let the mixture bubble until it thickened.

As for the side dishes, I had a large plastic tub of store-made potato salad complete with a can of freshly opened green beans. This would be some feast.

I had just set the table when Dad pulled in the driveway. He was already unbuckling his gun belt when he walked in the door.

"Hey, Donna, what smells so good?" He gave me a peck on the cheek.

"Chicken marsala," I announced.

"Sounds good." He put his gun belt on top of the refrigerator, just as he had when I was a toddler.

"Heard there was some excitement over at the Westbrooks' today," he chuckled. "Clay told me all about it after his interview with Vonnie and Evie."

"He interviewed Evie?"

Dad and I sat down and began to shovel the food on our plates. Dad continued, "Clay asked me which Potlucker I recommended as a good interviewee. I suggested you naturally, but he said he needed a fresh face. That's when I thought of Evie." Dad chuckled again. "Clay told me she bent his ear for an hour and a half."

I smiled and tried not to roll my eyes. "You don't say."

Dad grinned. "What I'd really like to hear is your version of this tale."

As we enjoyed the meal, I repeated the story, pausing for questions and laughter.

Later, after we cleared the table and washed the dishes, I pulled out the old framed photograph and sat down at the kitchen table. "Dad, take a look at this."

Dad sat down across from me and handed me a steaming mug of coffee, then took a sip of his. "Say, is this you and Vonnie Westbrook?" He laughed. "Why, just look at you two, fast friends since the beginning of time."

I pulled the oak frame, carved with forget-me-nots, from the Christi's bag and said, "I thought I'd reframe it for her birthday. What do you think?"

"Good idea." He turned the picture over, then slid the cardboard backing out of the old frame. "There's another photograph under here."

He pulled out what appeared to be an old wedding photograph and handed it to me. "What do you make of this?"

The yellowed photo showed a couple, a handsome Latino man dressed in a sky-blue suit smiling down at a petite blue-eyed blond who was holding a bouquet of tiger lilies. "That looks like a very young Vonnie," I said.

Dad nodded. "But the groom doesn't look a thing like Fred."

My chest constricted. "No, Dad, and as a matter of fact, the groom looks like a fellow I just met, a guy named David Harris."

"Harris?"

I slowly turned over the photograph. "Some Californian claiming to be searching for his birth mother, a Jewel something or other, said to be living in Summit View."

I looked at the back of the photograph and read the carefully printed words. Mr. and Mrs. Joseph and Yvonne Jewel.

The picture slipped from my fingers and floated to the floor.

"Let me see that," Dad said as he reached over and picked up the photo. He studied it for a moment, then looked back up at me. "If this doesn't beat anything."

I nodded.

"Somehow, Donna, I think you've just found David Harris's mother." He studied me for a minute. "So, what are you going to do?"

203

I was almost too stunned to answer. I slowly shook my head. "Honestly? I don't have a clue."

All I did know was that the only woman I had called my friend had betrayed me with a past she had failed to share. As I stared at the picture of the happy couple, my shock turned into anger. Could Vonnie be living a lie? Had she run out on her first husband after putting her baby, her own flesh and blood, up for adoption? That meant she was no better than my own mother. To abandon your baby . . . well, it couldn't get much lower than that.

Vonnie, to think that I admired you, loved you like a mother, thought you were special. Instead, you're the worst liar I know.

29

What secrets doesn't that girl know . . .

At least every other day, Clay drove from Higher Grounds to the courthouse before making his way to the newspaper office. He checked on recent arrests and various other unsavory Summit View activities.

Not that there was much, but it gave him an excuse to stay on top of things. To catch the more male-oriented gossip. To check on Donna, most of all.

He entered the door nearest booking, skimmed over the names scrawled in a large black leather book, noted that no one had been brought in over the past forty-eight, and then sauntered to the side of the building where Sheriff Vesey typically kept himself.

A quick glance to the left as he entered the room told him that Donna was not at her desk. Sheriff Vesey, however, was sitting at his, staring at the monitor of his computer, scribbling frantically on a yellow legal pad.

"Sheriff," Clay greeted, stepping into his office.

Vernon's head jerked up and he dropped his pen, laying his arm across the pad and his notes. Clay was quick enough to catch a word or two:

Harris.

California.

He narrowed his eyes at the sheriff. "Whatcha got going there?" he asked. Did Donna and her dad know something about Harris?

Vernon flipped the pad over. "Police business," he said, turning the monitor off.

Clay had missed his chance to read the screen by milliseconds. But his curiosity had been piqued, and for a reporter, that was everything.

Goldie

Breakfast Casserole

6 eggs
2 cups milk
1 ts salt
1 ts dry mustard
~ ~ ~ ~ ~ ~

1 cup shredded cheddar cheese
1 pound mild sausage
4 slices of white bread (cubed)
~ ~ ~ ~ ~ ~ ~ ~ ~ ~ ~ ~

Beat 6 eggs, add milk, salt and
mustard. Gently stir in 1 cup shredded
cheddar cheese, 1-pound mild sausage
that has been browned and drained, and
4 slices of cubed white bread. Place in a cold
Place in a buttered 9 x 13 casserole.
refrigerate over night. Place in a cold
oven set at 350 degrees and bake 45 minutes.

30

Marriage on Toast

It's another day, Lord, I prayed from my usual place at the kitchen table. *Another day of getting up early to talk to you, waiting for the annoying sound of my husband coming down the hallway of our home. Another day of hearing him say "Goldie, you got breakfast started?" about two seconds after he turns on* Fox and Friends. *And another day of pretending I don't know what's going on with him and Charlene Hopefield . . . of holding on to a marriage that's not really worth holding on to.*

Somehow, on the day I'd gotten the phone call from Lucy, the day I'd found the photograph of Jack and Charlene, the day Olivia had called wanting some stupid recipe for Lord-only-knows-what and come rushing over, my daughter had managed to talk me into staying with Jack.

"I'm leaving your father," I'd told her as soon as we were in the living room. I will admit I was dramatic about it, but in a subdued sort of way. I was sort of like Gloria Swanson coming down that long staircase at the end of *Sunset Boulevard*. I had no idea where I was going, but this was my defining moment. Every minute since the day I'd received my first piece of jewelry from Jack (other than my wedding rings, of course) had led to this one moment in my life.

"Mom, no," she'd said, plopping her slender frame down on the sofa opposite the chair where I was sitting. "Please think about this. For me, Mom," she pleaded. "And for Brook. Brook needs for his grandparents to be together."

208

I stood and moved away from her and into my bedroom; her entreaty was too much for me to be able to hear at the time.

She was fast on my heels. "Mom," she said, "I know this has been awful for you." I turned to look at her, noticing that her green eyes had welled up with tears and that it looked as though she hadn't even taken the time to brush the short curls of her red hair before coming over. I ridiculously wondered if she'd taken my grandson to preschool with her hair in such a tussle. "It's awful for me too. My gosh, my whole life I've known the truth about Dad," she confided.

"You have?" It was my turn to plop, and I did so on the bed. "I'm so sorry, Olivia. I should've left him a long time ago. I should've spared you all this pain."

Olivia crossed the room and knelt at my feet. "No, Mom. Don't apologize for his wrongdoings."

"And I shouldn't even be talking to you about this. After all, he's still your father."

"Don't apologize for that, either, Mom."

I threw my hands up and let them drop back down. "Then what are you saying, Olivia? This is where I am right now. I don't know what else I'm supposed to do."

"Have you talked to Dad about going into some kind of therapy?"

I laughed. "Here in Summit View? Where are we going to find a counselor in Summit View?"

Olivia fell back on her haunches. "Well, maybe not here in Summit View, but what about in Denver or even Vail?"

"Do you honestly think your father would drive hours to have someone tell him to stop sleeping with half of the state? Like that would make all the difference in the world?"

"Don't, Mom. Don't be so crude. What about the pastor? Counseling with someone like that?"

"Olivia, your father is an active church member. I can hardly imagine him sitting across from Pastor Kevin's office desk, talking about his adventures in adultery."

"Don't be so negative, Mom."

I stood, sidestepped her, and moved back out of the room and back into the living room. "Don't, don't, don't. Do you have any advice you can call proactive?" I called behind me, knowing she'd soon follow.

And she did. "I'm going to assume you've prayed about this."

I spun around. "Of course I have prayed about this!"

Olivia paused, crossing her thin arms. "Mom, I know you love the Lord . . ." She paused again for good measure. "I know you do. But sometimes when you pray—and I know because I've heard you—you do more whining to God than getting specific with him about what you need."

"Olivia Brook Dippel, I cannot believe what I'm hearing."

"Just think about it, Mom. Just think about it . . . and while you're thinking about it, think about holding on to your vows with Dad, okay?"

"What about his holding on to the vows he made with me? What is it they say? Cling only unto each other?"

Olivia looked at me with a furrowed brow. "That's cleave, Mom."

"Cleave?"

"Cleave . . . not cling."

I sighed. "Well, what in the world does that mean?"

She paused, thinking. "It means . . ." she said, bringing her hands together and lacing her fingers. "It means . . . well, I guess it means to cling."

"Well, your father has been clinging or cleaving or whatever you want to call it with someone else, and I'm sick of it."

"I know, Mom, just . . . please, don't do anything rash."

I promised her that I wouldn't, then—just as soon as she left—went back to Jack's office to look up *cleave* in the dictionary, only to discover it had two meanings. One was as an intransitive verb—to adhere firmly and closely or loyally and unwaveringly. The other was as a verb—to divide by or as if by a cutting blow. There was so much irony in the difference that I had to laugh out loud.

Do I whine, Lord? I prayed later. Do I? Is that what I've been doing all this time? If I have, I certainly haven't meant to. I only

210

wanted you to hear what my heart has been crying for such a very long time.

Well, maybe I have been whining. So let me get real specific with you. I need a miracle here. I ask you with all the reverence I have to bring Jack Dippel to his knees and back into our marriage the way he ought to be. Make it so he can't stand to look at another woman again. Make it so he wants to look at me the way I'm sure he looks at Charlene Hopefield.

The only thing I could do after that was wait. Of course, the news about Jan Moore made my problems seem trivial, giving me something to think about other than my life and the mess I'd made of it. It also gave Jack something he could actually discuss with me besides the stats from the Gold Diggers' football team. How horribly sad is that?

I heard the sound of *Fox and Friends* before I'd realized Jack had made it in to the living room. "Breakfast about ready, Goldie?" he called.

I closed my Bible quickly, picking it up and carrying it over to the kitchen counter. "Shortly," I called back. I heard a quiver in my voice, and I mentally kicked myself for it. *All right, Lord,* I offered up one last plea before I served the breakfast casserole (I'd just found the recipe in one of Lizzie Prattle's discarded women's mags). *It's been days and days since I asked you for changes, and not a thing in this world has changed. In fact, I'm not so sure that it hasn't gotten worse. But I'll trust you a little longer.*

I walked over to the oven and retrieved the casserole that had been warming there for the past half hour. I set it atop the stove, then methodically reached in the nearby cabinet for a plate. Jack entered the room just as I was pouring his coffee into a mug at the kitchen table. I glanced up at him momentarily, then returned my attention to pouring. "Morning," I said as politely as I knew how.

Jack was dressed in a dark blue sweat suit and warm socks, his standard fare for chilly mornings on the football field with his team. His silver hair was still unkempt, and he looked pale. For a fleeting moment I wondered what Charlene saw in him. Then again,

211

perhaps she'd never seen him so early in the morning. "Morning," he returned, sitting at his place at the table.

I returned the coffeepot to the coffeemaker all the while thinking, *Well, of course she's never seen him first thing in the morning. He's always come home, hasn't he?* Not once had he not returned.

I heard Jack's fork drop. "What is this?"

I turned from the counter. "What is what?"

He pointed to the casserole on his plate. "This. What is this?"

I stepped over to the table, to the opposite side of where he was, and clutched the back of a chair. "It's a breakfast casserole I read about in a magazine. It looks good." I tried to keep my voice upbeat. "Did you try it?"

"No, I didn't try it. It looks like eggs and cheese and some kind of meat product all mushed together."

I placed my fists on my hips. "Isn't that what a casserole is?" I asked. "A bunch of foods mushed together?"

"I like a basic breakfast, Goldie. You know that." He looked down again, then back at me. "Well?"

"Well what?" I shifted my weight slightly.

"Well, make me something I can eat. If I'm going to work every day to support you, the least you can do is make me a breakfast I like."

"Is that what you think? You think I'm just here to make you food so you can . . . what did you say? Support me? You don't support me, Jack."

Jack stood, grabbed the mug by its handle, and then banged it down on the table like a judge's gavel. Black coffee went everywhere, pooling along the tabletop and running in fat streams off the sides and down to the floor. "Now look what you made me do," he said. "Hurry up and clean this mess, Goldie."

I turned and grabbed a dish towel, then slung it at him. "You clean it up," I said, then turned on my heel and left the room.

"Now just hold up there, Goldie," Jack ordered, following behind me, leaving the spilled coffee to clean itself. "Look around you, why don't you, and don't you dare talk to me like that. Have you been watching Oprah or something?"

I burst out laughing in spite of my anger. Or, perhaps, because of it.

"That's it. You've been watching Oprah. She's been telling you to stand up to your husband, is that it? Well, I'll tell you what; when you make the kind of money that woman is making, you can throw dish towels at me all morning long if you want to." He slapped himself on the forehead. "Oh, but what am I saying? When was the last time you worked? Huh? Oh . . . let me think. You've never worked. Not a day in your life, at least not since you've married me and had me to take care of you."

"Excuse me? What do you call taking care of this house? Washing your dirty underwear? Being there for you anytime you needed someone to be there? Raising your daughter? What are you thinking—that being your wife has been some sort of cruise around the world?"

"Hey!" Jack exclaimed. "You don't like it . . ." He pointed toward the front door. "You know where the door is. Don't let it hit you on the way out."

I shook my head sadly. "Oh, and I'm sure you won't have any trouble finding someone to take my place. Some poor, poor, pitiful soul. Someone like . . . oh, let me think," I mimicked him. "Charlene Hopefield."

It was a delightful moment. I watched the pallor of his face grow ashy, then deepen to something akin to purple. "Who told you about Charlene Hopefield?"

I laughed again. "Oh, Jack. You pathetic man. Do you think I've been stupid all these years? I'm as sharp about your runnings-around as your mother was about your father's. And don't tell me you don't know about that."

Jack pointed to me. "You keep my mother out of this."

I snorted. "Oh, please." I turned and headed back toward the kitchen. "Go to work, Jack. Maybe you can meet Charlene in the teachers lounge before the school bell rings, eat yourself a stale donut, and toast your infidelity with a cup of coffee."

When I got to the kitchen I began to shake. It was only the lightest quivering at first, but as I heard Jack moving about—doing

213

whatever it is he does to finish getting ready for the day—it grew so violent I had to stop what I was doing and wrap my arms around myself. I took deep breaths, attempting to steady the erratic pounding of my heart. I thought about praying but decided against it. I was too angry at the moment. I had nothing, really, to say to God. Nothing except *Just let me get through these next few minutes, Lord. Just get him out of the house so I can think, why don't you?*

Jack left the house way before 7:00, giving himself plenty of time to get to work, where I imagined he would seek out his mistress. Maybe he'd tell her about my casserole. Perhaps they'd even laugh about it. Or he might even tell her I'd been disrespectful to him . . . how he'd spent all these years "supporting" me and now I was treating him like yesterday's trash. He'd say things like, "I told you, Charlene. My wife just doesn't understand me . . . doesn't appreciate me."

"I know, I know," she'd say, then slip her arms around him and kiss him deeply and passionately, the way he used to kiss me all those years ago by the pool in Washington, D.C., and in the early years of our marriage.

I touched my lips with the tips of my fingers. "I gotta get out of here," I whispered to no one. "I can't live like this anymore."

Two hours later—with the kitchen cleaned up and the bed stripped and remade—I arrived at Olivia's house with a large suitcase in one hand and an overnight bag in the other.

"Mom." She stood on the other side of the glass storm door, her eyes darting from my car parked in her driveway to the luggage in my hand. "What are you doing here?"

"Can I come in?" I asked.

She unlatched and opened the door. "Of course you can. I'm sorry. Goodness," she rattled as I stepped into the small living room of her home. Olivia and Tony live in a comfortable three-bedroom duplex owned by Tony's parents, who live, conveniently, on the other side. The rent is cheap, enabling my daughter to stay at home with Brook. I can certainly appreciate this for Brook's sake, but on this day I was wishing Olivia would do something to make herself financially secure, God forbid she be standing in Brook's living room one day, suitcase in hand. I set my luggage on the mocha-colored plush carpet as she repeated, "Mom, what are you doing here? What's going on?"

I turned and faced her. "I need a place to stay for a while."

"Oh, Mom. Come, sit down," she said, leading me to the over-stuffed red, blue, and green plaid sofa.

"I promise I won't get in the way and I won't stay here forever. I just need some time to find a job . . . to get my own place . . ."

"Mom." We sat, and she looked around the room, the walls of which were painted stark white, trimmed in maple. Olivia had stenciled a rolling train of red and blue flowers around the room and into the adjoining dining room, which was dominated by an antique oak table and matching sideboard and hutch.

I allowed my eyes to scan the room with hers, past the country teddy bears and porcelain figurines and hand-stitched quilts that hung from the walls, then back to her.

"I can help you around the house." She whipped her face back to mine. "Not that I think you need help. Goodness, look at this place. Early in the morning, and not a thing out of place. Where's my grandson?"

"He's at preschool. Mom, tell me what happened." She placed a slender hand on mine, which were one atop the other in my lap.

"I've simply had enough. I'm clinging, but he's cleaving—in the verb tense, not the other way it's used—and until we're both on the same definition of the word, I'm dying day by day and year by year. Affair by affair. I just can't live with a man who doesn't appreciate who I am or what I've been to him all these years."

Olivia was quiet before answering. "I understand, Mom. And of course you can stay here," she added with a sigh. "I'll call Tony at the shop, but I'm sure he'll be okay with it. You can stay in the guest bedroom. It's not fixed up real nice, but it's got a comfortable bed."

"Oh, Olivia," I cried, wrapping my arms around her, drawing her to me. "Oh, Olivia, I'm so sorry. I'm so, so sorry."

Olivia squeezed her bony frame into my softer one. "It's okay, Mom. It's all going to be okay," she said with a firm resolve, though I could hear the hurt in her voice.

I drew back to look at her. Sure enough, tiny tears were slipping down her cheeks, and I brushed them away with the tips of my fingers. "Now, now. Don't you cry too, or I'll never be able to stop." I forced a smile, the kind mothers manage to give to their children when the rest of the world seems to be going to pot. "And I promise things will get better." I took a deep breath, then let it out. "This will be a good time for us, my Olivia. I can help you with Brook . . . when he's home. When does he come home?"

"I pick him up at noon."

"Oh. Well . . . I'll take him to the park down the street after his afternoon nap and keep him in the evenings sometime so you and Tony can go out. You know, like on a date." I looked over my right shoulder, to the bar that wrapped around and divided the living room, dining room, and kitchen, then past it to the kitchen's maple cabinets and white tile countertops, unusually stacked with dirty dishes. "And I can help you prepare meals or clean up after we eat. I'm a good cook, you know, and I've always enjoyed taking care of a house."

Olivia coughed out a laugh. "Well, your timing couldn't be better," she said. "I could use some help in the kitchen right now."

"I noticed things seem to be a bit out of place in there. Is there a problem?" I asked.

She looked down at her lap. "No, no problem. Or, at least, just a temporary one. I'm just having trouble cleaning the kitchen." She looked back up at me. "Mom, I'm about two months pregnant," she announced. "We were going to tell you and Dad this weekend, but . . . well . . ."

I hugged my daughter again. "Oh, Olivia! How wonderful. Oh, how very wonderful."

Life goes on.

I found it hard to believe Saturday morning that it was time for another Potluck Club meeting. Hadn't it been only a couple of weeks since we'd had dessert with a brown bear? It had been a month since we'd met to pray, and I had two items for the prayer list: one, I would need prayer to continue to be strong in my resolve to make a better life for myself. This would be difficult for me to talk about—the girls still didn't know I'd left Jack. Two, I wanted to pray for Olivia's pregnancy. I hoped it wouldn't make Leigh feel strangely about her own upcoming arrival . . . which would be soon coming. I wondered what she planned to do after the baby arrived, or if she'd talked to the father at all since she'd come to Summit View.

Distressing as it was to think about Leigh raising a child without its father, I was so grateful to have a man like Tony Burke as the father of my grandchildren, not to mention the husband of my Olivia. Tony is a good man, a little shorter in stature than Olivia, but he's 100 percent proof that the height of a man doesn't make the man.

When Olivia told Tony that I needed a place to stay, he left his shop in the capable hands of his one and only employee and rushed right over. The shop, Ye Olde Antiques, is really within walking distance of their house—two or three blocks only—but that's not the point. The point is that he came.

He entered the house quietly through the front door, looked at me sitting there on his sofa nursing a hot cup of apple cinnamon tea, raked the fingers of one hand through his thick blond hair, then brought it down to rest on a square-shaped hip. "Mom," he said gently. "Ah, Mom."

He closed the door behind him, then joined me, sitting almost knee to knee. He gazed at me with his sweet blue eyes through small round glasses, placed a hand on my shoulder, and squeezed.

Words weren't really necessary, but I decided to use them anyway. "I won't interrupt your life for long, Tony. I promise. I know that as much as I loved Mother Dippel, I wouldn't have wanted her living with us for a long period of time when we were still honeymooning."

Tony smiled a crooked smile. "We've been married five years. We're hardly honeymooning."

I smiled back, raised my mug in a toast, and said, "Apparently you are. I understand I'm going to be a grandmother again."

"Olivia told you."

"She did."

"Where is she?" he asked, looking around.

"Taking a shower."

Tony nodded. "Well, I'll step back there and let her know I'm here. Meanwhile, you just know you're welcome to stay here as long as need be. I wouldn't mind some of your good cooking, maybe a little of your old-fashioned Southern dressing, and I know Brook will be thrilled to have his nana here."

I patted Tony's hand. "Tony, I'm not ready for anyone to know just yet about all this . . . so do me a favor and don't talk about it outside of this house, okay?"

"Not on your life." Tony's voice was so soft and kind; it was no wonder Olivia loved him like she did. No doubt Olivia has never wondered about or worried if Tony has roving hands and eyes. If the whole world fell into the sea and all that was left was Olivia, Brook, and himself, I suspect that Tony would be just fine with that.

Was it possible for a mother to be jealous of her own daughter's marriage? Well, maybe jealous isn't the word for it. Perhaps the right phrase is "tickled pink." I'm so blessed to know my daughter is in good hands.

But at the Potluck Club, I planned to ask that the girls pray for continued good fortune for my new little at-home family.

"Has Jack even called you?" Lizzie asked. We sat in our usual places in Evie's living room, going around in a circle, casting out our prayer requests like pennies in a fountain. *Please, Lord. Hear this one . . .*

"Oh, of course. He called later that day when he realized I wasn't at home to cook his supper." I had a tissue in my hand, and I began to tear at it. I kept my eyes focused on the white dust that flew about. "He figured I'd be at Olivia's. Not that I'd packed a bag and left him, but that I was just over there visiting. The notion of me leaving him has never once crossed his mind."

"I, for one, don't know what to say," Evie, who was dressed more fashionably than we'd ever known her to, broke in. Supposedly, she, Leigh, Lizzie, and Michelle had done some recent shopping in Silverthorne. "Yes, I do. What in Sam Hill made you wait so long?"

Donna had kept her jaw set most of the meeting, avoiding eye contact with everyone, including Vonnie, but at this she leaned forward, bracing her elbows on her knees and cracking her knuckles. "Much as I hate to admit it, Goldie, I'm with Evie on this one. I can't really say I'm surprised."

Donna wouldn't be. She knew so much more than the others, but, true to her profession, was keeping it all to herself, allowing me to tell only the parts I wanted to tell.

"Is Pastor Kevin aware?" Vonnie asked.

"Not from me, he isn't."

"What will you do tomorrow . . . for church?"

Church? I hadn't thought about church. I couldn't not go. Olivia and Tony, Jack and I had sat in our pew for the past seven years. Sitting there like a real family. Could I ask Olivia to choose which parent to sit with? Would that be fair? "I don't know," I whimpered, then felt Lizzie's arm slide across my shoulder.

"What did Jack say when he called, Goldie?" she asked.

I coughed out a laugh. "You know Jack. 'What are you doing, Goldie? What do you think you're doing? Throwing away a perfectly good marriage like this?' My question to him was, 'What makes this a perfectly good marriage? I stay at home while you run around?'" I looked about the room. "I don't guess it's been any secret that Jack has pretty much cheated on me since the day we married."

"I don't get it," Lisa Leann piped in. "I mean, I don't know you that well, Goldie, but you seem like such a dear lady. Is it that Jack is more interested in women who . . . how do I say this kindly? . . . fix themselves up a little more than you do?" Her eyes darted from one of us to the other as we each attempted to pull the stakes out

219

of our hearts. "I'm not saying that any of you are not attractive. You've all got a lot of potential, and I certainly tried to get that point across when I brought my little gift bags to you at the last meeting. But none of you have even contacted me about giving you a facial, and as of yet I haven't seen one of you with so much as a hint of lipstick on."

"Where do you get off talking like that?" Donna asked. For the life of me, I thought Donna was like a ticking time bomb that day.

Lisa shifted her weight in the chair, causing her shiny red leather pants to squeak. Her mouth fell open as though she'd been the one wronged. "All I'm saying is that a man likes to see a little color on his woman's face." She patted her cheek. "Who wants to live with a brown paper sack when you can live with a gift bag from Tiffany's?"

"Lisa Leann—" Vonnie's voice sounded like a warning.

"Now you just hold up there, Lisa Leann Lambert," Evie broke in. "I happen to know for a fact that your husband spends more time with Fred Westbrook than he does with what you obviously think is your pretty pout, so if I were you I'd watch what I say. Especially in my house."

"I didn't mean to cause such a—" I attempted to break in, but it didn't do much good. Lisa Leann nearly came out of her chair.

"You know, since the minute I came to town you haven't liked me, Evangeline Benson. And, for the life of me, I can't figure out why." Lisa Leann's face turned nearly as red as her dyed hair.

"I like you just fine," Evie barked.

Donna threw up her hands. "I could be in bed catching some z's right now and not listening to all this drivel."

"Oh, my goodness . . ." Leigh stretched out a bit and rubbed her swollen belly. Those of us who had given birth took note of the peak it formed in the middle and moved quickly.

"What is it?" Evie jumped to her niece's side, her writing pad and pen falling undetected to the floor.

Vonnie moved just as quickly.

"You're not in labor there, are you, Leigh?" Donna asked, standing from her chair but not approaching her. "I've got training, but I've never had to use it."

Evie turned on her. "Vonnie's a nurse, Donna. Remember?"

"I'm not in labor," Leigh said, taking in a deep breath and exhaling as though she were. "It's just a little Braxton Hicks."

"False labor," Vonnie reiterated. She looked at Leigh. "Are you sure?"

Leigh nodded. "This has been going on for a couple of days." She sat straight. "To be honest with you, the bickering in this room has totally stressed me out. I thought this was supposed to be a prayer group."

"Amen," Donna huffed.

What is going on with her, anyway?

The room grew silent, and eyes were downcast until Lizzie said, "You're so right, Leigh. Ladies, do you think we can get back on task here?"

Evie returned to her seat, picking up the pad and pen that had fallen to the floor in all the excitement. "We'll pray for you, Goldie," she said, her voice subdued. "Are there any specifics?"

I sniffled before answering. "Yes. I'm staying with Tony and Olivia—as I said before—but I can't do that forever. It's fine for now; as a matter of fact, Olivia is expecting again." A rush of excitement went throughout the room. I nodded and beamed. "Yes, yes. She's only a couple of months, and she's having some minor morning sickness, so my being there right now is a blessing. But eventually I'll have to find my own place."

"So, then," Lizzie said, "there's no chance of you and Jack reuniting?"

I shook my head. "I won't say yes or no right now. It's too soon. Olivia says we need counseling, and I guess we do." I paused. "I know we do." I chuckled. "But I don't know if Jack would ever consider it." The others in the group who knew Jack well nodded back at me. "And I need a job. So . . . if any of you know of work—"

"A job?" Lisa Leann cut in again, then scanned the room with her eyes. "And forgive me for breathing over here, but surely after all these years you're entitled to alimony. Why should you have to go to work at this stage of your life?"

"Alimony?" I asked. I hadn't even thought that far.

"If it were Henry, I'd take him for every nickel. Do you have an attorney?"

"I haven't really thought that far," I said, repeating my thoughts.

"Well, darling, you've got to think it before Jack does. I say we also pray that Goldie can find the right attorney." To my surprise, everyone agreed, Evie jotting it down on her pad of paper.

"Well, I think that's it for me," I said. "A job, a place to live, and—of course—Olivia."

"Let's be sure to pray for Jack too," Vonnie added.

"Do what?" Donna asked, narrowing her eyes at Vonnie.

Vonnie turned to her. "Donna, dear. When Jesus died it was for Jack's sins as well as Goldie's tears. A heart transplant in Jack could completely rewrite the end of this story."

Donna shrugged. "Yeah, well. Whatever. Personally, I'd rather chase a drunk driver on a moonless night." For the first time I seriously wondered about Donna's walk with the Lord, then mentally stopped myself from going there. Donna's faith was none of my business. Was it?

"Naturally we want to pray for Jan Moore," Lisa Leann piped in, oblivious to what I suspected everyone else in the room was sensing. Donna Vesey was hiding more than the fact she'd had to work a couple of altercations between my husband and his mistress.

"Of course we do," Evie said. "That certainly goes without saying." Everyone in the room, I'm sure, noticed the arrows that flew between Evie and Lisa Leann. Evie continued. "Girls, can I add something here?" She shook her head, fought back tears, then bowed her head before speaking again. "I know most of you remember my friend Ruth Ann. I loved Ruth Ann as much as I love my own sister, Peggy." Evie shrugged a shoulder. "I can't say

I understand it at all, but the Lord saw fit to take my precious, precious friend."

Leigh reached over and began to stroke her aunt's arm. The dam broke, and just like they said it was about time I left Jack, it was about time for Evie to break down. I've known her now for as many years as I've been married to Jack Dippel, and she's hurt over Ruth Ann McDonald's death in the deepest sort of way. It was enough to break anybody's heart, watching her sob over there in her chair, shoulders hunched and shaking up and down. "We prayed so ha . . . ha . . . haaaaaaard," she wailed. "And so I can't quite figure out how I'm supposed to pray now."

Lizzie shifted beside me. "Um, Evie?"

Evie wiped tears from her face with the palms of her hands as she looked across the room at the two of us. "What?"

"May I share something Jan shared with me the other day when I visited with her?"

Evie nodded.

Lizzie pressed her knees together and leaned over slightly, clasping one hand with the other. "Let me see if I can remember how she worded it. According to Jan—and she asked that I share this with you, by the way—she believes in four types of healing. There's the healing of the attitude that Paul talks about in 2 Corinthians. There's medical miracles, which are—indeed—miracles. There are supernatural miracles. And, the one healing we all have but rarely think about is our body's natural immune system." Lizzie cleared her throat and rolled her shoulders a bit, looking down at her tiny feet then back up. "But, you know, I was thinking about all this the other day . . . and I think there's a fifth healing. Jan knows it too, and even though she didn't say it out loud, there's no doubt in my mind she wanted to. In fact, she almost said it, then stopped herself."

"What is it?" Lisa Leann asked.

Lizzie looked directly at Evie. "Death, Evangeline. Death is the ultimate healing."

No one said a word, not a single word, but I started thinking about a song my mother used to sing when I was a child, and I began to hum it. All eyes turned to me.

"I don't know why, but I was just remembering the song," I explained.

Lizzie smiled at me. "It's a lovely old song," she said, then sang aloud, "In seasons of distress and grief, my soul has often found relief . . ."

I joined her. "And oft escaped the tempter's snare . . ." and then the others joined the two of us.

"By thy return, sweet hour of prayer!"

31

The woman is gone . . .

Clay Whitefield perched in his chair at Higher Grounds. He took a sip of coffee, placed the mug back on the table, then checked his watch for at least the sixth time in five minutes.

Any minute now the first car should be ambling by, indicating that the Potluck Club had ended. He wondered how much talk—or prayer, for that matter—had gone on about Goldie leaving Coach. He wondered, with a grin, if anyone had notified any black bears in the area.

Any minute now he'd see the evidence of another month gone by, another gathering of hens, and another offering of "prayer."

Any minute now, Donna would come in and give him the minute-by-minute details.

He looked at his watch again, then jerked his head upward as Lisa Leann's Lincoln slid past the window.

Any minute now . . .

A couple of hours later, he paid his bill and walked back to his apartment. Donna hadn't shown. He couldn't imagine why, but she hadn't.

Oh well, he thought. He'd have to get the news later.

Lisa Leann

Daffodil Cake

Ingredients:
1 can (1 lb. 4 oz.) Crushed pineapple
2 eggs
1 (tsp.) rum extract
1 lemon cake mix
1 pkg. Creamy vanilla frosting mix
1/4 cup butter
1/2 cup coconut

Directions:
Drain pineapple, reserving the syrup.
Combine pineapple, eggs, and 1/2 tsp. rum
extract in large mixing bowl.
(over)

32

Heated Showdown

How dare Evie attack my relationship with my husband in front of the entire Potluck Club? What did that old biddy know about marriage, anyway?

After our meeting, I fled for home in my Lincoln Continental. I looked into my rearview mirror and saw to my horror that mascara was running in black rivers down my cheeks. Seeing how pitiful I looked made me weep all the more, my shoulders quaking as I tried to keep my hands steady on the wheel.

"That old maid should rejoice," I said aloud. "She'll never know the heartbreak of having your 'pretty pout' totally ignored by your husband."

That made me cry harder, all the while wondering how Henry, the man of my dreams, had so completely cut me out of his life.

I had first met Henry when I was hired to be his secretary at Exxon. There he was, handsome and single and making the big money.

I was just out of college and ready to settle down. That first day I sat down in his office to take dictation, I was smitten. He was one tall Texan with curly black hair, big brown eyes, and the longest eyelashes you ever saw. The first time I heard him laugh at one of my jokes, I knew I could make him mine.

Whenever I'd bring one of my daffodil cakes to work, I'd waltz right into his office with an extra big slice. "Henry, I made this for you."

That got me noticed in short order. First it was flowers and then it was dinner, and when that man finally proposed to me in the Reunion Tower Restaurant in Dallas (the restaurant that slowly rotates on top a needle high above the city), my head didn't stop spinning until sometime after the kids were born.

The kids! How I missed them. My eyes instantly flooded, and I could hardly see to drive. One-handed, I dug a tissue out of my purse and dabbed at my tears.

How could Evie ever know what it's like to lose the one you love?

Sure, Henry still slept in my bed, but his body hardly ever reached for mine. A cry of anguish escaped my lips, and I tried to calm myself by taking a deep breath.

It hadn't always been like this. In our day, Henry and I had made the best couple ever, and I believe we were good for each other. He said he needed me because I spiced up his life. I needed him because he was my anchor. We spent a lot of time together, going to restaurants, enjoying movies, playing tennis. But he seemed to go into a permanent sulk when the babies came, probably because my attention was no longer fully his. He counterattacked by becoming even busier at the office.

Even then, he still loved my cooking. But gradually, over time, he seemed to have no time to sit down for a meal, whether with the kids or me. With his after-hours meetings and workouts at the gym, he'd sometimes crawl into bed well after I was asleep.

What could I do? I couldn't make the man love me or his family. I couldn't make him be a husband or a father, no matter how I begged or pleaded. I tried every tactic I could think of . . . until one day I gave up. So what if my loneliness made me become president of every organization to which I belonged. I was beginning to build a new life for myself. I grew so busy I didn't care if Henry had a permanent "Do Not Disturb" sign over his heart or not.

I ran my fingers through my hair, ignoring the fact that this gesture greatly disturbed my curls.

I couldn't help but feel sorry for myself. For now, I found myself with a husband who not only did not love me but also had taken me far away from the people who did. I began to weep all over again, not caring who saw me looking like a red-faced zebra. I was devastated.

To my relief, I pulled into view of my condo. It was only 3:00 in the afternoon and Henry wouldn't be home for a couple more hours. I could finish my cry and take a nice, hot shower. Refreshed, I could pretend that I didn't care that I was an outcast, spurned by my husband as well as by those I'd tried to befriend.

I hit the button on my garage door opener and drove my Lincoln inside. *Ohmygosh, what is Henry's Ford Explorer doing here?*

I cracked open the door to the house and quickly stepped inside. Let's see, where was he?

I heard noises in the kitchen and began to tiptoe past. However, when I saw Henry helping himself to a big bowl of my chicken and dumplings, so help me, I came at him like Chucky at that bear. "Henry Lambert, what in the name of Sam Hill do you think you are doing, eating the dish I prepared to take over to Jan Moore's house tonight?"

Henry, still wearing his fishing clothes, took a step back. He couldn't help but notice me now, breathing fire right in front of him. "What happened to you, Lisa Leann? You look like you've been in a train wreck."

I stormed past him and looked inside my Crock-Pot to survey the damage, which was irreparable. "How could you, Henry? What are the Moores going to eat for dinner tonight?"

Henry grinned in that exasperating way of his. "What about fish?"

Now, that was the wrong thing to say. I screamed, "Fish! Is that all you think about, fish?" By now I was totally out of control. I knew that as soon as I caught my reflection in the door of our stainless steel refrigerator. My scarlet face was covered with zebra war paint, and my hair stuck out in every direction.

Henry ventured innocently, "What's wrong with fish?"

Like I said, it's easier to let a cat out of the bag than to put it back in. But so help me, I couldn't contain myself. The cat was coming out, and it was coming out now.

"What do you mean, what's wrong with fish?" I shrieked. "If you love fish so much, you should have married one! Besides, if I was lucky enough to be a fish, then maybe I'd get a little of your attention!"

Henry's features faded from fear to amusement. "I don't know, Lisa Leann; you've always seemed like a rather cold fish to me."

Looking back, I think that remark was Henry's attempt to defuse the situation. However, his words snapped my last nerve. With anger, I backed my husband into the corner between the refrigerator and the stove. He leaned back, holding his spoon aloft while cradling his bowl of cooling chicken and dumplings to his chest.

"How dare you call me a cold fish when it's you who has left me in the cold! Not only that, you've uprooted me from my mother, children, and friends, and for what? So you can stand in an ice-cold river and fish all day?" I grabbed the bowl out of his hand and continued my shrieks. "Maybe you're happy ignoring me, maybe you've found your purpose in a fishing hook, but me, I've got nothing, not even you!"

With that, I tugged on the elastic waistband of Henry's fishing pants and dumped the rest of the chicken and dumplings down his trousers. Before he could react, I fled from the room and sprawled across the bed, sobbing hard. I knew at least Henry wouldn't touch me here.

As I boo-hooed, I could hear Henry in the kitchen cleaning up the mess. Soon, I heard the shower switch on.

By the time he was finished, I was sitting in my wicker rocking chair next to the bed, holding a box of tissues. Henry came out of the bath wrapped in his blue terry housecoat.

I don't think he saw me in the dim light until I whispered, "When did I lose you, Henry Lambert?"

He turned to me and shrugged. "We were all so busy. Though I have to blame myself for a lot of it."

A tear slid down my cheek. "Henry, I've missed you so much."

"Have you? I guess I've missed you too."

My heart skipped a beat. "Really?"

Henry nodded then sat down on the edge of the bed, just across from me. "I thought you'd given up."

"You and I, we've managed to achieve everything we could ask for in life. A beautiful home and great kids. We've even managed to save for our retirement. But somehow, we've forgotten our most important savings plan of all."

"What's that, Leann?"

"We forgot to save our marriage."

"I'm sorry for that."

"Me too."

I stood up and rummaged around on the bookshelf for a photo album labeled "Our Honeymoon."

I flipped the album open to a picture of a young, smiling couple, obviously very much in love. I handed the book to my husband.

"Henry, we loved each other once. Remember?"

Henry looked down at the picture, then back up to me. I reached for his hand and shyly asked, "Do you want to try again?"

"Do you?"

When I nodded, Henry surprised me by pulling me into his lap. I responded by wrapping my arms around his neck. Our eyes met, our lips touched, and Henry gently leaned me into the bed, where we relived the passion of long ago.

Later, Henry and I hurried around the kitchen as he taught me how to make trout amandine for the Moores. I pulled out a fork and took a bite of a pan-fried fish already cooling on a paper towel.

"I'd forgotten how good fresh trout is," I said, smiling up at Henry.

He smiled back. "Does that mean you're going to allow fish fries in the house?"

"When I don't have to eat alone," I challenged. "We really should take our meals together, you know."

"Agreed."

I smiled. I knew that our marriage needed a lot of work, but we'd definitely had a breakthrough. Plus we'd agreed to mealtimes together.

That night, Henry helped me deliver our fish fry to the Moores. Jan looked at both of us standing in her doorway and said, "You dears, we love fish. Thank you so much for your kindness."

We smiled at each other, then back at her. "We thank you, Jan, for the opportunity," I said.

Later, as we were driving home, Henry said, "Leann, I want to show you something." He stopped in front of a dilapidated Victorian house down on Main Street. Even the dim streetlights illuminated its poor condition. Its windows were boarded up, its paint peeling, and the roof looked as if it could use a little work. Henry said, "I've been thinking of making a real estate investment. Earlier tonight, when you said you'd lost your purpose, I couldn't help but think of this place."

"Why?"

Henry's eyes sparked. "What in the past five years has given you the most satisfaction?"

"Well, you already know the answer to that, Henry. It was helping Mandy plan her wedding."

"Exactly," Henry said. "I have to admit, you did a marvelous job."

I did a double take. "I didn't think you noticed."

"I did, and remember what I said to you at the time?"

"No."

"I said if you ever got tired of your choirs and clubs, you should consider going into business for yourself."

I was stunned. "As a wedding planner?"

"Why not? Not only do the locals have to plan their weddings, so do the tourists. Just the other day, an out-of-state couple got married not far from where I was fishing."

"Really?"

I gave that old two-story Victorian clapboard a second look. I just loved the steep roof, not to mention the ornate woodwork and trim. "You know, Henry, I see what you mean. I think this old place would make a great wedding boutique, complete with consulting services, of course."

Henry pulled the car back into the street and grinned. "I thought you'd say that."

I turned to him. "You know, that place will take a lot of work to make it shine. Are you up for helping me?"

"Well, as it was my idea, I'm willing to back it up with my hammer and paintbrush," Henry said.

It was going to take a lot of work to restore what we'd lost, and this old house that stood before us probably looked a lot like our current relationship.

But we had agreed to try. And just as this old home could be renewed with a paintbrush and hammer, our marriage could be renewed with care, courtesy, and a project we could tackle together. For the first time in ages, I hoped, I believed, it could.

I stared at my husband as we drove home in silence. I could just kiss him. Which I did, as soon as we got back to the bedroom.

33

What's she got going on . . .

Clay Whitefield looked out the window of his apartment. His brow rose as he tilted his chin just enough to stare through the slats of the blinds, taking in the scene of the Lamberts parked down the street. They seemed to be doing nothing more than staring at the old house he'd watched crumble to ruin over the years. "Hmmm," he mumbled. "What's up with that?"

The Lamberts were a nice enough couple, to his way of thinking, although it was obvious to him that they were living separate lives. Reporters had a nose for things like that.

He turned back to his desk and laptop. Bernstein and Woodward were sleeping, peacefully wrapped around each other and breathing in a rhythm only they could sense. Clay sighed as he sat, then frowned.

He hadn't seen Donna in days. He'd been hoping to get her opinion on the latest gossip in town: Goldie Dippel had finally left Coach. He'd cherish her thoughts, work hard to remember every word she said in reference to the situation, then write them in his notebook just as soon as she was out of view.

Donna, after all, had been the victim of a wife leaving her husband when her mother left her father. She'd be just full of a biased viewpoint . . . if he could just figure out where she'd been hiding herself.

Then again, Clay mused, when she read this week's *Gold Rush News*, she wasn't going to be too pleased with him, not pleased at all.

235

Evangeline

Sweet & Sour Chicken

Ingredients

- 1½ tsp. dried thyme
- 1½ tsp. paprika
- ½ tsp. cayenne pepper
- ½ tsp. ground allspice
- 1 tsp. pepper
- 3 Tbs. white vinegar
- 6 Tbs. olive oil
- 6 Tbs. soy sauce
- 6 Tbs. honey
- 4 skinless boneless chn breast

34

Scalding Story

The Monday morning sky was gray, a clear sign of the colder days to come. I both looked forward to and dreaded this time of year; the snowy white blanket capping the mountains and lawns is truly something to behold, but the brown slush that follows (not to mention the days stuck indoors) I am not particularly fond of.

When I walked into the kitchen, I found that Leigh was already there, toasting English muffins. She looked like she hadn't slept well, and I said so.

Leaning against the counter, she replied, "I didn't. This baby! It kicked all night." She rubbed the roundness of her belly, which I noticed appeared to have dropped a bit.

"You're dropping," I said, walking over to the refrigerator and pulling out the gallon jug of orange juice.

Leigh nodded. "I know. Dr. Henderson says it won't be much longer." Dr. Henderson, the ob-gyn from over in Breckenridge, had been treating Leigh since she'd arrived.

"I see." I poured my juice into a glass I'd taken out of the cabinet. "Leigh, don't you think we should talk about Gary?"

Leigh's English muffins popped up from the toaster, crisp and golden brown. "Not really." She pulled the muffins out, laid them on a nearby waiting plate, and then slathered them with margarine from a tub. She replaced the lid on the tub, but rather than place it back in the refrigerator, she slid it over a few inches. "There's nothing really to discuss." She shook her head. "That's not entirely true. I did speak with him a few nights ago."

"What?" I jerked the refrigerator door open, returning the orange juice, then stepped over and reached for the butter.

Leigh took a bite of the muffin, stuffing it in the side of her mouth. "He insists that I go back home before it's too late and I end up delivering out here." She chewed and swallowed. "He says it's not right for me to deprive him of the baby's birth. He says he's talked to Mom and Dad and—"

"He's talked with Peg and Matthew? When was this?"

"I don't know, Aunt Evie. Goodness, I don't know anything anymore."

I pointed a finger at my niece. "Now you listen to me, Leigh Banks. You do what you think is best and don't let anyone talk you into anything you don't want to do."

"Well, that's news. I thought you'd be all for me going back."

I took a sip of the juice. "Fine thing when a man doesn't say he misses the woman who is about to be the mother of his child. He's more worried about missing a birth? Not that I don't think he has rights, but let's keep our priorities straight. Besides, I don't want him pressuring you into doing something like moving in with him."

Leigh smirked. "No problem there, Aunt Evie."

I folded my arms across my middle. "Tell me something, Leigh. Do you still love him?"

Leigh didn't answer right away. Then she said, "Yes, I do. Very much. But I want it to be right."

The day continued to be gloomy. While Leigh rested for the better part of it, I finished up some paperwork until I grew tired and opted for a nap myself. Rather than returning to my room, I stretched out on the sofa, becoming less and less aware of the sounds of life from beyond the front window, and slipped into a frenzied dream.

Vonnie and I were back at college, but we looked as we look now. Everyone else looked like they did back all those years ago, but Vonnie and I had somehow managed to age. We were talking about our classes and about going to a pep rally later on in the week.

239

Then Vonnie pointed to a bench where the young man she'd been sitting with in the yearbook photograph sat smiling at the two of us. "Look at that," Vonnie said to me. "Isn't he a hottie?"

I woke with a jerk, sitting straight up, feeling strangely nauseous. *Dear Lord, what is it about that photograph that's got me feeling so odd?*

The following day I told Leigh I would be out most of the day, but I didn't say where I was going. Fortunately, she didn't ask. Maybe she thought I was going to the grocery store or something, I don't know, and at that moment I really didn't care. All I knew for sure was that for some strange reason the thought of my old friend Vonnie sitting on that bench with the dark-haired man gazing at her as though she were the world's best banana pudding bothered me. Since I'd discovered it, there'd been a few times I'd thought to ask Vonnie about it, but something always stopped me.

Maybe it wasn't my place to ask, maybe it wasn't even my place to know . . . but I wanted to satisfy my curiosity, and if driving to Cherry Creek College was what it took, then I would do it.

Within three hours of leaving my house, I had signed in as a guest and made my way over to the college library, where old yearbooks were kept, I suppose for posterity. I asked one of the librarians for the years 1964 through 1967, just to cover my bases, then took them to one of the many large oak desks and sat down.

The books were heavy and musty. I wrinkled my nose as I opened '65, slowly making my way through pages of faculty most likely all dead and buried now, miniskirts, and boys with long hair. There were a few photos of peace rallies and kids piled in VW bugs. Some photos made me laugh, and others brought feelings too poignant to linger over long, lest I begin to cry.

It was in the '65 yearbook that I found the photograph of the young man who'd sat with Vonnie on the bench. I ran my finger from the black-and-white school picture to just under where his name was registered. Joseph Ray Jewel, it read. Pre-med.

Joseph Ray Jewel. I let the name roll around in my head for a moment or two, but it didn't cause any memories to surface. Joe, perhaps? Ray? Joe Jewel? Ray Jewel?

Nothing.

I sighed, resigning myself to either hitting Vonnie head-on with what I knew or simply letting it slide. I closed the book, restacked the collection of yearbooks, then returned them to the librarian with a "thank you very much."

"Find what you were looking for?" she asked.

"Yes," I said, though in truth I had not.

I returned to my car and began the drive home, wondering what I would tell Leigh as to my long absence. Not that I had to tell her anything. At my age I should certainly be able to do what I please, when I please.

As I hit Summit View's city limit sign, I passed Donna Vesey in her Ford Bronco heading in the opposite direction.

And that was when it hit me. Something she'd said at the Potluck meeting when Vonnie had told us about Jan. "Hey, ladies, let me ask you a question," she'd said. "Any of you who've been in town a while know of a woman by the name of Jewel?"

I'd looked from Donna to the sofa, where Lizzie and Goldie exchanged blank glances. "No, why?" I'd answered.

"A few weeks ago I stopped a man from California. Name of David Harris. Nice-looking guy too," she'd added. "Thirty-five. Close to six foot. Black hair. Brown eyes. Looks Hispanic. Maybe Mexican. Mexican-American. Hard to say, really." Lisa Leann then made a crude statement about Julio Iglesias. Donna had continued. "Apparently he has a mother here. I'm thinking he was adopted and is trying to find her."

My hand clamped over my mouth as I inhaled deeply. Vonnie's sudden departure to Berkeley . . . her love for dolls . . . her favorite doll, Amanda Jewel—Jewel!—fit like the final pieces to a very large puzzle. "Oh, sweet Jesus in heaven," I declared. "Vonnie Westbrook, what have you done?"

I slowed my car, turning it around at the nearest section of the road that wouldn't get me hit by an oncoming car, then sped along, trying to catch up with Donna. When I came up behind her, I flashed my lights several times until I saw her gaze into her rearview mirror, then pull over. I pulled behind her, parking my car, then got out and came up to the driver's side of the Bronco. Donna had lowered the window, her forearm resting on top of the pane. She looked at me as if I'd lost my mind.

Maybe I had.

"What's going on?" she asked me. "Is it Leigh? Has she gone into labor?"

"We've got to talk."

"About what?"

"Do you remember a while back you mentioned a man who was looking for a woman named Jewel?"

I watched Donna's face grow dark. "Yeah. What about it?"

"I want you to drop it. If you see the man ever again, you tell him there is no Jewel here. Never has been."

Donna shook her head as though she couldn't believe what she was hearing. Something that sounded like a light snort came from her nose. "You women," she said. "You call yourselves Christians."

"I've lived here all my life, and there's never been a woman named Jewel here," I said, ignoring her dig.

Donna licked her bottom lip, then turned away from me, reaching for something in the seat beside her. When she showed me the old photograph of Vonnie and the man I now knew to be Joseph Ray Jewel, my mouth dropped open. "Yeah. Right," she said.

I reached for the photo, but Donna jerked it back, flicking it to the seat beside her. "That was a wedding photo," I said, wondering if my voice was registering the amount of shock I felt.

She looked back at me. "Looks like it, don't it? You're quite the detective there, Evangeline. If I ever see we need another deputy, I'll tell Dad to hire you." She looked face forward, then back to me within the span of a half second. "Are you going to tell me you never knew about this?"

"How did you get that photograph, Donna Vesey?"

"Are you going to tell me you never knew about this?" she repeated.

I folded my arms. "No. No, I did not."

"I don't believe you."

"Now you listen to me," I said, raising my voice. A car whizzed past me, and I inched closer to Donna's Bronco. "I don't know what this is all about, but I do know Vonnie. If she has kept this to herself all these years, there must be a good reason."

Donna's face grew harder still. "I thought I knew her. Apparently not."

I didn't speak for a minute. *Jesus, tell me what to say,* I prayed. "Donna, please. For Vonnie. Let's just keep this to ourselves until we can figure it all out."

"Tell you what, Evangeline," Donna said, returning her arm to the inside of the automobile and shifting to face forward. "The day I do what you tell me to do is the day I'll turn in my badge." She yanked the gearshift to drive and, without looking to see if traffic was coming, pulled back on the road and drove back down the highway, leaving me alone to wonder what to do next.

I somehow managed to get back to my Camry, sliding onto the bucket seat, feeling the chill of it penetrate through my slacks. I drove home in a state of shock, anxious to arrive there, to find my place of sanctuary. I needed peace and quiet if I was going to think everything through, to decide if I was going to call Vonnie or just let the chips fall where they may. It would have been different if Donna hadn't had the photograph.

The photograph! Where had Donna gotten that photograph?

Maybe I should call Vonnie, I decided as I turned into my driveway. *After all, if Donna knows, then perhaps others know as well.*

Like who?

Leigh was inching her way down the stairs when I came through the front door. "Where have you been?" she asked, stopping on the second step from the bottom. "I've been worried sick."

I removed my coat, hanging it on the coatrack. "I had to take a little trip." I avoided her eyes. "Are you hungry? I can fix us something to eat."

Leigh made her way over to me, and I brushed past her as she said, "No, I'm not hungry. I've been too concerned to be hungry."

I continued on into the kitchen. "You shouldn't have been. I'm a grown woman. I've lived here for many years without having to give a daily report as to my comings and goings, you know."

Leigh was behind me. "Sorry. I didn't know my love for you would be such a burden."

I spun around. "I'm not saying that. I'm not saying that at all." I didn't need this right now. I'd wanted time to think, not a challenge from my favorite—my only—niece.

Leigh's mouth was agape. "Aunt Evie!"

The hurt on her face caused my shoulders to drop. "I'm sorry. I've just got a lot on my mind." I turned to look at the stove. "I think I'll have a cup of hot tea. Join me?"

Leigh nodded. "I'll get the cups and saucers from the cabinet," she said.

When we were seated at the table, steam from our tea curling into the air between us, I said, "Leigh, have you ever had a friend—a good friend—do something that was totally out of character?" I fiddled with the handle of the teacup. "What I mean to say is: have you ever had a good friend do something that left you feeling betrayed?"

Leigh pondered the question for a moment before answering. "I can't really think of anything, no. Unless you include Gary's attitude lately, but I don't think that's what you're talking about." She narrowed her large eyes at me. "Is that what's going on? Has someone hurt you?"

"I—"

"Is it what Vernon Vesey did? A long time ago when he kissed Donna's mother?"

I looked up suddenly. "Oh, no, no, no."

She touched the top of my hand with her fingertips. "Because if it is—"

I smiled at her bravado. "It's not." She didn't look convinced. "Really, I promise."

Again, she pondered. "Is it Ruth Ann?"

"Ruth Ann? What in the world would make you ask a question like that?"

Leigh shrugged a shoulder. "I dunno. Some people feel a sense of betrayal when a loved one dies. Especially when a loved one dies before their time. You know what I'm saying?"

I took a sip of my tea before answering. "Well, I suppose you're right about that. I remember the way I felt when Ruth Ann died, as though she hadn't tried hard enough to stay alive. As though, if she really loved me, she would've fought harder." *My goodness . . . in comparison, those same feelings are very close to what I'm feeling now. Oh, Vonnie! How could you? How could you have gotten married, had a child, given the child up for adoption, and then . . . what? Divorced the father? Does Fred even know?*

"Does Fred know what?" Leigh asked.

I pinked; I'm just sure I did. "What? Oh. Did I speak out loud again?"

Leigh nodded.

"Nothing."

"Was there some connection between Fred Westbrook and Ruth Ann?" Leigh asked. She stretched out a bit and rubbed her abdomen.

"No! Of course not."

"Forgive me, Aunt Evie. I'm just trying to understand what you're asking me here."

I stood, picked up my half-consumed cup of tea, and placed it in the kitchen sink. "Let me know when you get hungry," I said. "I'm going to go lie down for just a few minutes. I'm too tired and too old to play twenty questions." I started for the door.

"Hey, that's cool. But you're the one who asked me, remember?"

I turned to look at her. She'd sat straight up—although as big with child as she was, I don't know how. "Asked you what?"

"About whether or not I've ever felt betrayed."

I thought about that for a moment. "So I did. You said you hadn't. Now, I'm going to go lie down. If you need me, knock on my door."

I didn't sleep. Of course, I didn't sleep. But at least my eyes were closed and my body was resting—or at least feigning rest. When I finally pulled my weary bones off the bed and walked back into the kitchen, I found Leigh pulling Chinese food out of a brown paper bag. We're quite progressive here in Summit View; we have one Chinese takeout restaurant, one Italian eat-in, and one Mexican. Add those to the "real food" menus at Higher Grounds Café, and we're a veritable buffet of international delights around here. There was a day when if you wanted sweet and sour chicken you had to first hope you could find a cookbook with it listed and then make it yourself. Not anymore.

Apparently Leigh'd had a yen for Chinese food. "I got you some honey chicken," she said. "I know it's your favorite."

I nodded. God love her heart, she was trying to appease my mood. "Thank you." I walked over to the cabinet and pulled out plates. "It smells good."

Leigh turned and rested her hips against the countertop. "I called Gary while you were resting."

I looked over my shoulder. "You did?"

"Mmmhmm." She scratched her belly.

"And?"

"Maybe praying for him is working. He's actually asking more questions about my well-being than harping on what he wants."

I placed the plates on the table. "Like?"

"Oh . . . questions like whether I'm getting enough rest. Have I gotten a doctor out here that I feel is competent, which I suppose is for my benefit rather than the baby's." She turned back to the little white boxes lined up on the counter. "Naturally he wants to know if I've made up my mind about returning home."

She picked up four boxes by the little wire handles—two in each hand—and walked toward me. I pulled my chair out from under the table as I asked, "Have you?"

Leigh sat, reaching for the box marked "S/S Ckn," which I assumed was her sweet and sour chicken she loves so much. "Nope."

I mouthed back "Nope," then spoke out loud. "There's no hurry. You're welcome to stay here as long as you want. Forever, in fact." I glanced over to the pantry door, where I'd always kept a calendar thumbtacked in place, as I reached for the box marked "Hny Ckn."

"Leigh, you've got a month left. I suspect we need to talk about setting a room up for the baby. Even if you decide you wanted to return to West Virginia, you shouldn't fly at this stage."

Leigh stabbed at a golden chunk of chicken on her plate, slipped it between her lips, and said, "I shouldn't have flown at seven months, I imagine."

I frowned. "Don't talk with your mouth full, Leigh Banks." I shook my fork at her. "And I suspect you're right about that."

She made a face at me and swallowed. "How about if, for now, we just get a bassinet that I can keep in my room? By the time we need more furniture, I'll have this all figured out."

"Let's pray so."

We ate in relative silence for the next few minutes until Leigh suddenly jumped and said, "Oh! I forgot." She stood and more or less waddled out of the room, then returned holding a tri-folded copy of the *Gold Rush News* in her hand. "Your paper was out on the front porch when I got home."

The *Gold Rush News*, our weekly newspaper, was instrumental in keeping Summit View's citizens apprised of the community's happenings. Since Clay Whitefield had become its ace reporter, the paper's focus had shifted somewhat to both national and international news as well, much to the chagrin of many of our residents. "If I want to know what's going on in Denmark," Fred Westbrook had said to Vonnie and me one evening when I was having dinner at their house, "I've always got the paper from Denver."

"Wonder if our bear story made it to the front page," I said, taking the extended paper from Leigh's hand. "I sure hope that Clay Whitefield quoted me correctly. Nothing worse in this world than having yourself misquoted by the local press."

She returned to her seat. "I'm sure he did just fine."

I unfolded the paper, laying the top half of the front page face-down, then pressing out the crinkles. "It was something, all right. I just hope that Clay Whitefield gave credit where credit is due: to Chucky!" I flipped the paper over, immediately spotting the color photo of Vonnie and her beloved dog. I laughed out loud, and Leigh leaned over a bit to see.

"Oh, look how cute Chucky is," she said. "Vonnie Westbrook and her heroic pal Chucky, a once-homeless bichon, rest easy at the Westbrook's backyard picnic table after being attacked by a bear," Leigh read the caption.

"Vonnie photographed well," I said, then felt myself grow a bit stiff. Vonnie . . . photographs.

Leigh pulled the paper a little closer to herself. "What's this about?" she asked.

"What?" I leaned closer to her, twisting myself a bit to see what she was pointing to.

"'Man Seeks Missing Jewel in Summit View,'" she read, pointing to a teaser box on the left-hand side of the front page.

"Jewel," I said. "Let me see that." I took the paper from her and read it for myself, continuing with "Story, Page Three." I sighed so hard the paper rustled at the force of my breath. "Oh no. Oh no."

"Aunt Evie?" Leigh asked. "What's going on?"

I didn't answer but instead read the very short article written by Clay Whitefield about a man—photo included of a young man who looked remarkably like the man I now knew was Joseph Ray Jewel—who was seeking to find his natural mother, his adopted mother (Harmony Harris, no less) having recently died of cancer. According to the article, Mr. David Harris believed that—because of information his dying mother had given him—his mother's first name was Jewel.

"That Donna!" I refolded the paper and slapped it against the table.

"What, Aunt Evie? What's going on?" Leigh's voice was nearing a squeal.

I stood, marched over to the wall-mounted phone, and dialed Donna's number. She answered after a few rings.

"I suppose this is about the newspaper article."

How'd she know it was me? "How'd you know it was me?" I asked her.

"Caller ID."

I could hear traffic in the background. "Are you in your car?"

248

"I am. Your call was forwarded to me, okay? Welcome to the new millennium." Her voice dripped with cynicism. I could hear the rustling of paper. "And by the way, I appreciated that shout-out you gave me in the bear story, and I quote, 'When I saw Deputy Donna Vesey leading the pack to the back porch rather than attempting to protect Vonnie, I knew we were in serious trouble.'"

I didn't respond to her sarcasm, instead focusing on the reason for my call. In any case, I wasn't sure what a shout-out was. "You're welcome, and yes, this is about the newspaper article, Donna Vesey. Let me ask you a question: have you flushed everything Vonnie Westbrook has done for you your whole life down the toilet?"

"Hold up—"

"Do you have no respect for a woman who has loved you like a mother . . . and the good Lord knows more than your own mother could have ever loved you?"

"Evangeline!"

"How long did it take you to run to Clay Whitefield after you and I talked?"

"Evie, think about what you're saying. You and I just saw each other today. Do you think I had time to call Clay and then he had time to print an article in a paper that probably went to bed sometime over the weekend?"

I stopped in my tirade. She was right there. Humph.

My silence allowed her the opportunity to continue. "I'm just as shocked and upset as you are. I had no idea." She paused. "I'm not saying I'm any less upset with Vonnie about all this, and I'm not saying I'm convinced you haven't known about it all these years."

"With God as my witness—"

"Save it, Evangeline. The question now is: what are we going to do from here?"

I looked out the kitchen window over the double sink. "You tell me, Donna Vesey."

She didn't answer right away. "I'm driving out in Vonnie's direction now. I only hope she hasn't seen the paper already."

I sighed in reply.

"And, Evie, just so you know, when I get my hands on Clay Whitefield, there's going to be a whole new story to tell come next week's paper. We may just have our first homicide in Summit View, Colorado, and I just may be on the other side of the law."

35

Don't get on her bad side . . .

Clay had been answering phone calls all day, or at least for the hours he'd been down at the Gold Rush News. Everyone thought they might know something about the missing jewel, but in the end, no one knew squat.

A few people had comments about the Potluckers, a few even asking how anyone could tell the members from the bear. One phone call in particular was about Ms. Benson's quote about Donna's reaction to the bear. That Evangeline. You didn't want to get on her bad side.

He'd driven past her earlier that day and seen her and Donna in what looked to be an argument. Donna looked pretty ticked. He wondered how long it would be before he felt the sting of her rebuke.

He chuckled. He couldn't wait.

Donna

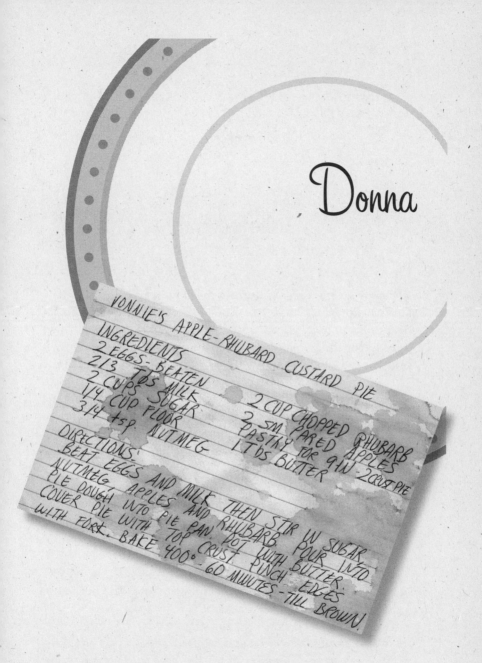

VONNIE'S APPLE-RHUBARD CUSTARD PIE

INGREDIENTS

2 EGGS - BEATEN
2/3 TBS MILK
2 CUPS SUGAR
1/4 CUP FLOOR
3/4 tsp. NUTMEG

2 CUP CHOPPED RHUBARB
3 SM. PARED APPLES
PASTRY FOR 9IN. 2CRUST PIE
1 TBS BUTTER

DIRECTIONS:

BEAT EGGS AND MILK THEN STIR IN SUGAR, NUTMEG, APPLES AND RHUBARB. POUR INTO PIE DOUGH INTO PIE PAN. DOT WITH BUTTER. COVER PIE WITH TOP CRUST. PINCH EDGES WITH FORK. BAKE 400° - 60 MINUTES - TILL BROWN.

36

Grilling Vonnie

The nerve of that woman, I fumed, *to tell me off twice in one day.* I put my clipboard onto the seat beside me. I'd been writing up a report on a tourist who had lost a wallet while shopping on Main Street. Poor thing. Unless a Good Samaritan found it, her credit card was probably already being swiped at the Frisco Wal-Mart.

I put my phone back into my console and shook my head. It was bad enough that Evie had dissed me in her interview about Vonnie and the bear. But to think that she thought I'd given Vonnie up to Clay Whitefield, well, that was unforgivable. I pulled onto Main Street but slowed down as I came to the Higher Grounds Café. Sure enough, there was Clay Whitefield's beat-up blue and gray jeep. I whipped my Bronco beside it, grabbed my copy of the *Gold Rush News*, and charged through the wooden door. The bell announced my arrival as I spotted my prey sitting at his usual table. He looked up from reading a copy of the *Rocky Mountain News*, happy to see me until he realized I was purple with rage.

"Donna, what's wrong?" He looked at the copy of the newspaper in my trembling hand. "Was it something I wrote?" He pulled out a chair. "Here, sit. Let's talk about it."

I sat down in a chair across from him.

"It's the article, isn't it?" he said. I narrowed my eyes as confirmation. "Honestly, Donna, I didn't think you'd mind that com-

254

ment from Evie about how you ran from the bear. I mean, who wouldn't run?"

"That's what you think this is about?"

I slapped the paper onto the table and pointed to the story about the "missing Jewel."

Clay looked at me wide eyed. "You know something about this?"

"My question to you is just how do you know?"

Clay leaned back in his chair and studied me. "I'm surprised you don't remember."

I cocked my head, in no mood to play games. "Pardon me? Remember what?"

"You were here the morning I interviewed David Harris, that guy everybody accused of being your boyfriend."

I leaned back and took a deep breath. "You were interviewing David Harris?"

"Well, yes. He called the paper and asked if I would run something to help him find his birth mother."

I put my elbow on the table and covered my eyes with my hand. "Of course, of course. How could I be so stupid?"

Suddenly, I realized Clay was pulling out a pen from his pocket. It hovered over his ever-ready notepad. "So, Deputy, just what do you know about his so-called 'missing Jewel'?"

I stood abruptly, almost knocking over my chair, and snatched my paper from the table. "That, my friend, is none of your business."

With that, I left the restaurant, mindful of Clay's scrutiny as I pulled my Bronco from my space. *Great job, Donna,* I scolded myself. *Why don't you alert the local press while you're at it?*

I sighed deeply, feeling absolutely drained. There were no two ways about it; it was time for me to have my little talk with Vonnie Westbrook about her son, one David Harris.

When I pulled up in front of her tiny, two-story, pink-and-rose-colored Victorian, I sat there unable to leave the safety of my truck. For the love of Mike, how was I even going to approach this topic?

Soon I saw her look out the etched glass window that graced the front door. She opened it and waved.

I halfheartedly waved back, watching Chucky dance at her feet. *How could she? How could this woman betray everyone she loved, especially me?*

I picked up the paper and my clipboard and pushed open my truck's door.

Vonnie spoke to me as I walked up the drive. "Donna, I knew you'd drop by on my birthday. I was just pulling out an apple rhubarb pie from my oven. I have some ice cream in the freezer. Why don't you come in and share a birthday slice with me?"

Great. I forgot it's her birthday.

I sat down at her kitchen table while she scooped out premium vanilla ice cream and put it onto two slices of warm pie.

She placed the pie in front of me, with one of her silver forks and a napkin.

I usually helped her in these preparations, but I could hardly move.

"So," she said, looking at me with worried eyes, "is everything okay? You seem kind of glum, dear."

"Is Fred here?" I asked.

"No, it's just you and me and the dog. Fred's still at work."

Her eyes fell on the copy of my *Gold Rush News*. "Oh, the article came out. Is that what you stopped by to show me?"

"Then you haven't seen it?"

Vonnie pulled out her reading glasses, which she wore on a chain around her neck, and put them on her nose. When she saw the picture of herself holding Chucky, she giggled with delight. "Oh, my! Just look at that, will you?"

She began to read the article, while I sat in silence, listening to her laughter. She looked up. "Donna, did you ever read anything so priceless? Though I do think the comment from Evie was uncalled for. You were trying to save us all."

I leaned back in my chair and stared at her.

She grew concerned. "Donna, you haven't touched your pie. Is everything all right?"

"No, Vonnie, everything is not all right."

"Tell me, dear," she asked with compassion. "What's wrong?"

"You can read it for yourself. It's in the article mentioned beneath the Potluck story."

Vonnie looked back at the paper. "A jewel theft in Summit View?"

I was patient. "Turn to page three."

The paper rustled, and her demeanor changed. Startled, she cried out, "What is this?"

"Don't you recognize him, Vonnie?"

Vonnie looked up. Her face was a mix of grief and panic. "Well, he does look like someone I used to know."

"You mean Joseph Jewel?"

Vonnie stared at me, absolutely stunned. "Joseph? You know about my Joseph?" She looked down at the article, then back at me. "This can't be. This can't be my son."

"Why is that, Vonnie?"

"My son is dead." And with that she broke down into hysterical sobs. I stood up and knelt beside her. She wrapped her arms around me and cried into my black leather jacket. "My baby is dead. Mother told me."

I held her until the sobs subsided, then pulled back. "Vonnie, your baby is not dead. He's very much alive and living in L.A."

Vonnie shook her head in disbelief.

I pulled David's card out of my pocket. "Here. See, Vonnie, I have his number. He wants you to call him."

"Oh no, no, this can't be. What would Fred say?"

I sat back in my chair while Vonnie dabbed her eyes with her napkin. "Fred doesn't know you were married before?"

"No one does. Mother said that would be best."

This just didn't make sense to me. "Vonnie, your mother didn't like Joseph?"

"She never met him." Vonnie looked down at her wrinkled hands. "She wouldn't."

I reached over and placed my hand on top of hers. "Why not?"

She tapped David's picture with her finger. "Donna, isn't it obvious?"

I looked down at the paper again, unsure of what she meant.

She changed the subject. "Donna, how did you find out about Joseph?"

"I took the Sunday school picture. It was meant to be a surprise. I was going to have it reframed. I had no idea it hid your secret."

"Then you saw my wedding picture?"

"I have it right here, in fact." I pulled the photo from beneath my clipboard.

When Vonnie saw the picture, she gasped. "Oh, Joseph." She held the picture to her heart. "Joseph, why did you leave me?"

"He abandoned you?"

"No, no. It was Vietnam. My Joseph was killed in action."

I sat back, stunned. Of all the thoughts that had gone through my head, I hadn't imagined the truth. I looked down at the ice cream, now melted into puddles around my pie. "Vonnie." I looked back up. "I'm sorry. I'm so very sorry."

37

She's hiding something . . .

He felt as though Donna had slapped him. Well, she may as well have. He couldn't imagine her fury over something so . . . something as . . . something that had absolutely nothing to do with her. Nothing whatsoever.

His brows shot so high they nearly blended with his hairline as he thought how he'd seen Donna and Evangeline in the midst of a heated conversation out in the middle of town. Did that have anything to do with the article about Harris? What was going on? Was Donna hiding something?

Clay jumped from his seat, reaching for the faux leather jacket he'd draped behind him earlier. Maybe, if he were lucky, he could catch Donna, find out where she was heading off to, and have enough fodder for his next chapter on the ladies of the Potluck.

Vonnie

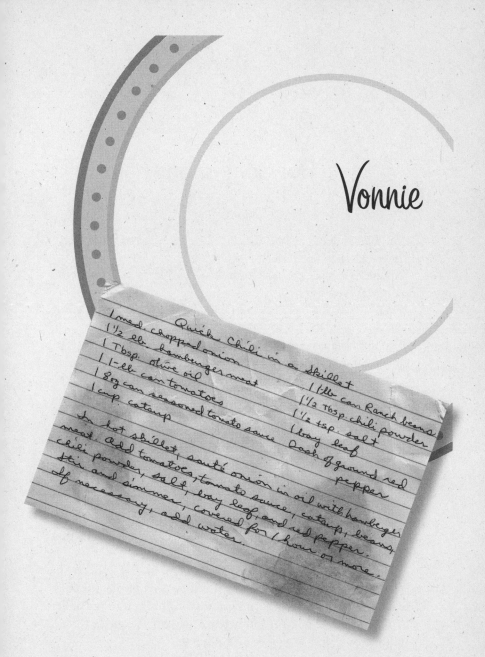

Quick Chili in a skillet

1 med. chopped onion
1½ lb. hamburger meat
1 Tbsp. olive oil
1 1-lb can tomatoes
1 8 oz can seasoned tomato sauce
1 cup catsup

1 lb can Ranch beans
1½ Tbsp. chili powder
1½ tsp. salt
1 bay leaf
Dash of ground red pepper

In hot skillet, sauté onion in oil with hamburger meat. Add tomatoes, tomato sauce, catsup, beans, chili powder, salt, bay leaf, and red pepper. Stir and simmer, covered for 1 hour or more. If necessary, add water.

38

Hot Confessions

Before Donna left, she put our untouched pie in the sink while I sat at the kitchen table, staring at the paper.

My son was alive and had been raised by Harmony Harris, the movie star? How?

Finally, I lay my head on the table and wept—for my Joe, for my baby, and finally for my mother's betrayal.

I sat up. *How could she?* I wondered, wiping my eyes on a napkin.

Just then, I heard Fred's truck pull into our driveway. I jumped out of my chair, knocking the paper and wedding picture to the floor. I picked them up and stuffed them into the nearby utensil drawer.

I was overcome with questions: what was I going to do about David, my mother, and my husband, not to mention dinner?

Quickly, I grabbed an onion from the kitchen counter and began to chop. I pulled out my electric skillet, dumped the onions inside, and turned the switch on high. The kitchen immediately smelled as if dinner were cooking. At the ruckus, Chucky rushed from his spot on the easy chair and sat at my feet, eager for any tidbits that might fall his way.

Ignoring him, I opened the cupboard and found a can of ranch-style beans. I thought I'd add the beans first to make the dish look like it was already cooking. I was pouring the beans into the skillet when Fred walked into the kitchen and gave me a squeeze. "Hey, famous lady. Everybody's talking about you."

I dropped the can into the skillet. "What?"

"Your picture in the paper!" He slapped a copy of the paper onto the kitchen cabinet next to me. "Have you seen it yet?"

I nodded, then fished the can out of my skillet, keeping my back to my husband. "Oh! Yes, I saw it."

"Say, you sound like you've been crying." He gently turned me to face him. "Those are tears. What's wrong, Vonnie?"

I stared up at him and simply said, "Goldie left Jack."

Fred gave me a peck on the forehead. "Can't say that didn't serve him right, from what I've heard. But don't let it get you down. Maybe this will help set things straight between them." He sniffed the air. "Smells good. What's for supper?"

"We're having chili, but I'm running behind schedule. Would you like a piece of my apple rhubarb pie while you wait?"

"Sounds perfect," he said, pulling a plate out of the cabinet. "Now all I need is the pie server." He put his hand on the handle of the utensil drawer.

"No! Wait! It's in the sink," I practically shouted.

"Okay," he said as he turned toward the sink and cut a big slice of pie. I handed him a fork from the dish rack on the counter, then leaned against the cabinet and took a deep breath.

Fred noticed. "Are you sure you're all right?"

I shook my head. "I think I'm coming down with a chill."

"Maybe I should finish cooking supper. Now, where's your big spoon?" Once again, he reached toward the drawer.

I playfully slapped away his hand. "Donna borrowed it. I'll finish dinner; you go sit down in front of the TV."

I pushed him toward the living room. When his back was turned, I picked up a magazine off the kitchen table and fanned myself. Whatever was I going to do?

I turned and looked at the man who had been a part of my life for more than thirty years. Sure, he wasn't Joe, but he was a good man, a kind man, a man I loved.

I shuddered. My private nightmare was soon to become common knowledge. For heaven's sake, the story was on the front page of the paper, just beneath my picture. People were bound to figure it out. Donna already had, and who else?

I touched my breast as if to still my rapid heart. If I didn't tell Fred, he would find out anyway. How would he take the news that I'd betrayed him with a secret past?

I opened the refrigerator door and pulled out the pound of hamburger I had defrosted. There was nothing else to do but cook dinner as I tried to figure this out.

Later, Fred helped me clear the table. I had already secretly moved the article and photo to my purse, to avoid any unpleasant surprises.

When everything was put away, I said, "I hope you don't mind, but I'm going to run over to see Mother."

"Vonnie, I thought you didn't feel well. Maybe you should think about going to bed."

"No, no, I'm fine."

Fred walked over to the hall closet. "I'll go with you then."

I stalled. "Oh, Fred, I really need to spend some time alone with Mom, if you don't mind."

Fred hung his coat back on the hanger. "Well, okay, but don't stay out so late. I'm kinda worried about you."

A few minutes later, I pointed my Ford Taurus out of Summit View and our secluded mountain valley and headed toward Frisco. Mom and Dad had retired to a tiny condo with a great view of Lake Dillon and the surrounding mountain peaks about ten years ago.

Back in the sixties, the powers that be had bulldozed the original Frisco town site, dammed Ten Mile Creek, and rebuilt the town just above what is now Lake Dillon.

When I pulled into the driveway, I froze. How would Mother respond to my demands that she explain the past?

When I rang the doorbell, Dad opened the door. "Vonnie! What brings you out so late?"

I gave Dad a kiss on the cheek. He was in his eighties, healthy and spry, though he battled high blood pressure. He'd retired from his job as pharmacist at the Gold Rush Drugstore, and that was almost two decades ago.

"I need to talk to Mom. Girl talk. Do you mind?"

He chuckled. "I can take a hint. I'll go into the living room and study for my Sunday school lesson. Your mom's in the kitchen. But I have to warn you, she's in one of her moods."

"Thanks, Dad."

"Who was at the door, dear?" Mother called when she heard Dad retreat back to the living room. I answered for him. "Mother, it's me."

She looked up and saw me standing in the doorway of the kitchen.

"Vonnie?"

I sat down across from her at the kitchen table, where she was reading a copy of the *Gold Rush News.* The paper was turned to the article on page three.

"Mother, do you know why I'm here?"

Mother burst into tears.

I was surprised at how frail she looked. Of course, she was in her eighties, but somehow, since I'd seen her a few days ago, she seemed to have shrunk. Her wrinkled face looked drawn, and her coloring was almost as pale as her snow-white hair.

"Vonnie, you've got to believe this when I say to you, I did it out of love."

I sat rigid in my chair. "We'll get back to that, Mother. First I want to know what happened."

Mother covered her face with her hands and began to weep. "Vonnie, I . . . oh, Vonnie!"

I sat quietly, listening to her sobs. Finally she was able to speak. "In a way, being found out is a relief to me. What I did, I did because I was a foolish woman. I couldn't accept that my daughter had married a Mexican man and was having a Mexican baby. I don't know. I figured it was for the best. You were young, you could get on with your life, have other children."

She looked up at me for support. I offered nothing other than my attention.

"I . . . I know what I did sounds dreadful."

I waited as she paused. She seemed to be trying to decide how to begin. Finally, she said, "Maria called me to tell me Joe died and that you were having the baby. At the news, I took the next plane from Denver to L.A. By the time I got to the hospital, you were in real trouble with your labor. Maria had remained faithfully beside your bed, but I insisted she leave. I told her it was my responsibility to take care of you. You probably don't even remember that, do you?"

I shook my head. "Not really."

"No small wonder. You were in shock; then with the drugs they gave you to relieve the pain of your labor, you were pretty much out of it. And really, it just about broke my heart to see you like that."

I stood up and got a box of tissues off the nearby writing desk and handed it to Mother. She took a tissue and held it tightly.

"You were so pale, so broken, and my heart broke right along with yours." She dabbed her eyes. "Shortly after I arrived, the doctor said you needed a C-section. You signed the papers, of course, but you really didn't know what you were doing. By then, I'd made my decision. With your husband dead and your heart broken, I didn't see how you could raise a child alone, especially a child of mixed race. So I called an L.A. attorney and talked about how we could put your baby up for adoption."

"What!? But you had no right!"

Mother sighed. "I realize that now." She stopped talking and looked down. "All I wanted to do was to take you home and make things better for you."

She sat silent until I said, "Go on."

"It seemed this attorney handled adoptions for the stars, and Joseph's baby seemed perfect for one of his clients. When the baby was born, the client, hiding behind shades and a hooded fur, took your son home to be his mother."

"But I never signed any papers. How could she take my baby if I never signed any papers?"

"You did. You were still heavily sedated. You thought you were signing a release for the baby's burial."

It took a moment before I could speak. I stammered, "But Maria, she wouldn't have allowed for that. How could you have gotten this past her?"

"By the time Maria got back to the hospital, everything had already been taken care of. Like you, Maria thought the baby was dead."

I leaned back in my chair, hardly able to breathe.

"Vonnie? Are you okay?"

"I don't know, Mother. I don't know." I stood up.

"Can you ever forgive me?" my mother asked, her eyes pleading with mine.

I simply couldn't answer.

I drove home in silence. When I entered the house, Fred was getting ready for bed. "Vonnie, you're as white as a ghost!"

I sat down on the edge of the bed. "Am I?"

Fred, dressed in his red plaid pajamas, sat down beside me. He placed the back of his hand on my forehead. "You don't seem to have a fever."

"Fred, something has come up. And before I tell you what it is, I want to tell you what you mean to me."

Fred wrapped his arm around me and drew me toward his shoulder. "There, there. It can't be all that bad, can it?"

"It can." I pulled away. "Fred, you've been a wonderful, faithful husband to me all these years. And I have grown to love you dearly."

Fred looked concerned. "But?"

"But there's something I never told you about my past. Something that has come back to haunt me."

"For goodness sake, Vonnie! What kind of past could you have had?"

"The paper. You saw the paper tonight?"

"Yes, we already talked about your article."

I walked toward the window and peeked between the blinds at the darkness. "But, Fred, that was only one of two articles that pertained to me."

"What, you entering the talent show at the Breckenridge barbeque cook-off next weekend?"

I turned back to face the man I loved and pulled our sitting chair before him, then sat down, reaching for his hand.

"Fred, the story about the missing Jewel. The boy looking for his mother?"

"Do you know her?"

I dropped eye contact and took a deep breath. Then I looked back into my husband's worried face.

"I do. And so do you."

"Then who is it?"

"I'm the missing Jewel. I'm David Harris's mother." I pulled out the wedding photo of me and Joseph Jewel. "I was married once before to a man named Jewel. I'm his widow, Fred. And the boy in the picture? David Harris is our son."

39

Can't figure her out . . .

Clay hardly slept that night. Woodward and Bernstein were especially loud scurrying about in the wood shavings and running on the wheel, but that wasn't why he couldn't sleep. It was more a feeling he couldn't shake, like he was on the verge of something big. Maybe even bigger than he could handle. But he just couldn't figure it out.

Around 3:00 a.m. he finally got up, made another cup of "at home" coffee, peered out the window at the silent street below, then settled in his chair and flipped on the television.

All the President's Men was playing on AMC. "Hey, guys," he said over his shoulder to the noisy gerbils. "You're on TV."

They neither noticed nor cared.

It was gonna be a long night.

Evangeline

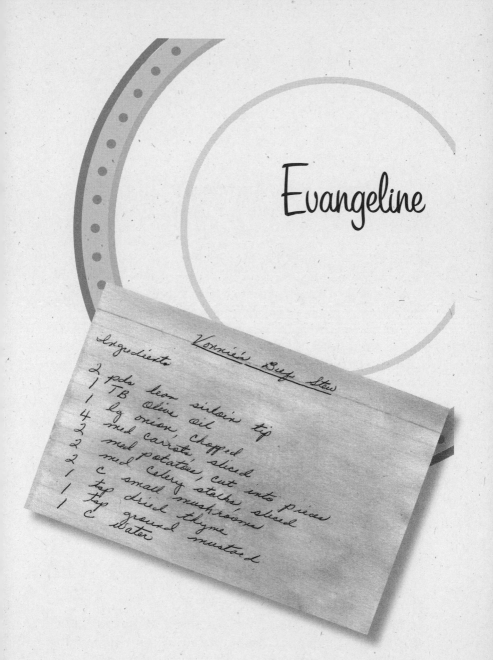

Vonnie's Beef Stew

Ingredients:

2 pds lean sirloin tip
1 TB olive oil
1 lg onion, chopped
4 med carrots, sliced
2 med potatoes, cut into pieces
2 med celery stalks, sliced
2 C small mushrooms, sliced
1 tsp dried thyme
1 tsp ground mustard
1 C water

40

Preserved Memories Shared

I heard the phone ring while I was brushing my teeth. It stopped after the second ring, so I assumed Leigh caught it. I turned the tapwater off and poised myself to listen for the sound of her voice calling me to the phone but didn't hear anything.

I dressed in the long denim skirt, turtleneck shirt, and patchwork denim jacket Leigh had picked out for me when we'd gone shopping with Lizzie and Michelle. I paused at the dresser long enough before leaving my bedroom to glance at myself in the mirror . . . and frowned. I looked like an old woman trying to pass herself off as being twenty years younger. I leaned forward to take in my reflection, patted at my hair for the sake of vanity, then pinched my already pointed nose.

I found Leigh in the living room looking out the front window. "Good morning," I said. "Anything happening out there I should know about?"

Leigh partially turned from the window, already shaking her head. "No, not really. It's definitely turning colder out there. The weatherman said we'd only see about midforties today."

"It's that time of year, all right."

She turned completely. "You look nice."

"I look silly."

Leigh moved toward me. "No, you don't." She stopped, taking me in fully. "You just need some accessories. What happened to the necklace and earrings we bought for this outfit?"

I brushed her away. "Oh, goodness. Leigh, women here don't fluff up so much. Haven't you noticed how they are? Airs are put on about as much as Maybelline. An updo is a ponytail." Leigh laughed, and for the first time I noticed that her eyes were a bit puffy. "Have you been crying?"

Leigh placed the palms of her hands on her cheeks. "Maybe. A little."

I touched her forearm. "What's wrong?"

Leigh shook her head, her eyes brimming over with tears. "I dunno. Maybe I'm just a little hormonal right now, you know what I'm saying?" She turned her head away from me, but I squeezed her arm, silently begging her not to turn away.

"Who was that on the phone?" I asked, wondering if the phone call and the tears were somehow related.

"Gary," she said in a whisper.

I watched her for a moment before continuing. Tears streamed down her cheeks, but she wasn't officially crying. "Let's go sit down on the sofa, shall we?"

We sat. I looked at her, and she, once again, looked out the window as though something or someone were about to show up. "Leigh? Talk to me, sweetheart."

She shook her head. "I dunno, Aunt Evie." The dam broke, and for a moment I simply allowed her to weep. When she was done she hiccupped a few times before whispering, "I just love him so much, Aunt Evie. I don't know that I've ever felt for anyone like I feel for him, and I can't imagine ever feeling this way again. He's the father of my baby, and here we are nearly an entire country apart, pretending we have nothing to hold on to." She splayed her hand over her stomach and rubbed lovingly.

"Tell me," I spoke softly. "Tell me why you love him so much."

She leaned her head against the back of the sofa, rolling her head toward me. Her eyes now danced. "Oh, Aunt Evie . . . he's so . . . so . . . deep down, he's truly wonderful."

"Deep down."

"Other than the fact that I'm pregnant with his child and unmarried, you'd like him. Did I ever tell you how we met?"

273

I shook my head. "No, I don't think so."

"He's a pharmaceutical representative. Very successful. I was in Daddy's office one day—we'd gone out for lunch together—and Gary was there, sitting in the front office waiting when we returned." She placed her hand over her heart. "My heart just went wild the minute I laid my eyes on him . . . and he felt the same way about me." She smiled. "He followed me to my car, asked me for my number . . ."

"Well, I hope you had enough good sense not to give it to him."

Leigh grinned at me.

"Leigh!"

"He's the most giving person you'd ever want to meet, Aunt Evie. He's not only handsome—did I tell you he looks like a six foot six Ken doll?" I shook my head no. "He does." She grinned again. "But that's not why I love him. I've never known anyone who is as giving as he is. He gives to so many charities, works with the homeless, helps build houses with Habitat for Humanity."

I pressed my lips together and nodded. "He sounds wonderful . . . in every way but one."

She sighed. "Maybe I'm being too hard on him."

I sat ramrod straight. "Now you listen to me, Leigh Banks. Don't you dare go soft on me here. Not at this stage in the game."

"I won't." Her voice was so soft I wasn't sure she'd even spoken.

"So what did he say this morning?"

Leigh shrugged her shoulders. "The same, more or less. Nothing's changed except that he actually said he misses me more than he anticipated. But don't you worry. I stood firm." She sat up and sighed. "By the way, where are you going so—how do you say it—gussied up?"

It was my turn to sigh. "I have to go see Vonnie."

Leigh was taken aback. "You act like that's a chore."

"Today it is."

"What's so special about today?"

I paused before continuing. "Leigh, if I tell you something, will you promise to keep it between the two of us?"

"You know I will."

I spent the next fifteen minutes explaining to Leigh what I knew about Vonnie . . . about Vonnie and Joseph Ray Jewel . . . and about Vonnie, Joseph Ray Jewel, and a young man named David Harris. Which, at the end of it all, wasn't much.

"So what are you going to do?"

I wondered about that very question myself. "Well, for starters I'm going to march myself out there this morning and talk to her. I don't have a clue as to what I'm going to say, but I figure that after all these years of knowing one another and loving one another like sisters, I owe it to her to be up front with her. I've wrestled with this and wrestled with this and I've prayed some more. And this is what's right."

Leigh leaned back again. "It seems to me you've got a lot of issues to settle. This thing with Vonnie, Ruth Ann's death . . . and Vernon Vesey."

Vonnie looked as though she'd been crying since the day she was born. She also looked like she'd slept in her clothes and that she'd lost her brush. She had what appeared to be one of Fred's handkerchiefs in her right hand, which she used to wipe at her nose and dab at her eyes.

I had to knock on the side door of her house—the one I've used for years—for a good five minutes before she answered, which she did without saying so much as a hello and then retreated back into the house. I let myself in, closing the door behind me, and followed my old friend into the family room, where she now sat in her favorite chair, holding Amanda Jewel.

"Amanda Jewel," I said.

Vonnie looked up at me with red-rimmed eyes. "That's right." She returned her attention to the doll cradled in her arms. "How'd you find out?"

I took a seat on the sofa, dropping my purse and keeping my feet planted firmly on the floor, pressed against each other. "Long story."

"Tell me about it."

I didn't say anything at first. "No, Vonnie. Why don't you tell me about it? Like you should have done when we were back at Cherry Creek."

"I couldn't back then, Evie," she whispered.

"But why not? We were friends, weren't we?"

She looked up at me so suddenly I thought her neck would snap. "He was Mexican-American, Evie."

I returned my thoughts just as forcefully. "It was the sixties, Vonnie. Good gosh, everything we'd ever thought was true went flush down the toilet. From the day Kennedy was killed in '63, not another thing made sense." I allowed a matter of moments to relive that fateful day in November, then finished with, "You could've told me."

Vonnie looked around her family room before looking back at me. "How could I tell you, Evie? What did you know about love? One kiss from Vernon Vesey did not make you the Elizabeth Taylor of Summit View."

I stood up and began to pace. "You know, I'm so sick of everybody bringing up that kiss from Vernon. Everyone thinks that just because I never quite got over it that means I don't understand anything else in the love and sex department." I pointed to her. "Well, I do. I might've locked my heart away early in life, but it kept beating. I was happy for Ruth Ann, wasn't I?"

Vonnie stood, still clutching her doll, and made her way to the kitchen, all the while saying, "That was different, Evie. Ruth Ann married Arnold McDonald, Summit View's golden boy." She stopped at the kitchen counter and turned to me. "Do you want anything? I've got some beef stew in the freezer I can microwave if you're hungry."

I stomped a foot. "I want the truth!"

"All right. I loved him. I loved him, I loved him, I loved him! God knows I loved him more than I've ever loved another human being my whole life . . . and yes, that includes Fred."

My hand flew over my mouth. How could she be married to a man she didn't love as much as her first husband? How could she share a bed with someone she wasn't able to give herself to completely? Maybe I wasn't as savvy in the love and sex department as I thought.

"If you're wondering if Fred knows, he does. He knows I loved Joe, he knows I married him, he knows I had a baby with him," she said quietly. "And," she added even more quietly, "he knows I lost it all."

I walked over to the kitchen table and pulled out a chair. "Well, Von, that's the part I don't understand."

Vonnie joined me at the table. "Are you willing to listen . . . to listen and not judge me?" she asked, setting Amanda Jewel in her lap as though she were a real child that could not be ignored or forgotten.

I looked at her for a good ten seconds before I answered. "Yes, I believe I am."

She told me the story—the whole story—of loving Joe, of marrying him, of losing him to the war. She told me about her mother's reaction to her pregnancy, of leaving for L.A. to live with Maria Jewel and learning to make Mexican tamales. She told me about the day she heard that Joe had been killed, about going into labor and giving birth, and then about her mother coming to tell her she'd lost the baby. "Why would I doubt her?" she concluded.

She was crying, and I was crying with her. "Have you spoken to your mother?"

"I have."

"And?"

"She's apologetic . . . begging for forgiveness . . . but . . . I need time, Evie."

"Of course you do. What about Maria Jewel?" I asked, but Vonnie only shook her head.

I fidgeted with the fringe of the woven place mat in front of me. "And Fred?"

Vonnie shrugged. "It's been difficult."

I couldn't look at her when I asked my next question. "What are you going to do about David Harris?"

I could feel the tension from all the way across the table. "He's my son and yet he's not. Did you know he was raised by that actress person?" I nodded, but I'm not sure she saw me. She continued, "He's my son and I don't even know him. Lord, what he must think of me."

I looked up then. "He came looking for you, didn't he? That must mean something. You owe it to yourself to see him . . . to talk to him. Vonnie, you owe it to yourself."

"We'll see. I have some praying to do on that matter, and I need to confer with Fred a little more, when he's not as emotional as he was this morning when we talked." Vonnie looked down. "What about the others, Evie? What do they know about all this?"

I waited for her to raise her chin and looked her in the eye. "Donna knows, but you know that." She nodded. "And Leigh knows. But to my knowledge, none of the other Potluckers have put it together."

"I don't know if Donna will ever forgive me."

I reached across the table and patted her hand. "Give it time. She's young."

"She feels betrayed. First Doreen," she said, sending a chill through me, "and now me."

I patted her hand again. "Give it time," I repeated. "One thing I can testify to is God's goodness where time is concerned."

Vonnie looked at me and smiled; it was a faint smile but a smile nonetheless. "Don't I know it. After all this time . . . I have a child. I have a son." She clutched Amanda Jewel to her breast. "My baby is alive."

41

She'll set you straight . . .

Clay's best attempts at following Donna were just that: attempts.
He'd covered nearly every street he could think to drive down but
hadn't seen her Bronco until some time later, heading back for her
bungalow.

He had managed to see Evangeline Benson's car parked in the
Westbrook driveway, not that it had anything to do with anything.
He smiled to himself though. Evangeline was probably setting
Vonnie straight on something or other.

Later that evening he watched several hours of mindless television. With each commercial he walked over to his desk, picked
up the PLC file, and flipped through it as though he were looking
for something, some clue, some single item in all his notes that
might give him an inkling as to what was going on with the ladies
of late.

But he found nothing.

Goldie

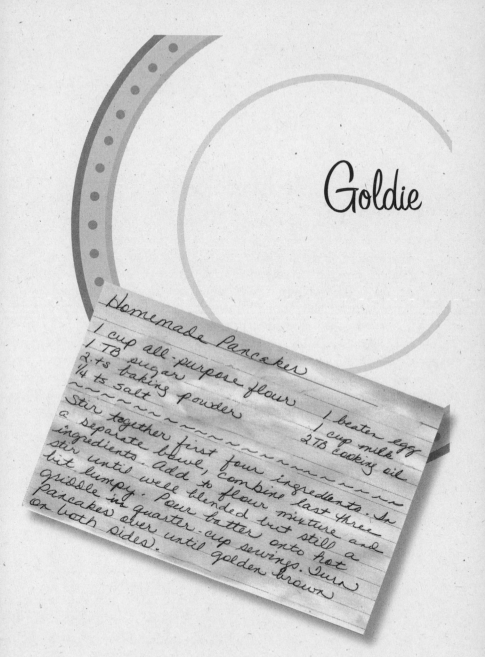

Homemade Pancakes

1 cup all-purpose flour
1 TB sugar
2 ts baking powder
1/4 ts salt
~ ~ ~ ~ ~ ~ ~ ~ ~
1 beaten egg
1 cup milk
2 TB cooking oil

Stir together first four ingredients. In a separate bowl, combine last three ingredients. Add to flour mixture and stir until well blended but still a bit lumpy. Pour batter onto hot griddle in quarter-cup servings. Turn pancakes over until golden brown on both sides.

42

Measured Steps

Olivia's morning sickness (that was really afternoon sickness) took a sudden turn for the worse on Tuesday afternoon, forcing her to ask me if I'd be willing to cook supper and clean up afterward. "That's why I'm here," I told her, and she gave me a look that read *No, that's not why you're here, but as long as you are . . .*

I cooked, served Tony and Brook, and checked in on Olivia, who napped fitfully in the master bedroom. Tony—stretched out in a blue leather recliner—watched television while I gave Brook his bath, dressed him, and then handed him off to his father, who then read him a story from *My First Bible Story Book* while I cleaned the kitchen. By the time we'd kissed Brook good night and I'd checked on my daughter one last time, I was too tired to do anything more than climb between the covers of the bed in what was now "Nana's Room." I hadn't closed my eyes more than a few minutes when the phone rang. Tony answered: "Oh, hi, Jack," followed by, "I think she's already gone to bed, but I'll check."

The closed door of my room cracked just enough to let in a muted shaft of light. I slammed my eyes shut, hoping Tony would assume I was asleep and not attempt to wake me, which is exactly what he did. When the door clicked shut, I reopened my eyes as though it would help me hear better.

"She is," I heard my son-in-law say, followed by, "No, I won't wake her for you, Jack. She's had a long day and she needs to rest . . . she's feeling a little sick and is in bed too . . . No, sir . . . No, sir . . . I will. Good night." I smiled, feeling blessed to have such a knight in shining armor, even if he was married to my daughter.

The following morning Olivia woke feeling well enough to get Brook ready for preschool. As soon as she left—leaving me alone in the house with a cup of coffee and the *Gold Rush News*—I curled up on the end of the sofa, spreading the paper out on the seat beside me. I read the article about Vonnie's dog and the bear, laughing out loud at the quote from Evangeline about Donna. *Lord, will those two ever have anything in common?*

I turned next to the classifieds, a one-page listing of houses for rent and for sale, lost and found items, legal notices, and—most importantly—employment. I'd never worked in my entire life, other than in my teen years back in the restaurant and at a medical office. There weren't any ads for medical clerks, and I was too old now for toting trays high over my head, too stressed to keep food orders in my head, so the "Wanted, Server" ad for Rosey's was out.

There were executive listings for Denver and Dillon, a few shops over in Vail and Breckenridge needing salesclerks. I could do that, I decided. I could sell stuff. I thought about the pay scale, wondered what minimum wage was now—which I'd make and which wasn't enough to put a roof over my head or food in my pantry. Maybe Lisa Leann was right. I needed an attorney.

My focus shifted from the employment ads to the advertisements. "Divorce Made Simple," one read. "Chris Lowe, Attorney at Law." Chris was the husband of Grace's pianist. Even thinking about Carrie caused me to flinch. Sunday I'd opted not to attend services at all, until I could make up my mind as to what to do.

I looked up to the wall clock. It was a little after 9:00; Olivia would be back any minute. I rose quickly, walked over to the phone at the bar, and dialed the number I'd read on the ad.

"Chris Lowe's office," a chipper voice said.

"Yes, hello. I . . . I need to set an appointment with Mr. Lowe, please."

"Your name?" the voice inquired.

I heard Olivia's car pulling into the garage. "Um, Goldie. Goldie Dippel."

"Oh, hello, Mrs. Dippel." I had no idea whom I was speaking with, and judging by the sound of Olivia's car door slamming, I didn't have time to find out.

"Yes, hello. I need to see Mr. Lowe as soon as possible."

Olivia was coming up the garage steps, closing the garage door using the remote control at the top.

"I can get you in early this afternoon if that works for you."

The back door opened. "It does, thank you. What time?" Olivia walked in, entering the laundry room off from the kitchen. I had a clear shot of her closing and securing the door with the dead bolt.

"Does 1:00 work for you?"

Olivia turned to see me with the phone pressed hard against my ear. "Hi, Mom."

I smiled at her. "Yes, that works fine for me," I spoke into the phone.

Olivia proceeded through the laundry room to the hall, which led to the back of the house.

"Do you know where we're located?" the voice asked.

"Main Street?"

"The corner of Main and Sixth. Across the street from the Church of Christ. We're on the second floor over the card shop."

"Thank you. I'll see you then." I replaced the receiver as quietly as I knew how, stepped lightly over to the sofa, and returned my attention to the paper still spread out before me.

Olivia entered just then. "Was that Dad on the phone?" she asked, sitting in Tony's recliner.

"No." I shook my head without looking over at her.

"Tony said he'd called last night but you were already asleep."

"Mmmhmm." I looked over at her. "Olivia, what do you think about my getting a job in Breckenridge in one of the little clothing stores?"

"Oh, Mom. Why don't you just wait to see what God allows?"

I looked back at the paper. "I'm not going to just sit and wait, Olivia. God provides, but he also expects us to work. He who does not work, does not eat," I said, quoting one of the verses found in Proverbs.

"But you don't need a real job; you're helping me out here." Out of the corner of my eye I saw her cross one leg over the other as if that settled that. "Just wait, okay? For me?"

I turned to look at her. "I can't do everything for you, Olivia. Some things I have to do for me. I need a job . . . no, I want a job. I want to feel useful to more than just my daughter or her husband or my grandson. Not that I'm not happy as a peach to help you, but I need to be my own person." I looked back at the paper. "For once in my life."

I stood on the sidewalk in front of the Alpine Card Shop at precisely 12:45, dressed in black slacks, a turquoise long-sleeved blouse, and a black jacket that did little to cut the cold coming in from down the mountains surrounding Summit View. Looking up, I saw an overhead window just below the Alpine-inspired façade jutting toward the blue sky. "Chris Lowe, Attorney at Law" was painted in picture-perfect lettering across the pane. I wondered how in the world I was supposed to get to the second floor. There didn't seem to be a door leading from the outside to the upstairs.

A customer exiting the card shop interrupted my silent wondering. "Hi, Goldie." I looked to see Carrie Lowe standing in front of me. I sighed, not needing this encounter. "Missed you on Sunday."

"Thank you," I said, hoping that just being polite would save me from having to say anything else.

"You didn't feel well?"

So much for not lying, Lord. "No, not really." Well, maybe not technically a lie.

"Going in the card shop?"

"Yes. Yes, I am." *I'm sorry, Lord. I don't mean to lie like this, but I'm just not ready for the whole world to know yet.*

Carrie smiled at me, tossing her long hair—secured by a large elastic band—over a shoulder. "Chris and I just came back from lunch over at the Pancake House," she continued, pointing to the card shop door.

285

"I was hoping to get him to go with me to Dillon this afternoon to look for new bedroom furniture, but he said he has a 1:00."

I felt my eyebrows rise. "Oh?"

She shrugged a shoulder. "Yeah. Oh, well. We'll go another time. I just had an itch, that's all."

I looked back up. "So that's where Chris's office is," I prodded her.

Carrie looked up too. "Yeah," she said, bringing her focus back to me. "The only thing I don't like about it is that you have to go through the card shop to get to it, and most of the time I can hardly get through it without finding some cute something or other for the house."

I smiled at her. "Well, let me get in there and see what I can find." *Sorry again, Lord, but you can consider this one an even exchange for the other line I thought was a lie. Apparently I am going into the card shop.*

I found a small staircase at the back of the card shop with a framed sign reading "Attorney's Office Upstairs" next to it. I took the steps deliberately, glancing down at my watch to check the time. I had only a few minutes before my appointment. I paused near the top step, thinking I could always turn right around and go back down. I didn't have to do this . . .

Ascending footsteps caused me to whirl around.

"Hi, Mrs. Dippel." It was the same voice I'd heard on the phone earlier, a voice I now recognized as belonging to Jenna Lowe, daughter of Chris and Carrie.

"Hello, Jenna." Jenna was a recent graduate of Summit View High; I remembered her as being one of Jack's star basketball players. "I didn't realize you worked for your father."

She smiled as she reached me, forcing me to continue my ascent into the attorney's office. "I've worked for Dad since I was in high school." She managed to step past me once we hit the landing. "You're just in time for your appointment. I'll let Dad know that you're here."

I took a seat in the nearest chair I could find, clutching my purse close to my abdomen. I crossed my legs, bobbed one foot up and down in time with the music coming from the overhead speaker, and looked about the room. There was a sofa table flush against a wall and covered in neatly stacked magazines—*Field and Stream, 4 Wheel Drive, Outside, Backcountry,* and *Skiing*—all the necessary periodicals for those who live in the high country, while only a Bible accessorized the coffee table in front of a forest green love seat. The walls were richly decorated with large matted prints of aerial-view snapshots photographed in Colorado.

"Mrs. Dippel?"

I jumped at the sound of Jenna's voice, standing and spilling my purse. "Oh, dear." I began to collect the various items rolling around on the floor.

"My dad is ready to see you now," Jenna continued.

I looked up at her, stuffing my purse with the retrieved escape artists, then stood straight and tall. "Thank you, Jenna."

I walked to the door she pointed to, entering to find a man I'd gone to church with for as many years as I'd been a citizen of Summit View. The interior of his office was pretty much the same as the outer office with the exception of the love seat. There was even a Bible opened on his desk. "Goldie," he greeted me, sunlight streaming in from the window behind him, nearly illuminating the white-blond hair he wore short and somewhat spiky. "Come in. Have a seat." He indicated a nearby chair, then returned to the one behind his desk. "How can I help you?"

I sighed deeply, allowing my shoulders to slump. "I've left Jack." Tears began to well up and spill down my cheeks. Chris stood and grabbed a box of tissues from a bookcase as he moved toward me. I took the entire box, saying, "Thank you," as he sat in the chair next to mine.

"Oh, Goldie," he said. "This is a part of my job I wish I never had to take part in. I know it hurts."

I nodded, blowing my nose as daintily as I knew how, considering how stuffed it had suddenly become. "I'm not saying I want a divorce, but I do need to know what my rights are. I have to think about financial support . . . things like that."

"Are you still at the house?"

"No. I'm staying with Olivia and Tony."

"I see. So you left the house."

"Yes." I looked him in the eye. "Is that bad?"

"No, no."

Chris stood and returned to his desk. "Goldie, is this because of Jack's . . ."

"Affairs? Yes."

"There's been more than one?" He picked up a pen and began to scribble on the yellow legal pad.

"There's been more than I can count. But," I looked down at my hands, "for the first time, Jack's seeing someone right here in Summit View." I looked back up to find my new attorney looking back at me. "I just can't live like this anymore."

Chris nodded, returning his attention to the pad. "Goldie, you've been married how many years?"

"Since 1975." I watched him make a notation on a yellow legal pad.

"Only one child?"

"Yes." Another jotting of notes.

"Can you tell me what Jack's annual salary is?"

I gave him the figure from last year's taxes. It probably wasn't anything close to what an attorney brought in, but it had kept us comfortable all these years.

"Have you ever worked outside the home since you were married, Goldie?"

"No," I said, "but I'm going to start looking for a job as soon as I leave here."

His head snapped to attention. "So this is serious enough for you to look for a job?"

I nodded. "It's serious enough for me to leave home, move in with my daughter, and then come to see you."

Chris leaned his forearms against the edge of the desk. "Had you ever worked before your marriage, Goldie?"

I nodded. "I waited tables in high school, then worked in a medical office for two years after that. Before I married Jack."

He rested his chin in the palm of his hand, causing the roundness of his cheeks to become rounder still. "Would you be interested in

288

working here? For me?" He sat up straight. "I know that's not why you came here, but Jenna has finally decided to go off to college in January, and I'll be in need of someone. We can work something out as far as my fee for representing you, and in addition I'll pay you twelve dollars an hour. Six months and I'll offer you a raise if you're still working out for me."

I swallowed. "I appreciate that, Chris. But I . . . I was also wondering about Jack financially supporting me . . ."

Chris chuckled. "Oh, don't you worry about that, Goldie. Jack's going to have to support you. You've got too many years invested in the marriage for him not to. The law requires it."

I sighed in relief. "Then I'd love to take you up on your offer." I pressed my hand to my chest, felt my heart pounding beneath the surface. "I'm not trying to take Jack for all he's worth, Chris."

"I know that, Goldie."

"But if I'm going to do this, I need to be able to support myself in every way possible."

"Can you start on Monday—allowing Jenna to train you for a couple of months? You'll be working Monday through Friday, 8:30 to 4:00. Wednesday's are different, though. You'll get off at noon. No weekends. How does that sound?"

I pressed my lips together, then smiled. "It sounds like a new beginning."

43

A working woman
after all these years . . .

Clay walked into the card shop. His mother's birthday was coming up, and he figured the least he could do was send her a card and maybe one of the little whatnots from the store. He and his mother had always been close, though they'd never showered each other with trinkets. But over the past couple of years he'd been able to give himself an A for effort in the gift-giving department.

Just as he entered, he saw Goldie Dippel coming through the door leading to the staircase, which led up to Chris Lowe's office. *Interesting,* he thought.

"Mrs. Dippel," he greeted her with a nod of his head and a dip of his cap.

"Clay!" She was visibly flushed.

He reached for a seasonal card and opened it, though he didn't really read it. "You okay, Mrs. Dippel?"

She wrapped her arms around herself. "I'm doing quite well, actually." She then smiled. "I just got a new job. Can you believe that? Me? Working after all these years?"

"I heard about you and Coach," he said, replacing the card. "Sorry to hear it."

Goldie Dippel touched his arm with her hand. "Don't be," she said. "I'd be sorrier to hear that I'd stayed."

Donna

EGG SALAD SANDWICH

6 HD-BOILED EGGS - CHOPPED FINE   1/2 tps. DRY MUSTARD
6 Tbs. MINCED CELERY   SALT & PEPPER
1 Tbs. SWEET PICKLE RELISH   1/2 CUP MAYO
2 Tbs. FREEZE-DRIED PARSLEY   2 Tbs. BACON BITS

MIX CHOPPED EGGS, CELERY, PICKLE
RELISH, PARSLEY, DRY MUSTARD, &
SALT & PEPPER (TO TASTE) IN BOWL.
STIR IN MAYO AND BACON BITS
REFRIGERATE TILL READY TO SERVE.
SPREAD ON BREAD. TOP WITH BREAD
SLICE.

44

Hashing Out the Meeting

It was 7:00 in the morning, and I was dressed in my uniform and getting ready for work. Thoughts of Vonnie kept seeping into my mind as I spread my egg salad onto toasted whole-wheat bread. I knew I should feel sorry for her, but I couldn't help but feel sorry for me. Vonnie was like my mother, more than my mother, she was like an angel, so I had thought. And to see her without her halo made me feel as if life no longer held anything for me. I mean, it wasn't wrong for her to marry Joseph Jewel. But it was wrong for her to keep it a secret from Fred, from me. In my opinion, that woman had been living a lie. And if Vonnie was a liar, then what was left? Truth? Ha! God? Humph. Nothing. Nothing was left. Learning of Vonnie's double life made me feel as if hope had just left on the last train to sanity, a train I had missed.

The phone rang, interrupting my thoughts. "Hello." My voice sounded even more monotone than usual.

"Donna, dear, is that you?" Vonnie sounded like she had a bad case of the flu.

"Yes."

"Donna, about my son."

Oh boy. "What about him?"

"Did you meet him?"

I sighed deeply. "I did."

"What was he like?"

I popped the plastic lid onto my container of egg salad and placed it back into the refrigerator. "I don't know, Vonnie. He seemed nice enough. He's a paramedic in L.A."

She sounded awestruck. "He's in medicine, like me."

I opened my drawer and pulled out my plastic sandwich bags. "I suppose that's true."

"I'm thinking of calling him. But I don't know. Fred's having a hard time with this news."

"That's understandable. I'm having a little trouble with it myself."

I could hear the pain in her voice. "Oh. Donna, I'm so sorry. I've hurt you too."

"I won't lie to you. This is the last thing I expected from you. To cover up your past, I mean. It makes me feel like you're not the person I thought you were."

"I guess I deserve that." She sighed. "I was wrong. Now, I'd like to make things right. But I need your help."

I tucked my sandwich into the plastic bag and dropped the bag into a small brown paper sack. "What can I do?"

"Could you call him? Arrange a meeting?"

"Sure, Vonnie, I can do that." I poured the remains of my fresh pot of coffee into my thermos. "I'll call him later today and see what he wants to do."

Vonnie sounded relieved. "Thank you, dear."

"No problem."

"And dear, I'm really sorry that I hurt you."

Later, on patrol, I stopped by a display for the *Gold Rush News* and got a fresh copy of the paper. The issues were good for a week, so it was still easy to find. I carried the paper back to my Bronco and skimmed through the article about the "missing Jewel" until I found the number. I dialed it on my cell phone.

When it rang, an answering machine picked up. "You've reached the home of David Harris. I can't come to the phone right now, but I'll be checking in for my messages, so leave your number."

"David? This is Deputy Donna Vesey from Summit View, Colorado. I've found Jewel. Call me for details." I left my number, hung up, and replayed his message in my mind. He must live alone. He didn't make any mention of a female counterpart or family.

I frowned. What did we really know about this guy? He could be some mass murderer. I'd make him play twenty questions before I'd let him near Vonnie.

After I ate my lunch in the church parking lot, a great place to hide from constant public scrutiny, I discovered my thermos was empty. I decided I'd stop by Higher Grounds for a fresh cup.

I took in my cell phone, just in case David should call back. I regretted my decision as soon as I saw Clay at his usual spot. Didn't that man ever leave?

"Hi, Clay."

He gave me a playful grimace. "Deputy. Are we still friends?"

I gave him a halfhearted smile. I didn't need to make an enemy of the local press, even if it was just Clay Whitefield. "I suppose. Sorry for the outburst."

Clay turned around in his chair and studied me. "Donna, I hate to ask, but you've got my curiosity up. Just who are you trying to protect?"

"Now, Clay, I told you I can't talk about it."

He looked disappointed. "Well, if you change your mind, you know where to find me."

I nodded and sat down at the counter. Sal instantly appeared. "Cup of coffee," I said before I realized she was already pouring me a cup. Was my routine that predictable? Just as I took my first sip, my cell rang.

"Deputy Vesey, it's David Harris."

I looked over my shoulder and saw that I had Clay's full attention. I didn't think he could hear David's voice, but he could hear mine.

"I've been expecting your call."

David's voice was full of hope. "You say you have information about my mother?"

"Could be. However, it's someone I happen to care about. So I'd like to ask you to tell me about yourself."

Holy cow, is Clay taking out his notepad? I stood abruptly. "Hang on." I turned to Sal. "Official business; I've got to take this call in my vehicle. Save my spot, will you?"

My eyes locked with Clay's on my way out. *That dog. He knows I'm talking to David Harris.*

I slipped into my Bronco and said, "I can talk now. So, here's my first question: are you any kind of pervert?"

"Ah, noooo."

"Do you have any steady relationships?"

"As in women? Well, my fiancée and I broke up not that long ago, so with Harmony gone, I've just got my buddies at work."

"I see. What about bad habits? Tell me about those."

"Not much to tell, I guess. I see what drugs, drinking and driving can do to those poor souls I've scraped off the freeway, so I'm not really into that."

"But are you a nice person?"

"Deputy, why these questions? You sound like you're screening me for a date."

I felt my face color. "Sir, I've just got a very delicate situation here, and quite frankly, I'm not too happy that you went to the press with this. It's caused a lot of heartache."

"That certainly wasn't my intention."

"Really? Exactly what were your intentions?"

"It's just that I'm at a place in life where everyone who has meant something to me has died or is dating my best friend. So, I'm feeling kinda lost, you know? I'm feeling like I've got to find myself, and the best place to start is to try to find my roots."

His fiancée took off with his best friend? "Bummer." I paused. *Okay, he sounds decent enough.* "Your mother, Vonnie, wants to meet you."

"Her name isn't Jewel?"

"No, that was her married name at the time of your birth."

"She and my dad were married? I kinda figured my mother was single."

"She was married, and she loved your dad."

"You mean my dad is still alive?"

295

"No, David. And Vonnie's remarried. Her new husband never knew about you or her previous marriage, until Vonnie read the article in the paper and she told him about it all."

"I see."

"She called me earlier today. She wants to know when you could return to Summit View."

He sounded excited. "I could be there by Saturday afternoon."

"Okay, call me when you get into town."

After I hung up with David, I called Vonnie back. "Vonnie, I've got news. You'll be meeting David Saturday night."

45

She'll beat you
at your own game . . .

Clay slapped his notepad back into his pocket, but not before he took down a few notes. Whoever called Donna, he had no doubt it had to do with the "missing jewel."

He watched her through the window of the café as she finished her call. It seemed she was asking a lot of questions. Making a lot of cryptic statements, none of which he could make out.

She ended the call, then made another, this time ducking her head so he couldn't make out the name of the person to whom she was speaking.

That little sneak, he thought. But she'd have to get up earlier than this if she thought to beat him at the detective game.

Evangeline

Cheese Enchiladas with Chili Sauce

Ingredients for Chili Sauce:

1½ pounds lean ground beef
½ cup chopped onion
2 tsp garlic powder
1½ tsp salt powder
1 tsp pepper
8 cups beef broth or bouillon
2 cans whole peeled tomatoes
3 Tbs. chili powder
1 Tbs. plus 1½ tsp. paprika
1 Tbs. ground cumin

46

Spicy Encounters

I had a mountain of work sitting on my desk on Thursday morning, and I was thankful for it. I needed something to keep my mind off everything that had happened in the past few days and weeks around Summit View. It seemed to me that with the arrival of Leigh at my front door that dark evening in September, life had simply turned upside down.

After a fitful night, I awoke Friday morning to the sound of enough clatter emitting from my kitchen to wake the dead. I sat up in bed, reaching for my mint-green, worn-completely-out-in-places chenille robe I'd bought sometime back in the eighties and I refuse to throw away. I drew my arms into the sleeves as I slipped into my bedroom slippers, then shuffled out the room, down the stairs, and to the kitchen.

Leigh had nearly every pot and pan from my cabinets perched haphazardly on the countertops. The water from the tap was streaming into the sink, various foods were set out on the kitchen table, and something—although I don't know what—appeared to be cooking on the stovetop. Leigh was scrubbing the bottom of a Corningware dish with a scrub pad, working so furiously one would think her life depended on it.

"What in the world . . . ?"

Leigh turned slightly from the sink. "Hi, Aunt Evie," she called over her shoulder, chipper as could be.

"What in the world!" I repeated.

Leigh smiled at me. "My pregnancy book says this is called 'nesting.'"

I walked over to the sink and turned the water down a bit. "Nesting?"

"Mmmhmm. It's when the mother-to-be has this sudden urge to clean everything, to get it ready for the baby's arrival." She threw the scrubbie on the ledge of the sink, then began to rinse the dish. "I woke up this morning with this urge to clean, clean, clean." She winked at me. "You keep everything so spotless around here, what I'm really doing is just recleaning, I guess you could say."

I turned to the stove. "And what's all this?"

"I also woke up with a craving for enchiladas, like the kind Maristela makes." Maristela has been Peg's cook since the boys were little.

I placed my hands on my hips and peered into a large Dutch oven with sauce simmering in it. "What, you just happened to have her recipe?"

Leigh pulled a dish towel from a chrome hanger near the sink and began drying the dish, flipping it one way and then the other. "I called home and got it."

I turned to look at her. "You called . . . you called home?"

She handed me the Corningware. "See? Sparkly as the day you bought it."

"Did you speak to your mother?"

"She answered." Leigh waddled past me to stir the sauce with a long wooden spoon resting nearby.

I placed the Corningware on the counter. "And?"

"And . . . we talked." She said the words as though she'd spoken to just anyone.

"Leigh, you've pretty much refused to talk to Peg and Matthew since you got here. Don't act like this is just any phone call."

Leigh laid the spoon down, waddled back over to the sink, and began to scrub another dish. "It was good, Aunt Evie. We talked for about five minutes . . . which, right now, is about all I can take of Mom."

301

"She's called me, you know."

"I know. She told me. She also said she asked you not to tell me. What's that all about?"

I shook my head. "She's just hurt, is all." I looked over to the coffeepot, which was half filled with fresh coffee. "I need caffeine."

"Sit down," Leigh said. "Let me get you a cup."

I complied. "So, you talked to your mother and got Maristela's recipe."

"Yep." Leigh placed a steaming cup of coffee in front of me. "I'll get the cream and sugar for you."

"Thank you." I watched her from over my shoulder. "How long does this nesting last?"

She opened and closed the refrigerator door, then set the creamer on the table before me. "I have no idea. I hope not for long, though, because this could get exhausting."

I decided to go back to the old subject. "Did Peg ask you about coming home?"

"I told her I'd talked with Gary," she answered, now placing the sugar bowl and a spoon before me. "And that I would not be making any decisions until after the baby is born." Leigh sat in the chair next to mine. "She's still more concerned about what the stupid neighbors are going to think or the women in her Junior League or whatever than she is about me."

I pointed the spoon at her. "That's not true, Leigh Banks. Your mother loves you very much and is very worried about you."

Leigh rose from her chair. "Ugh. Can we talk about something else, please?"

I sighed deeply. "Sure."

I heard the water being turned on behind me. "What's on your agenda for today?" she asked.

"I have some errands to run."

"Need company?"

I stared into the cup of coffee. "Not today."

Leigh turned. "What's going on?"

I looked over at my wise young niece. "I have some issues to settle," I said with a weak smile.

"You've got issues, all right." Her voice held the lilt of a tease. "Want to share?"

"Not really." I took a sip of coffee.

"Oh, come on! I tell you everything."

"No, you don't."

"Well, I would if you asked." She played a little stomping game with her feet. "Aunt Evieeeeeee. Tell meeeeeeee."

I stood, pushed the chair back under the table, and said, "I'll tell you when I get home, how's that?"

"You're a wicked woman, but I love ya." She threw a kiss at me by smacking at the air. I returned the gesture, then left to get ready for what could prove to be one of the most important days of my life.

I drove slowly down the winding driveway of All Saints Cemetery, the cold headstones forming a blur of silvery white on either side of the car. A multitude of vases filled with colorful silk flowers dotted the landscape. I passed the groundskeeper's cottage on my left. To the far right and up a hill was a white stone statue of Christ extending his arms slightly. Four or five fluffy sheep gathered around his sandaled feet, pressing into the folds of his robe. "Come to Me," read the caption etched into the granite beneath. "All Ye Who Are Weary and Heavy Laden and I Will Give You Rest."

I stopped my car nearby, waited a few moments before shutting off the engine, then opened the door. I continued to sit for a while, allowing the crisp late-October air to work its way into the Camry until I was forced to move.

Gravel crunched beneath my feet. My hands formed small balls as I wrapped my arms around myself; I was cold, not so much from the weather as the locale. I hated this place. I hated death. In some strange way, I even hated life.

I made my way up the grassy slope toward a headstone I'd long ignored. "Benson" it read. "Minerva Warren, Beloved Wife & Mother" on the left side. "Daniel Robert, Beloved Husband & Father" on the right side. Just under Daddy's name, in smaller lettering, was "Honorable Mayor of Summit View, Colorado."

Bits of dead grass had managed to find their way into the etching of letters. I bent down and blew, watching the bits fly up, then lie on the marble slab over the graves. I brushed the grass away with the palm of my hand, then stood, shoving my hands into the pockets of my coat. "Hey, Mama. Daddy," I said, then looked around to see if anyone else might be lingering about. I was completely alone. Just several hundred dead souls and me.

"I know I haven't been here in a while." I looked around again, then back to the slab. "I need to bring some new flowers out here, don't I? These are a little faded. I'll bring out an autumn arrangement next week." I sighed, as though waiting for an answer, then let a quick laugh escape me. "Oh, I can just hear you now, Mama. 'Evangeline Benson, how dare you let us lay out here for so long forgotten?' I'm sorry. I've not been mad with you or anything." I glanced farther down the path, nearer still to the statue of the Good Shepherd. "I've just been angry with Ruth Ann. That's really why I'm here, but I thought I'd stop by . . ." I paused. "This is so stupid. I can't believe I'm talking to you like this." I looked around again, then back down. "You couldn't help it that you got killed; I know that." Tears formed in my eyes, slipping down my cheeks. "Well, then. Um." I swallowed. "Daddy, I'm still working hard. And the house is holding up well." I took a step back. "I love you both. We didn't say that a lot when I was growing up, but I want you to know that I always have loved you . . . and I'll talk to you both later." I continued to back away until I'd returned to the path. I turned myself to the left, then proceeded up until I reached the headstone I'd not bothered to look at in many years.

"Hello, Ruth Ann." The wind picked up a few fallen aspen leaves that whirled about me. I shivered in the cold.

Arnold—or perhaps it had been one of their children—had placed a white wrought-iron bench near Ruth Ann's grave. I sat down on it, feeling the icy chill rush through me as I stared at her headstone until my eyes burned from not blinking. I would not cry . . . I would not cry. "How could you have left me?" I whispered, closing my eyes and resting against the back of the bench.

I felt more than heard something moving next to me. My eyes flew open. Ruth Ann, dressed in her favorite pink suit—the very one Arnold had buried her in—stood beside the bench. I jumped up so quickly I lost my step, coming back down hard to the bench on my rear end. I found my equilibrium and stood back up, taking several steps away from the apparition smiling at me. "Hello, Evangeline."

I pointed to the ghost. "You stay away from me, Ruth Ann McDonald." I turned my head from the left to the right and back to the left again. Could anyone see this besides me?

"No one here but us," she toyed.

"I'm not speaking to you," I said, pointing to her.

She smiled again. "Then why are you here?"

"To tell you I'm angry with you."

"Because?" She raised a perfectly arched brow.

"You left me! You left me in this awful place all alone!"

"What's so awful about it, Evie?"

"What's so awful about it? I'll tell you what's so awful about it. You were my best friend. We did everything together. There was nothing left for me when you left."

Ruth Ann took a step toward me. "Nothing? Seems to me you've done pretty well keeping yourself busy. The Potluck Club has flourished, I hear."

I threw up my arms. "What a motley crew we are. Lizzie's doing well, I suppose, but Goldie's left Jack, Donna Vesey gives me grief at nearly every meeting, Vonnie apparently married some man back in college who got killed in Vietnam but not before he got her pregnant, and she had the baby, thought he'd died, but now he's come to Summit View looking for her and God only knows if she'll even talk to him. You can just imagine what this has done to her relationship with Fred, not to mention with her mother, who apparently knew that the baby lived, but didn't want—"

Ruth Ann raised her hand. "I know all this, Evie."

"You do?"

She nodded. "How's Leigh?"

"You know about Leigh?"

She nodded again. "And Jan Moore and Lisa Leann Lambert."

I walked over to the bench and sat down. "Oh, Ruth Ann. Why haven't you been here to pray with me? What a mess we all live in down here."

Ruth Ann joined me on the bench, her body not touching mine. She looked straight ahead, hands folded in her lap, as she said, "You've been meeting to pray all these years, Evangeline. You, Lizzie, Goldie." She turned her head to look at me. "Von, Donna, and now Lisa Leann." She smiled a closed-lip smile. "You've got quite the little prayer group going, but you've forgotten to invite one very important person."

I furrowed my brow, unable to think of a single woman from Summit View who should be a part of our group. "Who?" I asked.

"You've forgotten to invite God." Ruth Ann shifted a bit, holding up a hand to stop the outburst she knew would fly out of my mouth. "Hear me out, Evangeline. When was the last time you truly prayed about anything? In faith?"

The tears I'd tried to keep at bay rose and spilled over again. "When I prayed for you to live." I jumped up. "Why'd you have to go and die on me, Ruth Ann McDonald?"

Ruth Ann remained seated. "Are you angry with me, Evangeline? Or God?"

I stomped around for a few good seconds before answering, "I'm mad with you both." I looked her in the eyes, realizing for the first time that she wasn't wearing those old, large-framed glasses . . . knowing her vision was crystal clear. My shoulders fell; my head bowed. "How could you?" I whispered. "I prayed so hard. How could God not have heard me? How could you have given up so easily?" I fell to my knees before her and began to sob.

Ruth Ann rose and walked over toward me. No sound came from her footsteps, but through my veil of tears I could see her tiny bare feet approaching. She stopped just in front of me. "God heard you, Evangeline. You prayed I would be healed, and I was." My shoulders shook almost violently from the flow of tears. "I've never felt so good in my life as I have in my death."

306

I looked up to see her smiling at me. "Shut up, Ruth Ann Mc-Donald," I said, suddenly hearing laughter forcing its way from way down inside of me. Ruth Ann knelt before me, laughing just as hard.

"Oh, Evie," she said, sobering. "You're still such a character."

I sat back on my rear end, rested my forearms on my knees, and looked around the serenity of the place. "Lizzie says there are five healings: a healing of the attitude, the natural immune system, medical science, miracles, and death."

"Lizzie always was the smart one."

I cut my eyes over to her. "What's it like up there?"

She smiled at me again. "It's pure heaven," she answered, and I rolled my eyes. "Well, you asked."

I sighed. "I surely did."

We sat for a few more minutes in complete silence; I'm not sure what Ruth Ann was thinking, but I was reflecting on the fact that life and death were such strange creatures. Goldie's marriage was dying, but her daughter was pregnant again. Our pastor's wife was battling cancer, but my niece was bringing life into the world.

"Hey," Ruth Ann said from beside me. "Do me a favor, okay?"

"If I can."

"When you leave here, go see Jan Moore. Spend time with her now . . . while you can."

"What do you mean, while I can?"

"The end of every day is filled with missed opportunities, Evangeline. Don't miss the opportunity to spend time with a really fine woman of God. Not so much for her but for you."

I bit my bottom lip. "All right. I will."

"Good. Now, then. Close your eyes."

"Why?"

"Don't question the dead, Evangeline. Just do it."

I closed my eyes and listened only to the silence around me. From somewhere, way far off, I thought I heard traffic; but it could have just as easily been the wisp of an angel's wings.

"Proverbs 3:5 says that if we trust in the Lord with all our heart and lean not on our own understanding, and in all our ways acknowledge him, he will direct our paths. Say that with me," she coaxed.

I did. I repeated the familiar Scripture three or four times until I realized I was no longer saying it with Ruth Ann but alone. I kept my eyes closed, sighing deeply. I was ready, I decided. Sitting in this place of death, I was ready to face Jan Moore. I was ready to face life.

"Evangeline?"

I opened my eyes quickly. I was no longer sitting on the ground but on the bench where I'd first closed my eyes. I was chilled to the bone, and Vernon Vesey was standing before me—one hand resting on the butt of his gun and the other hand on the bullet packs clipped to his belt. He wore his black leather officer's jacket; the sun glinted off the five points of his badge and danced in the coolness of his eyes. He tugged at the brim of his uniform cap. "Evangeline, are you all right?"

I looked around quickly. Ruth Ann was nowhere in sight, and I knew I'd only dreamed our conversation. But this apparition—my old friend Vernon—was real. "I'm fine, Vernon Vesey." I sat up straight as I spoke.

Vernon nodded toward the front of the cemetery. "I got a call from the groundskeeper. He was a little concerned about you sitting up here all alone for so long. Thought you might've had a heart attack or something."

"No. No heart attack. A heart transplant, maybe, but no heart attack."

Vernon frowned. "Say what?"

I patted the bench beside me. "Have a seat, Vernon Vesey. I have a question for you."

Vernon sat, the leather he wore pulling and stretching as he did so. He had put on a few pounds since we were kids.

I turned to look at him. "Answer this for me, will you? What was so special about Doreen McDaniel?"

Vernon shook his head. "Oh, heaven's above, Evangeline. Are you still singing that tired old song?"

I squared my shoulders. "I want to know. I need to know." I jutted my chin toward him. "Quite honestly, I believe I deserve to know."

Vernon turned enough to face me. "Evangeline, I was all of twelve years old. Boys twelve years old will do nearly anything when it comes to trying to . . . well, you know." I'm not sure, but I think he blushed. "Twelve-year-old boys like to think they've gotten to first base, if you don't mind my being so crude." He smiled at me with a hint of mischief. "Oh, that Doreen. She knew what she wanted from early on, didn't she? I suppose I was powerless to resist her wily ways."

I butted Vernon's shoulder with my own. "You got every bit of what you deserved in the end, if you ask me."

Seriousness brushed across his face. "I got Donna. That's the most important thing."

I nodded, turning to face forward. When I did, Vernon wrapped an arm around my shoulder, pulling me to him, then drew us both to rest on the back of the bench. He crossed his legs at the ankles, and I allowed myself to relax in his embrace. We sat like this for a few minutes before he broke the silence.

"Ruth Ann McDonald," he said. "Now there was a good kisser."

I jerked my head to look up at him, realizing immediately that he was teasing me with a lie. "Vernon Vesey, don't you dare talk ill of the dead."

Vernon reached up, ran a finger down the length of my nose, then up to remove his cap. "Evie-girl," he said softly. "I'm going to do something I've wanted to do since I was a boy." I felt his arm pulling me closer to him. "I'm going to kiss you like you've never been kissed before . . . and when I'm done, I just may kiss you again." We were so close I could smell the morning's coffee on his breath. "And then you know what you're going to do?"

I shook my head no.

"You're going to go home, get dressed, and I'm going to take you to dinner. After that . . . who knows?"

I closed my eyes, felt his lips against mine. It was—how did Ruth Ann put it?—pure heaven. *Vernon doesn't kiss like a chicken anymore,* I thought ridiculously. And then I wrapped my arms around his neck, for God and Ruth Ann and Mama and Daddy and all of Summit View to behold.

47

That woman is
a legendary kisser . . .

Well, I just wish you'd look at that, Clay Whitefield thought as he sat in his rundown jeep, parked just beyond the cemetery and well out of view.

He flipped open his notebook, scribbling thoughts and ideas as quickly as he could, then began to jot questions needing to be answered if he were ever going to write the story of the ladies of the Potluck.

Questions like: was the legend of Evangeline Benson and Vernon Vesey even accurate? Maybe their ill-fated prepubescent love affair hadn't ended with just one kiss. From the looks of things on the hillside, Clay would say those two might have been carrying on behind the backs of the good people of Summit View.

If that were true, could there be a possible tie-in with David Harris? Maybe he was their "love child." Maybe his original suspicions were way off track.

He shook his head. *Wait a minute, Whitefield. Harris has some Hispanic heritage . . .*

Did that mean, then, that Evangeline Benson may have been involved with someone else? Someone her parents would not have approved of way back in the love era of the sixties?

And—if so—who would be the one person most likely to know the answer to that question?

Clay snorted as he flipped the fraying cover of his notebook shut. "Well, that doesn't take a genius to figure out," he spoke into the cool air. He shifted in his seat and turned the key in the ignition, then shot a glance back up to where Vernon Vesey and Evangeline Benson were still hot in an embrace.

He breathed a sigh of relief. They hadn't heard the start of the jeep. He shifted the gearshift into reverse, backed up about a foot, then swung out onto the road. Sheer determination set the expression of his face.

With any luck Donna would be back at the café. With any luck the turning point of his story about the ladies was just at his fingertips, especially since he knew firsthand that Harris was coming back to town.

Donna

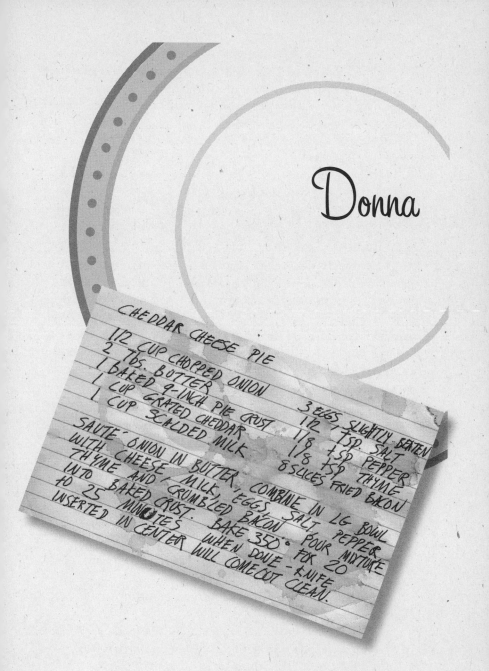

CHEDDAR CHEESE PIE

1/2 cup chopped onion
2 Tbs. butter
1 baked 9-inch pie crust
1 cup grated cheddar
1 cup scalded milk

3 eggs, slightly-beaten
1/2 tsp. salt
1/8 tsp pepper
1/8 tsp thyme
8 slices fried bacon

Saute onion in butter. Combine in lg bowl with cheese, milk, eggs, salt, pepper, thyme and crumbled bacon. Pour mixture into baked crust. Bake 350° for 20 to 25 minutes. When done - knife inserted in center will come out clean.

48

Half-Baked Attempt

As Clay's jeep was nowhere in sight, I'd decided to treat myself to a slice of Sal's cheddar cheese pie before the fun and games began. I ate my last bite still warmed from Sal's microwave and took a swig of what remained of my iced tea. I checked my clipboard. David was due in at DIA at 1300 hours, 1:00 civilian time, arriving on Frontier Flight 381. It took about three hours to get through the airport, the rental car agency, and up I-70 to this part of the high country, so I figured I'd get a call from him as soon as he got settled in the Gold Rush Bed and Breakfast. I checked my watch. As it was approaching 1630 hours, or 4:00 p.m., his call could come at any moment.

To my chagrin, Clay pulled up to the café in his old jeep. The bell above the door announced his arrival. "Good afternoon, Deputy Donna," Clay said as he walked in. He turned to Sal.

"The usual?" she asked as he nodded his head and sat down next to me at the counter.

"Got any news for me, Donna?"

I wiped my mouth with my napkin and turned to him. "Can't say that I do."

He gave me a sly grin. "A lot of intrigue going on around here, I'm told."

I pulled out my wallet and reached for a ten spot. "Well, then maybe you're the one who should be telling me what's new."

He leaned closer. "I've talked to David Harris."

I felt the color drain from my face. "Oh yeah? What did David have to say?"

"Well, now, that's actually confidential. However, I hear something is going down this afternoon. Right?"

I stood abruptly. "I don't know what you're talking about." I walked over to the register and gave Sal the ten. She handed me my change, and I walked back to the counter to leave the tip. "So, what are you planning to do, run an exposé on all this nonsense?"

Clay's eyes shone. "Something like that."

Without another word, I turned and left the café. *How could David call Clay? Had he given Clay Vonnie's name? I'm pretty sure I hadn't given David Vonnie's full name. But for gosh sakes, how many Vonnies live in Summit View?*

My cell rang as I climbed into my Bronco.

"Deputy, it's David. I'm at the hotel. Go ahead and call Vonnie and let her know she can meet me in room 109; it's a suite with a little sitting area."

"Not so fast," I said, feeling steamed. "I'm coming over to talk to you."

"Is everything okay?"

"That's what I'm going to find out."

I roared my truck through the heart of town and pulled into the driveway of the bed and breakfast. It was charming, really. A Swiss-alpine-styled Victorian, painted gray with white shutters and trim. Flower boxes filled with plastic red geraniums lined every spectacular leaded glass window. Lilly Deval, the owner and proprietor, had mothered this old mansion to this state of glory, decorating each room in period furniture and vintage-like wallpaper. I whipped into the driveway and found David Harris standing outside, waiting for my arrival.

"What's wrong, Deputy?" he called to me as I climbed out of the truck.

"That's just what I want to know." I walked up to him, standing toe-to-toe. "You've been talking to Clay Whitefield?"

He looked sheepish. "Well, he called me as soon as I talked to you yesterday. Said he'd heard I'd found my mother."

"That dog. He was eavesdropping on our conversation. But the big question is, what did you say to him? Did you give him Vonnie's name?"

"No! Since you said there'd been trouble, I decided not to tell him anything. But he does know I'm back in town. He saw me when I drove past the newspaper office."

Holy cow. I looked up and saw Clay drive past in his jeep. He tossed me a merry wave. That man was stalking me, and I had led him right to the site of the reunion.

I pushed David into the shadows. "Okay, change of plans. I cannot allow Vonnie's nightmare to become public."

"Nightmare?" David looked crestfallen. "Finding me is a nightmare?"

I looked at him hard then. Here David was, expecting to find someone to love, and he was suddenly faced with the worst possible rejection. On some level, I felt for him. After all, I'd been abandoned by my mother too. I can't imagine what I'd say to her if she suddenly showed up on my doorstep.

"David, I don't think it's you that's causing her pain. She didn't even know you existed."

"Now that just doesn't make sense. A woman knows if she's had a baby or not."

"It would seem so, wouldn't it? But I'll let her tell you all about it herself. However, first things first. We've got to come up with another plan. That was Clay who just drove by, and something tells me he didn't come without his camera."

He squinted against the afternoon sun as he looked down the street. "Clay is here?"

"I'm guessing he's parked not too far away, waiting to see who shows up. Quick, hop in my Bronco and let's see if he follows."

As I grabbed David's arm, I realized that Wade was standing at the front door of the hotel, his toolbox in his hand. I hadn't even noticed his truck. Lilly must have sent for him to do some repairs. I acknowledged him. "Hello, Wade."

Wade looked incensed. "Hello, Deputy. You and your boyfriend checking in?"

"Official business."

Wade gave me a sarcastic glare. "Oh, I see."

Ignoring him, David and I hopped into the truck and peeled out of the parking lot. I checked in my rearview mirror. Sure enough, Clay's jeep pulled out of a parking spot just down the block.

I reached for my cell phone and dialed Vonnie. "Sorry, Von, the meeting's been called off for tonight. We'll try again tomorrow."

49

That girl is always
one step ahead . . .

Clay knew when he'd been licked, even temporarily. He turned his jeep around and headed back toward his apartment. He parked, hurried up the stairs, then closed the door of his place firmly behind him. Woodward and Bernstein came to life, peering up at him with glassy eyes.

"Bad night?" he asked them.

Woodward waggled his whiskers at him.

"Well, you should've been with me today," he continued, throwing his notepad on the nearby desk. He reached for the boys' pet food, opened the cage, and gave them their nightly treat. "Ever hear the old saying, 'So close and yet so far away'? Well, that pretty much says it all for me. Donna was one step ahead this time."

He closed the lid. "But don't you worry, guys," he said, brushing the remaining crumbs from his fingertips. "Daddy's got a Plan B." He winked. "And it's a beaut!"

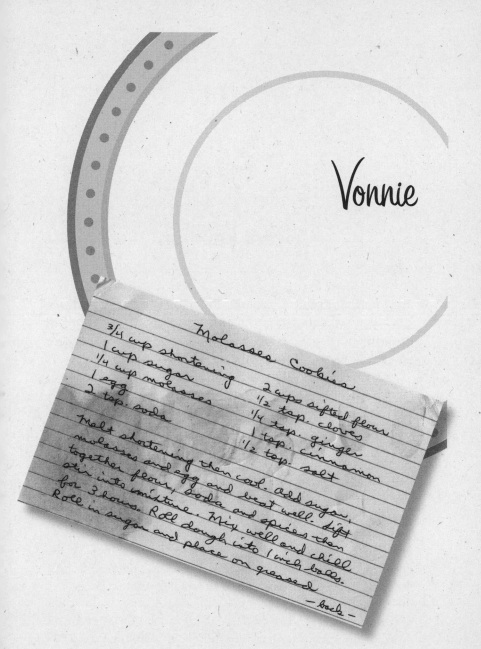

Vonnie

Molasses Cookies

3/4 cup shortening   2 cups sifted flour
1 cup sugar   1/2 tsp. cloves
1/4 cup molasses   1/4 tsp. ginger
1 egg   1 tsp. cinnamon
2 tsp. soda   1/2 tsp. salt

Melt shortening then cool. Add sugar,
molasses and egg and beat well. Sift
together flour, soda and spices then
stir into mixture. Mix well and chill
for 3 hours. Roll dough into 1 inch balls.
Roll in sugar and place on greased

— back —

50

Sweet Reunion

I was stunned at Donna's news that our meeting was off. Goodness, didn't that girl know what it had taken to ready myself for this moment? To have it delayed sent a shock of emotions throughout my system, but still I managed to ask, "Why?"

"It's Clay Whitefield. He knows David's in town, and he's following us."

I sat down hard on the kitchen chair, imagining what it would feel like to have my darkest secret on the front page of the *Gold Rush News*. I felt a chill shudder through me.

"Okay," I said. "You know best."

Fred walked down the stairs and stuck his nose in the kitchen. "Everything all right?" he asked.

I shook my head no. I whispered, "Tonight's meeting is off."

He stood, waiting for more news as I finished my conversation with Donna. But even as I listened to Donna's plans, I could not stop looking at this man with whom I had spent most of my life. He'd somehow changed since he had heard about Joseph and the baby. He seemed older, more serious, and a deep sadness had settled over him. At first, he'd asked a few questions, but for the most part he remained silent, simply saying, "This is going to take me a while to process."

That it was me who caused his pain practically broke my heart.

Donna was saying, "Clay won't be watching the church, he'll be busy watching David's hotel. So here's the plan. David's going to walk over to Higher Grounds Café for breakfast. We're sure Clay will come out of hiding and join him. Then when David gets up to go to the restroom, he exits the back door, cuts though the trailer park and into my waiting truck. Then I'll drive David to an undisclosed location. Clay will never know we made our escape until it's too late."

"Okay," I said, my heart pounding at the thought of the conspiracy.

Donna continued, "Here's what you'll do. Go to church as usual, then about fifteen minutes before the end of the service, slip out into the back parking lot, where I'll be waiting. I'll take you to David."

I nodded.

"Vonnie? Will that work for you?"

"Yes, dear."

When I hung up, I looked back at Fred. "The meeting's been postponed till tomorrow."

"How come?"

"I guess Clay Whitefield is standing by with a camera, hoping to find the 'missing Jewel.'"

Fred looked anguished. "I don't know if I'll ever be ready for the whole town to know about this."

I nodded, studying his drawn complexion. This was even harder on him than I had thought.

That afternoon, I was a nervous wreck. However, I did have the presence of mind to make my grandmother's molasses cookie recipe for my fifth-grade Sunday school class. It was our Sunday to celebrate the birthdays of the month, and it felt therapeutic to roll balls of cookie dough in sugar, then watch the cookies rise as they baked in my oven. I sighed as I used my metal spatula to scrape the cookies off the pan. How would I ever get through teaching that Sunday school lesson? The story of baby Moses being placed in a basket and set adrift on the Nile, to be found and raised by a princess, was more than ironic. Because when you think about it, that's just what had happened to my David.

My own baby had been set adrift in a strange state, to be raised by a princess of the entertainment industry. And now, just as in the story of Moses, David was returning to his roots. But how would Hollywood have impacted my sweet baby? I couldn't help but wonder. Did his princess mother love him the way I would have? Had she taught him right from wrong? Had she told him of God or helped him develop his character?

I shook my head. Harmony Harris's life had been one of glitter and glamour. To imagine her with a baby, my baby—it was unthinkable.

And now, a question loomed in front of me.

I was no princess but a heartbroken woman who had mourned the loss of her first husband and baby son for thirty-seven years. I would appear before my child with wrinkles, baggage and all.

I took a deep breath. What would David think of me? How could I ever compete against a princess?

Later that night when Fred was already in bed, staring at the ceiling, I pulled out a pair of socks and slipped them on my feet so my toes wouldn't freeze during the night. As I sat on the chair by the bed, I asked, "Are you ready to meet David?"

He shook his head. "You meet him first. This should be a time just for the two of you."

"Okay," I said. "Let's take separate cars to church. I'll leave from church to go to the meeting."

The kids at Sunday school were great as usual, though I teared up a time or two when I talked about baby Moses and the princess.

Afterward, I met up with Fred in the hallway and asked if we could sit near the back of the sanctuary during the worship service. "I'll have to slip out early," I explained. He nodded without really looking at me.

The choir opened the service with that dear old hymn, number 595.

The words seemed to lift off the page.

This is my Father's world,
O let me ne're forget
That though the wrong seems oft so strong,
God is the Ruler yet.
This is my Father's world;
The battle is not done;
Jesus who died shall be satisfied,
And earth and heav'n be one.

Lord, I silently prayed, *the wrong that's been done here, my mother's rejection of Joseph, Joseph's untimely death, the kidnapping of my baby, my lies of omission about the past to my husband and friends, it all overwhelms me. I'm only one small soul who cries out to you. You are my only hope.*

When Pastor Kevin stood to give announcements, he said, "Many of you have asked about Jan this morning."

I turned my eyes to the front pew where she always sat. For the first time, I realized her spot was empty. I looked back to the pastor.

"Things aren't going well," he admitted. A collective gasp escaped from the congregation. "Jan and I, we're asking for your prayers. We're keenly aware of your friendship, your concern. We're still holding on . . . trusting Jesus. No matter what, we are assured of his love and of his kingdom."

After that bit of news, there was no way I could concentrate on the message. Instead, I watched the minute hand of my watch slowly rotate to the appointed moment. Quietly, I stood, picked up my Bible and purse, and made my way to the door of the sanctuary, then outside into the bright sunshine. Donna was waiting for me in her Bronco.

I opened the door and climbed in. "Mission accomplished?" I asked.

She nodded, looking almost as nervous as I felt.

"Where are you taking me?"

"To my house. David is already waiting there."

I felt my stomach lurch. Soon I would face my past and look into the eyes of the baby I never knew.

We pulled into Donna's driveway, and my eyes filled with tears. I took a deep breath to steady myself. I would not break down. I couldn't.

Donna parked her Bronco behind her tiny rented bungalow. It was probably all of eight hundred square feet, including a kitchen/living room, a tiny bedroom, and adjoining bath. Of course, the place was small, but with the rent prices around here through the roof, what else could she afford?

She turned and looked at me. "How are you doing, Vonnie?"

I attempted a smile that somehow wouldn't appear. "I'm nervous."

Donna walked around the truck and helped me out. "David's nervous too, if that makes you feel any better."

She led me to the back door and pushed it open, and we were immediately in her kitchen. As my eyes adjusted to the dim light, I saw David rise from the table.

I froze. It was my son. My son, David Harris. The spitting image of his father. He was dressed in khakis and a black turtleneck, looking like the ghost of my beloved husband. He stepped toward me. "Mother?"

I felt the blood rush to my cheeks, and his image suddenly swam before me. I held open my arms and cried, "My son!"

He fell into them and held me as I wept on his shoulder. How long we stood like that, I have no idea. All I knew was that my son had come home.

Donna was quick to bring a box of tissues. When I finally pulled away, I discovered that David needed one as well. We sat at the table as Donna poured us both a cup of coffee, then disappeared into her bedroom.

At her absence, I could only stare at this man who so mirrored the man I had lost. "You look exactly like your father," I said.

"I do? Tell me about him."

"Joseph was the love of my life. He planned to be a doctor, you know, but got drafted to Vietnam. You, my dear, were the result of our honeymoon the weekend before he left for war."

A smile played on David's lips. I pulled the wedding picture from my purse and passed it to him. He stared at it as I continued.

"When I received the news that Joe had been killed in action, I became hysterical and went into labor. Not only was I in shock, your birth had complications. After the C-section, I was pretty much out of it. The next thing I know, my mother, who had been against the marriage, was by my side. She convinced me you had died. When I signed your adoption papers, I thought I was signing a burial release. Honestly? I didn't know you'd lived until I read the article in the paper. As soon as I saw your picture," I looked down at the photograph, then back at him, "there was no doubt as to who you are."

David put his hand on top of mine. "I've always known I was adopted, and through the years I've tried to imagine my history, but I never dreamed it was so tragic."

"David, if I had known you were alive, heaven and hell wouldn't have kept me from you. I loved your father with all my heart. If I had known his son survived, you would not have been adopted, you would've been a part of my life."

David squeezed my hand. "I believe you."

"I know another woman has raised you as her own. But I also know she's gone. It may be too soon to ask such a thing, but, David, with your permission, I'd like to be your mother."

David's eyes swam as he replied, "And with your permission, I'd like to be your son."

51

She's a woman of mystery . . .

Clay Whitefield awoke to a shaft of sunlight cutting through the blinds of his apartment and the sound of Woodward (or maybe it was Bernstein) taking his morning jog in the cage wheel.

He shot straight up, looked over at the old alarm clock he'd had since college days, and blinked hard. He blinked several more times, hoping that if he continued to focus on the clock's hands, they'd somehow turn backward.

They didn't. He fell back, rolled over on his side, and beat his pillow for good measure. He'd overslept. His alarm hadn't gone off and he'd overslept.

Clay reached for the clock, stared at its backside, and groaned loudly. He had set the timer, all right, but he'd forgotten to pull the alarm switch to the on position. A rarity, he'd slept till nearly noon.

His stomach growled. He'd missed breakfast—and if he didn't get up and dressed, he'd miss getting his seat at the café.

He swung out of bed and shuffled toward the bathroom. Ten minutes. Ten minutes was all he needed, and he'd be heading toward Sal's place. And maybe, if he had just a drop of luck left in him, there'd be some sort of buzz circulating about David Harris.

If not—to borrow from a famous book's ending—there would always be tomorrow. For today, the mystery of David Harris's mother remained just that. A mystery.

But tomorrow . . . ah, after all, tomorrow is another day.

Lizzie

Yellow Crookneck Squash Soup
1½ pounds yellow Crookneck Squash
1 onion
1 stick margarine
2-3 chicken Bouillon Cubes
2-3 cups Half-n-Half
Dash Salt and pepper
Curry powder

Slice Squash and onion. Sauté
in 1 stick margarine — until
very tender. Place in a food
processor, add bouillon cubes)

52

Trouble Boiling Over

Friday evening before our November Potluck, I sat in the living room of my home and stretched out on the Southwestern-patterned sofa with ends that reclined. I'd prepared a yellow crookneck squash soup that was simmering on the stove for the club meeting. Samuel was at the monthly financial meeting at Grace, Michelle was out on a date with a young man from work who seemed quite taken with her—and her with him—and I was alone.

Though a late-autumn storm was pouring down on Summit View, the night was blissful. No teenagers running down the halls, calling loud nonsense to one another, pushing their way in and out of the library, ignoring the old rule of silence. No computers humming, no phones ringing, just God and me, my favorite book of devotions, my Bible, and the journal Tim's wife had given me as part of my birthday gift.

The Scripture reading was from 2 Chronicles 7, the quote for the day from Hannah Whitall Smith:

> "If my people, who are called by my name, will humble themselves and pray and seek my face . . . then will I hear from heaven . . ." The greatest lesson a soul has to learn is that God, and God alone, is enough for all its needs.

I'm an underliner. When I read words and phrases that move me, I underline them. With my pen, I drew a straight line under the words *God is enough*. I pondered the sentence for a while, then set the devotional aside and pulled my journal in my lap.

Just then the phone rang. I glanced at the clock. It was nearly 9:00. Samuel might be calling to tell me he was on his way home, so I answered.

But it was Jan Moore.

"Lizzie?" she said, breathless.

"Jan?" Thunder rolled in the distance.

"Can you come here? To my house?"

"I can be there in about ten minutes. I'll just need to slip on some shoes." I was on the cordless, so while talking I headed for my bedroom closet.

"I'll unlock the front door," she said.

"Are you okay?" I asked. Moving through the house I passed windows that displayed the electrical show of the Lord on the other side. I flinched, knowing I'd have to drive in the storm.

"I am enough . . ."

"Kevin is at the meeting, and I can't get him to answer his cell phone. Maybe the signal is out, I don't know. No one is answering the phone in the church's office . . . and . . ." She drew in a deep breath. "I don't feel so well, Lizzie. I think I need to go to the hospital."

I opened my bedroom closet, reached up, and pulled a pair of slip-ons off a shelf where I kept my shoes. I dropped them to the floor, slipping my feet into them. "Have you called Doc Billings? An ambulance?"

"Doc Billings is meeting me at the hospital. I told him I didn't want an ambulance. If Kevin hears a siren, he might worry . . ."

Kevin has good cause to worry, I thought, but I didn't voice my concerns. "I'll be there in ten minutes."

Jan met me at the front door, dressed in a sky blue sweat suit that hung from her frail body. She wore a scarf around her head that pushed her thinning hair to her scalp. Her face was pale, but it looked as though she'd attempted to put on makeup.

She reached for me as soon as I opened the door, collapsing enough to let me know the situation was critical. I managed to get her to the car, all the while saying, "Have you tried Kevin again?" Water poured in streams from the umbrella I held over our heads, while our feet sloshed at the puddles that had formed during the storm.

She nodded but didn't answer. I helped her settle in the front passenger seat, then closed the door and hurried around to the driver's side. Opening my door I said, "I tried Samuel, but I'm having the same problem. I can't seem to get through." I shook the umbrella out, drew it closed, then dropped it at my feet, closing the door.

Jan laid her head against the back of the seat, rolled her head toward me, and mouthed, "Figures."

We arrived at the emergency room of the hospital within minutes. Doc Billings met us at the automatic sliding doors, saying, "Jan, I've called your oncologist in Denver. We'll get you settled here, then see where we stand, what we need to do from there." Behind him, an orderly stood behind a wheelchair, awaiting our arrival.

I continued to stand in the doorway, watching Jan as she was being wheeled into the recesses of the sterile emergency room. Doc Billings turned to me before following behind her and said, "Keep trying to get Pastor Kevin."

I followed the signs into the waiting room, where a handful of people waited either for their loved ones or to be called back for examination. In the far left was a small table with a phone, phone book, and table lamp casting a faint light on the corner. I walked purposefully over to it, picked up the phone receiver, and attempted to make another call to Samuel. The service was still down.

Setting my purse at my feet, I realized I was nearly soaked. A shiver went up my spine, and I heard the words from my devotional again. *"I am enough . . ."* I picked up the phone again, dialing Evie's house. She answered almost immediately.

"Evie, this is Lizzie. I just drove past your house and noticed that Vernon's car is there. Can I speak with him, please?"

"What's wrong, Lizzie Prattle?" Evie asked.

"It's Jan. Evie, I need to speak to Vernon right now."

I heard Evie call Vernon to the phone. When he said hello I asked him if he would drive over to the church. "Tell Kevin he needs to get here as soon as possible."

"Will do."

"And, Vernon. Ask Samuel to meet me here."

I called Vonnie, hoping she wasn't sleeping. It had been three weeks since her reunion with her son—three weeks of sorting things out with Fred and trying to determine how to let the community in on the various truths of her life—and I knew all this had caused her to be especially worn out.

"Von, Lizzie. I'm sorry to disturb you . . . I know you've had enough on your mind lately, but would you call the Potluckers and tell them Jan's at the hospital? We need to start a prayer chain."

Vonnie relayed that she would. "Should we come up?" she asked.

"I don't think so. I don't know if they'll keep her here or move her to Denver." I felt something wet slip down my cheek. I wondered if it was a tear or a drop of rain that had released itself from my scalp.

"Call me when you know something," she said.

"I will," I said, then hung up the phone in time to hear a nurse call my name.

"Follow me," she said. I picked up my purse and walked behind the nurse past dark corridors, through sliding glass doors, and then along a row of drawn curtains until one was pushed back for me to step past. "Here you go," she said.

Jan was lying on a gurney, raised slightly at the head and hooked up to as many machines as could possibly fit in such a small area. Her eyes were closed and her lips were drawn tight.

"Jan?" I whispered.

Her eyes fluttered open, and she lifted a hand to me. I took it immediately.

"Did you get Kevin?" she asked me.

"I called Vernon over at Evie's. He's going to the church to get him."

331

"Good," she mouthed, then smiled weakly. "Vernon over at Evie's . . ."

I squeezed her hand. "Yeah. Can you believe it? After all these years."

I watched as she blinked slowly and then—without moving her head—cut her eyes over to me. "Am I going to die?"

"No, Jan. Don't even say that." I leaned against the chrome sidebars of the gurney.

She ran her tongue over dry lips. "It's okay, you know." I squeezed her hand again. "Remember that day you came to the house?"

I said that I did.

"I said there were five healings."

"I know."

"But then I could only tell you four."

"I know, Jan."

"I wasn't ready to talk about the fifth."

"It's not necessary."

"But you knew, didn't you?"

"Yes. I knew."

A lone tear slipped down Jan's cheek. "Death," she whispered. "It isn't a punishment, you know, Lizzie. It's the victory we race toward. We're born, and God draws us to himself." She took a breath.

"Don't exhaust yourself," I pleaded.

"'Draw me' the bride said in Solomon's Song." Jan had something to say, and she obviously was going to say it. "I'm so grateful he did, Lizzie."

"I know. Me too."

She closed her eyes then, and for a moment I held my breath until she reopened them. "I'm going to walk on golden streets," she said, smiling. "I'm going to see the face of my Bridegroom." Her breath came in gasps.

"Jan, please . . ." I said, looking over my shoulder at the drawn curtain, wondering when Kevin would get there, and if he'd get there in time.

Jan squeezed my hand. "Not tonight," she said. "But soon."

I leaned closer to her. "Jan, I love you."

"I love you too."

By the time Kevin and Samuel arrived at the hospital, Jan was settled in a private room. Samuel and I decided to return home. "You can't really do anything more than you've done," Kevin said to me. "Except pray."

On the drive home—alone in my car with Samuel driving behind me—I thought about those words. Except pray.

"If my people . . ."

The words went through my mind as quickly as I drove across the intersections of road between the hospital and our house.

"I am enough . . ."

I began to recite the words over and over. *"If my people . . . I am enough . . . If my people . . . I am enough."*

When I turned in the driveway, I noticed a light on upstairs, indicating Michelle had returned. I glanced at the small digital clock on my dashboard. It was nearly midnight. Tired, I sighed deeply, pushed the remote control to open the garage door, and continued on in. Moments later I shut off the car, then looked in the rearview mirror to see Samuel pulling up behind me. I had lost him along the way but hadn't realized it. Somehow, it was okay. Samuel was not my source. He was not the one I clung to . . . or at least not the one I should cling to. My strength didn't come from him. Still, having thought he was right behind me . . .

Samuel shut off his car and climbed out. I followed suit.

"You okay?" he asked me. He reached back into his car and pushed his remote. The garage door began to descend with its noisy clatter.

I only nodded. If I spoke I might've broken down completely.

"Michy's home," he noted.

I nodded with relief. Samuel came up beside me, linked his arm around my waist, and pulled me toward the door leading into the house. Inside, he leaned over and kissed my cheek. Again, I only nodded. "I'm going to finish my devotional before I go to bed," I said. "That's what I was doing when Jan called."

Samuel patted my hip. "Don't be too long," he coaxed.

"I won't." I watched him walk through the kitchen and on up the back staircase, then turned and headed back into the family room, where my discarded Bible, devotional book, and journal lay askew where I'd been sitting earlier. I thought about preparing a cup of tea, then dismissed the idea. I had some things I wanted to say to God . . . to write to him in my journal. There was no reason to put it off.

"If my people," I wrote. *"I am enough . . . If we would simply pray, then you'll be enough. Is that it, God? Will you be enough if we lose Jan?"*

"Pray," Pastor Kevin had said. Pray . . .

"Start a prayer chain," I had told Vonnie. But why did it matter? I continued to write:

> Maybe prayer is my being ushered into the throne room of God, where I can tell him whatever is on my heart and he will listen. Maybe it's just that simple. God has not descended to me. I have ascended to him. All I know right now is that in prayer I can be safe in this room. I can be with my heavenly Father.

I paused, then continued.

> How could I have taken this so lightly before? I often wondered, "Why my child?" when it came to Michy's deafness. I cried out to God when I felt Tim had shamed me. I've questioned God on so many things over the years, I've been a part of a prayer group, but have I truly believed he heard me?

I shook my head no.

> So now I pray for Jan Moore, and I know others are praying too. The Potluck Club hasn't always gotten it right, but I know God has heard every one of our prayers. Evie's, Goldie's, Vonnie's, Lisa Leann's, and Donna's.

334

I nodded yes.

> Perhaps we were in need of healing even more than Jan.
> Jan's healing may or may not come about as we desire,
> but your desire is more that our hearts be healed than our
> bodies.

I closed my eyes, squeezing them so tightly I saw bursts of color. They burned and I was tired. Yet, somehow, I felt renewed.

"Prayer," I wrote, allowing myself one final line. *"What a concept."*

53

She's a true friend . . .

Clay had been on his way home from the newspaper office when he passed Lizzie Prattle's car. Lizzie had Jan Moore with her, and they turned into the hospital parking lot. Jan's head rested against the headrest. It seemed to him that it was tilted too far back for comfort, as though she were an old doll with a rubbery neck. Well, the situation didn't look good, but he knew Jan was in good hands with Lizzie. That woman was a true friend.

He slowed down the jeep. He wasn't much of a praying man, but he figured now was as good a time as any to offer up a line or two to the Almighty.

The jeep pulled off to the side of the road, and he bowed his head. "God," he ventured, then stopped. He wasn't used to this, wasn't even sure how to begin. "God," he tried again. "It's me. Clay Whitefield." He cleared his throat. "You may not know me well—okay, you know me pretty good, it's me not knowing you all that well—but I know you know Jan Moore. She's a good lady, God, and, um, I think she could use you right now." He cleared his throat again. "So, God? Be with her. That's about all I know to say." He opened his eyes, then closed them again just as quickly. "Oh! The Potluckers, God. They're going to be a little needy right now too. So . . . if you don't mind taking the time to sorta be with them right now too. Um, yeah, that would be nice."

Evangeline

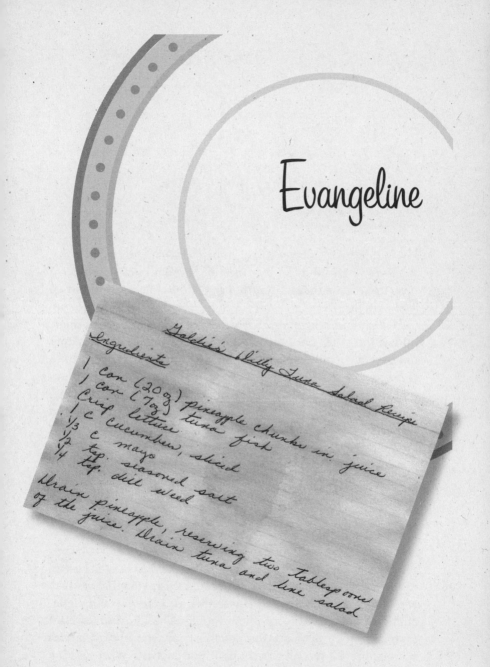

Goldie's Dilly Tuna Salad Recipe

Ingredients

1 can (20 oz) pineapple chunks in juice
1 can (7 oz) tuna fish
Crisp lettuce
1 c cucumber, sliced
1/3 c mayo
1/2 tsp. seasoned salt
1/4 tsp. dill weed

Drain pineapple, reserving two Tablespoons
of the juice. Drain tuna and line salad

54

Relishing Faith

It was quite a different group of women who gathered in my home for November's Potluck Club meeting. We'd all been through so many changes in the last month, had all learned our own spiritual lessons in life.

Lisa Leann has kept me on my toes, and don't think for a single minute I trust her, but I am at least willing to do my Christian duty in giving her another chance to prove herself to me.

The first thing she did that surprised me was throw a baby shower for Leigh at her home, which I will admit is lovely. The other thing is that she and her husband, Henry, bought the rundown Victorian on Main Street and are fixing it up to be Lisa Leann's new wedding boutique, a real first for Summit View. For the life of me, and I'd never admit this out loud, I am hoping to be her first customer.

Here's something else I'd never mention out loud: there's a new spring in her step, different from the old spring entirely. Lisa Leann has never been subdued—at least not as long as I've known her. But this is different. There's a glow in her cheeks that Mary Kay couldn't have possibly put there. My suspicions are that Henry should start his own—shall we say—cosmetic line.

Donna has continued to be a bit standoffish—both toward me and Vonnie. I know she's still a bit miffed with me for yelling at her after I assumed she was the one who'd gone to Clay Whitefield. I know now that this is not true, and I've apologized, but Donna's not taking it all so well. Of course, the fact that I've been dating

Vernon since my strange encounter-slash-dream on the hillside of All Saints hasn't helped much.

Leigh says that even when parents have been divorced as long as Donna's have, there's still a tiny trickle of hope that they will reunite. If another person enters the equation, that trickle all but dissipates. She also says that Donna could see me as the other woman in Vernon's life, and herself as the "other other" woman. Only Donna knows why there's such a wall between us, and all I can do is give it to God and hope he'll solve it in his good time. Lord knows I've done my best by the girl.

Faith is something I'm learning situation by situation.

Leigh was learning this too. Gary called every night but one, and that was last night. I'd never seen anyone struggle with the lack of a phone call since the days of my high school prom when I stared at a silent phone. By the time we turned in for the night, Leigh had gone from crying to saying, "Good riddance," though I don't think she meant that for a second.

God love Lizzie, she was really putting in the time with Jan Moore. She cooked for the family, helped Jan with the house, stayed with her during chemo treatments and while she was in the hospital, both here and in Denver. At first Lizzie was so dogged in her belief that Jan would beat cancer, but now I saw a new determination. Like me, Lizzie was coming to grips with death and God's will and how those two things interchange. Lizzie also was a virtual encyclopedia of information for us, making sure we all stayed informed on the latest cancer-fighting techniques. She even set up a "self-examination day" for us Potluckers. That's the day she called everyone first thing in the morning to remind us to do our exam while bathing and then called back later that night to confirm that we had.

According to Lizzie, everyone was A-OK.

Goldie's been going to work Monday through Friday at Chris Lowe's office. From what Vonnie says, she loves the job and she's happier than she's been in many years. She continues to live with Olivia and Tony. She told me they've insisted she stay until Olivia stops with the sickness part of her pregnancy. This will enable her to save some money to get her own place . . . if need be.

Of course, as soon as she arrived for the club meeting (and she was the last to do so), everyone flocked to her. "Has he called you?" Lisa Leann asked. "Suggested you come home?" She tossed her red head. "Now, I know I said you should take him for every penny he has, but now that I own my new shop, I say let bygones be bygones. And I think you should know I'm intending to do some wonderful things with wedding vow renewals at my new business. Lots of silver and gold and weaving in your original colors, that kind of thing."

Goldie was holding a tuna casserole, which I later learned was called dilly tuna salad. (In spite of her marital woes, Goldie continues to be a good cook, and there's not a soul here who isn't grateful for it.)

Goldie handed off the casserole dish to me, raised her hands for silence, and said, "Yes. Every day. Three times a day like clockwork. Knowing him, he's got it written down in his Daytimer. Call Goldie. Beg. Call Goldie. Plead. Call Goldie. Make promises you know you aren't ready to keep." Laughter followed Goldie's dramatic performance.

"And? What do you say to that?" someone asked, but I'm not sure who because I was already halfway to the kitchen.

Fortunately I could still hear the conversation, mainly because once I was out of earshot, I sprinted to the kitchen and back, nearly tripping over my own two feet.

"And nothing. He swears it's over with Charlene Hopefield, but I keep telling him that if he doesn't seek counseling with me, he can forget it, which is exactly what Chris has told me to say." She lifted a diamond and turquoise pendant from just below the hollow of her throat. "Here's the latest peace offering. I'm wearing it, but I'm not buying it, if you know what I mean." She grinned at us, dropping the pendant. "I no longer feel like I'm wearing his sin, but more my victory. Anyway, I'm enjoying myself right now." Goldie moved through the small crowd and continued, "I'm not saying I don't want my marriage to work, but I will admit to wanting Jack to suffer a little." Her eyes widened. "Not in a bad way, of course."

"What's wrong with a bad way?" Donna said. When all eyes fell on her in silence, she coughed out a laugh. "I'm kidding. I'm kidding."

Leigh left the little gathering about that time and went to the living room to sit down, saying, "This baby weighs an absolute ton."

Vonnie watched her closely. "You okay, Leigh?" she asked.

Leigh nodded an answer while rubbing her belly, looking a bit sad in my view. This particular day marked her official due date, and I could sense she was hoping the baby would make his or her appearance in a timely fashion. Vonnie walked across the room to her, laid her hand across her forehead, and said, "Don't worry. It'll come when it comes. You don't want to rush it. Believe me."

Out of all of us, Vonnie had made the biggest changes. I knew things with Fred were still tenuous, but I also knew she and her son—long-lost David Harris—were getting to know one another on a daily basis, mostly through phone calls.

Not everyone in town knew the truth about the "missing Jewel," but Vonnie's closest friends—the Potluck Club—knew . . . and we loved her in spite of it and because of it.

As we gathered in the living room I asked Lizzie, "What's new with Jan?"

Lizzie nodded as she sat, sliding the palms of her hands down the front of her slacks and then allowing them to rest on her knees. "Not so good. She's back at the hospital. Went in about 3:00 this morning. She's just so weak, and I'm not sure that she can hold on much longer." Lizzie pressed her lips together. "To tell you the truth, I'm not even sure she wishes to. She seems perfectly content to either live or die. She says that either way, it's all for him." Lizzie pointed upward with her index finger.

No one spoke for a moment; we just allowed what she'd said to be taken in by our spiritual hearts and minds, until Leigh asked, "What time is it?"

Donna gave her the time.

"Well," I said, "I for one feel better about the whole living and dying thing."

"How's that?" Vonnie asked, though she already knew the answer. Maybe she just didn't realize she knew the answer, I don't know, but I'd told her one afternoon as we shared a cup of coffee and our innermost thoughts.

"About three weeks ago I went to the cemetery."

"You did what?" Lizzie asked.

I raised a hand. "I know. It's the one place you'd rarely find me before . . ." I squirmed a bit. "Before Jan. But I have to tell you that her illness has caused me great distress. Not only because we might lose her to heaven but also because I had to finally come face to face with my anger over Ruth Ann's death. I blamed God for taking her, and Ruth Ann for actually dying." I took a deep breath. "Then I went out to All Saints and had myself a good, old-fashioned chat with her."

"Who?" Donna asked.

I looked at her as sweetly as I knew how. "Ruth Ann." I raised my brow. "Don't look at me like I'm crazy, Donna Vesey. Sometimes we just have to talk it all out to get to the truth."

Donna opened her mouth like she was going to say something, then closed it.

"I think it's wonderful," Lizzie said.

"Me too," Goldie said, then laughed. "You know, Olivia said to me that I don't pray to God but rather I whine to him." She shook her head sadly. "She was right. But no more! Now I tell God what's on my heart. I want to truly rejoice in the Lord always—"

"Amen!" we all said.

"And again I say rejoice!" Goldie finished. We all had a good laugh over that.

"So how do we pray today?" I asked when our laughter subsided. Nearby, Leigh let out a pent-up breath. I looked over at her, but she shook her head as if to dismiss me.

"What time is it?" she asked. When she noted our quizzical expressions, she said, "Sorry. Time feels like it's dragging today, you know what I'm saying?"

"I know what you're saying," Donna replied, then looked at her watch and told her. A whole five minutes had passed since the last time she'd asked.

"Prayer?" I inquired again, readying my pad and pen.

"Pray for Olivia's pregnancy," Goldie said. "And for Jack. And for Charlene Hopefield. God knows she needs it . . . and I really mean that."

From next to her, Lizzie smiled at Goldie, then patted her on the shoulder.

"Lizzie?" I asked.

"Pray for Jan." We all nodded as I jotted Jan's name down. "And for Tim. I don't know what, but I feel that something is up in Baton Rouge. Oh, and pray for Michelle. She's dating someone from work and seems to be quite happy about it, but a mother worries . . ."

I took note, then turned. "Donna?"

Though she rarely had a prayer request, this time Donna said, "Just pray God will give me the answers I'm looking for."

"Amen," Vonnie whispered.

"Von?"

"Well, of course pray for the changes going on in my life. I've got a lot of issues to deal with, as you know. At some point David and I will need to let it be known to the community at large that I'm his mother. If we can just keep Clay Whitefield off our trail long enough to make some decisions . . ."

I looked up at Donna, who gave me a "What?" look.

"We're all rooting for you," Goldie said, then shifted her gaze to the outside window. I wondered what had diverted her attention.

"Lisa Leann?" I asked.

Lisa Leann sat up straight. "Pray for my new business! I don't know when I've been this excited about anything, I just want it all to glorify God, and I'm as serious as a heart attack when I say that."

"Leigh, do you have any prayer requests?"

Leigh took a breath, paused, then took another one. "What time is it now?" she asked.

"For heaven's sake," Donna said, looking down to her watch. "It's five minutes since the last time you asked and ten minutes since the first time you asked."

Every woman in the room suddenly jumped.

"When did they start?" Lizzie asked.

"Are you hurting in your lower back?" Goldie asked.

"Your water hasn't broken, has it?" Lisa Leann piped in, to which I looked down at my mother's wool carpets in horror.

"Not too long ago, a little, and no," Leigh answered.

"Do I need to call an ambulance?" Donna piped in.

"I don't think so."

"We can take my Bronco, then. I'll use the lights if I have to." Donna turned for the front door.

"I'll get your suitcase," I told Leigh, touching the crown of her head with my hand. Deep down—where no one could see it—my soul was grinning from ear to ear. My baby girl—the daughter of my heart—was about to bring a new life into the world. It was such a marvelous thought, soured only by the sudden reminder that I would need to call Peggy and Matthew as soon as we reached the hospital.

It was the right thing to do.

When I returned to the foyer, the front door was open, and my five prayer partners stood around my niece. Instead of the clucking hens they'd all been when I'd left, they were silent and dumbfounded.

"What's going on?" I asked, then noted the young man standing on the other side of the threshold. He was six foot six and looked like a Ken doll. There was only one person this could be, and I suppose it was appropriate that he show up now of all times.

I pushed past the crowd. "You must be Gary," I said.

He looked down at me and smiled. "I am." Then, over to Leigh, the woman who was about to give birth to his child. "What's going on?"

"I'm in labor," she said. "I'll ask again: what are you doing here?"

Gary put his hand to his chest. "I came to be with you. I figured we'd wait out the baby's arrival together." His voice raised an octave. "Is it normal for babies to be born on their due date?"

Vonnie took a step forward. "Not normal, but it happens. Come on, girls. Let's get moving."

Donna ran up from the outside. A flurry of snow had begun to fall, and the flakes of it lay on her uniform jacket she'd obviously pulled out of the Bronco. "Ready?" she asked Leigh. "The Bronco's warming up, and I've already called in to the hospital."

With the help of Lisa Leann on one arm and Lizzie on the other, she took a step forward, Donna reaching for her.

"Hold on a minute," I said, shifting the suitcase from one hand to the other. I looked up at the man who'd come so far and just in time. "Let the father walk the mother to the car." I looked over at Leigh. "Okay?"

Leigh only nodded. Gary reached for her, supporting her weight by clasping her elbow and walking alongside her.

I rode shotgun in the front seat of the Bronco while Gary and Leigh rode in the back. With the blue light whirring atop the car (but, at Leigh's request, no siren), and snow bouncing against the hood and windshield of the car, Leigh did a lot of breathing she'd learned at the childbirth classes she'd taken before coming to Summit View. Gary said stupid male things like, "Does it hurt?" and "Do you need anything?"

"What are you doing here?" Leigh asked him, apparently for the third time.

"I wanted to be with you, sweetheart."

Leigh gritted her teeth. "Don't call me sweetheart!" She let out what sounded like a growl. "And why didn't you call me last night?"

"I . . . I was on my way here."

"Traveling by foot, were you?" Donna asked.

I cut a don't-get-involved look her way, although I knew it wouldn't do any good.

"I was struggling with it, okay? I've had a lot to think about . . . a lot to do."

"Ohmigoooooooosh," Leigh said. "What time is it now?"

Donna looked at the digital clock on the dashboard. "You're still at five minutes, Leigh."

"Is it supposed to hurt like this?" Gary asked again. I flipped the visor down so I could see him in the rearview mirror. His eyes met mine, and I gave him my best are-you-an-idiot-or-just-plain-stupid look. I think he caught my drift. I also noticed Leigh had clasped his hand and was squeezing as she huff-huff-huffed.

"Like what?" Leigh asked when her contraction had subsided. "Like what did you have to do?"

I kept my focus on the backseat. Gary reached into the pocket of his jeans with his free hand and extracted what appeared to be a ring box. Again, my soul smiled.

"Like this," he said, flipping it open. Both Donna and I turned in our seats.

The Bronco swerved, causing Donna to resume her focus on driving. I, however, kept my eyes on the rear of the car.

Leigh threw her head back. "You would pick now to do this. What's changed, Gary?"

"Me," he said. "I've changed. I love you, Leigh." He darted a look to me, then back to my niece. "Who is that woman?" he whispered.

"My aunt Evie," Leigh answered.

"Oh." He turned to me. "Hello, Aunt Evie. I'm Gary."

I squared my shoulders. "Well, I sincerely hope so."

He looked perplexed.

"Almost there, Leigh," Donna said, taking the turn into the hospital's entryway. I had to hold on to the side of my seat to keep from falling over. I could see the others in their cars following along behind us.

"Good," she grunted out.

"Marry me, Leigh. Marry me before the baby is born."

"Are you out of your mind?" Donna, Leigh, and I said in unison.

"Okay, then," he said, looking sheepish. "At least say you will before the baby is born."

"What's different, Gary?" Leigh asked again as Donna halted the Bronco, jerking me nearly into the floorboard.

Donna got out of the car and headed for the emergency room doors. An orderly pushing a wheelchair came out, followed by Vernon. "Dad! What are you doing here?" Donna exclaimed.

"I heard the call," I heard him answer. He looked over at me, and I smiled. He smiled back. "How are you doing, Evie-girl?"

"Dad, Leigh's the one in labor!"

346

Gary was talking while opening his door for himself and Leigh. "I met with your pastor. I'm joining the church."

"You're doing what?" Leigh asked as she settled herself in the wheelchair. "You think that's it? Joining the church?" The orderly began pushing her toward the open ER door and Donna Vesey.

Gary walked beside Leigh and spread his arms wide while still holding on to the ring box and ring. "No! I've given my life to God, Leigh. I have!"

Leigh let out another growl. "Arrrrrrrgggggghhhhh! What time is it now?" Her voice was swallowed by the closing of the automatic sliding doors.

Vernon came up beside the Bronco, reached inside the back for the suitcase, then leaned up to kiss me. "Getting out, or are you just going to sit here the rest of the afternoon?"

I realized then that I hadn't moved. I opened the door and climbed out. "This is almost too much for one day," I muttered. From a distance I could see the other Potluckers dashing up from the parking lot.

Vernon laughed. "Come on, Evie-girl. Let's go welcome a new life into the world."

I looped my hand into the crook of his arm. "I'm all for that," I said with a smile.

Faith Alexis arrived at 4:43 that afternoon. Gary and Leigh were all tears and smiles, and Leigh wore a beautiful diamond on her left ring finger. In the crook of her right arm lay Faith, and Gary stood by Leigh's side, which he'd not left during labor.

"Have you called your mother?" I asked Leigh.

She nodded. "She said you called after we got here. Thank you." She dipped her head to kiss the top of Baby Faith's head.

"They're flying out with my parents first thing tomorrow," Gary informed me, sitting at the right side of the bed.

"That's good. I insist they all stay at the house. You too, young man." Leigh closed her eyes, and I could tell it was more in contentment than exhaustion. Still, I felt it best for the new family to be alone. "I'm going to leave you three alone for a while," I said.

Leigh's eyes opened again. "Where are the rest of the girls?"

"Oh, they're still outside in the waiting area, waiting to get my report. They saw the baby earlier, right after she was born. But they've elected to hang around." I lowered my eyes a bit. "We also visited with Jan for a minute or two, but she's really not up for a lot of company."

Leigh sighed deeply. "I'm so sorry," she whispered.

I reached down and pinched her toes under the blanket. "Don't you think about it too much. You just enjoy these moments as a new mother."

"I will," she said, looking at Gary, who leaned over and pecked her on the lips.

I smiled at the three of them, thinking that life—right now—felt pretty good.

Hours later I stood at the nursery windowpane, looking in at my great-niece. There were three other babies there too, but (and I say this with all honesty) they were not nearly as precious as Baby Faith. I tapped on the window periodically, making those ridiculous sounds adults make when they think they're entertaining newborns.

Baby Faith neither acknowledged nor ignored me; she merely rested peacefully in her new, albeit temporary, home. Soon she would be in her own home, where she would be nurtured and could grow to be beautiful and healthy.

I closed my eyes, both happy and tired, and rested my forehead against the glass. I'd spoken to Peggy earlier, told her to plan to stay at the house—Gary's family too. She'd accepted. I told her there was something I wanted to tell her when she got here, but she wormed it out of me like she always does.

"I'm dating someone," I said.

"Who?" The sound of her voice was full of disbelief.

"Vernon Vesey."

"Vernon Vesey! After all these years?"

"Don't make a big deal about it," I said, pleading with her like I'd done when we were children and I'd told her about our one and only kiss . . . until now . . .

She promised she wouldn't, and then we said our good-byes.

It would be nice to have a houseful, I thought, then began to mentally check off everything I needed to do between now and then.

"Which one is she?"

I heard the voice behind me, and I jumped. Turning, I saw Pastor Kevin. He looked as though he'd aged ten years, if not ten years and a day, since the last time I'd seen him, which was only a few days ago. My "conversation" with Ruth Ann had led me to take time nearly every day to drop by the Moores' home—even if only to wash some dishes or dust the furniture for Jan or her daughter.

I turned back to the window. "Second from the left," I said, pointing. "Wrapped in pink."

"How precious," he said. I felt his hand slip along the top of my back and then rest on my shoulder. We stood silently, side by side, peering through a Plexiglas window at four new lives with so much ahead of them. *God only knows what heartaches and joys will come their way,* I thought.

"Life is a strange cycle, isn't it?" I said.

"That it is, Evangeline," Pastor Kevin said, squeezing my shoulder.

"How is Jan?" I asked.

Pastor Kevin was quiet for a long moment. Then he answered, "The battle is over. God won."

Unable to do anything, I continued to look straight ahead. Baby Faith squirmed, and for a moment I thought she was about to cry. Just as quickly, though, she calmed, drifting into sleep.

The Potluck Club Recipes

Brown Rice

1 can beef bouillon soup
1 can onion soup
1 cup rice
1 small can mushrooms or fresh cut-up mushrooms
2–3 pats of butter or margarine

Pour together in a greased casserole dish . . . you know, like Corningware. Put pats of butter on top. Bake at 350 degrees for 1 hour, covered.
Serves 4–6.

Evangline's Cook's Notes
If you can't make this dish, you can't boil water.

Best Oven-Barbecued Brisket

> 5–6 pounds brisket (or a 3–4 pound eye of round roast)
> 1 bottle liquid smoke
> garlic salt
> onion salt
> seasoned salt
> 1 tablespoon flour
> 1 oven bag
> 1 bottle barbecue sauce (onion flavored)
> ½ cup mild picante sauce

Trim fat from brisket. Soak brisket all night in 1 bottle of liquid smoke. The next day, season meat with garlic, onion, and seasoned salt. Put flour in oven bag and shake. Place meat and liquid smoke in flour-coated bag. Put bag into 2-inch deep baking dish. Place dish in 400 degree oven for approximately 15 minutes. Reduce heat to 200 degrees and cook 10–12 hours. Allow meat to cool in its own juice.

Drain juice and boil until thick. Add barbecue sauce and picante sauce and simmer.

Slice brisket. Place in a foil-lined pan and pour barbecue sauce over sliced meat. Heat at about 200 degrees for 1 hour.

Serves 8–10.

Lisa Leann's Cook's Notes

Start a day or two before to make the best barbecue ever tasted. My brisket got me into Woodland's Junior League, and I believe it helped me in my rise to becoming their president.

Mother Dippel's Chocolate Cake

> 1 cup shortening
> 1 stick butter
> 3 cups sugar
> 3 cups cake flour
> 4 tablespoons cocoa
> ½ teaspoon baking powder
> 1 cup milk
> 1 tablespoon vanilla
> 5 large eggs

Cream the shortening, butter, and sugar. Sift the flour (today you can get some cake flour that doesn't have to be sifted, so watch for that) with cocoa and baking powder. Add alternately to the creamed mixture with the milk, vanilla, and eggs, lightly beaten together. You'll want to beat this really good after each addition.

Bake in tube pan, coated well with a no-stick spray (Mother D. always used shortening and flour, but I don't think that's such a great idea in this day and time) at 325 degrees for 1 hour and 45 minutes or until done. (This is where the coffee and conversation come in.) Makes one very large cake for a very hungry family or group of friends.

Goldie's Cook's Notes
After being tired of hearing my constant pleas for the recipe, Mother Dippel finally caved and taught me how to make this delicious twist to the pound cake. Mother D. and I would often make this together, drinking coffee and talking about the latest installment of *The Young and the Restless.*

Spicy Apple Cider

> 2 cups water
> 2 cinnamon sticks
> 1 tablespoon whole cloves
> 2 quarts apple cider
> 1 lemon, sliced thin
> 1 orange, sliced thin
> ½ teaspoon whole allspice

All I do is combine water and spices in a large pot on stove and boil. Then I strain the mixture and pour the spiced water into my Crock-Pot. I add apple cider, lemon, and orange and cook over low heat till warm.

Makes 10 cups.

Donna's Cook's Notes

Of course I know how to cook. After all, I cooked for Dad most of my childhood. In those days, my best friend in the kitchen was my mother's old Betty Crocker cookbook, but nowadays I get most of my recipes from the Internet.

Apple Cinnamon Bread

1 cup water
5 tablespoons apple juice concentrate (frozen)
½ cup applesauce
1 teaspoon cinnamon
1⅓ tablespoons brown sugar
½ teaspoon salt
2 cups whole wheat flour
3 tablespoons Vital gluten
2 cups bread flour
2 teaspoons yeast
1 extra tablespoon of flour if baking at high altitude

Bring ingredients to room temperature and pour into bread machine, in order. Select "sweet bread" and push start.

Lisa Leann's Cook's Notes

There is nothing that smells better on a cold morning than apple cinnamon bread. I used to make it for my kids every week. It was a Lambert house favorite. My, how I miss those days.

Oven-Fried Eggplant

½ cup fine dry bread crumbs
2 tablespoons grated Parmesan cheese
¼ teaspoon salt
¼ teaspoon pepper
1 eggplant
¼ cup mayonnaise

Combine first 4 ingredients in shallow dish. Peel eggplant and cut into ¼ inch slices. Spread both sides with mayo. Dredge in bread crumbs. Place on a lightly greased baking sheet. Bake at 400 degrees uncovered for 10–12 minutes or until browned.

Serves 4–6.

Lizzie's Cook's Notes

My sweet, sweet Aunt Bettye gave me this recipe many years ago when I was visiting her in her Atlanta home. I took one bite of this scrumptious dish and told her I absolutely had to have the recipe.

Homemade Vegetable Soup

    1 large can V8 juice
    1 diced medium onion
    1 bay leaf
    1 small can tomato sauce
    2 packages mixed veggies
    1 cup macaroni
    Mrs. Dash to season

Place ingredients in a large pot. Slow simmer for several hours.

Goldie's Cook's Notes

This is another recipe given to me by my mother-in-law. I can still recall the day she made it for the first time. Of course, with the Dippel clan of men, she had to double the recipe. You'll want to cook this in a large pot and let it simmer all day. Perfect for cold days . . . or cold hearts.

Mexican Tamales

> 5 pounds lean pork or beef, cooked and shredded
> 6–7 pounds fresh masa (corn flour)
> 1½ pounds lard
> 1 tablespoon salt
> 1½ pints red chili sauce (store-bought)
> 1 bundle oujas (corn shucks)

Completely cover the meat with water, add salt to taste, then slow boil in a large covered pot until completely done. Next, cool the meat and save the broth. When meat has cooled, shred it and mix it into the chili sauce. While meat is boiling, clean the oujas with warm water.

To make the masa, you can mix by hand or use a hand mixer. In a large bowl, mix the masa, lard, salt, and enough broth to make a smooth paste. Beat till a small amount (1 tsp.) is able to float in a cup of cool water. Spread masa, ⅛- to ¼-inch thick, onto the oujas. Add a small amount of meat and roll up. Fold up ends of ouja and place (with the fold down) on a rack in a pan deep enough to steam. Add 1–2 inches water, cover with a tight-fitting lid, and steam about 1½ hours.

You can substitute or mix the beef or pork with chicken or fried beans.

This recipe will make 4–5 dozen Mexican tamales.

Vonnie's Cook's Notes

This recipe takes me back to a different time. Though the people in that time are long departed from my life, I think of them whenever I mix the masa. You'd think creating this dish would be too painful, but to tell you the truth, it's my favorite way to remember those I'll never forget.

Mama's Broccoli Casserole

2 10-ounce packages frozen chopped broccoli
1 cup mayo
1 cup sharp cheddar cheese
1 can cream of mushroom soup
2 eggs
1 cup crushed Ritz crackers

Boil broccoli for 5 minutes, then drain and allow to cool.

In a separate bowl, mix mayo, cheese, soup, and eggs. Add broccoli to mixture; stir well and then place in buttered cooking dish. Sprinkle Ritz cracker crumbs on top. Bake at 325 degrees for 35 minutes.

Serves 6–8.

Evangeline's Cook's Notes

One taste and you'll know why this was Ruth Ann's favorite broccoli casserole recipe. How I wish she were here to eat it one more time. (By the way, Mama always made this for both Thanksgiving and the day after, cutting up the leftover turkey and adding it to the mixture. Beats a turkey sandwich any old day of the week.)

Lasagna

2 pounds ground beef
1 clove garlic, minced
1 tablespoon parsley flakes
1 tablespoon basil
2 teaspoons salt
1 can tomatoes
1 6-ounce can tomato paste
1 16-ounce package lasagna noodles
1 teaspoon olive oil
2 12-ounce cartons cottage cheese
2 beaten eggs
2 tablespoons parsley flakes
2 teaspoons salt
½ teaspoon pepper
½ cup grated Parmesan cheese
1 pound mozzarella cheese

Brown meat, drain off excess fat. Add next 6 ingredients, then simmer until mixture becomes thick. I find this usually takes about an hour.

Cook your noodles in boiling water with a teaspoon of olive oil and some salt. Drain and rinse with cold water.

Meanwhile, combine cottage cheese with next 5 ingredients. In a 13-by-9-by-2-inch pan, make layers of this mixture, then noodles, and then mozzarella cheese, followed by meat mixture. Repeat. Bake at 375 for half an hour.

Serves 12 (3-inch square per serving).

Lizzie's Cook's Notes

On days when you have little else to do, make this up and, once cooled, seal and freeze. Perfect for last-minute luncheons, church socials, or days when you're forced to visit friends who are dying.

Sal's Denver Omelet

1 tablespoon butter
¼ cup chopped onion
¼ cup chopped green bell pepper
⅛ cup chopped ham
⅛ cup chopped bacon
3 eggs
1 tablespoon cream
⅛ teaspoon salt
⅛ teaspoon pepper
3 drops Tabasco sauce
¼ cup shredded cheese

Sauté onion, bell pepper, ham, and bacon in hot skillet with butter. In a small bowl, whip eggs lightly and add cream, salt, pepper, and Tabasco sauce. Add mixture to sautéed mix and let omelet brown on one side. Flip over and brown on the other side. Cover top with cheese, fold omelet in half, and serve.

Makes 1 large serving.

Donna's Cook's Notes

One of these babies first thing in the morning keeps me going till my late afternoon lunch break. It's one of my favorite ways to start the day.

Indian Chai Tea

3 teabags black tea
4 cups water
1 3-inch cinnamon stick
1-inch piece of gingerroot cut into 4 slices
½ teaspoon cardamom seeds
½ teaspoon black peppercorns
½ teaspoon whole cloves
1 teaspoon whole coriander seeds
1 cup milk
honey

Bring water to boil. Add spices, cover, and simmer 20 minutes. Add teabags and steep 10 minutes. Add milk and heat to drinking temperature. Be careful not to boil. Strain mixture through a clean cotton dish towel. Serve with honey to taste.

Lizzie's Cook's Notes
Years ago, when I volunteered at a nursing home in a nearby town, I was treated to India chai tea in the afternoons by one of the precious ladies I visited there. I hadn't thought of drinking it again for years now and was thrilled when I learned that Jan had the recipe and actually enjoyed drinking it in the afternoons.

Lisa Leann's Cinnamon Rolls

1 cup water a little warmer than room temperature
1 egg
3 cups bread flour
¼ cup sugar
2 tablespoons powdered milk
1 teaspoon salt
5 tablespoons butter, softened
1 teaspoon instant yeast
⅓ cup butter
½ cup vanilla ice cream
½ cup brown sugar
½ cup butter, softened
1 tablespoon ground cinnamon
½ cup brown sugar

Preheat oven to 350 degrees. Pour water, egg, bread flour, white sugar, powdered milk, salt, 5 tablespoons butter, and yeast into your bread machine. Set machine on the "dough" setting and turn on. As dough mixes, melt ⅓ cup butter in a small saucepan. Add brown sugar and ice cream and boil for two minutes to create caramel sauce. Pour sauce into bottom of lightly greased 9-by-13 pan.

When the bread machine has finished preparing the dough, place dough onto lightly floured surface. With rolling pin, shape dough into a rectangle, then spread with softened butter and sprinkle with cinnamon and brown sugar. Roll rectangle into a "log" then pinch edges to seal. Cut log into 12 rolls and place in pan of caramel. Allow dough to rise (about 45 minutes) until doubled in size.

Bake approximately 20 minutes, until golden brown. For high altitude baking, add 1 tablespoon of flour to the dough.

Vonnie's Cook's Notes
Use Lisa Leann's secret weapon carefully. She tells me it's a powerful persuader.

363

Chicken Marsala

4 boneless chicken breasts
½ cup flour
2 tablespoons butter (not margarine)
2 cups thinly sliced mushrooms
3 tablespoons chopped green onions
2 tablespoons olive oil
1 cup of marsala wine
½ cup chicken broth (canned works well)
salt and pepper to taste

Melt butter in skillet and sauté green onions and mushrooms. Remove mushrooms and onions from pan and set aside. Next, use mallet to pound chicken until thin. Dredge chicken in flour, then sauté in olive oil until thoroughly cooked. In saucepan, add wine, chicken broth, mushrooms, green onions, salt and pepper, and heat until bubbly, about 3 minutes. Pour sauce over chicken and serve.
Serves 4.

Donna's Cook's Notes
This turned out to be a tasty recipe, and I loved using the mallet. I'll have to remember to cook this whenever I feel especially frustrated—pounding chicken is a great stress reliever.

Breakfast Casserole

6 eggs
2 cups milk
1 teaspoon salt
1 teaspoon dry mustard
1 cup shredded cheddar cheese
1 pound mild sausage
4 slices of white bread (cubed)

Beat eggs, add milk, salt, and mustard. Gently stir in shredded cheddar cheese, sausage that has been browned and drained, and cubed white bread. Place in a buttered 9-by-13 casserole dish. Refrigerate overnight. Place in a cold oven set at 350 degrees and bake 45 minutes. Serve and watch it disappear!

Goldie's Cook's Notes
According to the women's magazine I got from Lizzie, this recipe is the favorite Christmas morning recipe of a famous Christian radio talk show hostess. I tried it once, and I have to admit it's both easy and delicious!

Daffodil Cake

> 1 can (1 pound and 4 ounces) crushed pineapple
> 2 eggs
> 1 teaspoon rum extract
> 1 lemon cake mix
> 1 package creamy vanilla frosting mix
> ¼ cup butter
> ½ cup coconut

Drain pineapple, reserving the syrup. Combine syrup, eggs, and ½ teaspoon rum extract in large mixing bowl. Add cake mix. Beat 4 minutes, then fold in drained pineapple. Spoon into 2 greased 9-inch round cake pans. Bake at 350 degrees for 40–45 minutes. Cool 10 minutes, then turn cake out of pan. Cool another half hour. Prepare frosting mix by adding butter and ½ teaspoon rum extract. Spread ⅓ of frosting between the layers, then sprinkle with ¼ cup coconut. Frost cake with remaining frosting and sprinkle with remaining coconut.

Follow instructions on cake box for high altitude directions.

Lisa Leann's Cook's Notes
I'd forgotten about this recipe, and really, I think it's one of the reasons Henry fell in love with me.

Sweet and Sour Chicken

6 tablespoons olive oil
6 tablespoons soy sauce
6 tablespoons honey
3 tablespoons white vinegar
1½ teaspoons dried thyme
1½ teaspoons paprika
½ teaspoon cayenne pepper
½ teaspoon ground allspice
1 teaspoon pepper
4 skinless boneless chicken breasts
2 cups hot cooked white rice

Preheat oven to 375 degrees. Combine oil, soy sauce, honey, vinegar, thyme, paprika, cayenne pepper, allspice, and pepper in a shallow baking dish; mix well. Pierce both sides of each chicken breast with a fork. Place in baking dish; turn chicken several times using tongs.

Bake chicken, basting several times with sauce, for 30 minutes. Spoon rice onto a serving platter.

Arrange chicken over rice. Drizzle a small amount of sauce over chicken. Serve remaining sauce on the side.

Serves 4.

Evangeline's Cook's Notes

Well, if you're a glutton for punishment and the local Chinese restaurant just doesn't "do it" for you, here's the way to do it at home. It takes longer, but I'll have to admit it does taste better.

Apple-Rhubarb Custard Pie

  2 eggs, beaten
  ⅔ tablespoon milk
  2 cups sugar
  ¼ cup flour
  ¾ teaspoon nutmeg
  2 cups coarsely chopped rhubarb
  2 small pared apples
  pastry for 1 9-inch, 2-crust pie
  1 tablespoon butter

Beat eggs and milk, then stir in sugar, flour, nutmeg, apples, and rhubarb. Pour into pie dough in pie pan. Dot with butter. Cover pie with top crust. Pinch edges with fork. Bake at 400 degrees for 60 minutes or until brown.

Donna's Cook's Notes
Some of my favorite things about autumn are the fresh apples and rhubarb. Of course, this pie is even better when Vonnie makes it and offers me a warm slice.

Quick Chili in a Skillet

    1 medium chopped onion
    1½ pounds hamburger meat
    1 tablespoon olive oil
    1 1-pound can tomatoes
    1 8-ounce can seasoned tomato sauce
    1 cup catsup
    1 1-pound can ranch beans
    1½ tablespoons chili powder
    1½ teaspoons salt
    1 bay leaf
    dash of ground red pepper

In a hot skillet, sauté onion in oil with hamburger meat. Add tomatoes, tomato sauce, catsup, beans, chili powder, salt, bay leaf, and red pepper. Stir and simmer, covered for 1 hour or more. If necessary, add water.

Serves 6–8.

Vonnie's Cook's Notes

I know this chili takes a while to simmer, but I can get it off to a pretty quick start when I need to.

Vonnie's Beef Stew

2 pounds lean sirloin tip
1 tablespoon olive oil
1 large onion, chopped
4 medium carrots, sliced
2 medium potatoes, cut into pieces
2 medium celery stalks, sliced
2 cups small mushrooms
1 teaspoon dried thyme
1 teaspoon ground mustard
1 cup water
1 cup dry red wine
1 16-ounce can no-salt-added stewed tomatoes
3 tablespoons all-purpose flour

Cut meat into cubes (first, trim the fat away). Heat olive oil in a large soup pot over medium heat until hot. Add beef and quickly brown on all sides. Add remaining ingredients except flour. You'll want to add salt and pepper to taste and then reduce heat to simmer. Simmer for an hour or until beef is cooked and vegetables are tender.

Combine a cup of the stew broth with flour in a small bowl. Mix with fork or whisk and add to stew. Continue heating another 10–15 minutes or until thickened.

Serves 8.

Evangeline's Cook's Notes
Vonnie usually makes a large batch of her stew and then freezes it for quick meals in several small microwavable containers. Pop them in the microwave and, voila, there's a meal you don't have to fuss over.

Homemade Pancakes

    1 cup all-purpose flour
    1 tablespoon sugar
    2 teaspoons baking powder
    ¼ teaspoon salt
    1 beaten egg
    1 cup milk
    2 tablespoons cooking oil

Stir together first four ingredients. In a separate bowl, combine last 3 ingredients. Add to flour mixture and stir until well blended but still a bit lumpy. Pour batter onto hot griddle in quarter-cup servings. Turn pancakes over until golden brown on both sides.

Buttermilk: prepare as above, this time reducing the baking powder to 1 teaspoon. Add ½ teaspoon baking soda to first set of ingredients. Substitute buttermilk for milk. You can also add a little extra buttermilk to thin the batter.

Buckwheat: prepare as above, this time substituting ½ cup whole wheat flour and ½ cup buckwheat flour for the all-purpose flour. You can also use brown sugar rather than white sugar.

Nutty orange: prepare as above, but this time add ½ teaspoon each of baking soda and ground cinnamon to the first set of ingredients. Instead of milk, use orange juice. Fold in ½ cup nuts into the batter before pouring onto griddle.

Goldie's Cook's Notes

If there's one thing Summit View is known for, it's the Pancake House. Not only do they have the yummiest, fluffiest pancakes that folks around here eat for breakfast, lunch, and dinner, but the pancakes also come in four varieties: buttermilk, buckwheat, nutty orange, and, of course, plain. I begged the owner of the Pancake House for the recipe . . .

Egg Salad Sandwich

6 hard-boiled eggs, finely chopped
6 tablespoons minced celery
3 tablespoons sweet pickle relish
2 tablespoons freeze-dried parsley
½ teaspoon dry mustard
salt and pepper to taste
¼ cup mayonnaise
2 tablespoons bacon bits

Mix chopped eggs, celery, pickle relish, parsley, dry mustard, salt, and pepper in bowl. Stir in mayonnaise and bacon bits. Refrigerate until ready to serve. Spread mixture on slice of bread. Top with slice of bread.

Makes 2 cups, enough for 6 sandwiches.

Donna's Cook's Notes

This is a simple recipe that I can make in advance. Of course, I get tired of the same sandwich, day after day, so I like to mix it up with a good ol' ham sandwich now and then.

Cheese Enchiladas with Chili Sauce

CHILI SAUCE:
1½ pounds lean ground beef
½ cup chopped onion
2 teaspoons garlic powder
1½ teaspoons salt
1 teaspoon pepper
8 cups beef broth or bouillon
2 cans whole peeled tomatoes
3 tablespoons chili powder
1 tablespoon plus 1½ teaspoons paprika
1 tablespoon ground cumin
⅓ cup cornstarch
⅓ cup water

In a large saucepan, brown ground beef with onion, garlic powder, salt, and pepper. Drain. Add broth, tomatoes, chili powder, paprika, and cumin. Mix well, breaking up tomatoes with large spoon. Bring to a boil. Reduce heat and simmer uncovered for an hour.

In a small bowl, mix cornstarch and water until cornstarch is completely dissolved. Gradually add to chili sauce, stirring constantly. Continue cooking 5 minutes.

ENCHILADAS:
16 flour tortillas (6 inch)
vegetable oil
6 cups shredded cheddar cheese
1 cup chopped onion
1 cup shredded American cheese

Turn oven to 350 degrees. Heat about ½-inch oil in a small skillet, until hot but not smoking. Quickly fry each tortilla in oil to soften, about 2 seconds on each side. Drain on paper towels.

In a large bowl, combine cheddar cheese and onion. Mix well. Spoon ½ cup cheese mixture down center of each tortilla. Roll up and place seam side down in 2 11-by-7-inch baking dishes. Top with chili sauce. Cover with foil.

Bake 10 minutes or until hot.

Remove foil, sprinkle with American cheese, and continue baking 2 minutes or until cheese melts.

Evangeline's Cook's Notes
I could eat these three meals a day. And I have. Seriously . . . I have!

Cheddar Cheese Pie

½ cup chopped onion
2 tablespoons butter
1 baked 9-inch pie crust
1 cup grated cheddar cheese
1 cup scalded milk
3 eggs, slightly beaten
½ teaspoon salt
⅛ teaspoon pepper
⅛ teaspoon thyme
8 slices fried bacon

First, sauté onion in butter, then combine in large bowl with cheese, milk, eggs, salt, pepper, thyme, and crumbled bacon. Pour mixture into baked crust. Bake at 350 degrees for 20–25 minutes. When done, knife inserted into the center of pie will come out clean.

Baking time will take longer at higher altitudes.

Donna's Cook's Notes

There's something about this cheese pie that is very satisfying. Sometimes it's all I can do to stop at one slice. I should probably start making it at home, but then, why go to the effort when I can get it at Sal's?

Molasses Cookies

¾ cup shortening
1 cup sugar
¼ cup molasses
1 egg
2 teaspoons soda
2 cups sifted flour
½ teaspoon cloves
¼ teaspoon ginger
1 teaspoon cinnamon
½ teaspoon salt

Melt shortening, then cool. Add sugar, molasses, and egg and beat well. Sift together flour, soda, and spices, then stir into mixture. Mix well and chill for 3 hours. Roll dough into 1-inch balls. Roll in sugar and place on greased cookie sheet. Bake at 375 for 8–10 minutes.

Yields 4–5 dozen 2-inch cookies.

Vonnie's Cook's Notes

This recipe has been in my family for more than a hundred years. My grandmother made it for my mother, my mother made it for me, and I'd always thought I'd make it for my own children. Now, who knows? Maybe my dream will come true.

Yellow Crookneck Squash Soup

1½ pounds of yellow crookneck squash
1 onion
1 stick margarine
2 chicken bouillon cubes
2–3 cups half-and-half
dash of salt and pepper
curry powder

Slice squash and onions. Sauté in 1 stick margarine until very tender. Place in a food processor, add bouillon cubes, and blend till smooth. Pour into sauccpan and stir in half-and-half until desired consistency. Season with salt, pepper, and dash of curry to taste. This may be served hot or cold.

Serves 4.

Lizzie's Cook's Notes

Years ago I was invited to a special luncheon with my sweet Aunt Janice. She made tuna salad and this squash soup, which she served with fresh fruit on the side. This is an excellent yet simple recipe . . . a favorite in cold weather or hot!

Dilly Tuna Salad

> 1 can (20 oz.) pineapple chunks in juice
> 1 can (7 oz.) tuna fish
> crisp lettuce
> 1 cup cucumbers, sliced
> ⅓ cup mayo
> ½ teaspoon seasoned salt
> ¼ teaspoon dill weed

Drain pineapple, reserving 2 tablespoons of the juice. Drain tuna and line salad bowl with lettuce. Toss tuna, pineapple, cucumbers. Pour into bowl. Blend mayo, salt, and reserved juice. Pour over salad. Sprinkle with dill weed.

Serves 4.

Evangeline's Cook's Notes
I'd never had anything quite like this before, but I was glad that after all the Potluck Club rush, it was left behind in my fridge. I ate it for dinner the night baby Faith was born, the night Jan entered heaven.

Acknowledgments

Eva Marie Everson—I would like to begin by thanking Linda Evans Shepherd for the opportunity to work with her on this project. Linda, I can still see myself sitting in BWI, trying to catch a nap as I waited for a delayed plane, answering my cell phone and hearing you rattle on about this neat little idea. A "let me think about it" and a while later, and we were off on an adventure we couldn't have imagined then! Thank you, girlfriend, for thinking of me when you first caught the vision for "the girls"!

Thank you to my husband, who didn't mind my going off to the high country of Colorado for more than a week to work on this project and who cooked/grilled all our meals.

Thank you, Paul and Jim Shepherd, for sharing your wife/mom and the cabin for quite a few days. Thank you, Laura, for not staying "mad" too long upon our return. We'll try to keep the time away shorter from now on.

Thank you, Deb Haggerty, for introducing me to Linda, with whom I have discovered that I'm funny.

Thank you to my mother, my grandmother, and my aunts—Bettye and Janice—for the recipes. You know how much I hate to cook.

And thank you to the members of Word Weavers. You're a great group of critiquers.

Linda Evans Shepherd—What can I say about my dear friend Eva? Let's see, as she's paying me to compliment her I can tell you she's really, really cool and a *fantastic* writer. Okay, so she's not paying me, but she's still really, really cool and a fantastic writer, and one of my dearest friends.

I would also like to acknowledge those who thought Eva and I, two strong and determined women, could not write a whole novel together. What were you thinking? Not only did we do it once, we did it again with the next installment of the Potluck due out next year. What fun we've had living dual lives with our Potluck characters.

Of course I would like to acknowledge our families, who have so sweetly let Eva and I lead double lives. Paul, you're the best. To my son, Jim, you're one great kid. And daughter, Laura, you're the most beautiful eighteen-year-old girl in the world. You may not be like other girls, but your joy and sweet spirit are so precious to me. Thank you for all the wordless songs you sing to your mommy.

And finally, thank you, God, for allowing me so many blessings and the privilege of writing this book with Eva.

The Authors—we would like to thank our wonderful editors, Jeanette Thomason and Kristin Kornoelje, as well as the rest of the Revell team! Thank you so much for believing in a project such as *The Potluck Club*, for "seeing" the girls as easily as we do.

Thank you to the awesome women of AWSA (Advanced Writers & Speakers Association) who have prayed us through illnesses, family crises, blizzards, and rewrites. You're the best!

A very special thank you to the town of Frisco, Colorado (aka, Summit View!) for being our prototype. A really, really special thank you to Frisco's Butterhorn Bakery & Café (Higher Grounds Café) for those midafternoon lattes we have grown accustomed to.

Another thank you to the Summit County police department for giving us the inside scoop on your world as we filled out the reports on Eva's lost wallet. Who knew the event would end up in a book?

And, finally, a huge thank you to our Heavenly Father, to our precious friend and Bridegroom Jesus Christ, and to the Holy Spirit, who binds us together as sisters in him by whom we pray.

About the Authors

Linda Evans Shepherd has turned the "pits" of her life into stepping stones following a violent car crash that left her then-infant daughter in a year-long coma and permanently disabled (see LindaAndLaura .com).

Linda is the president of Right to the Heart Ministries and is also an international speaker (see ShepPro.com), radio host of the nationally syndicated Right to the Heart radio, occasional television host of Daystar's Denver Celebration, the founder and leader of Advanced Writers and Speakers Association (see AWSAWomen .com), and the publisher of Right to the Heart of Women ezine (see RightToTheHeartOfWomen.com), which goes to more than ten thousand women leaders of the church.

She's been married twenty-six years to Paul and has two teenagers, Laura and Jimmy.

Linda has written more than eighteen books, including *Intimate Moments with God* (co-authored with Eva Marie Everson from Honor/Cook), *Tangled Heart: A Mystery Devotional* (Jubilant Press), and *Grief Relief* (Jubilant Press).

Award-winning author and speaker **Eva Marie Everson** is a Southern girl who's not that crazy about being in the kitchen unless she's being called to eat some of her mama or daddy's cooking. She is married to a wonderful man, Dennis, and is a mother and grand-mother to the most precious children in the world.

Eva's writing career and ministry began in 1999 when a friend asked her what she'd want to do for the Lord, if she could do any-thing. "Write and speak," she said. And so it began.

Since that time, she has written, co-written, contributed to, and edited and compiled a number of works, including *The Shadows Trilogy* (Barbour Publishing) and *Sex, Lies, & the Media* (co-written with her daughter, Jessica, and published by Cook Communica-tions). She is a Right to the Heart board member and a member of Christian Women in Media & Arts and a number of other organizations.

A graduate of Andersonville Theological Seminary, she speaks nationally, drawing others to the heart of God. In 2002, she was one of six journalists chosen to visit Israel. She was forever changed.

JOIN THE POTLUCK CLUB

To read more about the authors
or to find additional recipes, visit:

www.PotLuckClub.com

A Sneak Peek
at the next adventure of the Potluck Club

Clay Whitefield burrowed under the musky blankets, eking out an attempt at a few more minutes of sleep before heaving himself out of bed. The weight from the quilt his grandmother had made upon his arrival into the world laid over him like the history of her people, the Cheyenne. But his grandmother and her people were the last thing on his mind.

Outside the window of his second-story flat, the town of Summit View, Colorado, was coming to life. With or without him. His boss, the editor and publisher of the *Gold Rush News*, was most likely sitting at his desk by now, wondering when Clay would amble in. Shifts were changing at the hospital and down at the sheriff's department. Children were preparing for school. Sally Madison, owner of Higher Grounds Café, had already unlocked the doors to her establishment. Larry, her cook, had slapped a heap of lard onto the flat grill, readying it for the morning specials. One of Sal's girls had started the coffee. The very thought of it brewing interrupted Clay's dreams, and his nose twitched.

He opened one eye. Across the room on a scarred table, his gerbils, Woodward and Bernstein, lay wrapped around each other as though they were one. Nearby, his laptop sat at attention, the screen saver banner sliding across its face, teasing him.

Clay Whitefield, it said. Ace Reporter.

He'd worked last night until the early hours of the morning—thus his attempt at sleeping in. The big story of his career had kept him up, driving him toward a completion he feared would never come. This story—this single story—had tickled his imagination when he was a child, encouraged him to do well when he'd gone off to the University of Northern Colorado to study journalism, and propelled him back to his hometown upon graduation.

It was the story of a group of women who called themselves the Potluck Club. But it was more than their monthly gatherings that kept his fingers to the keyboard and his pen and notebook in an ever-ready position. It was their past secrets and current escapades.

It was, most particularly, their youngest member.

Because Clay Whitefield believed with everything his journalistic heart had in it that Donna Vesey was carrying the deepest secret of them all.

Don't miss what's brewing in the next Potluck Club book, coming Summer 2006